A VALENTINE TREAT FOR YOU!

A PAIR OF ENCHANTING ROMANCES BY TWO OF TODAY'S MOST BELOVED ROMANCE WRITERS—FOR ONE LOW PRICE!

NOELLE BERRY McCUE
Only The Present

"The coffee will be done in about five minutes, Daniel," Maureen said as she walked unsteadily past him. Just as she was about to reach the safety of the chair, she stumbled ignominiously, and Daniel's hands reached out to grab her forearms.

"Honey, I think you need a cold shower. Let me help you." He drew her into his arms, and as his hands reached behind her and lowered the zipper of her dress, Maureen stiffened in shock.

Giving her a wry look, and kissing the tip of her nose, Daniel whispered, "Go on before I change my mind and decide to get in the shower with you."

ANNE N. REISSER
The Face Of Love

"All right, Breck. You win," Andrea said. "Spell out your terms." Her voice was passionless and level, reflecting her sudden numb acceptance of the unbelievable.

"I won't prosecute your father," Breck began. "He'll be forcibly retired, but no criminal charges will be filed. It wouldn't look right if I prosecuted my father-in-law."

Andrea's head jerked up. "Father-in-law?" she repeated.

"Of course. You weren't interested in any other arrangement. You'll get a ring and I'll get…you. I'm paying a high price for you, Andrea. See that you're worth it."

Other Holiday Specials From *Leisure Books:*
A WILDERNESS CHRISTMAS
A FRONTIER CHRISTMAS
AN OLD-FASHIONED VALENTINE
A VALENTINE SAMPLER

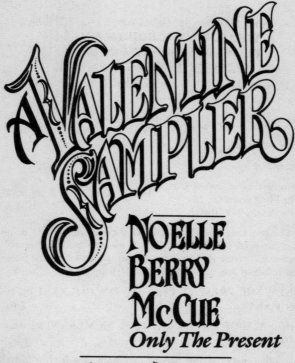

A VALENTINE SAMPLER

NOELLE BERRY McCUE
Only The Present

ANNE N. REISSER
The Face Of Love

LEISURE BOOKS NEW YORK CITY

A LEISURE BOOK®

February 1994

Published by

Dorchester Publishing Co., Inc.
276 Fifth Avenue
New York, NY 10001

Printed in the United States of America.

NOELLE BERRY McCUE
Only The Present

CHAPTER ONE

The fog rolled in thick, spreading a muffled curtain over the small car as it inched its way slowly toward the Bay Bridge. Maureen sat with tensed hands perspiring as she gripped the wheel of her Volkswagen tightly and slowed the car down once again. The radio was playing softly, but her nerves were stretched to the screaming point and she was hardly aware of the soothing rhythm in the background. She was near to the toll plaza now, but the fog was so thick it was difficult to see any landmarks. Peering out the window, she strained to see the outlines of the Oakland army base, which she knew should be there, but like a magician's trick it had completely disappeared. Not even the large smokestack in the foreground that burned natural gas was visible.

A relieved sigh whistled through her tensed mouth as she saw the lights of the toll plaza ahead wavering ghost-like with the distorted images only thick fog, especially San Francisco fog, created. Maureen knew that in the swirling gray mass distances were deceptive, but she felt as if she had been driving for hours. Coming to a stop, she handed her money over to the uniformed attendant quickly, giving him a fleeting smile as she drove away, and not noticing the bemused smile he gave her in return.

Usually Maureen enjoyed the long drive into San Francisco, especially during the long summer days. She didn't leave for work until eight o'clock at night, which meant the traffic wasn't heavy as it was during normal commuter hours, and during the summer it was still daylight, which was an added bonus. Maureen tried to relax her grip on the steering wheel. She gently rubbed her strained neck muscles, comforted by the soft brush of her thick hair against the back of her hand. It was a normal feeling, whereas she had been behaving stupidly with her emotions for the past few minutes and feeling an abnormal amount of fear.

After all, she was no stranger to fog, so why behave so irrationally about driving in it? The truth was obvious: Maureen Connolly is a blubbering coward! Smiling, Maureen forced herself to control her thoughts a little better than she had up until now. Peering to her right, she just managed to catch a glimpse of the towers of local radio stations through a momentary opening in the fog. Somehow the sight cheered her, for there was always the hope that the fog would lessen up ahead, though she knew that was unlikely. She wished suddenly that she could see the little mud hens floating about in the water. She had always loved watching their antics whenever a break in the bridge permitted her to glimpse the green-gray swells of the ocean below, and on a night like this she couldn't help childishly resenting their absence.

Reaching over, Maureen adjusted the volume of the radio. She needed a lot of noise to dispel the silence around her. Being alone in the fog always had this effect on her. She had to be realistic. The mud hens are still there bobbing up and down in that cold water; the San Francisco skyline is still there, its tall buildings looking lonely and majestic perched upon tall hills and surrounded by water; the people haven't suddenly disappeared. Maureen chided herself, trying to stifle the thought that she was the last person alive in the whole world.

"Thank God!" Maureen breathed thankfully as she reached the tunnel under Treasure Island. Traversing the long well-lit tunnel, Maureen didn't increase her speed, preferring the claustrophobic underground tunnel to the fog any day. Largely man-made, Treasure Island had always fascinated her. The ability of mere man to so change the work of nature amazed her, but in this case man had created something worthwhile, not destroyed the work it had taken nature billions of years to create. This small mountain of earth was developed for the 1939 World's Fair, and since then, it had been used mainly by the navy. The main part was an island in truth. It had been added to and extended to blend so naturally, it was impossible to tell where man and nature mingled.

Leaving the tunnel, Maureen was relieved to see that the fog was slowly beginning to disperse. Though she still couldn't see into the distance very well, she could just barely make out the gray supports of the bridge, and at least the line dividing the lanes was clear now. Peering through the remaining grayish wisps of fog to catch a glimpse of Alcatraz was clearly a waste of time, but now she was able to see the faint outline of the tops of the city's buildings. The mist swirled, letting her glimpse a landmark and then quickly smothering it again in its protective blanket. She was just able to make out the tallest, the Transamerica Pyramid Building, but the top of the cone wasn't visible, giving the impression of even greater height, as if it disappeared into the clouds. Looking quickly to the right, Maureen was unable to see Coit Tower, but she could just make out the outline of the Golden Gate Bridge behind it, its long string of fog lights glowing eerily as if suspended in space. Imagining Coit Tower, which used to be the tallest landmark in San Francisco, Maureen smiled. She remembered the day her father had taken her there when she was a little girl. They had climbed to the top, and he had held her up so she could see the breathtaking panorama spread out around them. She remembered how awed she had been when he had explained the history of Coit Tower as well as the history of some of the older buildings around and behind it. Her father had made history come alive for her that day, and she still thrilled to the memory. He had described the 1906 earthquake and holocaust so vividly that the child she had been then had trembled in his arms. She still could almost see and smell the flames that had nearly destroyed the city, and she still felt the well of pride in the exploits of the brave men who had

11

fought the fires that ravaged the city. Coit Tower, looking like a large replica of the practice towers still used to train firemen, was a fitting tribute to their courage.

From long practice Maureen automatically turned off onto Broadway and negotiated the horseshoe curve before the street straightened. As she rounded the curve she could just catch a glimpse of the Bay Bridge. It seemed even closer than usual, but that, she knew, was due to the murky fog, which still persisted in spreading clinging tendrils around the massive structure. Passing Sinbads restaurant, its exterior looking dingy in the diffused light, Maureen sighed. This drive seemed interminable, but there was the World Trade Center ahead, so she was almost home free. Thank goodness she didn't have far to go once she reached the Embarcadero. It was a wonder she had made it this far, and in an excess of relief she saluted the World Trade Center as she sailed past, her confidence growing and encouraging her finally to pick up speed. The mellow gray stone building looked rather sinister in the growing dimness, but its history wasn't at all dubious. In fact—Maureen smiled at her thoughts—it had been nothing worse than an embarcation point for travelers in the past and was still sometimes called the Old Ferry Building.

Humming under her breath, Maureen turned into the parking lot used by club personnel, mainly because it stayed open all night, but really because it was several blocks from the main nightlife area and was usually not very crowded. After locking the car, she began to walk briskly, the scent of the ocean wafting through her nostrils. Her long dark hair blew damply around an oval face endowed with almost striking beauty by high cheekbones and a dusky rose complexion. A small smile tickled her mouth as she walked under the lights, but she quickly wiped her face free of all expression as she approached the stranger coming toward her. Passing the rather too handsome man with her face assuming a haughty expression foreign to her, Maureen was relieved to see his smile drop as his face hardened coldly as he walked quickly by. Probably couldn't wait to get away from her, but she couldn't help that; she had too much trouble repelling the men at the club without trying to worry about being picked up by a stranger on the street, and she couldn't risk him following her into Grady's.

Reaching the large carved oak door of the club, Maureen grasped the handle and entered. It was dimly lit. Turning left, she avoided the entry into the club proper and entered a room for employees only. Walking down the hall, she soon reached her dressing room, the door painted a garish yellow with a glittering star just above eye level. Maureen shook her head laughingly. Since two of them shared this little box of a room, and those two were the club's only performers, she and Gaye had good-naturedly taken the ribbing of the club's other employees. With a reminiscent grin Maureen turned the handle of the dressing-room door and walked through, thinking fondly of Grady and his little practical jokes. How lucky they all were to work for a man like him. His heart was as gold filled as his teeth!

"Hello, Gaye. Sorry I'm late." Maureen glanced apologetically at the pert blonde grinning at her through the mirror.

"That's okay, honey. I took your show for you, so sit down and relax, you've plenty of time."

"Gaye, whatever would I do without you? Was Grady mad?"

"You've got to be kidding, Maurie. Grady might yell at the rest of us like a bear with a sore head, but not at his little Maurie," she replied without rancor, smiling at her good-humoredly. "Anyway," Gaye continued with a laugh, "what else was he going to do, spit nickels?"

"Oh, Gaye!" Maureen chuckled in response. "Your phraseology leaves much to be desired."

"Don't I know it, honey!"

Sitting down at her dressing table beside Gaye, Maureen removed her coat and draped it over the back of her chair while she proceeded to put on her makeup. Blending in a foundation cream, she caught Gaye's expression in the mirror.

"What's the matter, Gaye? You look like the world's coming to an end. Having trouble with Harry?"

"Him!" Gaye retorted forcefully, pouting her lips and blowing a distinct raspberry.

"Gaye, you know you're crazy about old Harry!" Maureen mocked with a graceful gesture of her hand.

"Yeah, the bum! Why I had to go and fall for someone without the sense to appreciate me, I'll never know."

Gaye continued talking, but the flow of words went pleasantly around Maureen without really penetrating her consciousness as she carefully applied a thin streak of eyeliner to accentuate her already slumbrous dark eyes. Putting down the eyeliner, she began brushing on charcoal mascara to lengthen her thick, lustrous lashes. Absentmindedly she thought how glad she was her lashes were naturally long. She would hate to have to wear this thick stuff all the time like some of her friends. Normally during the day she wore no makeup at all, and she always felt her face was clean and healthier without all the artifice. Apparently her mother had been right when she had cautioned against wearing the covering makeup that had been so popular among her friends during her teenage years, for her skin was clear and petal soft, unlike that of some other girls her age whose pores had enlarged, giving a coarsened appearance that was quite aging.

Putting down the mascara brush, Maureen looked worriedly at Gaye whose words were finally penetrating her consciousness. What she said shocked her, even though they had been expecting something of the kind. Poor Grady, he loved San Francisco, had lived here all his life, and worked hard for all he had. Maureen felt dreadfully sorry for him but even sorrier for dear Mrs. Grady. The last couple of years her asthma had become so much worse, in spite of all the specialists she had seen. How awful she must feel now that they were certain she would never be better in this climate. It would be a wrench for them to leave the home they loved so well, which sat high on a hill offering a panoramic view of their beloved bay. How they would hate leaving, but she knew Grady wouldn't find it as difficult as his wife. If the change meant keeping his beloved Grace with him, he would relocate with a song in his heart. Thinking of the truly

14

devoted couple, Maureen sighed. To love and be loved like that was the greatest treasure life could offer two people. She had once loved . . .

Abruptly Maureen stood up, determinedly banishing thoughts of the past. Pulling off her wool slacks, she turned her face away from the revealing image in the mirror. Bending, she removed her calf-length black boots and reached for her panty hose, smoothing them over her long slender legs and up to her waist.

"Darn, I should have waited to put on my makeup." Maureen's words were muffled as she carefully pulled her gray turtleneck sweater over her head. Swinging her hair free, she slipped into her jersey dress, the clinging folds hugging her dainty yet curvaceous figure. The dress was beautiful against the olive of her complexion, its shimmering folds a flaming orange that deepened or lightened in color depending on the light and the movement of her body. It was deceptively simple in design, but she always felt self-conscious wearing it, with its mini length showing more of her legs than she was used to, and the fabric gently molding her curving hips and fanning upward, not covering as much of her softly rounded breasts as she would have liked.

"Here, honey. Let me help you with that zipper." Gaye walked quickly around Maureen, who was struggling frustratedly with hands behind her back.

"Thanks, Gaye, I feel like a contortionist every time I get into one of these outfits." Maureen laughed with a small quiver in her voice, causing Gaye to smile reassuringly at her.

As Gaye studied Maureen she couldn't help seeing the doubt in her friend's face when she regarded her reflection in the mirror. Gaye knew Maureen better than almost anyone else and understood how much the girl hated flaunting her femininity, even though it was good for the business. She knew that when Maureen, with her dark Spanish looks, walked in front of the audience with her black hair flowing loose to her waist in rippling waves, she created a sensation. Gaye's own blues singing was greatly appreciated, but Maureen put them in a trance with her

15

softly sexy voice singing potent Spanish love songs. Funnily enough, she was popular with women as well as men. Her obvious innocence somehow penetrated her performance and was fully appreciated by the females, while the men wove daydreams around the apparent promise in her eyes and voice. When the two of them occasionally sang together, Gaye too was caught in the aura Maureen seemed unconscious of creating, and during those times Gaye felt that she was in the presence of greatness. She knew they made a startling foil for each other, and it was during times like those that she knew how strong was her love for the lovely, artless child Maurie was. Gaye was in her mid thirties but old in the ways of the world. It was odd she'd never felt jealousy, only a warm protectiveness for Maureen, but then there was something about Maureen that inspired such a feeling in nearly everyone who came to know her well. Gaye knew better than anyone how tough life had been for Maurie up until recently, but it hadn't embittered her. She still exuded cheerfulness and a genuine fondness for people, and they loved her for it!

Putting an arm around Gaye, Maureen turned so they both faced their reflected images.

"We're both gorgeous." She laughed, giving Gaye's slightly plump waist a squeeze.

"You're right, honey . . . we'll knock em dead!" Gaye turned her head to smile warmly at Maureen.

"I just hope Grady appreciates us!" Maureen spoke in mock doubt, secure in the warm knowledge of their boss's very real affection for them.

"Humph! He appreciates anyone who puts money in his pockets," Gaye growled with a laugh before moving away from Maureen.

"Poor Grady." Maureen echoed Gaye's laugh and began to brush her hair. "Sometimes I think he's a frustrated father, the way he worries about us. We're awfully lucky, Gaye, especially me!"

As she spoke the words, Maureen knew how true they were. Life had been a constant struggle for her before she came to work at the Miramar. At times she had despaired, terrified she'd lose Katy, but now most of the pressure had been taken from her shoulders. The last couple of years had left their scars—she was fully aware of that, especially when she remembered the long nights slinging hamburgers on a grill at an all-night joint. She would come home to shower, spend a couple of hours with Katy, and have an early lunch; then she would take Katy to Nonna's again before rushing to her other job as a waitress for a four-hour afternoon shift. Sometimes she had been so tired she just didn't think she could go on any longer, but when she held Katy and heard her little baby laugh, it had all seemed worthwhile. She couldn't have managed at all without her neighbor, and Maureen still shuddered to think of what she would have done if Nonna hadn't cared for Katy. Working two jobs, she'd had to sleep after her four-hour shift, before getting up at eleven to start all over again at midnight, which meant that Nonna had cared for Katy for all but that precious few hours in the morning. How awful those days had been after her parents' tragic deaths. Katy had been a totally unlooked-for bundle of joy to herself and her mother and father, and when they had died in an automobile accident, Maureen couldn't consider letting the authorities take Katy, though she had been pressured to do so. Katy was the only thing she'd had left from what had once been her family, and she belonged with her and no one else.

Meeting Gaye and Harry had changed all that—Maureen smiled in memory. The pace and strain had inevitably taken their toll of her health. One day, coming down with flu, she couldn't afford to take time off from work and had just placed a lunch order on the table when she passed out cold as she turned to walk away. When she had regained consciousness, she was in the back room of the restaurant with a very frazzled boss waving a paper in front of her, and her customers standing there looking worried.

That had been her introduction to Gaye and Harry. They never had gotten around to eating that lunch, she remembered with a smile. They had insisted on taking her home, and considering the extremely weakened condition she had been in at the time, it was no wonder Gaye and

Harry had succeeded in taking over with so little resistance on her part. Their sympathy and understanding had breached the defenses she had held in for so long, and once their kindness had eaten through that facade of aloofness she had assumed for self-preservation from the blows life had dealt her, she had talked and cried herself out, seemingly unable to stop the flow once started. Together Gaye and Harry had cared for her and Katy until she was on her feet again, and then Gaye had taken her to meet Grady, whose soft heart had been as touched by Gaye's account as Gaye's and Harry's had been.

Grady had given her a job in the office of the Miramar. Having heard her singing one day during a break and then learning from Gaye that she could play guitar as well, he had given her a raise and put her to work in the club proper. He had needed to pull a few strings because she was only nineteen, but Grady had believed in her ability and her talent. He got around the no-one-under-twenty-one-allowed law by having her perform in the dining area of the club, not in the bar itself where Gaye performed.

In a few weeks she'd be twenty-one. Maureen sighed. Already she had worked at the Miramar for nearly two years, and her self-confidence was growing by leaps and bounds. Grady had hinted at future plans to put on a gala performance marking her coming of age, but Maureen felt uneasy about the whole thing. Being underage had been the best excuse possible for not fraternizing with her customers. Grady was not the type of boss who insisted his girls should drink with the clientele between shows—he was too protective of them for that; but some men could get nasty with a few drinks in them, and she would hate to lose the protection of being underage. Having had one disastrous love affair when she was seventeen, Maureen felt it would be a long time, if ever, before she let herself become involved with a man again.

A frown marred the perfection of her darkly slanted brows as she remembered the naive and trusting child she had been, and she grimaced when she bitterly recalled the heartbreak that had followed the loving. Maureen gave a tiny toss of her head and deliberately turned her thoughts from old memories. Instead, she thought of how satisfying life had become. Life had really been looking up for her and Katy since she had met Gaye and Harry and started working for Grady, and she would never cease being grateful for the change. Why was she wasting her thoughts on bad memories when she had so much to look forward to! Maureen smiled, thinking of Katy. It just didn't seem possible the little minx would be three years old in a few months. She and Nonna were already looking over brochures for a good nursery school for her to attend a couple of hours a day. They both felt Katy needed other children of her own age to play with, and it would spell Nonna, which was even more of an incentive for Maureen.

Nonna loved them both dearly, but it was becoming more and more obvious to Maureen that her old friend was finding Katy more than a handful. For that matter, she did herself! Maureen's mouth curved in a small smile of satisfaction. Already at not quite three Katy knew her alphabet, could count to ten, loved her books above any of her toys, and had the vocabulary of a much older child. Her precociousness did have drawbacks though, for she was becoming something of a terror, and sometimes Maureen couldn't help thinking Katy needed a much firmer hand than she or Nonna provided.

Maureen looked up as the light above her dressing mirror began blinking. Only five minutes until she went on. Quickly turning and running the comb through her hair, she parted it in the middle and tried smoothing out the slight curls on the sides caused by the dampness of the fog. She sighed and immediately was caught by a huge yawn, which she tried unsuccessfully to muffle with her hand.

"Maurie, what time did that little devil wake you up this morning?"

"The same as always, eight o'clock," Maureen grimaced.

"Honey, you know what happened before when you tried burning the candle at both ends," Gaye warned her worriedly.

Laughing at Gaye's disapproving frown, Maureen felt ashamed of herself a moment later when she saw the hurt look in Gaye's eyes. She quickly tried to reassure her.

19

"It's not as bad as it sounds, Gaye. I'm in bed at three, up with Katy at eight o'clock, but I do sleep another couple of hours later on. You know Nonna watches me like a hawk. She only lets me get by with my routine so I can spend part of the day with Katy, but after lunch she insists Katy have her nap at her house so I can get more sleep, and keeps her there until nearly dinnertime. There's really nothing to worry about, so don't . . . please!"

Gaye turned and wrapped her pink velour dressing gown around her waist and tightened the sash with a little jerk, giving a disdainful sniff as she did so. Turning again to Maureen, she shook her head.

"I don't know how you manage, honey. It's such a long commute to San Leandro. Why don't you get an apartment here in the city?" Gaye questioned for maybe the hundredth time. Maureen smiled as Gaye broke into her usual arguments for getting them all to move to the city, but found it impossible to be annoyed by her well-intentioned friend. It was so nice to be wanted and cared about, so Maureen patiently went through her arguments again.

"Gaye, you know what anything with a yard would cost, and I don't want Katy in an apartment. We've been through the reasons before, and deep down you agree with me, now don't you?" Maureen questioned teasingly.

"Well, maybe I do, Maurie," Gaye admitted grudgingly. "But it sure would be nice if you were closer to Harry and me. We worry about you driving all that way so late at night."

Maureen gave Gaye a swift hug, and Gaye teasingly expelled the air from her lungs in a whoosh before hugging Maureen back affectionately.

"Gaye, you know I'd rather live closer to you, don't you?"

"Oh, go on! I know why you won't move into San Francisco, and much as I hate to admit it, your reasons are good ones, Maurie. I'm just being selfish!" Gaye exclaimed with a grin.

Maureen knew her reasons were sound, and she thought of the cheery little home she had made for herself and Katy. Their house was really two houses, with a wall separating hers from Nonna's, with two separate entrances. Maureen had privacy, and both homes had their own fenced-in backyards, which was ideal for a small child. They were part of several identical units and formed a cul-de-sac set well back from the street, with a large communal tree shading the front yard. The only disadvantage Gaye could see was the long, late night . . . or rather the early-morning commute, which Maureen had to agree with in all honesty.

Maureen turned to walk to the door, guitar in hand. It was a Martin and her most treasured possession. A gift from her father for her twelfth birthday, it seemed to bring back his image every time she played it. They had been so close, and he'd seen she had the best instruction possible, but looking back, she felt that she had learned most from her father, who had himself played flamenco and Spanish guitar. A tender smile crossed her face as she thought of him. Of mixed Spanish and Irish descent, he had been tall and lean with a gentle manner—a dreamer really—but with a hot temper when aroused. Maureen was lucky, for she inherited her mother's gentle but firm common sense attitude to life, and her father's love of music. She had to be honest with herself. She, and Katy too, had also inherited his seething temper. Neither of them were easily aroused, but when they were, they both found it hard to let go of their anger, which wasn't a good thing. Opening the door she couldn't help thinking that, temper or no, her parents had left a wonderful heritage, especially the love of music both she and Katy shared. God willing, she hoped she could leave Katy with as much. How she wished Mother and Father were still here to hand their legacy of love direct to Katy, instead of secondhand by her!

"See you for coffee later, Gaye?" Maureen smiled back at her friend. "Or will Harry be coming tonight?"

"Of course we'll break for coffee, you nut. You know Harry considers himself lucky to have two good-looking girls hanging on his every word," Gaye joked, smiling at the thought of her gentle, slightly chubby Harry. Still smiling softly, she undid the sash of her dressing gown and reached for her second costume of the evening.

"Gaye, if Harry could only see you in that, he wouldn't be so shy about proposing!" Maureen teased, one eyebrow quirked roguishly. Gaye quickly grabbed a hairbrush, raising it in the air threateningly as Maureen laughed and made a quick exit through the door, closing it quietly behind her.

Maureen walked quickly down the white-painted hall, her long silky legs and softly flowing hips swaying. Reaching the door at the end marked Office, she entered, walking smoothly across to the other door, which led into the main dining area. She reached up on the wall to the right side of the door and pressed the little signal button that would let Jack, the bartender and lighting man, know she was ready. In the bar area, which was set to the left of the office door, Jack saw Maureen's signal and unobtrusively turned the dimmer system on the far wall, lowering the lights in the restaurant and bar area slowly and quietly, causing the patrons to babble expectantly.

Maureen entered, reaching the end of the bar, which was just a recessed alcove separated from the main dining room by a large Spanish-style archway. As Maureen reached the special platform Harry had installed for her she glanced through the dimness and heard the familiar cacophony of sound, like a muffled roar, prevalent in any large restaurant in the world. She smiled to herself. Sitting, she braced her right foot on the rung jointing the legs of the stool, crossing her left leg swiftly over her right and smoothing her dress self-consciously. After all this time she was still unnerved by the thought of all those invisible eyes staring at her. She pulled her hair free, and it rippled in a satiny cascade down her back, nearly reaching her waist. Bracing her guitar firmly upon her lap, she gave a little nod in the direction of the bar area, and immediately an orangey-gold spotlight played over her still figure.

A hush came over the room as the diners looked toward the beautiful girl sitting there so quietly, her beauty cast in an almost unearthly glow. Although Maureen couldn't see the faces of the people because of the lowered lights, she swept her glance slowly around the room, marshaling her thoughts and trying to gauge the mood of her audience.

The people waited in excited expectancy, the breath caught in their throats; little shadows—cast by small candles set in exquisitely molded amber glass in the center of each table—danced over their darkened features. The anticipation in the room increased until it could almost be felt, and only then did Maureen begin. Slowly her fingers began moving in a soft caress over the strings of her guitar, poignantly strumming the refrain of a Spanish ballad. Gently her voice began to fill the air with a haunting quality. As she performed—eyes closed, head thrown slightly back, showing the long alabaster perfection of her lovely throat—Maureen became a child again. There she was in their warm living room, the firelight flickering over her father's intent face as he listened to her play. There now, she was playing for her father, singing with him, loving him. The sad longing in her voice flowed in waves around her audience, and as the tears clouded Maureen's eyes the women in the audience openly wiped their own, and the men found it suddenly difficult to swallow. No one in the room could tear his eyes away from Maureen —so lonely and lost to the world around her.

She sang song after song. There was no attempt at applause between songs, as if the audience just couldn't bring itself to interrupt the magical flow of music. The high arched ceilings of the large room and the muting effect of the microphone gave a slight echoing quality to Maureen's voice, which in turn gave the music an almost cathedrallike sound. On and on she played, her long slim fingers moving faster and faster, now slower, languidly, now building again to a crescendo. Her fingers seemed to possess a life of their own. Suddenly they stilled, and Maureen moved off fluidly into the shadows as the last haunting notes wafted through the air. For a heart-stopping moment no one moved, and then a great roar of sound followed her as the audience rose to their feet.

The sound went on, rising even louder as Maureen appeared again, her head lowered in a slight bow, a tired smile on her mouth, and a vague look in her eyes, as if she had just returned from a world long lost to her. Maureen then turned to melt into the anonymity of the shadows, but as she began to move away toward the exit, a larger shadow detached itself from the wall, blocking her way. Glancing up into piercingly cold gray eyes, Maureen gasped disbelievingly and moved slowly backward, her hand outflung in protest. The man approached sinuously, like some leashed beast of prey, not speaking but seeming to pierce her soul with his eyes and stab her heart with the disdainful smile upon the chiseled mouth.

"God, no!" Maureen whispered, her eyes never leaving his face, a face she had thought never to see again. In her tortured gaze he became larger and darker; and as he reached for her and caught her in his arms, in her mind, now numbed, he seemed to merge with all the other shadows in the darkened room. With a despairing cry she felt herself enfolded in the endless darkness of arms her frantic thoughts knew she must escape.

CHAPTER TWO

"Maurie, oh, Maurie, honey, wake up!"

Maureen could hear Gaye's voice. Funny how far away she sounds, she thought, and why are my ears buzzing? Tentatively she ran her tongue over her lips, trying to identify the taste that lingered there. Ugh. She'd always hated the taste of brandy. Why in the world would she have drunk the stuff? Slowly her eyes opened, and she blinked bewilderedly at the frowning Gaye bending over her and attempting to pour more of that revolting liquid down her throat!

"No . . . no more," she gasped, grimacing as a small but revivifying amount of the alcohol trickled down her throat like liquid fire. "What happened?" she asked.

"Okay, honey. Just take it easy." Gaye quickly replaced the stopper and set the small glass container on the table beside the couch. Gently she reached out and brushed a few wisps of damp hair out of Maureen's face. "You fainted . . . are you all right?"

"Yes, I'm fine," Maureen murmured doubtfully. Suddenly she sat up as memory returned, looking jerkily around the dressing room. Raising her hand to shade her eyes from the harsh light of the naked bulb overhead, she uncurled her legs from the small couch, which they used for relaxing between shows.

"Where's Daniel, Gaye? I know I saw him, I couldn't have imagined it." She frowned, almost doubting herself.

She couldn't help hoping all of this was some horrible nightmare, and she held her breath waiting for Gaye's reply.

"You mean Mr. Lord? He's waiting in Grady's office," Gaye replied as she helped Maureen, who had suddenly whitened, to lie back against the cushions that she had piled under her still-whirling head. "Honey, you could have knocked me down with a feather. You never mentioned knowing Daniel Lord."

Gaye straightened, looking at Maureen curiously. "Where'd you ever meet him?"

"It's a long story, Gaye," Maureen replied, running a shaking hand over her hair. She hated keeping secrets from Gaye, who was the best friend anyone could ever have, but she didn't think she could bear to go into a long explanation now. "I don't want to see him!" Maureen looked up at Gaye, and the bitter expression on her face startled her friend.

"But Maurie, do you know who he is? He's one of the most important men in the city. They call him the lord of the financial district, and I for one wouldn't want to make him angry by giving him any orders!"

Maureen walked over to her dressing table and sat down. "Please, Gaye!" she pleaded. "Tell Mr. Lord I'm indisposed or something. Just make any excuse, or tell him the truth, I don't care. Only I won't see him—not now, not ever!"

Her thoughts were distracted, disjointed, and she couldn't understand her own feelings of panic. Pain she'd buried deep was welling up inside her again, and she couldn't bear it! Maureen questioned her feelings and realized she felt sick, sick to her stomach, and what was worse, sick to her very soul.

Gaye opened her mouth to argue but, seeing Maureen's distrait look, changed her mind.

"Okay, honey, I'll tell him, but he won't like it . . . he's not the type of man you can put off forever," she replied, then left quietly.

Gaye's words—little did she know it—cut through Maureen like a knife. With a muffled sob, she placed her hands over her face. "Oh, God! How well I know what kind of man he is," she murmured aloud as memory flooded back.

Her father had run an antique shop that dealt in the restoration of musical instruments, mainly stringed. She had loved to help him, she remembered with a sigh. His shop was small, but he was well known in his field, and never seemed to lack for business.

Her father and mother had a comfortable life, and she herself had never lacked for anything, especially love. Thinking back, she could pinpoint the exact time things began to change. Her father began to look harassed and worried, unlike his usually cheerful self. Her mother, too, had been tense, as if waiting. Finally her father told her he had made some unwise investments, and unless he could get a loan, his business would fold. Maureen was appalled, she had had no idea things were so bad, for even the shop was mortgaged, as well as their small home.

Out of desperation her father had made an appointment to see a prominent and influential financier in San Francisco. It was a last resort—she realized that now—but at the time it was their only hope, albeit a small one.

Maureen licked her dry lips, swallowing convulsively. How different her life might have been if her father had never given in to her pleadings, never taken her with him that day nearly four years ago. Four years. She shook her head with a sigh. It seemed like yesterday.

She could still see that waiting room in the outer office, could still smell the roses in the graceful vases that stood on either side of the large white leather couch she'd perched on so tensely. The walls were paneled in a grayish white that gleamed with a pearly glow as the sun stroked its smooth surface. The deep pile carpet was a smoky blue-gray which blended with the subdued atmosphere of the large room. Subdued, that is, except for the drapes, covering nearly half of one wall, drawn to let in the sunlight. They were a vivid turquoise, in a material she could only guess at, that fell in pleated folds from ceiling to floor and rippled with aquamarine highlights.

The large double doors through which her father had

disappeared opened as he returned. As soon as she had seen his face, she had known the worst. He had looked pinched and gray as he'd slowly walked across the room to sit beside her. Shaking his head, he had tried to smile, she remembered. Placing his head against the back of the couch, he had made an attempt to explain coherently. His eyes closed wearily. Because the house and shop were both mortgaged, he'd explained, he had no collateral, and Daniel Lord did not appear to suffer fools gladly. Well, he really couldn't blame Mr. Lord under the circumstances, he had sighed; but she had become blazingly angry. To think of all the years of good business upon which this high and mighty Daniel Lord could make his judgment, all the good years of devotion and hard work! Well, she'd show him!

Her father had tried to remonstrate with her, but she wouldn't listen. To this day she could not remember what had given her the courage to do what she'd done next, unless it had been her anger driving her. Many times, over the years, she had wished to turn back the clock, wished to have the chance of never having to live through those next few moments.

After going with her father to the lobby, she had used the excuse of having forgotten her purse and, leaving her preoccupied father to wait, had sped back to the office. She had walked through the waiting room, entered the inner office, and demanded to see Mr. Lord. The secretary had relayed the message, although less aggressively, and Maureen had been asked to go in.

She hadn't known what to expect when she had entered the office of Daniel Lord, certainly not the man himself. Having forged ahead on her emotions, she had become suddenly tongue-tied when the man standing before the large bay window turned toward her. When he had requested that she be seated, she had done so, mainly because her legs felt as if they would no longer hold her up, she remembered. He was the most devastatingly attractive man she had ever seen. Dark thick hair, bronzed skin, steel-gray eyes framed by long thick lashes. Her breath had caught in her throat, heart inexplicably pounding, when he had turned those piercing eyes upon her, their gray depths shaded as they slowly traversed her body, from the tip of her toes to the top of her head.

He had realized almost immediately his effect on her—of course he had. Daniel Lord hadn't gotten where he was at thirty-four without meeting many women along the way, and using them. As soon as he had seen her come through the door, he had been determined to have her. Used to getting what he wanted no matter what the cost, he hadn't been particularly concerned with how he achieved it, and even now the knowledge made her bitter. How flattered that first look of his had made her feel. If only she had known then what she had later so painfully learned!

So he had turned on the charm, Maureen remembered. The dinner date he proposed, to discuss her father's situation, had only been one of many assignations with Daniel. He was sophisticated and assured, and she had fallen more and more in love with him as the days passed, but he had kept their relationship very undemanding. Throwing a casual arm across her shoulders, taking her arm as they walked. She had been frightened of his motives at first but had soon begun to trust him completely, and to long for him to love her, to know the feel of his kiss. How very foolish the young can be, thinking they can change the world, or because they love . . . thinking they must necessarily be loved in return. Like crazy moths flying so confidently toward the light that attracts them, only to burn themselves up when reaching their goal.

That was the way it had been for her with Daniel, she realized now. For as soon as he had sensed her desire for him—desire that had frightened her in its intensity—he had subtly begun playing upon her emotions with finesse, until she had become a quivering mass of uncertainty.

Slowly he had changed his tactics. How calculated it all seemed now, so why had she been too dumb to see it then? Maybe dumb wasn't the right word, for it was not intelligence that she had lacked, but experience in emotional involvements, for boys her own age had never appealed to her. She had preferred the company of her father and actively avoided dates with boys from school after the first few boring attempts had failed to appeal to her. Yes, she thought disgustedly. Couple her lack of experience with the stars in her eyes when she looked into Daniel Lord's . . . and disaster was inevitable. When they dined, he would look into her eyes and allow his gaze to travel to her mouth, making her tremble with emotion. As they danced he would hold her closely against his lean, hard body, letting her feel his maleness against her as they swayed together, moving his hands over her back, caressing her hips while pulling her even closer. Bending his head, he would feather light kisses across her closed eyes and down to her flushed cheeks, stopping just short of her mouth, and a gasp would escape her as the tip of his tongue quickly flicked out to caress the tiny dimple his lips discovered there.

Soon Maureen had forgotten everything but Daniel. Nothing else had mattered to her, and she had lived only when she was with him. Even her father's worries had ceased to be important, she remembered with shame. She had known Daniel would take care of everything because he loved her. She had been unable to eat or sleep and, with her emotions burning her up, began living on her nerves. Yes, Daniel had been very clever, and he had known almost to the minute when she had finally reached the breaking point. Never would she forget the day the whole beautiful dream had come crashing around her, shattering her heart and all her youthful hopes like shards of splintering glass.

The day had begun with such blissful promise, Maureen remembered with a look of pain crossing her features as she tormentedly covered her face with her hands. She had met Daniel at his office, and they had gone to the Japanese Tea Gardens in San Francisco, where they had spent several wonderful hours walking hand in hand through the well-laid-out meandering paths. She had gazed blissfully at the beautifully designed trees and shrubs, with the smell of the blossoming flowers drifting around them like a benediction. They had lunch at a little outdoor restaurant set upon a raised platform. Pressing her hands even tighter over her eyes to try to hold back the tears, Maureen recalled how she hadn't had eyes for anyone but Daniel, and the other people milling around and below them had been as unsubstantial as ghosts. There had only been his eyes looking into hers, the feel of his hands caressing her fingertips.

Daniel knew the Oakland Bay area rather well, having business contacts on both sides of the bay, and for dinner he had taken her to Charlie Brown's. She remembered very little of the drive, but one building seemed to stand out in her memory. It stood next to a modern high rise, an old white building with a small bell tower on top. Having admired the quaintness of the small two-story churchlike building, how chagrined she had been when Daniel had pointed out that it was a funeral parlor. They had laughed together hilariously. Recalling the bittersweet memory, Maureen couldn't seem to stop the tears overflowing her eyes and trickling through the fingers covering her face. Then, their laughter had seemed another indication of a shared love, but now she couldn't help thinking of the long-forgotten incident as an omen of the death of that love, a warning of what was to follow.

Charlie Brown's was located at Edgewater West, with condominiums behind that spread out toward the San Francisco skyline sprawling out in the distance. In the foreground were the Berkeley mud flats, which had become quite a tourist attraction with their remarkable driftwood sculptures. Though not located in Berkeley itself, Daniel had explained, they were so named because of the hippies from that area who came to express themselves artistically with whatever they could pick up lying around. The sculptures had been amazingly realistic, particularly a train and a truck that looked as if they were moving as the car sped past, and a little windmill that turned crazily in the breeze.

After dining at Charlie Brown's, they had gone to nearby Tia Maria's to dance. It had been very late when they had left the overheated atmosphere and stepped into the car park, and the night air was cold owing to the closeness of the bay. She had stumbled. Only Daniel's arms had prevented her from falling, and with a muffled intake of breath he had molded her body to his and then kissed her, and even now she trembled at the sensations the memory aroused. His mouth upon hers had been hard and passionate, his head moving sensuously back and forth, playing with a devilish certainty upon the trembling uncertainty of her own. Nothing had prepared her for the arousal that fired her body as she felt Daniel's mouth against hers.

Raising her head, Maureen stared tormentedly at her reflection, placing her fingers against her lips. Daniel had played with her mouth, running his tongue teasingly over her closed lips until her emotions had left her gasping for breath. When he had whispered, "Open your mouth, baby . . . like this," and smilingly pressed down upon her full lower lip with the tips of his fingers, she had eagerly complied. Dear God, how can the memory of that kiss still do this to me? Maureen shivered, shaking her head in an agony of recrimination as she thought back to that heart-stopping moment. Daniel had stared into her eyes for a moment out of time. Then his head had moved slowly toward hers, his eyes darkening as his slightly parted lips had captured hers again, his tongue entering her mouth, causing the world to spin around her head as she'd pressed her heated body even closer to his, his caressing hands causing shivers of delight to course through her bloodstream in a never-ending sequence.

That kiss had seemed to go on forever, and it had been impossible to stop the blood from pounding through her— as it did even now at the thought of it. She had stood in a seething daze while Daniel ended the kiss, and placing his lips caressingly upon the side of her neck he'd huskily whispered, "Let's go home," and slowly walked her to the car.

Maureen grimaced at the image of her young eagerness. She'd been achingly willing Daniel to kiss her again, but he had begun to drive back immediately, much to her disappointment! He had driven to a strange block of apartments in the Embarcadero and parked his car in an underground stall. Maureen hadn't realized until that moment that Daniel was taking her to his apartment when he had whispered "Home," and by the time she awoke to the fact, it was too late to make an excuse to really go home—at least a plausible one. She had been frightened then, remembering his kiss, but had wordlessly allowed him to help her out of the car. By this time her churning emotions had had a chance to subside somewhat, and she'd felt like what she was—a rather naive young girl afraid of the unknown.

Reliving those moments, Maureen wondered now why she had gone with Daniel to his apartment, but then she knew the answer. She had been afraid of losing him by showing her uncertainty! With a bravado she was far from feeling, she had feigned a sophistication and nonchalance she had been rather proud of at the time. When they had entered the elevator, Daniel's arm caressingly around her waist, he had begun a desultory conversation with the elevator boy, who was dressed in a ridiculous uniform with a pert hat cocked at an angle on his head. That hadn't been the only pert thing about him, Maureen remembered, a blush staining her cheeks. When the doors had opened at the top floor, Daniel's glance had momentarily been diverted, and in that instant the boy had glanced at her, looking her up and down suggestively and winking. Once again now, Maureen writhed in embarrassment, knowing what he'd been thinking from his too expressive face. She'd rushed quickly ahead of Daniel, feeling her whole body burning in embarrassment.

Maureen glanced slowly around the reflected duplicate of the small dressing room that had become so familiar to her in the last year. The door was behind her, with the large fitted wardrobe slightly opened to her left. She wanted to look at these things, to try to hold on to the present, but glancing down at the bottles and lotions on the table in front of her, she was again lost in the past, seeing other rooms, rooms she didn't want to remember!

Daniel had a suite on the top floor of a large high rise. As she had entered through the door he had held open for her, her feet had felt the softness of the sumptuous gold carpeting upon the floor, and her gaze had quickly registered the pale orange velvet modular sofa unit across

33

the sunken living room. It was arranged cozily in a semi-circle in front of a large plate-glass window. Daniel pressed a switch upon the wall and the gold draperies had opened fully, with a soft shushing sound, to reveal a wall consisting entirely of glass, with sliding doors in the center opening onto a patio, which had delighted her. With a cry she had crossed the living room and gone outside. The fragrance of flowers had been all around her, for the patio had been designed as a miniature terrace garden, where flowers of every description bloomed, along with potted trees and shrubs.

Walking to the railing, she had been enchanted by the view; but Daniel had followed her and slipped an arm around her shoulders, and she had shivered, the jacket to her sleeveless pantsuit having been discarded when she had entered the apartment. Remarking that she would catch a chill—for though it was then early summer, the nights in San Francisco could be surprisingly cold—he had led her back into the warmth. Going to the far wall, he pulled a carved figure on the paneling, and natural cedar panels had swung aside to reveal a wet bar set in a recessed cavity in the wall. Sitting on the couch, she had felt self-conscious, and grateful to be holding something when Daniel placed a drink in her hands. Then he fixed a stronger one for himself. He had been drinking rather a lot, but because he showed none of the obvious effects, she hadn't thought much about it until it was too late!

He had walked behind the sofa, turning on the stereo as he passed, and Maureen had felt, rather than heard, the soft blues record as the plaintive melody had filled the air. Daniel, sensing her nervous withdrawal, had placed her empty glass upon the smoked-glass top of the modern coffee table and then drew her into his arms. As they danced he talked quietly and soothingly, reassuring her and calming her with ease. Her fears had been subdued so easily. Even now, as she thought about how trusting she had been, she couldn't help the self-disgust that welled up inside her. When Daniel had kissed her, she had responded with all the innocent fervor of her loving young body and soul.

34

Maureen picked up the brush lying in front of her and absently began running it through her hair—an action that usually calmed her—and then glanced frowningly into the mirror. Her memories were rather vague about what had occurred after that, she realized with surprise. It seemed as if one minute they had been dancing and the next she had been lying upon the sofa, Daniel leaning over her. Even now she couldn't remember the time in between.

All she remembered clearly was the feel of Daniel's passionate mouth ravaging the parted softness of hers, his hands strong and hard on her body, sending a kaleidoscope of sensations tearing through her.

He had murmured, "God, I want you," while with deft fingers he had unbuttoned her blouse. Her breasts had hardened and firmed under the magic of his lean fingers, her breath coming from between the warm fullness of her parted lips in choking gasps. His mouth had followed his hands, sending shivers of delight coursing through her, but when he began unfastening the waistband of her slacks, warning lights had exploded in her brain.

Suddenly seeing an image of herself sprawled in such abandon, she had grasped Daniel's demanding hands and moaned, "Please, Daniel, not until we're married. Stop, please. I've never . . . oh, don't!" As she struggled in earnest her sobs had rung out harshly in the quiet room, mingling with the sound of Daniel's panting breath.

Placing the brush upon the table, Maureen closed her eyes in agony, totally rejecting the memory of Daniel's anger, the terrible fury that he had released upon her unsuspecting head. He had dragged her back into his arms, kissing her shaking mouth violently while his hands roamed with savage possession over her protesting body. He had told her he had no intention of marrying her; he wasn't going to be caught in that trap by a little tease like her.

He said many things that awful night, she thought bitterly. Finally she had fought free of his arms, but in the tussle he had fallen and knocked himself unconscious. Sobbing, she had run out as if all the hounds of hell had been at her heels. She had gone home to the haven of her father's understanding arms, pouring out the whole story in near hysteria.

Rubbing her aching temples with nerveless fingers, she knew that in spite of the hurt and terror she had experienced at his hands, she had been unable to hate Daniel. She made excuses for his behavior in her own mind and had waited, in an agony of wanting, for him to come to her and tell her it was all some ghastly mistake.

They had moved from San Francisco into Oakland shortly after that terrible night, and she had nearly become ill as the weeks went by with no word from Daniel. Finally she had talked her father into contacting him, and Daniel's complete rejection of her pleas had finally made her realize what a fool she had been.

He had left her to face the future alone, without showing her the decency of even meeting her face to face. He had relayed his message through her father, and from that moment she had begun to hate him with a hatred that was almost unbalanced in its intensity.

Her hate had been almost a blessing in disguise, she realized now. Staring at her reflection in the mirror, Maureen again saw the remnants of that hatred glinting in her eyes. It gave me the courage to pull out of my apathy then, to piece together what remained of my shattered life . . . it will do the same for me now, she vowed silently.

"What in hell do you mean, you won't see me?" A voice behind her grated harshly. Maureen's head jerked up as she stared in disbelief at the grim-faced man standing there.

Licking lips suddenly dry, she stammered, "I—I didn't hear you come in."

"Obviously not," he replied, his eyes piercing her from across the room.

Standing and turning to face him, she tilted her chin in a defiant angle. "What are you doing here, Daniel? You must know we have nothing to talk about."

"Well, honey," he replied, his eyes glancing caressingly over her rounded body. "It's never been talking I was interested in where you were concerned."

"No, I know exactly what you were interested in, Daniel, but you can just think again!"

"God, you're even more beautiful than you were four years ago, baby!" Daniel's voice was soft as he leaned indolently back against the closed door.

"Your opinion doesn't matter to me in the least, Daniel, and don't call me baby," she replied, while pondering the changes the years had made in him. She remembered his tall muscular figure so well. Never had she believed she would see him again, and now it was the same man, yet different. His voice was deeper than she remembered, and she realized there were lines in his face that hadn't been there before. The gray hairs now silvering his temples gave him the look of someone for whom the last few years hadn't been easy. Probably too much big business, and too many women!

Seeing her thoughts revealed in her face, Daniel walked slowly toward her, and Maureen felt her body stiffen in response.

"My opinion used to matter a lot, Maurie," he said, reaching out and running his hand caressingly down her arm.

Jerking free of his touch, Maureen said, "Don't touch me, Daniel. I don't like it."

"You used to like it when I touched you, honey," he mocked hatefully, but Maureen felt a surge of pleasure as the clenching of his fist told her the scathing words had hit their mark.

"That was a long time ago, when I was young enough to think I could ever love a man like you. I'm a big girl now, and thanks to you, I learned quickly." Maureen tried to make her voice emotionless and hard—as his was —and was disgusted with herself for letting him see her bitterness. Knowing Daniel, it would just give him a weapon to use against her.

"It's true you've changed, Maurie. I never thought I'd see the day shy little Maurie would be on a stage, flaunting her body for all comers. Or is it just the highest bidders you take on?"

Gasping at the insult, Maureen whirled around, an arm raised to slap that mocking smile off his face.

He caught her wrist: "I think not, sweetheart," and jerking her arm, he forced her close against his body.

Struggling, Maureen cried, "Let me go, I hate you," as he tightened his arms around her body, trapping her arms at her side.

"I just wanted to say I'm buying, honey," he whispered. "I knew the minute I saw you again I hadn't gotten you out of my system."

"Please don't, Daniel. I'm not what you think, let me go!" Desperately Maureen struggled in his arms, knowing the old soul-destroying attraction was still there between them.

He hesitated for a moment, but he didn't want to believe her words. All he knew was he wanted her like he'd never wanted another woman before or since meeting her. With a groan he parted her mouth with his.

Maureen fought from responding to the mouth ravaging hers, but when his tongue forced her lips apart and entered her mouth, she went limp. The kiss went on and on, his mouth hardening and lengthening, moving caressingly from side to side, coaxing a response.

Maureen began to tremble, feeling a fire shoot through her limbs, and struggled again, desperately trying to hide her emotions. To her surprise, Daniel immediately released her.

Shaking, Maureen stared at him and asked piteously, "What do you want, Daniel?"

"You're not the innocent young virgin now, you know what I want, honey," he replied, his voice quiet as he stared grimly into her eyes. "You ran out on me once, Maurie. I won't give you the opportunity again."

"I never ran out on you," Maureen heard herself scream at him, and with a visible effort won some measure of control. "You threw me out, Daniel!"

"Don't give me that!" Daniel sneered cruelly, running an angry hand through the thickness of his hair. "I was drunk that night, Maurie!"

Meeting the scorn in her eyes, Daniel had the grace to

look away in embarrassment, much to Maureen's surprise. "All right . . . I behaved like a swine, but for someone who supposedly loved me so deeply," he said to her sarcastically, "you sure didn't believe in giving me a chance to make things right with you. You just ran out without a trace, and all the detective agencies in the city couldn't trace you or your family."

Dear God . . . Daniel is telling the truth! One glance at his face told her that. But it just isn't possible, he has to be lying. Her father had said . . . Suddenly it all fell into place, and Maureen couldn't bear the hurt the discovery caused. Her father had been so angry on that night, Maureen remembered. It hurt to think her beloved father had lied to her, but she had to make herself understand his point of view. He had hated Daniel for hurting his little girl, and he must have felt he was protecting her by keeping Daniel away from her. With these thoughts Maureen forgave him, and some of the hurt melted from her heart.

Walking over to her dressing table on trembling legs, Maureen again sat down. She knew now that Daniel would never believe she wasn't what he thought. He really didn't remember . . . it must have been a combination of drink and that crack on the head, she thought hysterically. A night that had almost destroyed her, and he couldn't even remember! Maureen nearly laughed aloud at the irony of it, but not quite!

"Why now, Daniel? Four years ago I loved you more than life itself, no matter what you think, but you didn't love me. Why come back now, to destroy the life I've built for myself?"

Lighting a cigarette, Daniel drew the smoke into his lungs and exhaled slowly. His eyes narrowing in an insolent scowl, he replied, "It's taken me this long to find you, Maurie . . . to find you working in a place like this!"

Spine stiffening in outrage, Maureen gripped the edge of the dressing table. "Just what do you mean by that?"

"I made it clear from the beginning what I thought."

"This place is perfectly respectable, and for your information I sing for a living, Daniel, nothing else!"

Suddenly feeling the need to move around, Maureen got up and rummaged in Gaye's drawer for the ashtray her friend kept there for Harry. Handing it to Daniel, she said bitterly, "I work here because here's where the money is. I got tired of slinging hamburgers, of working two jobs to have enough money to live on." Drawing a deep quivering breath and turning her back toward him, Maureen whispered, "I have more than myself to support, Daniel. I have my sister's future to think about."

"I didn't know you had a sister, Maurie. You never mentioned her," Daniel said, puzzled. Then anger darkened his face. "Why in hell isn't your father supporting her, and you too for that matter?"

"He's dead." Maureen stated the words baldly, her voice little more than a whisper. Daniel heard the despondency behind it, and his face softened.

"I'm sorry, I didn't know."

"She . . . Katy was born just a few months before my mother and father were killed in an auto accident." Maureen couldn't help the tears that came to her eyes as the remembered pain of that terrible time lashed out at her once again, and she felt vulnerable before Daniel's piercing gaze.

Walking across the room, Maureen stopped in front of the sofa where Daniel was sitting. "There are a lot of things you don't know, Daniel . . . and I won't waste your time or mine by telling you. I know what you think of me, have always thought . . . but I just don't care. I only want you to realize one thing. You killed whatever feelings I had for you, and I don't want you anymore."

Silence hung like a heavy pall over the room, so intense it was almost tangible as Daniel stared at Maureen, his face harsh in the dim light. Taking a deep breath, Maureen could no longer stand his accusing gaze and turned her back to him, fully expecting him to leave quietly.

I should have known better, she thought with a start as Daniel came up behind her, his hands reaching out ruthlessly to grip her arms and spin her around. Stunned, she looked into his eyes in disbelief, angry words choking her throat. Before she dared give them utterance, Daniel shook her, his hands trembling in reaction.

"Can't you get it through your head that it doesn't matter to me what you want?"

Maureen gasped, staring up incredulously into Daniel's face. What she saw reflected in his eyes made her realize his words hadn't been said in anger alone—he meant every word! Her mind churning furiously, Maureen tried to think of some way out, something that would scotch Daniel's plans once and for all, for he wasn't the kind of man to let anything or anyone get in his way once his mind was made up. It would take more than her own reluctance to convince him, and suddenly a solution came to her, if she dared use it.

"Daniel, I know my wishes have never mattered to you," she said, her voice scathing, "but they do matter to Jack, and I think he's the only one with the right to decide when and if I marry."

"Who said anything about marriage," he sneered.

"Jack," she replied, her eyes lighting in triumph.

Maureen held her breath, waiting for Daniel's reaction, and it wasn't long in coming.

"You mean Jack Cummings, the bartender here?" Daniel's voice was soft, and she was bewildered by his reaction.

"Yes . . ." Maureen's voice involuntarily faded as she mumbled her reply, for as she looked into Daniel's eyes she realized the softness of his voice had been a cover for his true emotions, and what she now read in his eyes caused her to shiver in sudden fear.

The gray eyes glinting into hers left little to the imagination about what he was thinking, and she knew without a doubt she had failed. Compunction for the harm she might have inadvertently caused Jack smote her, and she trembled convulsively under Daniel's tightening fingers.

"Please, you're hurting me," she whispered, trying to twist out of his punishing grip.

"You don't know it, Maurie, but you and your Jack are living in a dream world."

Sudden anger overriding caution, Maureen blurted out, "He loves me, Daniel, something you will never understand." Looking into his eyes, she summoned all the scorn her voice was capable of: "Why should I be a rich man's temporary mistress when I could live as another man's wife?"

Daniel flinched at her words. As he stared at her angry face he nearly gasped aloud at the savagery of his own emotions at the thought of her slipping out of his grasp. He had to forcibly restrain himself from trembling at her closeness like any callow youth. He didn't know why, but the idea of her belonging to any man but himself was poison to him, and this was something he had certainly never counted on. Summoning a cold smile to allay her fears, he controlled the almost violent urge to use threats against her so-called fiancé to gain his objective. It would, he knew, give her one more reason to hate him, and he needed time to think of an alternative.

"All right, Maurie . . . I get your point," Daniel said quietly, walking to the door. "I hope you'll enjoy being a poor man's wife, honey." His voice mouthed "poor" sneeringly, then he left, closing the door behind him.

Maureen stared at the door in stupefaction, hardly daring to believe she'd won. Elation coursed through her veins at the realization that she'd outwitted the mighty Daniel Lord. She could hardly believe her ruse had worked, and she sighed in relief. Bless Jack . . . he doesn't know it . . . but right now I could almost go ahead and marry him.

Thinking of Jack caused a worried frown to mar the smoothness of her forehead. It wasn't fair laying this on him, for he'd been a very good friend to her, and she knew he loved her, or at least thought he did. He was the only man she'd dated since Daniel, the only man that didn't want any more from her than she was able to give. Really, Jack is more like a brother to me, she mused. As soon as he had realized that she couldn't love him in the way he'd wanted, he had set out to be the very best of friends.

When he had taken her out, Katy had come along, too. They had had delightful trips to the San Francisco Zoo, and several times had taken picnic lunches to the rolling

42

green expanses of Golden Gate Park. For the first time in her life Maureen had known what it was to be really carefree in the company of a man other than her father, and now she sighed for what was past. She didn't want Jack hurt, and vowed she wouldn't implicate him in this mess any more than she already had. Her mouth tightened in determination. I'll fight Daniel fair and never again use a friend to slink away from my own problems, she thought, disgusted at her actions.

CHAPTER THREE

The sun's rays burned hotly on the sands as Maureen reclined beside Gaye on the colorful blanket spread out beneath them. Looking out over the expanse of water, she watched the swells break against the shore, spewing white foam in their wake.

A few feet away Katy was playing with her bucket and spade in the patches of water left from the receding tide. Glancing at her, Maureen thought about how ideal this beach was for small children.

Santa Cruz beach has a natural windbreak of towering rocks and beside them runs an inlet which fills with water at high tide. When the tide recedes, it leaves little sand-water pools for very small children, and a wide expanse of shallow sun-warmed water, for swimmers who want to paddle around without battling surf. Without warning, a sun-browned body in a minute blue-flowered bikini hurled itself into Maureen's arms.

"Maurie . . . when can we ride the horsies?" Katy questioned in a pleading voice, spreading wet sandy arms wide around Maureen's neck.

Maureen loved the feel of those little arms, and a wealth of emotion surged through her as she hugged Katy close. She couldn't have made it through this last couple of weeks without her—and all the everyday diversions a small child could cause—and she was more grateful for Katy than ever before.

Daniel had been to the club on several occasions, but she had only heard about his visits secondhand. Gaye had told her he'd been in talking to Grady, but when questioned, Gaye had been rather evasive as to the reasons. Maureen frowned momentarily.

She was still on tenterhooks, wondering what Daniel's next move would be. He had left in a towering rage, she remembered fearfully. He hadn't spoken another word to her after her dismissal of him—just walked out quietly, his mouth a grim white line in his pale face.

That's what worried her so much now, she realized. If Daniel had raged at her, or even argued, she could have understood. It was his very quietness that unnerved her, for she knew Daniel well enough to know he wasn't a man to accept defeat easily, if at all.

"I don't know where you two get the energy," Gaye groaned, watching Maureen wrestling with Katy. She smiled as she heard the child's delighted giggles. Levering herself lethargically into a sitting position, she yawned. "All this sun and sea air makes me feel like a marshmallow."

"Aunty Gaye, me wants a marshmallow," cried Katy, wriggling out of Maureen's arms and throwing herself at Gaye.

"Now you've done it, Gaye!" Maureen laughed, brushing the sand off her arms.

"We don't have any marshmallows, honey," Gaye told Katy, giving her a hug, "but Aunty Gaye will give you some juice," she coaxed, reaching for the Thermos.

"Don't want juice!" Katy frowned determinedly. "Katy wants marshmallow," she told Gaye firmly, her lower lip jutting out warningly.

Correctly reading the signs in the small girl's face, Maureen decided to get Gaye off the hook. With a droll look for her friend, she promised, "Honey, you eat your sandwich and drink your juice. Then, if you finish all your lunch, Aunty Gaye and I will take you to ride the merry-go-round."

Katy's stormy face instantly cleared. Sitting down beside Maureen, she took the sandwich Gaye handed her in her chubby hands. "If I eat the crust, can I have two rides?"

Maureen caught the sly glance on Katy's face, but for the sake of peace decided to ignore it. "Well, we'll see if Aunty Gaye can hold up that long." Gaye grimaced as she heard Maureen's words.

"That means yes," Katy sighed happily.

"Don't talk with your mouth full," growled Gaye.

"You're going to be the death of your Aunty Gaye yet." Maureen laughed, rumpling Katy's tangled dark curls.

Unwrapping her own sandwich, Maureen smiled at Gaye and then began to eat. As she watched Katy carefully eat the center out of her sandwich half, she couldn't help wondering if there was really any reason to smile. Katy was becoming thoroughly spoilt and was already much too used to having her own way. Sighing, Maureen quickly finished her meal, brushing the crumbs from her legs.

As if that were a hidden signal, she and Gaye jumped up and began clearing away the mess, walking the few feet to a garbage receptacle, which was already nearly crammed full.

With lunch finished and all their paraphernalia stuffed into an oversized beach bag, Maureen and Gaye made their way with difficulty—stepping over and around reclining bodies—to the steps leading up to the Santa Cruz boardwalk. Katy was running ahead, spewing sand in her wake.

"Stop right where you are, young lady," Maureen called in alarm, not wanting to lose the child in the crowds lining the boardwalk. Katy, hearing the warning in Maureen's voice, suddenly stopped running and grasped Maureen's hand, looking up at her with a beguiling smile. Maureen couldn't help returning the smile, though she knew the good behavior was less in response to her authority than it was to the promised merry-go-round ride. Katy, being a logical child, wasn't about to blow a good thing by misbehaving.

Reaching the top of the stairs, Maureen grabbed Katy's sticky hand.

"We'd better get to the bathroom first, okay?" Maureen looked down at Katy with resignation. "Then we can change and wash this little sand crab up," Maureen stated, glancing at Gaye for approval.

"Sounds good to me, Maurie," Gaye said, levering the bag farther up on her shoulder.

"Let me carry that for a while."

"Honey, you have enough to do just keeping up with quicksilver Katy," Gaye replied firmly, swinging the bag out of Maureen's reach.

Gaye glanced at Maureen, noting the dark circles under her eyes, the tension around her mouth that the weekend hadn't entirely erased. She had hoped the time away in the sunshine and sea breezes would be a good rest cure for Maurie. As Maureen tiredly lifted the excited little girl in her arms Gaye looked away. Though they were enjoying themselves, Maurie still had a haunted look in her eyes when she thought herself unobserved, and Gaye had a good idea Daniel Lord was behind it. A man usually is, she thought cynically.

Maureen noticed the surreptitious glances Gaye was giving her, and groaned inwardly. Though she had tried to hide her tiredness from Gaye's discerning eyes, there was no way to hide completely the dark smudges beneath her eyes. She knew Gaye must be near to guessing at least part of the truth, and she felt her friend's hurt at her own reticence. Maureen wanted, at times like this, to confide completely in Gaye, but something always stopped her. Pride probably, either false or otherwise, but she knew it wasn't pride alone. Maureen had learned independence in a hard school, and letting it go, even to confide in a beloved friend like Gaye, didn't come easy. Oh, well, she thought with a sigh. Maybe it's for the best!

Gaye pushed open the heavy door to the dingy bathroom with difficulty. It was large, cavernous, and not particularly clean, with double rows of stalls running to left and right. Maureen shivered in the cool air, running to stop Katy from crawling under an occupied cubicle.

After changing into shorts and a halter top which left the golden expanse of her midriff bare, Maureen wished she had two sets of hands as she washed and dressed a wriggling Katy in a yellow sunsuit and bent to fasten small white T-strapped sandals on her dimpled baby feet.

Glancing down at her sleeveless body shirt and long white slacks, Gaye glanced at Maureen's long brown legs and grimaced.

"You're going to give me a complex in those things, Maurie."

"Why didn't you wear shorts, Gaye? It's too hot for slacks, and we are at the beach, after all," Maureen said questioningly as they left the coolness of the bathroom.

As the rays of the sun seemed to attack with renewed ferocity, Gaye groaned, then sighed wistfully.

"Honey, if my legs looked like yours, I'd never wear anything else," she quipped, disgustedly surveying her short plump limbs as they walked toward the merry-go-round.

Maureen just shook her head and laughed. "Vanity, vanity!" Her attention on Gaye for the moment, Maureen's laughter was choked off midstream. Katy, seeing her chance, had quickly made her bid for freedom, and Maureen clutched Katy's hand tighter when it seemed likely to be jerked out of her grasp.

Later, watching Katy's excited face as she waved to them, the merry-go-round whirling her past in a blur of color and hurdy-gurdy sound, they both smiled at the delightful picture the child presented, Gaye nearly as proud as Maureen.

"She never gets enough, does she?" asked Gaye, with a little chuckle.

"Never, but I was the same. I remember coming here with Mother and Dad," replied Maureen reminiscently. "I had a favorite blue-and-gold horse, and I'd make my father wait until I could have that particular one . . . none other would do." Maureen laughed at the memory. "You should have seen my father running around after that horse, trying to get to it before someone else did. He'd lift me up with a scowl on his face, embarrassed because people were staring at him and thinking he was probably a little crazy. At least Katy's not that particular!" Maureen laughed again, more at the horrified look on Gaye's face as she imagined herself running to catch a certain horse for Katy.

After literally dragging the crying child off the merry-go-round at last, Gaye suggested they walk to the far end of the boardwalk.

"We can have an early dinner at the coffee shop there, okay?"

"Good idea." Maureen smiled. "Then we can put Katy right to bed, she's exhausted now . . . as you can hear," Maureen agreed drolly, with a glance at the still-screaming Katy as she tucked her protesting small hand more firmly in hers.

Suddenly Katy pulled free from Maureen's restraining grasp and ran on ahead, for she had spotted the marionette show just past the coffee shop. She hopped up and down in excitement, her despair over leaving her beloved "horsies" forgotten now that a new interest had caught her volatile attention.

"Oh, no! I'd forgotten about that," Maureen groaned with exasperation.

"It's all right, honey. This way we can get her to eat her dinner by bribing her with the puppet show," said Gaye, bending to tell the child.

Maureen laughed in admiration. "Now you know my secret!"

Straightening, Gaye winked. "Honey, I always say survival of the fittest means you're a quick learner."

After a light meal of soup and toast, eaten while they tried to talk over the noise of the arcade opposite, and then sitting through the clever marionette show, Maureen and Gaye began the long walk across to the boardwalk's exit. Going down the ramp toward the parking lot, Maureen thought what a super day it had been for her and Katy.

This weekend had been just the medicine she'd needed. Though she hadn't completely relaxed, she had come close to it, probably because she knew Daniel was nowhere near. Her nerves, she realized now, had been stretched unbearably while she anticipated with dread the confrontation with Daniel she was sure would come. As each day had passed, she'd felt like a little mouse trapped in a corner, with the cat ready to pounce.

Reaching the car, they stowed their things in the trunk and drove off. As Gaye traversed the few blocks to their motel, Maureen held Katy's soft body in her lap.

"Poor baby's so tired," she whispered as she placed a soft kiss on the child's smooth forehead, brushing her soft curly hair back with her lips. "She's half asleep already, Gaye. It's been a big day for such a little girl," she reiterated softly.

"Huh, I know just how she feels!" Gaye exclaimed. "I don't know about you, honey, you're used to it, but it's been a big day for this particular big girl, too." Gaye laughed.

"Not tired either," Katy mumbled indignantly, the sleepy treble lost as Gaye's startled laughter rang out, her glance going to Maureen in disbelief.

Back in the motel, Maureen quickly bathed the tired little girl, dressing her in fuzzy pink pajamas with feet slightly cracked from repeated washings. They're really much too warm for this time of year, she thought fondly, bending down to kiss the slightly damp head and breathing in the baby smell she so loved, but Katy had the habit of kicking off her covers in the night, so they were practical.

Tiptoeing out of the bedroom with its double and single beds, Maureen left the door open a crack and also left the light on in the tiny hall in case Katy woke up in the night. Being used to a night-light in her small bedroom at home, Maureen knew it was a good precaution. Katy was such a light sleeper. She had a habit of coming half awake, and, if aware of the dark, waking fully.

"Do you want to play cards, or just watch some television?" Gaye asked as Maureen entered and threw herself tiredly into a chair.

"To tell you the truth, I'm too tired to do much more than shower and climb into bed myself. Sorry, Gaye . . .

51

but I was actually envying Katy a few moments ago."
Maureen yawned, smiling her regret.

"Well, you go right ahead, don't think you have to entertain me, Maurie. After all, the more rest you get, the sooner you'll be your old self."

"I don't know what in the world is the matter with me lately. I'm sorry I'm such a wet blanket, Gaye." Maureen, trying to stifle another yawn with her hand and failing, looked at Gaye with a guilty expression on her mobile face.

"Honey, I don't want to pry, you know that, but can I ask you a rather personal question?" Gaye asked warily.

Maureen tensed in the chair, afraid of what Gaye would ask. She had told her a rather sketchy version of her past association with Daniel. She'd only told Gaye they'd parted after an argument. What if Gaye suspected more than she'd been told, and openly asked her? She could never lie to Gaye, she'd been too good to her, but knowing Gaye's protective instinct where she was concerned, she didn't want to complicate things. She realized, with a sense of wonder, that it was Daniel she was trying to protect. She just couldn't bear to hear Gaye decrying what Daniel had done to her, even though she herself did it. Gaye had a heart of gold, but she did tend to be outspoken when her dander was up. Well, it's up to me alone to see that the past remains just that . . . past. There's no point raking up all that again now, for any reason. She was getting paranoid about the whole thing anyway. What made her think Gaye's question would even concern Daniel? Disgusted with herself for letting Daniel pop in and out of her thoughts like a bogeyman, Maureen smiled at Gaye, nodding affirmatively before she had a chance to change her mind.

Seeing Maureen's assenting nod, Gaye took a deep breath and said, "Honey, what will you do when Grady sells the club?"

Hearing the unexpected question, Maureen almost visibly sagged with relief. It would teach her to expect the worst!

"I guess I'll go back to waitress work, unless the new owner keeps me on, Gaye," she answered quietly.

"That's what I was afraid you'd say," replied Gaye with a worried frown. "You know you can't take the hours you'd need to work in order to support yourself, not with Katy getting to be such a handful! Honey, won't you reconsider moving to Nevada with Harry and me? You know . . . you can make big money working in those clubs . . . especially with a voice and a face like yours."

Maureen thought over Gaye's words but knew she wouldn't follow her friend's suggestion. The last couple of months had seen so many changes in her once snug existence, not the least being Harry's long anticipated proposal to Gaye and their plans for settling in Nevada when they married. Maureen was glad for Gaye's sake, but she just wouldn't horn in on the beginning of their married life together.

The other big blow had come almost simultaneously with Gaye's big announcement, she mused, pulling at the fullness of her lower lip. Grady's wife, an asthmatic, had been steadily having more, and more severe, attacks. After the last, which had nearly cost her her life, Grady had come to the club from the hospital, calling them all in his office. He had explained her condition to them, saying the doctor had recommended a different climate, and he was looking for a buyer for the club. They'd all understood, of course, and sympathized with poor Grady, but it had still been a shock. Maureen sighed, a frown marring her face. It seemed to her that since Daniel had walked back into her life, he'd brought nothing but trouble with him!

She had already been approached by two other clubs, once the news was out, but she couldn't bear the thought of the life it would involve. Sure, I would make enough money, but the truth is, I'm scared, she admitted to herself. She'd been protected with Gaye and Grady. The other clubs would expect her to do more than sing for her supper, she thought cynically, and she would rather go back to waitressing than have to mingle with customers and fend off the advances of strange men.

"Gaye, you know I appreciate the offer, and I know you're worried about Katy and me, but—"

53

"I know, Maurie . . . you think you'd be a problem, but Harry and I . . . we want you."

Getting up, Maureen walked over and gave Gaye a quick hug. "Don't worry, Gaye. I promise I'll consider your offer, but don't count on my agreeing. Who knows, maybe I'll meet the man of my dreams who'll carry me off into the sunset, with Katy tucked up in the saddle bag." Maureen laughed, trying to interject a happier note into the conversation.

"Huh, I think you already have!"

Stiffening, Maureen asked, "What do you mean?"

"Maurie, I said I wouldn't interfere, but you've been so different since that night. I—I'm sorry, honey, but I have to ask, did Daniel Lord ask you to marry him when you knew him before? Don't answer if you don't want to. Just tell me to shut up and mind my own business."

"It's not marriage he wants!" Maureen said baldly, before she had time to think.

"Oh, honey . . . I'm sorry for putting my big foot in it, but would you marry him if he asks?"

"No . . . you don't understand everything, and I just can't go into it now . . . but he doesn't love me, Gaye."

"But Maurie, think of the life you could have, the security for you and Katy . . . he obviously wants you now, and eventually he might want you enough to ask you to be his wife. God . . . I know of a lot of women who'd love to be in your shoes, marriage or no marriage."

"That's the trouble, Gaye. He does want me, but I'm just not made that way. I couldn't face myself in the mirror every morning . . . knowing I was his mistress. A man like Daniel would make me his thing, his possession, even if he did eventually marry me. I wouldn't have my own identity anymore."

Maureen thought how true the words were as soon as they were spoken, even if that truth hurt. She knew her refusal was the right one, for both her and Daniel; no other decision was possible. Maybe someday he'd really love someone, she thought with a small pain in her heart, which puzzled her. When and if that day comes, she knew only too well, that woman would be the luckiest in the world. She had seen Daniel both in passion and in anger, but was there also any possibility of Daniel ever really loving a woman? With genuine love to temper and guide him, would he be a different person . . . no longer the domineering male bent on acquiring, uncaring of the cost to himself or anyone else?

Maybe she could have been the one to unlock all the secrets Daniel kept deep inside him. . . . Maybe once, but not now, she thought sadly. He'd destroyed all hope of that when he had showed his contempt of her as a person, both in the past and also at their last meeting. With him, she would feel she had to fight to keep her own identity, and that was no way to begin a relationship, even if he did offer her marriage. Marriage should be two people sharing hopes, and dreams . . . sharing thoughts and leaning one on the other. Daniel would exploit her need to lean, without letting her into his own heart and mind, and she couldn't live like that. She knew she needed to be herself, as well as an extension of him. She guessed it all boiled down to needing to be needed as well as wanted, and Daniel needed no one but himself, she concluded bitterly.

"Oh, Maurie . . . I understand what you're saying, but I still think you're crazy," Gaye told her bluntly. "How about Jack, Maurie? You know he's crazy about you."

"Number one," Maureen smiled, "he hasn't asked me. Number two, and more important, I'm not crazy about him, at least not that way."

"But, Maurie—"

Maureen laughed, shaking her head at a disappointed Gaye. "You know I look upon Jack as a very dear friend, but I could never love him enough, and he's too nice a man to cheat in that way. Anyway, he thinks he loves me, but he's really in love with the idea of having a wife and family, Gaye. That makes him rather vulnerable to any girl, especially one like me with a little girl he's crazy about to start things off."

"Isn't that all to the good?"

"It would be if I could love him as he deserves to be loved, but I can't and never will."

Sighing, Maureen walked toward the bedroom. Reaching the doorway, she turned. "I know you think I'm crazy, Gaye, but I just can't sell myself short. Maybe I'm asking for too much, but . . . that's just the way I am. Don't worry so much," Maureen said on a lighter note. "Don't you know it'll cause wrinkles?"

Going along with Maureen's mood, sensing her desire to end the conversation, Gaye jumped up to stare in mock horror at her reflection, smoothing imaginary wrinkles. Laughing, Maureen called out her good-nights as she entered the bedroom. She did not see the sober look that crossed her friend's face as she watched Maureen leave the room.

After a quick shower Maureen prepared for bed. As she climbed into the double bed she thought of her conversation with Gaye. Yawning, she sensed worriedly that tonight would be like all the other nights spent thinking of Daniel, and worrying over the future. But the sea and sand having done their work, she fell into a deep sleep almost at once.

Maureen wasn't aware of the hours that had elapsed before a very worried Gaye finally joined her. For Gaye the night was a long one, as she wondered what Maureen's reaction would be when she found out the name of the club's new owner. What really frightened her, though, was the motivation of Maureen's new boss.

That night, relaxing at home in her robe and slippers, Maureen sighed at the welcome sight of the familiar comforts around her. She felt more rested than she had for a long time.

Their weekend trip had ended wonderfully. They had packed and left early because they wanted to stop at Santa's Village on the way through the mountains. Katy had been so thrilled with the rides, and she herself had been delighted with the little chalets nestled beneath tall evergreens.

After spending a couple of hours seeing everything— or nearly everything—there was, they had eaten a picnic lunch and again started for home.

Maureen sighed luxuriously, leaning back in the chair

56

and rubbing her aching feet. The rest of the trip had passed quickly. Luckily it had been Katy's nap time, she thought with a weary smile; so she and Gaye had been able to talk without any distractions, for the tired little pumpkin had slept all the way home.

It was more than time she got to bed. Rising, Maureen stretched and felt her muscles protest. She must be getting old and creaky if one weekend at the beach could do this to her. Suddenly her body tautened in alarm as she heard the firm knock on her door. Looking through the window, she gasped as she saw Daniel standing there. Letting the curtain drop, she leaned weakly against the door. She contemplated pretending she was asleep, but he would have seen the lights. Oh, God . . . give me strength, she prayed despairingly as she released the catch on the door and opened it wide.

She'd thought of him so much, seeing him at last was almost an anticlimax; and now she watched mesmerized as he crossed over to the couch, moving with his curiously pantherish stride.

"May I sit down?" he asked casually.

"Yes . . . yes, of course," Maureen stammered in agitation as she closed the door and sat down again in the chair, glad that it was on the other side of the living room.

"For the love of God, Maurie," Daniel exclaimed with anger. "Come over here, I need to talk to you."

Nervously Maureen rose and joined him on the farthest end of the couch, sitting with her feet tucked defensively under her.

"What do you want, Daniel?" she asked with a desperate attempt at calm. "It's late, and I'm tired."

"Damn it, Maurie! I'm not here with rape in mind, if that's what you're worried about," Daniel spat out.

"You couldn't prove it by me," she replied bitterly, looking down at her clenched hands. Forcing herself to relax the tense grip on her robe, she again glanced up at him.

Seeing the almost savage expression in his eyes, she quickly averted her gaze from his . . . staring instead at the smooth brown column of his throat . . . admiring

57

fleetingly the silver ankh necklace nestled against his bronzed skin.

"Maurie," he said, subduing his anger with visible effort. "I've spent the last few weeks getting my affairs in order. I've given you the time you needed . . . now I'm tired of waiting. It's time for you to stop acting like a child," he stated, his chiseled mouth firming uncompromisingly.

"Your affairs?" Maureen shot back tauntingly. She was foolishly playing with fire but could not stop herself. She was more angry at being told she was childish than she'd have believed possible, but Daniel had always had this effect on her. One minute he would, by a look or a touch, arouse her to passion; the next she would be stammering in fury at some chance word or attitude. Even in their halcyon days his attitude had often provoked her, but she had meekly kept silent, like a timid mouse, for fear he would leave her, she remembered cynically.

"Damn you, Maurie. What the hell are you implying?" Daniel's furious tones jerked her rudely out of her reverie.

"N—nothing, Daniel," she stammered, realizing she had gone too far.

There was nothing to gain, she realized, in antagonizing Daniel further. Glancing at him to see the effect of her placating words, she noticed the muscle twitch in his cheek, a sure sign that he was about to lose control.

As her agitated gaze took in his lean, muscular figure, the silk shirt open to the middle of his chest—Maureen's senses reeled from the sexual magnetism he still exerted over her. She couldn't subdue the sensations that were sweeping over her as she saw the mat of dark hairs on his chest, agonizingly remembering the feel of them against her as he'd pressed his passion-warmed body to hers.

"I've made tentative arrangements for our wedding two weeks from now, Maurie," Daniel stated baldly, drawing in his breath and clenching his jaw tensely as he stared at the incredulous expression crossing her face. The very quietness of his words gave them a certain force.

Maureen swallowed with difficulty, then walked deter-

minedly to the door. As she opened it, she looked pointedly at him.

"Please leave, now! I've told you . . . I don't want you,
Daniel."

Maureen couldn't help it, she had never before felt such
anger and disgust. His so-called proposal rose like bile in
her throat, threatening to choke her. Taking deep, ragged
breaths to calm herself, Maureen stared at Daniel who
lounged at his ease on her couch. How dare he come in
here, without a by-your-leave, and expect her just meekly
to accede to his demands, as if she were a puppet he
could manipulate at will, or as if no woman, least of all
her, could resist the chance of becoming his wife. True,
at one point in her life that would have been the epitome
of all her dreams, but no more.

How could he calmly make plans like this, expecting her
to acquiesce, especially when she'd deliberately led him to
believe she was in love with someone else? It just didn't
make sense—unless she hadn't been convincing enough?
No, Daniel had been convinced, she was sure of that.
Fluctuating emotions crossed her face like fleeting shadows
as she nervously debated with herself regarding Daniel's
present attitude. Staring at his face, Maureen tried to read
a clue to his quiet sureness, but his expression gave nothing away. His very calmness was more frightening than
his anger. She was determined to break that calm of his
if it killed her.

Taking a deep breath for courage, she said, "With
nothing but bitterness between us, how long do you think
it would be before you resumed your . . . activities?"
Hearing the sneer in her voice, Maureen was appalled at
her own daring, and she saw Daniel's body stiffen. She
had been more successful than she'd hoped!

Daniel leaped from the couch and strode toward her.
Grabbing her arm, he jerked her against the hard masculine length of his body. Her involuntary response to their
closeness caused his expression to change, and as his eyes
darkened for a reason other than anger Maureen cursed
her stupidity in not keeping a tighter control over her

traitorous body. Furious with herself, she knew she'd lost any advantage she might have gained.

Seeing the passionate warmth of his look, Maureen began to struggle as his arms closed around her and his head lowered toward hers.

"No!" she gasped, turning her head to escape his mouth. His lips pressed hotly upon her neck—when the sweetness of her lips was denied him—leaving trails of fire where they pressed against her flushed skin.

With a kick of his foot Daniel slammed the door . . . pressing her against it with the weight of his body. Parting her robe with his hand, he groaned as his mouth traveled over her scented skin, to cover the throbbing aureoles of her breasts.

"Maurie?" Maureen tensed as the frightened cry rent the stillness, only the sobbing rasp of their mingled breath disturbing the quiet.

"Daniel . . . let me go!" Maureen cried struggling in panic. Tearing herself out of his arms, she clutched her robe to hide her nakedness from his gaze. With a little sob, and very little dignity, she stumbled into the room to soothe the frightened child.

Bending over Katy, Maureen gathered her damp little body in her arms. Still emotionally shaken, she could feel Daniel's presence behind her in the small room.

What if Katy hadn't cried out? she thought, torturing herself with images of what might have happened. What price freedom then? Dear God, why does he have this power over me? All he has to do is be in the same room to sap all resolution. If she was to survive, Maureen knew she must keep him at arm's length, or farther if possible!

"Who's that man?" Katy questioned loudly. Having walked over to sit on the opposite side of the bed, Daniel faced Maureen and Katy, taking in the delightful picture they made.

"Who do you think I am, sweetheart?" Daniel questioned softly, before Maureen had a chance to answer the child herself. Reaching out, he gently smoothed a hand over the child's fine dark hair.

Katy stared at him with large dark eyes so reminiscent of Maureen's they made him catch his breath. Seemingly coming to a decision, Katy asked, "Are you a daddy?"

"No, honey. I'm not that lucky." Daniel smiled.

Maureen gasped in wonder at the singular sweetness of that smile. Daniel's face had miraculously softened. This was a side to him she'd never seen before; she had never dreamed he even liked children.

Katy pulled away from Maureen. "Don't you have a little girl?"

"I don't, honey . . . but I'd like a little girl more than anything," Daniel said, surprised himself at how true those words suddenly were.

"My daddy's in Heaven."

"I know, honey, and I'm sorry. Anyone would be lucky to have a little girl like you."

"You can be my daddy," she stated trustfully, holding out her arms to Daniel, who took her from Maureen's protesting arms firmly and placed her gently upon his lap.

"Katy . . . that's enough. It's time you were asleep!" Maureen could do nothing about the high nervous pitch of her voice, could do nothing to curb the tension assailing her.

She was amazed and a little frightened at Katy's reaction to Daniel. She had never known her to behave like that toward any stranger, especially since she was unused to many men around. It seemed she wasn't the only Connolly to be susceptible to Daniel's particular brand of charm, she thought with irony. He was certainly exerting himself now, and she bitterly conceded his success.

For once Katy chose to ignore Maureen's express demand, letting Daniel hold her even closer. Lifting her arms to cling to his neck, she said winningly, "He's my daddy now, aren't you my daddy?"

As Daniel looked into the child's eyes, a strange emotion choked him, something he'd never before felt for another human being, and his arms tightened almost convulsively around Katy's slight frame.

His eyes bore into Maureen's, a warning in their depths, before he again bent to Katy and whispered: "That's just what I'm planning to be, Chicken. Now . . . I think Maurie's right . . . Bed for you."

Giggling at this form of endearment, Katy allowed herself to be resettled. After kissing Maureen, she held up her smiling face for Daniel's kiss. Tiptoeing from the room, she whispered in a sleepy little voice, "Wait till Nonna sees my daddy!" Contentedly she snuggled deep under the covers, her nightmare of moments ago forgotten.

"Daniel, how dare you?" Maureen cried angrily, following him to the door.

His hand on the knob, he turned to her. "You'll find I'll dare a lot of things, Maurie. You may not want me, although you gave the lie to that a few moments ago in my arms," Daniel stated dryly, causing a hot flush to stain Maureen's cheeks. "But that little one in there does. I didn't lie to her, Maurie. You're her sister, but you're obviously a mother to her, and as soon as you're my wife, I will be her daddy!" Daniel's tone was savage, and Maureen quailed at his determination.

"You just won't accept no for an answer, will you? The all-powerful Daniel Lord just can't bear to fail." Maureen's words were bitter, and crossing her arms over her breasts, she hugged her shaking form. "You'd destroy my life, and possibly Katy's, to assuage your own egotistical pride, your obsession."

"Maurie, that I want you is beside the point, even if I only wanted you for my mistress with no permanent ties." Daniel smiled cruelly at her, setting her teeth on edge. "You yourself scotched that idea by throwing this Jack character in my face. If you were married to him I wouldn't have a chance in hell of having you, for believe it or not I don't bed married women!"

Maureen gasped at his honesty, a chagrined expression crossing her face. So much for my smoke screen, she thought hysterically. It had just burst into flame in front of her eyes.

"Maurie, I need a wife, you need a home . . . someone to take care of you and that little girl in there. I need a hostess, a family, while you need security for both you and Katy. We have a lot to offer each other. Can't you stop acting like a hurt and bitter child long enough to see the advantages?" Daniel spoke softly, stroking an index finger across her cheek, which was wet with angry tears.

"What about Jack . . . doesn't he have any say in this?" Maureen knew she was grasping at straws, but she had to do something.

"None!" Daniel's voice was coldly controlled as his hand began to curve around the nape of her neck.

"Don't touch me!" Maureen sobbed, jerking her face from the insidious warmth of his hand. "That's your answer to everything, but damn you . . . I won't be just another of your possessions kept for your own personal use!"

Opening the door, Daniel turned to her with a steely glint in his gray eyes. "I'm finalizing the arrangements. I'll notify you as to time and place as soon as the last details are complete," he said, surveying her insolently. "Oh! Don't think you have any choice, Maurie. I don't want to force you, but you know me well enough to know I get what I set out to get . . . and I'm not very particular as to how."

Maureen stared in horrified fascination at the muscle pulsing in his cheek as she heard the implied threat in his voice.

"I see we understand each other." Daniel smiled, then closed the door quietly behind his retreating figure.

Maureen stared at the closed door, eventually dragging herself into the bedroom. Suddenly nausea overcame her, and with a despairing cry she rushed to the bathroom.

Once the spasms had passed, she bathed her face, grateful for the cool water against her heated cheeks. After lethargically pulling on a nightgown, she crawled beneath the chill sheets, her body shivering more from the violence of her emotions than from the cold. As she stared into the darkness her brain went round and round, trying to find an escape. But as the agonizing hours passed, she knew there was no way out, as Daniel had known the minute he walked through the door tonight.

CHAPTER FOUR

Maureen felt awful as she dragged herself to work that evening. It had been a particularly difficult day. Katy had been naughtier than usual partly, she supposed, because the child was disappointed their weekend had come to an end, and partly because she sensed her own emotional turmoil.

Either way, she had lost all patience more than once, especially when Katy insisted on talking of nothing but her "new daddy." Poor Katy had been glad to get to Nonna's by the end of the day. Maureen grimaced as she entered the club. Well, she thought optimistically, at least the worst is over. Little did she realize how prophetic those thoughts were.

After the last show a voice hailed her as slowly she prepared to enter her dressing room.

"Hey, Maurie," Jack yelled down the hall. "Grady wants us all to meet in the office."

"Can't it wait until I've changed, Jack?" Maureen asked, wearily pushing back her straying hair.

"Sorry, honey," he replied, placing a comforting arm around her shoulders and walking with her toward Grady's office. "He wants us to get everything straight with the new owner. I just hope none of us need to look for a new job. They're not easy to come by, with unemployment the way it is," Jack sighed, his usually ready smile replaced by a worried frown. "Anyway, I've gotten kind of attached to the old place!"

As Maureen followed Jack into Grady's office she worried about Jack's words. Suppose Grady was wrong, and the new owner didn't want her to stay on? Oh, darn! Why does life have to be so complicated? she questioned herself, biting the inside of her lower lip.

Lately everything seemed to be going wrong—even her beloved baby seemed to be getting out of hand. She sighed. Katy, she knew, needed a firm hand, but both she and Nonna tended to spoil her. If she lost her job, she really didn't know how she'd manage. Her brave words to Gaye had been mere bravado, she realized despairingly, said partly to reassure Gaye but mainly to convince herself.

Now Daniel's threat was hanging over her, too. She knew it wasn't an empty one, and her tormented mind had grown exhausted with the effort of thinking of a way to get away from him. Whatever he'd meant by his parting words, Maureen knew that whatever ace Daniel had up his sleeve was a good one. He seemed so sure of her compliance, so terribly sure!

Maybe Daniel was bluffing, she thought hopefully. That he was determined to have her was in no doubt, and now that he'd met Katy his determination would be even stronger. She had to admit to herself the beginnings of the strong attraction Katy had for Daniel, the first tenuous threads of love in a man she'd always thought incapable of that tender emotion. For Katy, who had never known her father, it was the attraction of a very little girl to a strong man, Maureen thought with a despairing grimace. Even she hadn't realized how much Katy wanted a father, and she had been closer to the child—she and Nonna—than anyone.

The only avenue open to her was to take Katy and run far and fast, but that was out of the question. For one thing, how would she manage to support them in a strange city, without friends? If she went to Nevada with Harry and Gaye, she knew she'd have no trouble, but Daniel would be sure to check there first. Bseides, she remembered Daniel saying once that he had several business ventures in that city and was even part owner of a casino there.

The other worry was Nonna. She knew it would break her heart if she and Katy left her; Maureen couldn't bring that kind of pain to her dear friend. There has to be another solution, she thought for the hundredth time. She totally rejected the obvious one—marrying Jack. He had been so loyal and understanding when she'd told him about her conversation with Daniel, but it would be a mistake to marry where the love wasn't equal on both sides. After all, that was exactly what she had against marrying Daniel, wasn't it? Maureen questioned herself yet again. She had been very tempted to take Jack up on his offer. At least then they'd be safe and cared for, she and Katy. She had argued with herself, but looking into Jack's honest kindly face, she had known she couldn't take the chance of hurting him, for he deserved someone who loved him.

As she smiled up at Jack, who gave her a friendly wink in return, Maureen knew her decision had been a wise one. Entering Grady's office with Jack's arm still draped casually across her shoulders, Maureen sighed with regret. Why couldn't she be in love with Jack? Why were cold gray eyes always there in front of her when she looked at another man, making it impossible for her to really give her love as she had once before? Maureen was relieved to see Gaye hurrying toward her. Maybe her volatile friend could cheer her up. She smiled at the thought and waved to Jack as he crossed the room to join another group.

"Maurie, there's something you should know before Grady gets here," Gaye said to her, her voice breathless.

Maureen walked over and sat on the edge of Grady's large pinewood desk. Her fingers caressed the rough wood as she wondered sadly how she'd feel seeing someone else sitting behind it.

Maureen turned her attention to her friend, noting Gaye's worried frown.

"What is it, Gaye?"

"Oh, honey! It's the——" Gaye began, stopping abruptly as she heard the door open behind her. Too late, Gaye thought, seeing Maureen's face pale as a horrified gasp escaped her.

"No!" Maureen whimpered. "N—no, it can't be!"

"You all right, honey?" Gaye asked, placing a protective hand on Maureen's shoulder.

"I'm okay," she whispered. "Oh, Gaye . . . why didn't you tell me sooner?" As she spoke, her eyes never left the tall man standing beside Grady, his figure seeming overlarge in the small office.

So far, he had ignored her presence, shaking hands with the other club employees as Grady, beaming, made the introductions. How stupid not to have put two and two together, she thought disgustedly.

Now she understood Gaye's evasiveness and her worried expression upon hearing that Daniel wanted her to be his mistress. Her friend was afraid he'd bought the club to get her in a position where she'd be forced into complying, she realized with a desire to laugh hysterically bubbling inside her.

Poor Gaye, how relieved she'd be if she knew Daniel asked me to marry him after all. If it was up to her, Gaye's mind would never be put at rest, but she knew suddenly that it was out of her hands. Daniel was too strong; he had too many tricks up his sleeve.

Of course Grady was pleased. He had worried about the job security of his employees, most of whom had been with him many years. He'd been elated, she remembered, when he'd told them the new owner wanted nothing changed. Jack was to be the manager, and as long as they did their work as they had in the past, he would be grateful if they all chose to stay.

Grady hadn't been the only one elated at the news. They had all—she swallowed painfully—breathed a sigh of relief. Only I had reservations, she recalled with a grimace, wondering if the new employer would be the chase-around-the-desk type.

She wasn't vain, but her looks had caused her trouble

68

before—she'd had to leave several waitress jobs for that very reason. She sometimes felt good looks in a woman were more a liability than an advantage, causing a woman to be seen as a face and a body . . . not as a person with a mind to go with them. That kind of thinking led her straight back to Daniel, and Maureen couldn't help the mocking laugh that escaped from between her lips.

"Oh, honey!" Gaye groaned, replying to Maureen's earlier question. "I thought I'd have time to tell you sooner," she pleaded, drawing her arm around Maureen in a swift hug. "I wanted you to enjoy the weekend, and there wasn't anything you could have done about it. I'm sorry you found out this way."

"It's all right," she smiled, returning Gaye's hug. "You were right. It would have spoiled my weekend, all right, and I know I wouldn't have been able to change anything by worrying about it."

Tension gripped her as she saw Daniel's tall figure walking slowly toward them. Consciously unclenching her fists, she strove to project a calmness she was far from feeling.

"Gaye," Daniel said smiling. "Grady needs you to help dispense the goodies." He pointed to the canapés and champagne being wheeled in by white-coated waiters with beaming faces.

Looking at Maureen doubtfully, but seeing her reassuring nod, Gaye replied, "Okay, Mr. Lord . . . will do."

"The name is Daniel." He grinned.

Responding to his charm—she was still hopeful that his intentions toward Maurie were honorable—Gaye walked away, leaving Maureen and Daniel alone.

"Excuse me." Maureen began to move past Daniel. "I'll just go help Gaye." As her steps quickened, Daniel's arm reached out to clutch her wrist, stopping her in mid flight. Filled with a sense of frustration, she gasped in surprise.

"Maurie, they can manage without your help," he said sharply.

Pointedly looking down at the lean fingers clutching

the softness of her upper arm, Maureen shot Daniel a murderous glance, expecting him to release her. As her eyes met the cold gray glance she felt the warm hands tightening upon her skin. His mouth softened sensuously as he fixed his eyes—the pupils enlarging—on her.

Maureen's breath caught in her throat, then came out in little gasps as she stared at him. A warm rose color flushed her dusky gold skin as she felt the tips of his fingers caress her arm with erotic intent.

Jerking her arm free of the insidious seductiveness of his touch, she could still feel tiny flickers of flame around her nerve ends. Maureen stayed where she was, realizing the foolishness of flight. Daniel wouldn't be beyond carrying her out of the room screaming, in front of everyone.

Suddenly Daniel was speaking in a low rumbling voice, telling her the wedding, her wedding, was set for three days from today, instead of the two weeks he'd originally decided upon.

"You don't believe in giving me much time, do you, Daniel?" Her bitterness at his high-handed planning of her life showed through.

"I told you, honey. There's nothing to decide. You'll marry me, all right," he said firmly. "Get all ideas of your boyfriend out of that beautiful little head of yours, Maurie. You're mine, and you'll stay mine!"

"What makes you so damn sure, Daniel?" Maureen tossed her luxurious hair angrily. His whole attitude grated on her, but she knew that he had won, and she had to face the truth about herself—that part of her wanted to stop fighting. Never to have to worry anymore, to be able to hand over some of the terrible burdens she'd been weighted with for so long. Realizing the direction her thoughts were taking, Maureen stiffened her resolve, feeling disgust at her own weakness. No, she wouldn't give in, not through selfishness. Daniel had made her suffer in the past; she couldn't trust him not to do it again. Why should everything he wants just fall into his lap when he crooks his little finger? Let him do the suffering for a change!

"You think I gave any credence to that threat you

made?" Maureen thrust out her rounded chin belligerently, bravely covering the lie.

"I know you did, honey. You know me well enough to know I don't make idle threats." Daniel's voice was harsh, his tone uncompromising.

Studying his closed expression and tightly compressed lips, Maureen breathed a sigh of relief.

"You were bluffing, Daniel," she murmured, her face softening with the beginnings of a smile. "You don't really have anything to threaten me with."

"Look around you, Maurie."

As Maureen looked at him quickly, she saw him hesitate before he spoke again, seeming to swallow with difficulty.

"Your friends have been good to you, haven't they?" His face was closed, his lids shading his eyes so she couldn't read the expression in them. "It would be a pity if all the happy anticipation for the future they're showing now was changed, wouldn't it?"

"What do you mean?" Maureen's voice was little more than a whisper as she stared up at him.

"I own the club, I could very easily close it down . . . for good."

"You wouldn't . . ."

"You obviously care a lot for Jack"—Maureen flinched at the sneer in his voice—"and all your other friends who work here. I've been hearing them sing little Maurie's praises this last few weeks. Cross me, Maurie, and I'll close the club and refuse them, right down to the last employee, any kind of a work reference. In other words, they'll be finding it difficult, if not impossible, to find work."

Maureen stared at him in fascination, knowing he was more than capable of following through with his threats.

"Daniel . . . they've never harmed you," she said chokingly, her eyes dilating in dismay at his threat. She knew with a dreadful certainty he meant every word.

Maureen closed her eyes, her face whitening. He'd thought of everything; but then, Daniel knew how to play a winning hand. She realized now that she had been

71

right all along. Daniel had played her along, letting her win small hands, only to stack the deck against her in the end.

Looking around the room at the smiling faces, she saw Grady's and stared intently at him. She saw the tender look he bestowed on the frail woman sitting there, saw the small shaky hand caress his arm in response. Feeling a lump forming in her throat at the touching demonstration of trust and affection, Maureen knew she had to play Daniel's way, even though she despised him for it.

"What do you want me to do, Daniel?" Maureen asked him quietly, her tone resigned.

"We'll announce our engagement now, Maurie!" Seeing she was about to protest, he cut in swiftly, telling her they'd do it his way or not at all. "We'll do as I said, and announce our engagement—that way it will be a double celebration."

"I—" she began, but he stopped her words with a look. Maureen's glance roamed his face swiftly, seeing the determination written there. Tightening her lips and tiredly nodding her head, she sent him a look that held all the disdain she felt for him at that particular moment.

"Good, we understand each other," he whispered, stiffening under her glance. He took her arm in his firmly and led her toward the group of people who had been speculating about the two of them. Gaye and Jack, however, had been sending glances their way that were more worried than speculative.

As they approached the center of the group Daniel glanced swiftly at the various expressions on the faces of those assembled there, before making his announcement. He looked into the face of his new manager, Jack Cummings, rather more intently than was necessary. The large boyishly freckled face gazed frowningly into Daniel's, an unspoken message passing between the two men, and at least on Daniel's part there was an armed truce as they shook hands. Jack mumbled his congratulations and moved away, and his expression clearly spoke of mixed feelings, including a sense of loss as he gazed at Maurie before moving away into the crowd. As Daniel watched him walk to the other side of the room his mouth tensed and his face hardened. Jack turned, raising a drink to his dry mouth. As he did his eyes met Daniel's, and he drew in his breath at the savage warning there!

Her face fixed in a smile, she murmured the accepted inanities until she thought she'd scream. As the tension mounted within her she began to wonder how she had gotten into this situation, how things had gotten so out of hand.

Wiping a shaking hand over the perspiration beading her forehead, she looked across the width of the room at Daniel. Sometime in the last half hour or so they'd become separated by the crowd. Not that it could be called a crowd, though with the heat and the noise, the dozen or so people certainly felt like one.

As Maureen gazed across the room Mrs. Grady's conversation merged into the background; her consciousness was now submerged in thoughts of Daniel. He was leaning casually with one hand braced against the wall, a cigarette in his other hand. His lean muscular legs were resting at an angle, and as she watched he guided the cigarette slowly toward his mouth. He bent his head as he listened intently to Harry, who had arrived a few minutes earlier and stood with his burly arm around Gaye. She'd give a lot to know just what Daniel was saying to hold Harry's attention so completely. Whatever it was, it was certainly causing Gaye's husky laugh to peal out, and her eyes sparkled. Maureen chided herself for feeling left out as she watched the cozy little trio. After all, the farther away she was from Daniel, the better she liked it!

For someone who couldn't stand the sight of the tall, magnetic figure across the room, she was having increasing difficulty tearing her eyes away from him. Watching as Daniel put the cigarette against his firmly molded lips and drew the smoke into his lungs, something strange happened to Maureen, strange yet achingly familiar. All of a sudden it was as if he'd reached out and caressed her. She could almost feel that sensuous mouth upon hers.

Daniel looked up and encountered her unguarded eyes

upon him, and she looked quickly away to murmur further inanities to Mrs. Grady, who thankfully was unaware of Maureen's lack of attention. She was breathing rather fast and hoped no one would notice the breathless quality in her voice. She couldn't help her agitation, for in the split second that her eyes and Daniel's had met across the room, she had read intense desire in his. Caught unawares, she was terrified that he might have read an answering passion in her own eyes.

Maureen jumped as she felt hard arms steal around her and a husky voice whisper, "Come on, honey. I'll take you home." Murmuring apologies, she was conscious of Daniel's muscular arm encircling her waist as they walked across the room calling smiling good-nights to everyone.

As they walked to Daniel's car Maureen stammered nervously, telling him she had her car. "There's no need to drive me home, Daniel. It's late, and I know you must be tired."

"So solicitous for my welfare, darling?"

"Oh, there's no use talking to you!" Maureen exclaimed, disturbed at the nearly hysterical tone of her voice, which seemed to be babbling in her own ears.

Daniel seated her in his car and slid in beside her. "Give me your keys."

"M—my keys? What for?"

Closing his eyes in exasperation he replied, "I'll have Blake collect your car tomorrow."

Momentarily diverted, Maureen asked unnecessarily, "Oh, is Blake still with you?" Blake had been Daniel's chauffeur, butler, and right-hand man four years ago. Fiftyish and balding, he would often pick her up when Daniel was kept over at a meeting, and she had grown very fond of him. Although completely devoted to Daniel, Blake had, nevertheless, tried in an oblique way to warn her.

"The keys, Maurie." Daniel spoke softly, his hand reaching out.

Maureen gave him the keys after a small search

through her bag, avoiding contact with him as she placed the keys in his palm.

"Thank you," he said, starting the engine and backing out of the stall.

"I don't know about you, but I'm hungry. We'll stop for a bite to eat, then I'll drive you home."

"All right," she replied, though the thought of food made her choke. Moistening her dry lips with the tip of her tongue, she glanced out the window unseeingly, conscious of his disturbing gaze.

Daniel drove through the teeming San Francisco streets to cross through the financial district. Glancing around her, Maureen realized they were on Merchant Street. As they approached the Blue Fox Maureen, still in her working clothes, was glad Daniel hadn't given her time to change into casual slacks and sweater. She had never dined here, but she'd heard of it. A continental restaurant, it was one of the world's great dining establishments. Over about thirty years it had been converted from a one-room eating place into the exclusive restaurant it was today.

Daniel walked around the car, handing the keys to the valet, then opening the door for Maureen. Nervously stepping out, she avoided his hand, walking quickly ahead of him. Entering, Daniel placed a guiding hand under her elbow, leading her toward the smaller of the three rooms, located in the center of the restaurant. Almost instantly a man approached whom she took to be a waiter—only to realize it was the owner himself. Daniel apologized for their lack of reservations but was smilingly and vociferously vetoed while they were immediately seated in a quiet corner. As Daniel, after introducing her as his fiancée, quietly talked with this man he apparently knew well, Maureen glanced around her. The room was lavishly appointed with high-backed velvet chairs, mirrors placed strategically throughout, and gold and crystal chandeliers, the whole blending together in a rather opulent and highly tasteful decor. She felt out of place and a little self-conscious as she caught a glimpse of the furs and jewelry of the women around her.

After the waiter had taken their order, and the proprietor had smilingly left for another table, Maureen glanced across at Daniel, wanting but unable to say something to break the silence between them. To her relief the waiter chose that moment to return with their drinks, and Maureen thankfully sipped hers. It was surprisingly good, and she thirstily drank half of it down.

"Hey, Maurie! That's not water you're drinking," Daniel warned.

In a mood of petulant defiance, Maureen finished her drink and asked for another.

"Okay, honey. It's your funeral." He gave her an infuriating smile as he signaled the waiter. "Just don't blame me later for getting you drunk!"

"I'm not a child," she snapped, angered by that mocking smile. "Just quit treating me like a baby."

"Believe me, I have no intention of treating you like a baby, Maurie . . . quite the reverse, in fact." Daniel's eyes traveled over her body. Flushing, Maureen found she couldn't hold his gaze, and looked down quickly, staring intently at the design on the tablecloth as if it held all the secrets of the universe. At that moment the waiter returned with his second drink, and Maureen clenched it as Daniel's laugh reverberated in her ears.

Maureen had been able to eat more of the meal than she'd thought herself capable of doing. The unaccustomed alcohol had relaxed her. Daniel, much to her relief, had talked only about the commonplace and told her about his plans for the club; and as she finished the last bite of the delicious *médaillon de boeuf aux champignons* she realized with amazement that she had been unconcernedly chattering away, forgetting her earlier resentment.

Daniel waived dessert and ordered liqueurs instead. Remembering her love of chocolate, he ordered her a crème de cacao, which she found to be delicious, with its rich chocolate taste. As she finished it Maureen felt her head begin to spin annoyingly. Frowning at the unusual sensation, she heard Daniel's laugh from quite a distance away. After paying the bill and unobtrusively leaving a tip that would pay for her nylons for a month, he took her arm firmly. She stumbled as they reached the cold air outside.

Seated again in the heated car as they drove across the Bay Bridge, Maureen felt sleepy and had to fight to keep her eyes open. She was all floaty and felt as if she hadn't a care in the world—which was a very welcome change from the way she had felt earlier. Her lips curled in a silly smile. She didn't see the intense glance Daniel, who'd had very little to drink, shot at her . . . or the satisfied smile curving his mobile mouth. . . . If she had, she might have started to worry all over again.

Looking vaguely out the window, Maureen chuckled suddenly.

"What's so funny, baby?"

"T—the b—bridge." She giggled, cocking her head to look upward at the massive structure. "It—it looks like a ship turned upside down a—and inside out."

"You're right, honey . . . it does." His laugh rang out thoroughly, and he reached out and pulled her unresisting body closer to him in a swift hug.

Feeling the warmth and solidity of his chest beneath her cheek, Maureen snuggled even closer, closing her eyes confidingly, and unconsciously placing her hand upon his upper thigh. She fell asleep almost instantly, so didn't feel Daniel's body stiffen in surprise.

As he looked down at Maureen's bent head Daniel moved his arm from around her slowly, lifting her gently until her head was resting more comfortably on his shoulder. Her other hand he left where it was as he picked up speed. With teeth gritted he drove as fast as was safe, feeling that warm little hand burning through his clothes, sending shock waves through his body.

If Maurie could read my thoughts now, he mocked, she'd probably jump from the car. God, I want her, he thought savagely, as he felt her softly sensuous body close to his, unconsciously moving against him, increasing his growing desire.

Looking down at her shining dark hair nestled against

his shoulder, its scent wafting up to him, he whispered, "You won't be treated like a baby, sweetheart, but like a woman. My woman!"

Maureen slept as contentedly as a baby, unknowing of the turmoil she was causing as they traveled irreversibly closer to her home.

CHAPTER FIVE

Daniel was soon turning onto the Nimitz Freeway, and as they passed Oakland, spread out around them, Maureen sleepily awoke from her short nap. Realizing suddenly that she was half lying on Daniel's muscular form, she moved away, gasping in dismay.

Still fuzzy under the effects of the alcohol, she bewilderedly glanced around her. Surprised to find they had come so far, she recognized the Mormon Temple set proudly on the hill in the distance like a far-off castle of old. It was a fairly new structure, and she remembered how awed she'd been when her father had taken her on a tour many years before. The inside was as large and elaborate as the outside—and had seemed huge to the small girl she'd been then. It had left a lasting impression, although her memories were vague, which was only to be expected. Of course, it had only been open to the general public for a short time. A pity, she thought. She'd love for Katy to see it as she had.

With a start Maureen realized Daniel was pulling into the back parking area of her home. After locking the car, Daniel walked with her to her door, his arm casually flung about her shoulders. Taking the key from her trembling fingers, he opened the door, and Maureen walked ahead of him into the living room, automatically reaching for the switch on the wall to the left and thus bathing the room in startling light.

Unsteadily, Maureen walked into her small kitchenette and reached for the coffee percolator.

"Make yourself comfortable." She spoke over her shoulder to the man standing there. Why in the world did I say that? Heaven forbid! She noticed him glancing around her small but homey living room and knew he was really studying it this time. The circumstances of his last and only visit hadn't exactly been conducive to relaxed scrutiny. At least everything is tidy, she thought in relief, trying to see it through his eyes.

She wondered what he was thinking? Probably the same as he'd think of her car. She smiled, trying not to laugh at the comparison. Though both had similar features of German design, her little Volks had never driven as quietly or smoothly, not to mention as fast, as his Porsche. His car was like a leashed beast, just waiting to pounce, and as the thought came to her a little giggle finally escaped.

"Share the joke?"

Daniel's voice behind her made Maureen jump like a frightened rabbit. There was some underlying quality in the tone that made her flush in confusion. Stammering slightly, she told him her thoughts, and he replied mockingly, "Kind of like its owner, hmmm?"

His inference brought the flush even more vividly to her cheeks, and she gave Daniel a speaking glance. He laughed, a rich full sound that seemed to make the kitchenette seem even smaller.

"Oh, Maurie! You rise to the bait so well." He chuckled.

Turning back again into the living room, Daniel draped his coat over the back of the one easy chair the room boasted—a rather lumpy and dilapidated rocker Maureen had picked up at a garage sale—and then looked around the room intently.

Maureen would have been surprised at his thoughts. The kitchen was admittedly small, but she had used cheerful paint and wallpaper in yellows and browns throughout, which made it seem to Daniel to be warm and pleasing . . . a nice room to go to at the beginning of the day.

But looking at the blendings of blues, greens, and golds on the coverings for the rocker and sofa, which he knew had seen better days—especially when he felt the lumps as he gingerly lowered his large frame into its over soft surface—he realized Maureen had, with limited means, created a haven of warmth and harmony. In effect, a home, and thinking of the opulent but rather cold decor of his professionally decorated apartment, he wondered how it would look in a few months after Maurie got to work on it. The more he thought about it, the more determined he was that they should have a house, with plenty of room for Katy to run around in. He would put his real estate agents to work on it immediately.

Smiling to himself, Daniel allowed his gaze to wander around the room, quickly taking in all the little personal knickknacks that added to the room's charm. There were pictures on the walnut end table, along with flowers set in a pale blue vase on a drum table in front of the window. Curious, he walked across the room to examine them. Bending, he saw two people pictured, with a leggy young schoolgirl between. He recognized a younger version of her father, of course, but it was the twelve- or thirteen-year-old Maurie that held his attention. She was beautiful even then, he mused smilingly, putting the picture back in place.

His thoughts were interrupted by the sight of Maureen coming very cautiously into the room.

"The coffee will be done in about five minutes, Daniel."

"That's fine, I could use a cup before I make that long drive back."

Smiling, trying to appear poised but failing dismally, Maureen walked unsteadily past him. Just as she was about to reach the safety of the chair, which seemed farther away than usual, she stumbled ignominiously, and Daniel's hands reached out to grip her forearms.

"Honey, I think you need a cold shower." He smiled

down at her. "Why don't you go and freshen up while I watch a little television?"

"W—with you here?" Maureen squeaked, realizing her mistake as she saw his mouth tighten.

"Look, in three days you'll be my wife," he told her angrily. "What will you do then, Maurie? Only shower when I'm at work?"

"We're not married yet . . . and it's possible something will prevent it," she said to him, angry at his mocking question.

"We made an official announcement tonight, or have you forgotten already?" A thread of steel ran through the softly voiced question.

Seeing his expression, Maureen suddenly capitulated. "All right, I think I will freshen up," she mumbled, despising herself for her cowardice and pulling herself from Daniel's hands.

"Let me help you," he said, reaching out for her again and drawing her into his arms. As his hands reached behind her and lowered the zipper of her dress Maureen stiffened in shock. Giving her a wry look, and kissing the tip of her uptilted nose, he whispered, "Go on, before I change my mind and decide to get in the shower with you." As Maureen almost ran from the room Daniel's laughter followed her.

Daniel turned and absentmindedly switched on the television, at which point his attention was caught by another picture. Smiling tenderly, he held it in his hands. It was obviously Katy at about two years old. Was she ever a little honey, he thought. Maurie must have looked just like her at that age, and he considered the children they might have.

Maurie liked children, if her attitude toward her sister was anything to go by. He was an only child, and he hoped she also favored the idea of a large family. It had been lonely for him growing up, and he wondered fleetingly if she too had suffered that particular type of aloneness before Katy was born. He rather doubted it, for she'd come from an environment of love, whereas his had been one of strife in which he had been used as an implement of torture by two people who had come to hate each other.

He wondered why, with a background such as his, he wanted to marry Maurie. He should have learned a lesson from his parents' example and steered clear of that entanglement, but taking a good look at his own involvement with Maurie, both past and present, he knew this just wasn't possible. She'd gotten under his skin, and there seemed to be no getting her out. He couldn't risk losing her to Jack, for if she married him, he wouldn't be able to reach her with any amount of threats then.

He didn't kid himself—he couldn't honestly say he loved her. God, he didn't know what love was, and he certainly didn't think he had it in him to love. All he knew for sure was he had to have Maurie. She has to belong to me alone, he thought savagely. When he heard her sing again tonight, he'd been more sure of that than ever before. He remembered the intense jealousy he'd felt hearing some of the more lewd comments from the bar; he'd had to restrain himself forcibly from physical violence. He had to have the right to control her earning her living in that way . . . he wanted to be the one with the right to look at her, to touch, to possess. Determination once again washed over him as he realized his mind was turning to sensual thoughts.

When they had finally arrived at her home tonight, Maurie had seemed so unsure of herself, so childlike, it had effectively killed his ardor. Now, especially after her comment earlier—when he'd sensed the engagement wasn't real to her—he was determined that she be in no doubt as to its reality. Walking toward the doorway through which Maurie had passed, his eyes were twin fires, and his mouth curved sensually.

From the bedroom Maureen had heard the television set go on. Nervously looking back over her shoulder, she debated upon the wiseness of taking a shower with Daniel in the other room. The flushed, sticky feeling of her body convinced her, and she quickly stepped out of her clothes. Walking swiftly to the yellow and gold tiled bath-

83

room, she locked the door behind her, breathing a sigh of relief.

The slightly cool spray on her overheated skin was blissful, but with a sense of urgency she quickly rinsed and stepped out of the shower. Having dried herself, she wrapped the large bath towel sarongwise around her body and walked to the mirror to brush her slightly damp hair.

Smoothing the curling dark tendrils back from her flushed cheeks, she thought back over the events of the evening. What chance had she and Daniel of any happiness? There was too much she had to forget, too much he had already forgotten. A cynical frown marred her forehead. Sighing despondently, and feeling inertia overcoming her, she turned and entered the bedroom.

That's strange, she thought, puzzled. She could have sworn she had left the light on. She closed the bathroom door and walked toward the light switch. A voice rent the dimness of the room.

"Leave it off, and come here."

Gasping aloud, Maureen whirled around, her heartbeat accelerating, a trembling hand at her throat. Peering across the room, a large shadow detached itself from the chair beside her bed.

"D—Daniel," she stammered foolishly. "W—what's the matter? What are you doing here?"

His hands reached out for the tiny lamp on her nightstand. The room was now bathed in a pale rose glow.

"I said . . . come here! Or would you rather I came after you?" he said demandingly.

In a daze, Maureen walked slowly toward him, one hand clutching the towel, as if it were the support for her unsteady legs. She knew he would make good his threat, what she didn't understand, or couldn't make her curiously unfunctioning brain grasp, was why her feet seemed to be carrying her toward him at all.

As she approached his still figure his hands reached for the softness of her upper arms caressingly.

"What do you think I'm going to do, sweetheart?" he said in response to her question.

"I don't know what you think you're doing, but I know what you're not. I think you'd better leave, Daniel . . . now!" Her eyes looked scornfully into his.

She knew one didn't demand of a man like Daniel and get away with it, but her evening was suddenly culminating in a rage inside her. Her earlier feelings of trapped helplessness gave impetus to the furious emotions tearing through her now, and she was uncaring of his anger, which, as she looked into his face, she knew she was arousing.

His eyes encompassed her towel-draped figure with burning intent, and his mouth, which had been tight with anger at her remarks, once again curved sensuously.

"Honey, it's a long drive back to the city, and I'd rather spend the rest of the night here with you," he whispered, his thumbs caressing her arms in a circular motion.

"You despicable rat! You've been planning this all along, that's why you insisted on driving me home," Maureen gasped, the tears starting behind her eyelids.

"Think what you like, you'll think the worst anyway, Maurie, and where's the harm? We'll be married soon, why shouldn't we begin the marriage tonight?"

"Because I don't want to, that's why. I don't want to begin it at all . . . and now I know I can't . . . no matter what you threaten!"

"I think that was a very foolish statement to make, Maurie. You'll realize that very shortly," Daniel warned, anger at her rejection beginning to gnaw at his insides. "I think after tonight you'll be more than happy to marry me."

Seeing the desire beginning to burn in his eyes, Maureen whirled, intent upon escape. His hand gripped her arm savagely, making her cry out as she was jerked against his hard body, his arms crushing her to him. His hand twined itself in her hair, pulling it until the tears forced themselves from her eyes. Her head jerked back, her lips parted in a noiseless moan of pain, as his lips cruelly covered hers.

Maureen's head reeled as she struggled against him. Managing to tear her lips free of his brutally punishing mouth, she cried, "For the love of God, Daniel. Let me go, please don't do this."

Looking down at her pleading face, Daniel replied, "No, Maurie . . . I can't let you go. After tonight, you'll marry me all right, your prudish little soul won't allow you to do anything else."

As she heard the steely tone of his voice Maureen knew it was too late. Daniel would never change his mind. It was as if her threat of not going through with the wedding had reacted on him like a match put to dry grass. What a fool she was, for now she had truly inflamed him, bringing out the complete savagery she had often sensed was within him.

Holding her struggling body more tightly against him, Daniel whispered, "We've talked enough. I told you I'd have you, whether you wanted me or not. It's time you learned I mean what I say . . . this seems to be the only way I can convince you, honey."

"No! I won't let you," Maureen screamed at him in a fine rage, her dark eyes shooting sparks of fire.

"You can't stop me!" Daniel growled, kissing her frenziedly. "Baby, don't fight me . . . I'll make it good for you. I don't want to hurt you, Maurie."

The seductive timbre of his pleading voice robbed Maureen of the breath remaining in her lungs. Holding him off with one ineffectual hand against his rapidly pulsing chest, she stared for one indecisive moment into his face as her own pulse quickened in remembered yearning for this, the only man who had ever meant anything in her life, outside of her father. Just for a split second did her resolution waiver until she thought of Katy, and the power she would place in Daniel's hands if she capitulated. Purposely remembering the bitterness instead of the brief sweetness of the past; deliberately conjuring up visions of the misery knowing Daniel had cost her, gave her the strength to resist him once again.

As he felt her struggling even harder in his embrace Daniel's hands tightened involuntarily upon her soft body.

His hands began to slacken as he stared into the tormented eyes in front of him, until he heard her bitter whisper.

"You could never make anything good for me, Daniel . . . you never will, at least . . . not with my consent."

Finally goaded beyond endurance, his emotions spinning out of control as they never had before, Daniel pulled her soft form against his, his mouth finding the softness of hers unerringly. His mouth ground against hers with unbearable pressure, and Maureen tasted blood in her mouth. As he forced her lips apart to plunder within she knew he tasted it too.

During the struggle the towel had dropped to the floor in a heap. She felt the roughness of his chest hair against her softly rounded breasts, unable to push him away with her hands locked to her sides. The buckle of his belt dug agonizingly into her narrow waist as his hands arched her to him, and with a moan of pain escaping her bruised lips, she kicked at his legs.

Stooping, Daniel lifted her in his arms, hands sure under her warm curved thighs, and with his mouth still locked to hers, he walked purposely toward the bed.

Laying her down, Daniel held her easily. Maureen was nearly limp from the violence of the last few minutes, but when she felt the hard virile body press hers into the softness of the bed, she realized she was too weak to fight anymore.

"Don't . . . you'll hate yourself even more than I'll hate you, Daniel," she pleaded, her head thrashing from side to side.

Groaning low in his throat, Daniel faintly heard her exhausted words. Lifting his head from the scented hollow of her shoulder, he registered only her stillness. Mistakenly taking this to mean acquiescence, he forgot everything else as he gazed at the silken perfection of her dusky gold body beneath him.

"God . . . you're more beautiful than I'd even imagined," he groaned low in his throat, as his hands began a sensual exploration, his mouth again taking urgent possession of hers.

Exultantly he heard her moan and felt her involuntary response to his expert fingers. As he faintly heard that low sound and felt her begin to tremble in his arms, he frantically began to increase his demands on her quivering body.

Think of something else, she told herself, anything else. Work, music . . . don't give him the satisfaction of responding. As the moments passed he became less gentle in his passion, and Maureen could feel a deep, responding passion burning throughout her awakened body. Only Daniel had ever made her feel like this. A silent sob was building in her tightened throat. God, I can't tell him now, he'll never believe me. This was all he wanted, had ever wanted from her—the bitter thoughts churned unbidden to her mind—and a relationship based only upon a physical need was not what she wanted. She wouldn't give him a hold on her by telling him anything, not after this. She would keep her knowledge to herself, or he'd use it against her to hold her to him, or to hurt her even further!

Dear God, hadn't he made her suffer enough? No, she was damned if she'd let him do this willingly, and tried to ignore the sweet torment of his hands upon her.

The sob that had been trying to escape finally broke through her throat, and she didn't seem able to stop, as sob after sob followed the first, tears coursing down her pale cheeks. All the pent-up emotion of years was contained in those heartrending, almost hysterical utterances. Her small fists hammered uselessly upon his chest, and the tears and the fluttering of those hands against him brought Daniel to his senses faster than a douse of cold water, effectively stifling the heat of his passion.

"Dear God, Maurie . . . what have I done?" Daniel whispered in an agony of remorse.

Sitting up in the bed, the pillows behind her where Daniel had placed them, Maureen couldn't answer him. With dilated eyes staring ahead unseeingly, teeth chattering in shock, she clutched the bedclothes tightly against her shaking form.

Daniel rose from the bed and quickly pulled on his

discarded clothing. As he left the room Maureen tried to hate him, but even that was denied her. Trying to think back upon what had almost happened, she found her mind curiously blank.

Maureen could smell the aroma of coffee, and it seemed like days since she'd brewed it, not hours. She looked up to find Daniel standing beside her, his hand outstretched. Absently taking the proffered cup and carrying it to her bruised lips, she sipped thankfully.

Taking the empty cup from her unresisting hands, Daniel lowered himself once again to sit beside her, a muscle jerking in his cheek as he felt her cringe, her beautiful tear-wet eyes looking at him fearfully, bewilderedly. She looked to Daniel as if she had lost her last friend in the world, and he bit down upon his lower lip savagely.

He spoke gently: "Maurie, why didn't you tell me?"

"You wouldn't let me, and you wouldn't have believed me, Daniel . . . you're like all men. Just because I work as I do for a living, and look as I do, you all think I sleep around. All part of the job, isn't that what was driving you?" Maureen sighed lethargically. "Well, it doesn't matter now, anyway."

"You know damn well it matters, Maurie. You . . . I never imagined it was fear—"

"That I was afraid because of innocence, not perversity?" she whispered, a small warning devil inside her driving her on. Daniel, misinterpreting the hysterical outburst of a few moments ago, had given Maureen her solution, and God help her, she had to use it.

"Why'd you bother to stop?" she asked bitterly. "Physically I'm the same as when you began, but that's just a technicality, thanks to you. I'm just another of your women now!"

Violently rejecting her remark, he cried, "Damn you . . . no!"

Hearing the tortured sound in his voice, Maureen closed her eyes on her own lying guilt as she cried, "Oh, yes, I am, Daniel. You took what I would have given, and I can't ever forget or forgive that." As she spoke the words she consoled her conscience with the thought that

what she was implying was true, only four years too late!
"I'll marry you, Daniel," she continued, "but I want you
to understand one thing. On the day you try to do this
to me again, I'll leave you."

Maureen knew her bluff was a long shot, but she had
to try it. There was no other way, and once she was
his wife she couldn't live with the thought of his violence
. . . and she couldn't cry rape then. She wanted to laugh
at the incongruity of her thoughts, or cry . . . either
would bring some measure of relief.

"Why bother to marry me at all, Maurie? I'm a normal
man, I couldn't promise to exist under those childish
conditions." Daniel spoke through tightened lips, his face
whitening under the force of her scornful words.

"You don't leave me much choice, do you? You were
even low enough to threaten me with the livelihood of
people who have been good to me if I didn't give in to
your demands. Isn't that reason enough?" Maureen turned
her face away from his gaze, knowing he would never
let her go, and looking down at her hands clenched in
her lap.

She could feel his eyes take in the bruises his lovemaking had caused; and risking a quick upward look she
saw a muscle in his jaw jerk in response to his thoughts.
She couldn't believe he really cared for her, not after
tonight. Desire her . . . yes, she could believe that, for
if she had learned nothing else in her relationship with
Daniel, past and present, it was the physical power she
held over him, not to mention his over her.

"Maurie, what do you want from me?" he cried, bury-
ing his head in his hands and running his fingers through
his hair.

"Nothing, Daniel. That's the point I'm trying to make.
I just want you to get out of my life and leave me alone,"
she said to him, a spark of hope burning inside her, only
to be dispelled at his next words.

Raising his head to stare intently into her face, he replied, "You know I can't do that, baby . . . especially
now."

"What's so special about now?"

Raking his disturbing gaze over her face and the outline of her body beneath the sheet, he told her harshly, "You belong to me."

As she heard his words Maureen marveled at the traitorous response of her body. She knew what had happened was wrong on Daniel's part, but in a way she'd been at fault. If only the present wasn't so distorted by the past!

Maureen turned her head to glance at Daniel's averted profile, and she couldn't doubt his suffering, which surprised her. To a self-assured man like Daniel, being driven to lose all control is in itself a torment, she thought with a deeper perception than she had dreamed herself capable of.

In an honest attempt at self-awareness, Maureen admitted she still loved Daniel. The very fact that he had lost control, that his actions hadn't been premeditated as she'd accused, was his saving grace. That, and the deeprooted knowledge of her own body's momentary encouragement to his caressing mouth and hands.

How could she blame him totally, when for those few crucial moments she had forgotten herself in his arms? But that didn't alter the situation, she realized, lying back against the pillows in sudden weariness. What had happened tonight, as well as what had happened in the past would always color their relationship. Without love on both their parts, and trust of him on hers, there could be no good relationship between them. She'd give him what he wanted, if he still wanted it with the conditions she imposed, and in every other way she'd try to be a good wife to him.

"I don't belong to you, Daniel. I've never been an object you could buy . . . maybe now you'll believe me," she said, finally responding to his earlier assertion.

Gritting his teeth, he told her, "I've never tried to buy you, you're not some little tramp I hired for a night."

"You could have fooled me!"

"Damn you!" His earlier gentleness now gave way once again to anger. Maureen always seemed, sooner or later, to bring out the worst in him.

"You'll marry me whether you want to or not, without any damn threats on your part. God, the thought of you has driven me crazy for years . . . Tonight was just the culmination of a hell of a lot of frustration!"

He gripped her arms, and the sheet slipped down around her waist. Seeing the rose-tinted perfection of her firm breasts, Daniel's eyes darkened again in response to the beauty of her body.

"You still drive me crazy, and I'm not sorry this happened, Maurie, just the way it did!" Daniel groaned, slowly drawing her into his arms. "Honey, forget tonight, your fear of making love," he whispered. "I'll be gentle with you, Maurie. This time will be good for you . . . just let me love you."

As she heard his huskily coaxing voice all the hurt and disillusion exploded inside her tormented brain. All the emotions seething inside her for the last few weeks came to the surface, and she lost what little control over her temper she possessed.

Fighting and twisting in his arms, she cried, "Haven't you hurt me enough? Don't touch me . . . I hate you! I'm not a thing you can use!" To Maureen, the mere fact that he wanted her again proved he cared not for her feelings but for his own satisfaction. He wanted to assuage his guilt for what happened by taking her, and making her respond fully, but she couldn't let him. She couldn't lose what little self-respect he had left her.

Sobbing, she felt herself being gently laid back. As his weight lifted from the edge of the bed she rolled over, hiding her face in the pillows.

From across the room Daniel's furious voice carried over the sound of her muffled weeping.

"All right . . . have it your way for now, Maurie. In three days we'll be married, and you'll belong to me legally. I'll make no promises for the future, but I will do my best to wait until you've grown up!" Daniel spat the words out, his voice freezing the sobs in her throat.

"Just remember, you'll belong to me, you'll be my wife. I'll pander to your ridiculous fears for a while, Maurie, but eventually I mean to have you, in every sense of the word!"

As the intention behind his words smote her she feared more than ever for the future. Maureen despised his attitude, and his power over her. She was determined he wouldn't have it all his own way, and at least she had bought herself a little more time. She would hold off his possession of her as long as possible, because she just wouldn't let herself become another object for him to own, and the sooner he realized that, the better. The winning of a minor skirmish had made her rather brave. Why, then, as she heard the controlled slam of the door closing behind him, did her teeth clench and a fearful premonition grip her shaking limbs? Glancing at the closed door, which suddenly seemed to represent her relationship with Daniel, Maureen uttered a dejected moan, feeling very old, and very, very tired. Her thoughts fusing and floating toward sleep, she wondered if she would live to be old, and if she did, would she ever . . . ever be wise?

CHAPTER SIX

The sun filtering through the closed chintz curtains in her room awakened Maureen. Sleepily she gazed up at the flickering shadows as the sun rippled through the trees outside her window, to dance enticingly against her walls.

With a groan, Maureen stretched her lissome young body before unwillingly getting out of the bed. She was unwilling to face the day, as she had been unwilling to face many of the days since Daniel's advent into her life.

Looking at the clock on her bedside table, she gave a startled gasp as she realized the lateness of the hour. She should have been at Nonna's over an hour ago to pick up Katy.

She ran to the closet and discarded one outfit after another, wondering at her contrariness. Normally she wasn't so fussy about what she wore, but the thought that Daniel might drop by at any time made her more critical than usual, she realized, momentarily disgusted with herself. Mutinously grabbing her oldest pants and blouse in defiance of her own thoughts, she entered the bathroom.

After showering and donning gray wool slacks and a white and gray tank top, Maureen gave a quick brushing to her long, sleep-tousled hair. Looking at her reflection in the mirror, she automatically reached for her makeup box, her hand stilling in midair. Setting her lips in an angry line, Maureen slammed the box back in place on her vanity table, determined to look as plain and unattractive as possible. Let him come. Maybe luck will be with me and he'll change his mind, she thought wryly, not believing her own thoughts for a moment. With a shrug of her slim shoulders, she stormed out of the house and marched over to Nonna's next door.

Giving a sharp knock on Nonna's door, Maureen walked in, sure of her own welcome. Nonna had told her not to bother knocking, she remembered with a smile, and she'd teased the older woman, saying she didn't want to walk in on her with a boyfriend. Nonna had reacted beautifully—Maureen chuckled—as she'd shamed Maurene in voluble Spanish, something she did only when she was emotionally distressed. When she'd seen the dimple peeping through onto Maureen's cheek, Nonna had become shamefaced and entered into the spirit of Maureen's teasing, her plump frame shaking with laughter.

"Nonna, I'm sorry I'm so late, I overslept," Maureen called. "Where's Katy?"

"Niña's playing in backyard," the older woman replied, her lips tightly controlled, features set in her normally sunny face, as she suddenly turned away from Maureen.

Puzzled, Maureen sensed the hurt hostility emanating from Nonna. Her eyes followed the robust figure as it bustled into the kitchen. Following, Maureen pulled out a kitchen chair, her eyes never leaving the disapproving back of the gray-haired woman.

"Nonna, what's wrong?"

"You ask Nonna that?"

"Are you going to tell me, Nonna, or must I guess?" Maureen asked in exasperation.

"I don't mean to pry, but I see that man go in with you last night," she mumbled in a shaky voice as she turned to stare at Maureen. "I thought you good girl, but Nonna know he leave very much too late."

Suddenly the old woman's face began to crumple, and she threw the long white apron over her face, her body rocking back and forth.

"Nonna, please don't cry . . . it wasn't like that!"

Maureen cried, running to throw her arms around Nonna's trembling form.

Comforting her friend, Maureen felt a tremendous, even though illogical, anger against Daniel for being the cause of her dearest Nonna's pain. Murmuring soothing nonsense, Maureen forced the apron away from Nonna's watery eyes, compassion in her own.

"Oh, Nonna . . . that's what I came here to tell you. That man was Daniel Lord. I knew him years ago when my father and mother were alive." Her eager words fell all over themselves in her haste to get them out. "He . . . he wants to marry me, Nonna."

"He knows about Niña?" Nonna questioned.

"Yes, he knows everything." Maureen replied, her eyes falling from the old woman's piercing stare.

"I know!" Nonna explained smilingly. "He's choice of your father, *sí?*"

Realizing the interpretation the beaming woman was putting upon her past acquaintance with Daniel, Maureen sighed, her mind going over all possibilities. Why worry dear Nonna? Why worry her unnecessarily by telling her the truth? At least one of us should have our illusions.

"Yes, Nonna. He's my *novio*, and we're to be married this weekend," she explained quietly.

"Oh, Maurie! I so ha—happy for you. Now you have someone to look after you and Niña," she exclaimed, hugging the younger woman to her. "I am a silly old woman for doubting my Maurie, forgive please?"

"There's nothing to forgive, Nonna . . . I understand," Maureen said.

Suddenly the reality of the situation forcibly hit Nonna, and her face whitened as she clutched at Maureen.

"H—he won't take you and the little one away from your Nonna?" The appeal in Nonna's voice was pitifully obvious.

Oh, God! She'd never discussed Nonna with Daniel. Maureen bit down on her lower lip in consternation. Smoothing a gentle hand over the shaking form, Maureen knew she would have to tell Nonna a little white lie, and if Daniel didn't like the end result, which she was sure he wouldn't, then he'd just have to lump it.

"Nonna, I've told Daniel all about you, and we . . . we want you to come and live with us," she told her, one finger crossed behind her back.

The white lie was worth it, Maureen thought with a smile as she saw the transformation it worked upon the old woman's face. Her expression was incredulous at first, and then, when she saw the corroboration in Maureen's reassuring smile, joy radiated from her whole body.

"This man, he is good man, yes?" Nonna frowned momentarily, then answered her own question, thus saving Maureen the necessity of replying:

"Yes . . . he must be good man to want Niña and her Nonna, too!"

"Well, he wants both of you," Maureen ascertained staunchly. "Will you come, Nonna? We'll probably live in San Francisco for the present, in an apartment. Will you like that?"

"Nonna, she would like living in a barn, anywhere, so long as she could stay with her *chicas,*" she replied, wiping the last traces of her tears away with the corner of her apron. "We have coffee, and some of Nonna's *pasteles* for lunch later, yes, *linda?*"

Only Nonna could call me pretty and make me feel so warm and loved, Maureen thought gladly. Daniel would just have to take Nonna, that's all, he'd just have to. Nonna was like the grandmother she never knew, and she couldn't just abandon her; and if she faced the truth, she needed Nonna more now than ever. To her, Nonna would represent normality in a life gone suddenly topsy-turvy, and when she was married to Daniel, she would need all the familiar loving comfort she could get. Her love for Nonna was great, and if Daniel couldn't accept that, and Nonna, he could go jump in a lake. Hearing her own thoughts, Maureen mocked at herself. She was certainly brave when Daniel wasn't around!

Maureen turned down Nonna's offer of *pasteles* for lunch, much as she hated to. Nonna had gradually turned

98

Maureen on to Spanish food, and *pasteles* were one of her favorites. Made with green bananas, and stuffed with pork, pepper, seasonings, and black olives, they were delicious. She preferred hers plain, as did Katy, but Nonna laced hers with generous amounts of her special red chili sauce. Maureen had tried that once, and once only, she remembered with a grimace, and the end result had left her gasping with tears pouring down her face. How Nonna had laughed at her, thumping her energetically on the back.

Drinking her coffee, Maureen let Nonna's excited chatter flow over her, responding to her many questions evasively, while her brain seethed. She decided she must talk to Daniel, her guilty conscience regarding her friend's evident happiness getting the better of her.

After explaining to Nonna that she must call her *novio*, Maureen went back home with the older woman's eager acquiescence ringing in her ears. Picking up the phone, she hesitated momentarily, her hand poised in midair. Taking a deep breath, grasping at what little courage she had, Maureen dialed Daniel's number. She never questioned the fact that her fingers dialed the number automatically, if she had she might have wondered why, after all these years, she so readily remembered.

She heard the phone reverberating in her ear, and after the third ring, was nearly ready to put the phone back on its receiver. No one's home, she thought with an inordinate amount of relief, when to her consternation the phone was picked up at the other end.

A familiar voice spoke into the phone, and Maureen felt a certain affection creeping into her voice as she said, "Hello, Blake, do you know who this is?"

"Miss Maureen, I'm terribly glad to hear your voice after all these years," Blake replied, genuine warmth in his rather thin voice. "How have you been, Miss Maureen?"

"Fine, Blake . . . thank you for asking."

"May I offer you and Mr. Daniel my sincerest congratulations, with every wish for your future happiness?"

The sincerity in Blake's voice, who she felt had been her one true friend all those years ago, brought the sentimental moisture to her eyes.

"Thank you, Blake. Umm . . . is Daniel there by any chance?" Maureen regretted the quiver in her voice, but Blake luckily didn't seem to notice.

"Why, yes, he just came in a few minutes ago. He was just telling me about your imminent wedding, and I was so pleased." Then, lowering his voice to a whisper, he said, "You'll be good for Mr. Daniel, Miss Maureen . . . and the little one, well, she'll be good for all of us. My, we'll be a real family, won't we?" Blake questioned, not really expecting an answer. "Wait a moment, Miss Maureen, and I'll fetch Mr. Daniel."

"Maurie, you wanted to speak to me?" It seemed to Maureen, when she heard the rich, resonant tones of Daniel's voice on the line, that all the thoughts that had been buzzing around in her head suddenly fled. For the life of her, she couldn't think of a thing to say, and embarrassment flooded over her. Thankful that Daniel couldn't see her blush, she was even more thankful when Daniel's amused voice drawled, "Maurie, you called me, remember?"

Her temper snapping her out of mental inertia, Maureen said abruptly, "Of course I remember who called Daniel. I was just distracted by something . . . there's no need for sarcasm."

"Well?"

"Well, what?"

"Maurie," he said, his tone exasperated in the extreme. "In about half a minute I'm going to come over there and strangle you."

Marshaling her thoughts, Maureen muttered, "I want you . . . I mean I want to see you." Stammering to cover her initial slip, she wondered what in the world was the matter with her, why a simple phone conversation with this man threw her into such confusion? I'm acting more like a child than a grown woman, she thought in disgust.

"Baby, I like 'I want you' better," Daniel replied in

100

a low voice. "With an invitation like that I'll be right over."

"After last night you ought to know better than that, Daniel."

"That's a low blow, Maurie. I've tried to apologize . . . what do you want, my blood?"

"This is important, Daniel." Maureen knew the frustration she was feeling was evident in her voice, and she resented Daniel, knowing he was fully aware of his ability to get a rise out of her so easily, and hating herself for the twinge of guilt that assailed her.

"Believe me, honey . . . what I have in mind is important too . . . especially after two cold showers," he mumbled softly. Hearing her swift intake of breath, he forestalled the tirade he knew was imminent. He asked, "Will twelve thirty be all right for you?"

"That'll be fine," she replied, taking a calming breath.

"I'll tell Blake to fix lunch for Katy, but you and I will eat out." Daniel surprised Maureen into further speechlessness.

"But—" Maureen began, only to be stopped by Daniel's next words.

"Bring clothes for her, Maurie. I'll be keeping her with me tonight."

"Now wait just a minute, Daniel," she said, once again to be stopped before she could continue.

"No, Maurie, you wait a minute. I want to get to know the child before we're married, not after. I want it to be the two of us, can you understand that? After all, it's not fair to spring everything on her all at once, is it?" He spoke softly, leaving her with little choice but to agree. Katy did need to adjust to Daniel's presence—she realized that; but as she hung up the phone, she couldn't help feeling resentment at his high-handed attitude.

Attempting to marshal her thoughts, she stared down at the phone, perplexed. "He makes me so mad I could scream," she muttered. Giving herself a mental shake, she stomped off toward the bedroom. As she began making the bed her thoughts lent frantic haste to her movements, causing her to trip on the trailing end of the bedspread. Rubbing her bruised arm, which was already showing a faint purple tinge, she gingerly picked herself up off the floor, anger distorting her mouth.

"I must get a hold on myself," she mumbled, and taking a deep breath, she managed to finish making the bed, if not with its usual wrinkle-free perfection, at least creditably. After dusting the bedroom furniture, and straightening the dresser top, she glanced around the room, pleased with the outcome. Looking at the clock by her bed, she gave a gasp. Knowing Daniel, he was probably halfway there, and she still had the front room and kitchen to straighten.

By the time Maureen heard Daniel's car pull up in front of her place, she had managed to give herself a quick once-over, as well as the house. She had twisted her smooth hair into a chignon, its coiled smoothness heavy on the back of her neck, and changed into a simple dark blue wool dress. She was vaguely dissatisfied with the dress; it was so old, but it was one of the few that had held up over the years. She was unaware, as she opened the door to Daniel's knock, of the way the straight shift style clung to and molded her superb figure, the tiny cap sleeves and rounded scooped neckline showing off her golden arms and the glorious length of her neck.

She was also unaware of Daniel's swiftly indrawn breath, for she turned immediately, with a stammered apology, to get her coat from the bedroom closet. As his eyes followed the unconsciously provocative sway of her body across the room he felt a constriction in his chest. Taking a deep breath, he was again in control of his wayward emotions.

He opened the door for her to pass in front of him, murmuring softly, but impersonally, "You look lovely, Maurie." Smiling her thanks, she passed him, and as he caught the subtle hint of her perfume, his face muscles tightened, and he had to restrain himself from catching her up in his arms. Sensing his mood, she glanced up at his face, her own eyes widening in alarm as she saw the passion in his eyes. A puzzled frown crossed her face only seconds later, for his expression was once again blandly impersonal as he turned toward her once she had locked the door behind them. She must have been mistaken. The thought gave her much relief.

"Where's Katy?" he asked, a thread of steel running through his voice as he glanced at her.

"S—she's at my neighbor's," she blurted out. "Daniel, d—do you think we could have lunch on this side of the bay, a—and then come back for Katy? I—I didn't have time to ready her clothes, and she'll need a bath before she goes with you, and—"

"Whoa, slow down, honey." He smiled, inordinately relieved she had not been trying to defy him. "That'll be fine, but won't she kick up a fuss about leaving with me?"

"Oh, no . . . she's asked about you continuously," she replied without thinking.

Glancing up at him as she spoke, she was amazed at how her thoughtless remark caused his face to soften, and suddenly it occurred to her that Daniel was a singularly unloved man. Maybe being unloved in his life was the reason for his being so unloving. Maybe if she showed him affection in a physical way, the only way he seemed to understand, instead of always fighting him, he would begin to . . .

Turning toward Nonna's quickly, she hastened her steps in case Daniel could see the thoughts chasing across her mobile features. Lord, he always could read my face, she thought, knocking on Nonna's door. Over her shoulder she spoke to Daniel, who was still bewildered by her sudden flight.

"I'll just tell Nonna we're going, and let Katy know she's going with you tonight, Daniel. I—I'd like you to meet Nonna, too, if you don't mind?" she questioned rather timidly, still trying to regain her composure.

"I don't mind, sweetheart." His smile turned to shocked incredulity as the door opened and a short, plump body, speaking rapid Spanish, hurtled itself into his arms, dragging his head down with strong arms to place kisses upon his cheeks. As he looked at Maureen—who was doubled

103

up in laughter, with her hand over her mouth to stifle her giggles and her eyes dancing in merriment—he vowed to get even with her.

Holding the little gray-haired lady with weeping eyes as he ushered her into her home, he whispered to Maureen, "Just you wait, my girl," his eyes holding hers intently. She lowered her own from the wicked promise in his, suddenly finding it hard to breathe.

How can he act like last night never happened? Not twelve hours later, and he has the audacity to flirt with her, and to appear lighthearted to boot. Maureen knew she was deliberately trying to summon the anger she'd felt last night to counter the effect this smiling, friendly, and too handsome man was having on her solar plexus. Her eyes unwillingly encountering his gaze, she nearly gasped at the devilish light in his eyes. It was as if there was an open communication system between them, and she flushed when she realized he could read her thoughts once again.

"I'll go get Katy." She spoke quickly, almost stumbling from the room in her haste. Opening the back door, she walked quickly through into the backyard and stopped, dismayed at the sight that met her eyes. There was Katy, of whose appearance she was inordinately proud, sitting quite happily digging in a veritable quagmire, seemingly with more mud on her than under her.

"Oh, no!" she muttered distractedly. "Why today?" Glancing up from her earnest endeavors, Katy spotted Maureen, a delighted smile breaking out on her chubby face.

"Maurie, come see my moot," Katy babbled happily, her smile faltering slightly as she saw the expression on Maureen's face.

"That's *moat*, darling," she corrected automatically. No wonder Katy had questioned her so thoroughly when she had read her the story about the castle. She sighed. Knowing the child's fertile imagination, she should have been prepared for something like this. Resigned, she duly admired the long muddy trench around Katy, her mind abstracted, trying to think of a way of smuggling her home before Daniel caught sight of her. If she could just rush her through the gate, and give her a quick wash, she thought there might just be enough time . . . if she hurried.

"Daniel," Katy squealed, and rushed past Maureen before that appalled young lady could bring herself to move to stop her. Maureen closed her eyes, afraid to turn around as she heard the impact of a small body hitting a much larger one, and cringed when she heard the muffled grunt that followed. She turned slowly, and her eyes widened as she saw a once immaculate Daniel, his white slacks and blue velour shirt now spackled with mud, hugging Katy's wriggling body tightly in his arms and returning her earnest little kisses enthusiastically.

When he lifted his head finally from the child's stranglehold on his neck, Maureen gasped. Holding her face rigid, her breath coming in choked gasps, she thought of anything save the two she quickly averted her face from. Oh, no . . . she didn't dare look again! Making the mistake of taking just a quick peek, she could no longer stifle the laughter that was welling up inside her, and once again she was overcome with mirth at Daniel's expense.

"Just what's so funny, Maurie?" Daniel questioned threateningly, while Katy rested contentedly in his arms, one small arm thrown confidingly around his neck, as she too stared in puzzlement at Maureen.

"Daniel," she gasped, "there's just a little mud on your face. I—I didn't mean to laugh, I'm sorry." Maureen ruined this polite speech by once again giving way to a choked giggle.

"That's two I owe you, my girl!" he stated emphatically, taking out his handkerchief and wiping the mud off his cheek. Maureen walked up and, taking the cloth from him, wiped the remaining mud off his very formidable nose, her eyes still irrepressibly mirthful. As their glances met she quickly stepped back in no little confusion, as she returned the soiled cloth, wincing at the involuntary touch of her fingers upon the warm skin of his hand.

Registering his mistaken interpretation of her grimace as being distaste at even the most casual of physical contact with him, his face tightened. He wondered how in the world he was going to get her over her fear of him. Not that it wasn't his own fault she felt disgust, he did, too, when he remembered his treatment of her last night. But damn it, he wanted to have no marriage of convenience with Maurie. He'd just have to tread warily or she'd run from him again, and he couldn't risk that. His arms involuntarily tightened around the child.

Daniel glanced ruefully down at his no longer immaculate clothes. He looked up at Katy and realized the child was also looking at his soiled shirt, her lower lip trembling and tears forming in her eyes as they met his.

"I dirtied you," she mumbled as a large tear slipped down her cheek, leaving a dirty little trail on her sad face.

Wiping the tear away, he smiled tenderly at her. "It'll wash, Chicken." Glancing wickedly at Maureen, he said, "Maurie will just have to give us both a bath, hmmm?"

"Will you, Maurie . . . please?" Katy asked in delight, her baby face once again wreathed in smiles.

The warning signs on Maureen's expressive face were plain to read, and Daniel burst into laughter. "Uh, oh, Chicken . . . looks like we're in trouble," he teased, backing away from Maureen.

"Maurie, don't you 'pank my Daniel," Katy said with a fierce frown. This again proved too much for both Maureen and Daniel, who were doubled up with mirth when Nonna opened up the door, smiling tearily at the happy little family. Calling to tell them lunch was ready, she gasped and her hands flew to her cheeks as she caught sight of Daniel and Katy.

"No . . . no . . . no," she chanted. Alternately clucking and scolding in both Spanish and English, Nonna ushered the unrepentant duo into the bathroom, her remarks never ceasing as she sponged what she could off Daniel's clothes; then she left him to deal with the rest while she took over the ablutions of Katy, who needed rather more done to her. Gratefully Maureen handed

Katy over to Nonna's tender hands, for she had caught a glimpse of herself in the mirror over the sink and realized the mud had somehow managed to transfer itself to her dress and face; and as if that wasn't bad enough, her hair was falling down. Glaring at the amused Daniel reflected behind her, she quickly washed and tidied herself as well as possible; her hands—made all thumbs under Daniel's gaze as he leaned against the wall watching her frenzied attempts—fumbled with her hair. Still scolding, Nonna led Katy out of the bathroom.

"Why don't you leave too?" Maureen said, glaring at him through the mirror.

"Do I bother you, honey?" he questioned, his eyebrows raised. Truth to tell, he just wanted to look at her but was quite enjoying the reaction he was getting. Laugh at me, would she, the little devil? So it makes her nervous when I stare at her, does it? Well, I'll just get a little of my own back!

As Maureen glanced toward him again she was appalled to see him sauntering toward her, the strange light in his eyes giving her some inkling of his thoughts. Stiffening, she felt his hands on her shoulders, turning her. Closing her eyes, expecting his anger for the way she'd dismissed him so peremptorily, she was startled into incredulity when she heard his low chuckle. Her eyes flew open in amazement, only to have her gaze flounder as she saw his eyes openly caressing her body.

Thinking he had no right to look at her like that, with the deliberate intention of embarrassing her, she began indignantly to pull away from his confining hands when he unexpectedly pressed his body against hers, levering her against the basin and reaching around behind her. She pushed at his chest to no avail and was so preoccupied she failed to hear the water running behind her. With a wicked grin Daniel began energetically to wash her face with a washcloth, leaving her gasping at the coldness of the water. His lower body still pressed into her while he held her neck with one hand, making it impossible for her to turn her spluttering face away from his extremely damp ministrations.

"Hold still, Maurie. There's just a tiny bit left on your nose," he whispered, laughing at the outraged expression on her face as he deliberately ground his thighs closer into her softness. Suddenly seeing the humor of the situation, she relaxed, realizing Daniel was just getting his own back. She gave him a sheepish smile, conceding victory to him for this round.

As he felt her body relax, and gazed bemusedly at the little dimple peeping out from beside her mouth, Daniel forgot what he was doing and even why he was doing it. Glancing downward at the curves barely displayed by the scooped neckline of her dress, he quickly dropped the washcloth behind them. He took a deep breath, and all humor quickly drained from his face.

Staring intently at Maureen's lovely face upturned to his, eyes closed again to further facilitate his ablutions, he quietly and gently reached out his hand to caress her neck with the lightest of touches. Opening her eyes in alarm, Maureen found herself drowning in his gaze, and she seemed to see a question in his eyes as she realized that for the first time in four years she didn't want to run from him—quite the opposite, in fact. She remained perfectly still while a small, shy smile glinted from the corner of her mouth.

At her smile Daniel's own lips curved tenderly, and with a slow movement he lowered his mouth to hers. She felt the first tender touch of his mouth caressing hers, his fingers on the vulnerable softness of her neck and shoulder. Something warm and tender unfurled inside her lonely heart, and she melted against him, tentatively returning his kiss.

Feeling her response, he nearly lost all control. Dear God, he thought, doesn't she know what she's doing to me? Then, just in time, he realized that she truly didn't know. That's where he'd gone wrong before, for in her innocent responses to him he'd read experience and had treated her like any other woman he'd had, which had only frightened her. Lifting his mouth from hers with reluctance, he moved his lips gently to her cheek and the soft skin at the side of her neck, nuzzling there, satisfied when he felt her breath quicken and a tiny shudder go through her taut body.

Maureen became aware of the effect Daniel was once again having on her emotions, and began to pull away from the tantalizing delight of his mouth on her heated skin. She was surprised even slightly chagrined, when he immediately let her go.

"We—we're in no condition to go out, Daniel. Would you mind very much eating here? Nonna has just taken it for granted, and it would mean a lot to her," she muttered in some embarrassment, lowering her eyes from his too knowing gaze.

"I'm certainly in no state to go out, and I am getting rather hungry," he replied matter-of-factly, giving her a quick kiss and moving away from her completely.

"Shall we go?" Daniel smiled, awakening an answering smile in her as he led her out of the room and headed for the kitchen. Thinking of that smile, he knew he had handled the situation correctly for a change, and felt rewarded when he remembered her momentary, but definite, response to his kisses.

Maureen didn't see the mocking smile that crossed his face, a smile that was full of confidence in his own ability to wear down her defenses. I'll go slowly with her, he thought, watching as she walked ahead of him toward the kitchen. Soon she would be his wife, and with the satisfying thought came the certainty that with his own particular powers of persuasion, there would be no refusing him when he finally had her convinced her place was in his bed!

CHAPTER SEVEN

"Honey, I could sure stand to rest my aching feet," moaned Gaye, with a reproachful grin at Maureen. Smiling in response, Maureen clutched her packages closer, trying to juggle them to a more comfortable position. All in all, she thought in satisfaction, it has been an extremely hectic but rewarding day. She had been shopping for her trousseau and was now more than thankful to fall in with Gaye's suggestion.

"Let's stow these things in the trunk of the car, and then go get an early dinner. All right with you?"

"Sounds great, honey, but I'm paying," Gaye affirmed. "After all, I didn't have time to give you a wedding shower, so the least I can do is give you a bachelorette dinner." She laughed, giving Maureen a wink.

"I know there isn't any use arguing with you, so I'll just say thank you nicely. Now, where shall we eat? I'm starting to feel empty." Her tone cheerful, she smiled at Gaye while putting her packages in the trunk of the car and laughed aloud as her friend groaned after dropping hers on top of Maureen's.

"Somewhere we can have a quiet drink before dinner, honey," Gaye begged, rolling her eyes upward in exhaustion.

"You took the words right out of my mouth!"

As Maureen drove slowly through the crowded shopping park Gaye glanced at her fondly, thinking that a sweeter, more considerate girl had never lived. It was only poetic justice that Maurie was to marry a sought-after man like Daniel Lord. After all the poor kid had to struggle through, she deserved to be one of the lucky ones. Thank God, Maurie would never have to pinch pennies again or worry about Katy's future. Daniel Lord was more than capable of taking care of them both. Of course, Maurie did have an inordinate amount of stiff-necked pride. Gaye wasn't blind to her friend's faults, but that was all to the good really, so long as Daniel knew how to handle her. She had a sneaking suspicion he was learning fast. She smiled at the thought.

Interrupting reveries with a start, Gaye said, "Maurie, how about us going to the Blue Dolphin? It's a super restaurant right on the Marina . . . you'd love it, as crazy as you are for watching sailboats!"

"You're sure it's not too expensive, Gaye?"

"Sure I'm sure."

"It's not a fancy place, is it? I'm not really dressed for dining out."

"Maurie, I really feel like going all out tonight. What say we go to your place first and get all dressed up? You have that new sexy pantsuit, and I have that rather fetching dress I bought. It's your last night as a single girl, and we could have kind of a last fling together," Gaye begged.

"All right, Gaye . . . it does sound like fun." Maureen couldn't help giving in to Gaye's pleadings, and it really did sound good. Just to go and glance out at the boats in their moorings and to rest their feet sounded heavenly, especially resting their feet!

Allowing herself to be caught up in Gaye's enthusiasm, she began to feel excited herself. She realized how much this meant to Gaye, and wasn't about to spoil her friend's pleasure in her marriage, even if she herself could get none from it. Dreading tomorrow, she was only more than willing to do something different, not relishing the thought of sitting at home worrying, as she'd been prone to do these last two days. As she turned back on to Hesperian Boulevard, heading toward home, she told Gaye she was just in the mood to dress up, and felt rewarded by the smile on Gaye's face. Something about that smile puzzled her momentarily, though. Had Gaye seemed relieved? She quickly forgot her disquieting impressions as the car picked up speed. She needed to focus all her attention on the road as she made her way through the heavy traffic.

Gaye could feel Maureen's finely drawn tension and remained quiet, looking out the window of the little Volkswagen. Maureen was more than grateful for her friend's intuition. Feeling the wheel smooth beneath her moist palms, she realized she'd be thankful when all this rush was over. She'd been in so much confusion lately, especially since that impromptu lunch at Nonna's two days ago.

Two days? It seemed to have happened much longer ago than that, but she knew it was because so much had been accomplished since! Remembering the relaxed laughter of that meal brought a pleased smile to her face. She'd seen yet another side of Daniel that day, and it was one that she had more than liked. He had been so tender with Katy, who had insisted upon being at her most demanding that afternoon, not wanting to share Daniel's attention. He had handled her beautifully, she had to admit, and had soon settled her down. Occasionally he whispered some little secret in Katy's ear, which threw her into fits of giggles. He talked to Nonna and herself, but still he had managed to make Katy feel included. As a result Katy ate more, and behaved better, than she ever had done before—or so it had seemed to her and Nonna, the two of them constantly glancing at each other in astonishment.

Just the memory of his tender handling of Katy, which seemed almost instinctive, set Maureen wondering if what she feared about Daniel's influence upon Katy could ever materialize. Surely Daniel seemed to have a far easier time getting what he wanted from Katy than from her; but then, Nonna had soon been eating out of his hand too, she remembered, grimacing at the trend her thoughts were taking. Daniel is one of those men who charm without trying, and Nonna was no exception to the rule.

He had praised Nonna's cooking, saying it was better than any he'd eaten in Mexico, and she'd been lost. As if that wasn't enough, he'd thoroughly taken the wind out of Maureen's sails by taking for granted that Nonna would make her home with them, and though it was what she wanted, Maureen felt resentful, which wasn't logical. She sat like a fool in openmouthed surprise as he further sealed his sainthood in a traitorous Nonna's eyes by lapsing into fluent Spanish.

From then on, as far as Nonna was concerned, Daniel was approved wholeheartedly. Nonna was old-fashioned in her beliefs, and Daniel knew it and could see the love the old woman had for "her children," and oh, how he used it to his advantage, at last managing to seal the engagement irrevocably in Maureen's eyes. There was no going back from then on, for to Nonna, a betrothal was as binding as a marriage.

There was no way she could have killed the joy shining in Katy's eyes either. She had known the child had taken a fancy to Daniel, but hadn't fully realized the extent of it. Katy had quietly crawled up on Daniel's lap and cuddled there, rubbing her small hand over his face and whispering something to him she was unable to hear. She didn't think she would ever forget the sight of him bending to answer the child, hugging her close as he did so. As the adults quietly talked practicalities, Katy trustingly fell asleep in his arms. She had risen to take her from him, but he'd looked at her almost fiercely, and had insisted upon placing Katy in bed himself, gently removing her clothes without waking her and tenderly placing the blankets around the sleeping child.

Upon returning to the room, Daniel swiftly took all the plans for moving and so forth out of their hands, shouldering all the burdens. With a quick phone call, he arranged for the moving men to come and also arranged the storing of Nonna's treasures, insisting upon bearing the expense. Within two hours he had everything planned to the last detail, for both her and Nonna, and Maureen felt even more resentful as events moved swiftly away from her.

It seemed that once he got his finger in the pie, there was no pie left! Daniel had of course realized her attitude, and when the subject of Maureen's clothes and wedding dress came up, he very wisely conceded to her wish to pay for everything herself. He—she smirked disdainfully at the thought—would have had her fitted at the finest salons in San Francisco! Well, her wedding outfit might not be the most expensive, but he couldn't have found a more beautiful dress and veil if he'd consulted the finest fashion houses. The thought of the lovely ivory and lace Empire gown now hanging in her closet ready for tomorrow gave her a great deal of satisfaction.

It was really a blessing Daniel insisted upon taking Katy, for it had given her the rest of that day to shop for her wedding dress, which she found at Sherry's in San Leandro, the first place she looked. Thank goodness, it fit perfectly! The only alteration had been to the hem, which had to be shortened to calf length. She doubted the gown could have been ready in time if it had needed extensive alterations; but as it was, she was able to pick it up this morning.

Entering the parking space in front of her home, she had to pull around a large moving van in front of Nonna's. They hadn't wasted much time. But then, when Daniel Lord gives the orders, they are followed to the letter, she thought spitefully, including herself among the followers. As she and Gaye got the packages from the back of the car, they caught a glimpse of Nonna bustling about, giving expert advice to the experts, and she and Gaye smiled at each other, turning to wave to the happily smiling Nonna before entering the house.

Here, too, was evidence of change, for all of Katy's things were in labeled boxes ready for the movers. Seeing her living room turned topsy-turvy gave her a jolt, for this had been home for so long. In their way they'd been very happy here, and she felt fear at leaving her safe, familiar little home. She picked up a stray teddy bear and stuffed it into the top of the large box from which it had fallen.

She missed her baby, and talking on the phone to her wasn't the same as having her close. She and Katy had never been separated for this long before, and suddenly she longed to hold her, with a yearning that was startling in its intensity. She was jealous, she realized with a feeling of self-disgust, but she'd never had to share Katy in this way before, so maybe there was some justification.

Changing with Gaye, amid much chatter and laughter, Maureen tried to keep her plunging mood from her friend's notice, and she must have succeeded, because Gaye's spirits seemed to soar ever higher as she excitedly made plans for the evening. She was glad, for she owed it to Gaye, especially after having dragged her around the stores since early this morning. What the heck, she thought, her own spirits rising to the occasion. If you can't beat 'em, join 'em! Laughing aloud, she threw herself into the preparations, thus managing to keep worrisome thoughts at bay.

Later, entering the Blue Dolphin, with its glass cases holding various interesting displays, Maureen checked her coat, and she and Gaye spent a few minutes admiring the curios and jewelry on display. Leaving Gaye to admire a silver bracelet with jade inserts, she moved into the foyer, where she noticed the arched entry to the right and approached it, curious.

Standing just under the arch, she looked past her at a large room filled with people. To the far right was a bandstand, and she was surprised to see a small dance floor directly in front and beyond that an area with tables, some with white cloths and place settings for diners and others without for those who were using the facilities of the bar only.

What caught and held her attention, though, were the glass windows that circled the entire room. She allowed her eyes to roam at will and was amazed at the view. Outside, there seemed to be literally hundreds of pleasure craft of every description and size imaginable, giving the impression the restaurant itself was moored among them.

There were large power launches, with upper stories making them appear slightly ungainly. As if to add to this impression there were the myriad sailing vessels, lines sleek and graceful, with a fluidity of design that left her gasping in admiration for the unknown nautical architects.

Maureen's rapt attention was broken by Gaye's voice calling her, and with a sigh she reluctantly turned away to follow her upstairs set against the wall on the left side of the foyer. She was puzzled, presuming they'd be dining if not in the bar area, then farther down in what she guessed was the main dining room. Oh, well, probably the place was full, or maybe the view was better from upstairs.

Turning a corner after reaching the top of the stairs, Maureen halted in stunned amazement as cries of "Surprise, surprise," rang in her ears. Flabbergasted, she sent a speaking look to Gaye, who laughed, literally dragging Maureen into the room.

There was a cacophony of sound as voices babbled out all around her in a surging tide. Literally all her friends from the club were there, even the woman who came in to clean, and quite a few she didn't recognize, probably spouses or dates. Maureen's eyes filled with weak tears as she felt the genuine affection and warmth radiating out toward her from these friends who had come to mean so much to her; and with a muffled sob, she felt Gaye's arms go around her shaking body, finding comfort in the fact that Gaye's eyes were moist too. Slowly she pieced together the fact that Daniel had closed down the entire club to allow them to give her a combined shower and engagement party. He had even arranged transportation for those who had no way to get there from the city, and it was obvious to Maureen that everyone was wildly prepared to enjoy himself.

The knowledge that Daniel had arranged all this somewhat dulled Maureen's happiness, though why she should be such an ungrateful beast, she couldn't understand. This desire in herself to mitigate Daniel's effect on her life, to score off of him if possible every chance she could get, was both childish and undignified, she told herself. After all, if she took everything Daniel did and said with suspicion, always looking for ulterior motives, what chance would their marriage have? She knew he was trying, and the least she could do was meet him halfway, but her fear of possible consequences seemed to form an impenetrable barrier where her emotions were concerned. All she seemed able to accomplish was perfecting an outward facade for other people, as she was doing now, and that just wasn't good enough, she realized in trepidation.

She wasn't the type of person who could bear putting on a smiling act all the time for the benefit of other people while knowing herself to be unhappy. Eventually the real situation between the two of them was bound to show, and there would be those who thought she'd allowed herself to be bought, for some people never looked beyond the surface facade to discover the real motivations of those they gossiped about. Daniel was very much in the limelight, for he was a figure who, owing to his very forceful personality, and not a little to his good looks, was constantly in the news. What if she cracked under the strain of their relationship? Feeling the way she did about Daniel, that curious bond of love and fear that bound her to him, would she be able to bear his using her for his own ends, his indifference to her as time went by and the newness of passion wore off . . . his other women? No one looking at my smiling face would guess the doubts and fears tormenting me, she thought wryly, so maybe there is some hope for the future after all.

The champagne had been flowing pretty freely by the time dinner was served, and Maureen, her mouth dry with nerves, drank more of the sparkling beverage than she was used to. Without her being aware of it, attentive waiters were there to refill her glass before it was half empty, and as she sat down at the head of the long line of white-clothed tables her head was swimming alarmingly.

Looking down the tables at her friends, she noticed that one face was conspicuously absent. He probably couldn't be bothered to attend! Then suddenly it didn't seem to matter in the least, as the bubbles in the champagne spread through her bloodstream. What's the use of worrying about anything, she thought with a giggle. Gaye, from her place on Maureen's right, was looking at her with a slightly solicitous air.

"I'm q—quite fine, Gaye," she stammered, trying with difficulty to focus on Gaye's wavering image.

"Honey, I do believe you're ripped," Gaye said in amazement. "How much of that stuff have you downed?"

"A—a few glasses, and I am not," Maureen denied.

"Not what?"

"Not ripped," she said indignantly.

"I'd sure like to know what you'd call it, then," Gaye replied. "You'd better begin eating, and no more wine for you, my girl. Daniel will wring my neck if he sees you like this, so you'd better sober up fast."

"Will he?"

"Will he what?"

"See me?"

Sudden comprehension crossed Gaye's features when she heard the childish question, realizing Maureen thought Daniel wasn't coming.

"Honey, he'll be here a little later, don't fret. He's with Harry, taking care of some last-minute details that have cropped up," Gaye explained, rewarded by a lightening of Maureen's features.

"I—I didn't realize," she said sheepishly, lowering her confused gaze from Gaye's knowing look.

"Well, technically the bridegroom isn't supposed to see the bride the night before the wedding, you know."

"I never thought of that."

"Well, Daniel did, but it seems he knows you better than I thought," Gaye said dryly.

"What do you mean?" Maureen asked, picking up her fork and beginning to eat with enforced nonchalance.

Pouring black coffee from the large urn on the table, Gaye watched Maureen place a few more bites into her mouth. As Maureen sipped the hot beverage slowly, Gaye smiled her satisfaction and finally replied to Maureen's earlier question.

"Daniel told me to keep an eye out for you until he got here, and told me he would have to break tradition under the circumstances, or you'd think he couldn't be bothered to attend. Seems as if he was right," Gaye remarked disapprovingly. "What I can't understand is why you're always thinking the worst where he's concerned."

"Gaye, believe me, there are reasons. I—I try not to let my attitude show, but I'm not a very good actress, I guess."

"Honey, the only reason I notice is because I've grown so fond of you over the years, and the last few days Harry and I have grown close to Daniel, too," Gaye said, frowning. "Don't you worry, everything will work out for the best, Maurie. Just you remember, Harry and I are your friends if you ever need us."

Gaye's kindness was almost her undoing, her emotions being so volatile, and her eyes misted over. Gaye was such a dear. She must have been curious about the suddenness of this marriage, and about why Maureen had agreed to marry Daniel in the first place—her earlier attitude had been so obvious—but Gaye had never questioned her motives. That's really the mark of true friendship, she thought, blind faith in another person. If only she had half of that faith in Daniel, she wouldn't feel so much despair over the thought of tomorrow, and all their tomorrows.

Dinner finished and the tables cleared, Maureen was further astounded when waiters came, piling gifts upon the table in front of her. Maureen opened each one carefully, reading each card aloud. She was especially touched by each handwritten message. She wouldn't in any way spoil the party for anyone by letting them see her trepidation, and any nervousness attributed to her would be brushed off as natural for a soon-to-be bride, she hoped. In fact, when she unwrapped Gaye's present last of all and pulled out a delicious negligee in white, so cobwebby thin as to seem almost transparent, everyone roared in delight at the flush that stained her cheeks and neck, and that seemed to her to be spreading all over her body. Quickly returning the lacy confection to its box, she stammered her thanks and quickly sat down again.

"Gaye, how could you?" Maureen hissed, sending Gaye a killing glance.

"Don't blame me, honey. It was Harry's idea," Gaye replied, chuckling. "He'll be mad as fire he wasn't here to see your face."

"Well, thank God Daniel wasn't! I can just picture his amusement."

Turning to look at Gaye as she spoke, Maureen was arrested by Gaye's widened eyes, and to her amazement she saw Gaye look quickly down at her coffee cup, her face working convulsively. While Maureen stared at Gaye's face in puzzlement, Gaye once again raised her eyes to Maureen. Quickly looking behind Maureen, Gaye could no longer control the mirthful gasp that escaped her. Bewildered, Maureen looked out over the faces now laughing uproariously, and hearing a rustling of tissue paper beside her, she stiffened and slowly turned. There stood Daniel, and— Oh, no! He was holding up her night-dress and slowly running his lean hand over its lacy folds. Face beet-red, she snatched the gown from him in a frenzy of embarrassment, much to the amusement of their guests.

Maureen shoved the lid on the box properly this time and stared down at it, her discomfiture intensified by Daniel's amused chuckle, and his warm breath on her ear as he bent down to whisper, "Very pretty, sweetheart," while sealing his words with a warm kiss on the side of her neck.

The firm pressure of his warm mouth, open on the softly vulnerable spot of silken skin beneath her ear, increased her shyness to an unbearable degree. Pulling back from the provocative caress, she gasped and turned, chattering about trivialities to Gaye. For the life of her, she couldn't make sense of her own words, and Gaye, realizing she needed a breathing space to quiet her tumultuous emotions, gave her the diversion she needed, bless her!

121

"There, Harry Davis, I hope you're satisfied with your little joke," Gaye said. "You men go get yourselves some food, maybe that'll soothe your perverted sense of humor."

Laughing, Harry raised his hands in alarm and shot Daniel a look that clearly said "Women!" They then sauntered off to order a quick meal—Harry's arm draped around Daniel's shoulders so that the two presented a united front announcing "We men stick together." Maureen now had the respite she so desperately needed.

As she laughed and talked with the other women—the men having gravitated to Daniel and Harry—Maureen felt revitalized. To her it seemed as if the whole party had come alive, and glancing toward Daniel, she knew she hadn't just imagined it. His dynamic presence, so darkly attractive and self-assured, did have a definite effect upon the men standing around him; and looking around at the faces of the women, she noticed they too were stealing quick glances toward the man whose personality seemed to ooze out around them.

Daniel made a laughing remark Maureen couldn't catch, but listening to the laughter of the men, and seeing the rapt attention on their faces, she thought suddenly that this was the secret to Daniel's success in business. He had the ability to be a ladies' man, with his harshly aloof sensual magnetism, while still retaining an aura of intense masculinity that made him a man's man.

As he finished his dinner Daniel listened to a mild argument between Grady and Harry about baseball. His attention wandering, he looked up and encountered Maureen's dark eyes upon him, though she quickly flushed and looked away. Staring across the room at her, he felt his emotions, always quick to surface when she was near, begin to stir. God, he thought, blood pounding in his temples, breath quickening. She's enough to send a man's blood pressure sky-high.

Narrowing his gray eyes, he appraised her pantsuit, the material silky and clinging lovingly to the lush curves of her figure. In a soft yellow, it was halter-necked, with a deep plunging vee, and was practically backless, showing off the golden-skinned beauty of the girl wearing it. The color seemed to strike sparks off her dark hair, flowing loose and silky to her waist. Daniel's breath caught in his throat at the thought that this time tomorrow night he would have the right to twist that glorious hair around his own body. Stirred by the sensuality of his thoughts, he jumped up and suggested they all head downstairs to dance. Startled, those around him broke off their own conversations to stare at him in surprise.

The rest of the evening was a sheer delight for all. Downstairs, in the foyer, Daniel spoke quietly to the maitre d', who immediately led the party to a group of tables located directly in front of the bandstand. The band was very good, and though they started the evening out playing soft, sentimental dance tunes, they picked up the beat as the evening wore on.

Laughing at the sight of Grady, Harry, Gaye, and Emma, the cleaning lady, out on the dance floor attempting to learn the hustle from some exuberant youths, Maureen was suffused with warmth toward Daniel for arranging for her friends to have such a good time. She hadn't spoken much to him. As host, he was busy partnering his guests while she often took the floor; but they hadn't as yet danced together, for which she'd been relieved.

Turning to him now, she whispered, "Thank you for my party, Daniel."

"Don't thank me," he returned. "All I did was arrange the details and make sure everyone had a way to get here, that's all. That is, other than closing down the club for the weekend."

"B—but Daniel," she stammered. "You mean you didn't—"

"No, honey," he interrupted. "You don't realize how much you mean to people, Maurie. You have a habit of selling yourself short. I've been hearing things about you from your friends that make me ashamed of my thoughts about them, but especially about you. Now I understand why you felt so secure and safe at the club. Those people out there chipped in together to give you and me this party. They love you, Maurie."

123

"Daniel, I'm so ashamed. I—I didn't realize, I just assumed . . ." Maureen's face softened as she looked with new eyes at her friends.

"Let's give them something for their money, Maurie," Daniel whispered, bending toward her and turning her face toward him. His lips found hers, and Maureen clutched convulsively at his arm, the muscles taut beneath her hand. Feeling her response, Daniel nibbled at her lips, causing them to open slightly in further submission. Breath mingling in a warm tide, she shivered as she felt Daniel's tongue parting further the quivering sweetness of her mouth.

For Maureen, time and place had ceased to exist, and all she could hear was the blood pounding loudly in her ears. She didn't know if the kiss lasted ten seconds or as many minutes, so confusing was the heat coursing out through her body to her numbed brain. Daniel's kiss hardened, and she thought she would faint as she felt his tongue circling and teasing her own, sensations welling up in her so intensely she moaned aloud.

As he felt her loss of control, not to mention his own, Daniel pulled his mouth reluctantly away from hers and pressed his hot forehead against her own, his eyes closing convulsively, his breath coming in gasps. All at once cheering and clapping broke out, and with dazed eyes Maureen and Daniel saw the delighted faces of the people around them.

"Everybody loves a lover," Daniel muttered, while Maureen hid her face in his shoulder. Kissing the top of her head, he turned to the others with a grin. "There are times when friends, especially such friends as all of you have proved to be to Maurie and me, are wonderful to have around. But the way I feel right now, I wish you'd all go to the devil," he told them audaciously. Roaring with laughter, they all cried, "Kiss her again, Daniel, don't mind us," and with a shake of his head and a grin he promised, "Wait for tomorrow. Once she's my wife I won't be able to stop, but I get the feeling if I kiss her again, she'll be too scared to marry me."

Maureen didn't know how she ever got through the rest

of the evening, but evidently she made rather a good job of it, for no one seemed to guess at the quaking fear inside her. "Too scared to marry me . . . too scared!" Daniel's mocking words reverberated through her head time and time again, and she knew she wasn't scared—she was terrified. She couldn't cope with her ambiguous feelings toward Daniel, nor with his lack of feeling toward her.

Oh, he appeared to care in front of others, and she was grateful to him for the pretense, for it quite effectively settled once and for all any doubts there might be about why she was marrying him. Her abandoned reaction to his kiss had convinced even Jack—she flushed at the thought, for he avoided her gaze whenever he could.

Finally it was over, and once she was alone she was totally unable to give vent to her feelings. Fear was like a lump in her throat. She wanted to cry, but even tears were denied her. After a cool shower, for the night was oppressively warm, she huddled like a child under the covers, her mind too disturbed to sleep.

Morning found her heavy-eyed and depressed as she was awakened by a pounding on her door. "Go away," she moaned aloud. Wrapping her homey wool dressing gown, a relic of her teens, around her, she stumbled through to the front room, dodging boxes as she passed.

"Honey, if Daniel sees you like that he'll turn tail and run," Gaye joked, bursting into the room like a whirlwind.

Maureen brushed her hair from her face. "I wish he would!"

"Maurie, you've just got bride jitters." Gaye laughed. "Come on, you'll feel better after a shower and a little food."

Gaye firmly pushed Maureen through to the bathroom. "You shower, and I'll fix you a light breakfast, honey . . . how's that sound?"

"Fine, Gaye. I'm sorry to be such a pain."

"That's okay, honey," Gaye said, giving Maureen a quick hug. "If anybody understands, I do . . . I'll be in the same boat myself in a couple of weeks!"

"That's right." Maureen laughed, trying desperately to fall in with Gaye's exuberant mood.

"Sure . . . we'll have you fixed up in no time!"

To Maureen's surprise, Gaye's words proved true. Within an amazingly short time they were climbing into the gleaming silver-gray Cadillac Daniel used when entertaining customers. Maureen was grateful for its air-conditioned interior, for the August morning was stiflingly hot. Even with the air-conditioning her skin felt clammy against the gray leather upholstery.

The church Daniel had chosen was large and rather functional-looking, not her idea of a church at all. As they parked in front of the modern low building, she thought its only saving grace was the giant oak trees softening its exterior with dancing shadows.

"Oh, Gaye! I feel sick."

"Maurie, calm down. There's nothing to be afraid of, honey."

Worried, Gaye noticed the pallor of Maureen's face, the faint smudges beneath her eyes.

Maureen hadn't noticed the man driving the car, but as Gaye tapped on the panel separating them from the driver she gave a visible start as he turned around.

"Oh, Blake!"

"Miss Maureen, you look beautiful." Blake's smile turned to a concerned frown as he noted the almost panic-stricken look in Maureen's eyes.

"Blake, I c—can't go through with this!" Maureen's teeth chattered.

"You must, Miss Maureen—for the little girl's sake, as well as Mr. Daniel's." Blake's quiet but firm voice had the desired effect, as their eyes met in a long look of total understanding.

"Mr. Blake, is that right?" Gaye questioned, rummaging in her purse and bringing out a small brown vial.

"Just Blake, ma'am."

Maureen raised her head from the back of the seat, suddenly conscious of her faux pas.

"Oh, I'm sorry," she apologized. "Gaye, this is Mr. Blake, or just Blake, as he prefers. He's Daniel's friend and man-of-all-trades." She smiled. "Blake, this is my best friend, Gaye."

126

"Blake, I'm glad to meet you." Gaye grinned, receiving an approving smile in return. Gaye glanced at Maureen, then back to Blake. As their eyes met she whispered, "Can you get me some water?"

"Certainly, Miss Gaye. There will be glasses set up for the luncheon in the adjoining building. I won't be a moment."

Gaye talked soothingly to Maureen. In a very short time Blake returned with the water.

"Here, Maurie . . . take this." Gaye pressed a small capsule in Maureen's shaking hand.

"What is it?"

"Just something mild to settle your nerves," Gaye replied quietly. "I was afraid you might need it, so I brought them along just in case."

"You know I don't like taking—"

Gaye wouldn't let her finish her sentence. "Just this once," she pleaded. "For me?"

Maureen smiled and obediently placed the pill on the back of her tongue, washing it down with the water Blake handed her.

"Just sit here and rest. We have a few minutes," Gaye murmured.

"Miss Gaye?"

Gaye's head turned from her contemplation of Maureen, and she glanced inquiringly at Blake.

"I would suggest the small dressing room just off the vestibule for the purpose," he said quietly. At Gaye's questioning glance Blake mouthed the word *photographers,* and Gaye bit her lip, glancing outside nervously.

"That's all we'd need," she whispered in disgust.

Unobtrusively they ushered Maureen out of the car and led her quickly up a path and through a side door. As the door closed behind them Gaye saw three men with camera equipment slung over their shoulders hurrying up the path, and she breathed a sigh of relief before quickly locking the door behind them.

From then on, everything that happened seemed a jumble of confused impressions to Maureen, almost as if they weren't happening to her at all. Gaye's pill had

127

calmed her; in fact—she smiled at the thought—it had nearly made her comatose.

There was the ceremony, with Daniel looking solemn and totally unfamiliar to her in a dark suit and tie. She did not falter as she walked up the aisle to him, her mind concentrating on the surprisingly beautiful interior of the chapel. There were tall gold candelabra on the dais, which was plain except for the masses of fragrant blossoms adorning the altar. Tall stained-glass windows covered the whole wall behind the altar, and the sun filtered through to cast dancing prisms of colored light upon the stark white cross atop a raised platform at the center.

The whole effect was soothing, and holy, and throughout the ceremony Maureen glanced upward at the minister's face, a feeling of peace stealing over her.

Afterward they posed for the professional photographer Daniel had hired, while their guests assembled next door to be seated for the luncheon.

The only event to jar Maureen's newfound calm occurred when they left the hall after the buffet luncheon. She had eaten very little and, after a whispered word in Daniel's ear from Gaye, had drunk only water. As they ran to the car amid the cries and good wishes of the crowd following them, there was a barrage of flashing lights. Maureen stumbled in surprise, and Daniel grabbed her arm, shouldering his way past the raucous reporters and shielding her with his body. Her arm hurt from the grip of his fingers, and he almost threw her in the car, quickly locking her door and running around to the driver's side. As he jumped in opposite her Maureen flinched as another flash went off beside her.

Seeing her startled movement, Daniel quickly drew away from the curb, and Maureen shook with relief.

"I'm sorry you had to go through that, honey," he apologized quietly, glancing at her in concern.

"My God, does that happen often, Daniel?"

"Not if I can help it, Maurie."

Maureen felt aware of him beside her with every nerve in her body. "W—where are we going?" she questioned nervously, not daring to look at him, her finger feeling curiously weighted by the lovely ring, which symbolically tied her to this stranger beside her.

"A friend of mine has a place in Pescadero, right on the beach," he replied. "I think you'll like it . . . and we can relax."

"Pescadero . . . that's near Monterey, isn't it?" Maureen knew very well where it was, but something warned her that silence would be more nerve-racking than speech at this point.

If Daniel guessed why she chattered so much during the two-hour drive, he never let on, replying to her questions in a firm voice and pointing out different landmarks as they drove down the coast.

Grateful for his voice piercing the quiet of the car, Maureen allowed her thoughts to roam as she took in the splendid grandeur of rocky sand dunes, the misty sea air, which as they drew nearer to their destination became fog-laden, and the pounding gray-green surf.

They passed Pebble Beach, thus called, Daniel explained, because instead of sand small rocks, polished smooth by the friction of the seawater, covered its surface.

Soon Daniel turned down a private road, and after about five minutes a cabin came into view. She was surprised at its rough-hewn exterior, for she'd expected something grander.

"Like it?" Daniel's question drew her out of her reverie.

"Oh, yes!" Maureen spoke without thinking, her enthusiasm caught up by the scene in front of her. The cabin was nestled cozily between huge conifers, their green branches spreading over the cabin, shading it from the sun. To the left she could see a path through the trees, and as Daniel unloaded the trunk she wandered over curiously.

The path twisted down to the beach rather steeply, and she changed her mind about descending. She doubted her white heels were quite the thing for exploring.

Going back to the cabin, she entered gingerly, her nervousness returning. Daniel was crouched in front of a huge stone fireplace, and soon she smelled delicious pinewood as the flames caught and danced merrily against the dried wood.

"I put our bags in the bedroom, honey." He pointed behind him. "Through there."

"Thank you," she whispered, and slowly walked through to the one other room the cabin boasted—she had noticed a tiny kitchen as she passed. "One bedroom," she moaned aloud. Oh, why hadn't she questioned Daniel? She couldn't spend days alone with him here, she just couldn't. Her eyes encompassed the only furniture the room possessed, a large tallboy with old faded wood and too many drawers, and a double bed covered with a huge quilted coverlet.

Hopefully Maureen tried the door on her right, but it only opened up into a rather functional bathroom, with an old claw-footed bathtub. There was a mirror over a cracked basin, and though stark, she noticed absentmindedly, everything was scrupulously clean.

She turned into the bedroom once again, to stop short in dismay. Daniel stood there, leaning negligently with one hand grasping the carved bedpost, his suit jacket slung carelessly over his other arm. Their eyes locked, and Daniel's features hardened as he saw the panic she was trying so hard to conceal.

"Thinking of running away?" he drawled.

The words were so true, she flinched as if she'd been struck. With innate pride she at once straightened and lifted her head. "You needn't be afraid I'm going to run out on you, Daniel. A bargain is a bargain. Just don't think I'm going to agree to be anything but your hostess, that's all. All you've left me is my pride, you've taken my freedom and everything else, even Nonna and Katy," she told him in fierce tones, no less effective for being whispered. "I won't let you use me against my will, for if you force me I promise I'll hate you! You wanted a wife, but I never wanted a husband . . . remember that," she said, fear making her lash out.

Maureen felt trepidation over the way she had spoken to him, but she just couldn't stand another moment. She had to make it clear to him that she couldn't bear to have

130

him touch her! Obviously, he had never believed her protestations, not to the extent he obviously did now. She couldn't help the fear she felt as he stood there tight-lipped, a grayish pallor appearing around his mouth.

As Daniel looked at Maureen he was at first furious and then puzzled. Why was she so afraid of making love? What had happened to cause that look of a startled doe trapped and staring down the barrel of a hunter's rifle? He knew he'd given her reason to be afraid of him, and even more reason to hate him, but even so, her reactions were too intense, her fear too violent . . . almost abnormal. He cursed his past actions, but they couldn't be undone. If he took her now, as much as he longed to, it would be by force, and the thought of that was like bile in his throat. No, he decided, her first time should be something to remember with wonder, not revulsion. Daniel sighed for the nights here that now they would never share.

"Maurie, a bargain is a bargain, as you say . . . and I'll keep mine," he told her, all traces of anger wiped from his voice.

Startled but hopeful, Maureen stared at him, and the words she tried to speak wouldn't come.

"How about fixing some dinner, wife? I'm hungry."

"Yes, y—yes," she stammered. "As soon as I've changed."

"Good," he said, turning to leave the room. "I'll sleep in the other room, Maurie. You can relax, all right?"

"Thank you, Daniel. I—" Maureen was stunned by his sudden about-face, by this new understanding Daniel who was such a stranger to her, but she was sublimely grateful for the respite. She realized it was just a respite when he spoke from the doorway, a hint of the old familiar Daniel in his voice.

"I'll give you the time you need, Maurie . . . time for you to grow up and become a woman—my woman. But I haven't the greatest amount of patience when there's something I want, and I want you," he said, his words causing her eyes to widen in fear. "But I want a woman in my arms, Maurie, not the struggling child of the other night, so I'll give you time. I hope it'll be enough time for you, but if not I'll have to take what you won't give freely, and I can guarantee the next morning you'll be more woman than you ever dreamed it possible to be."

His promise was a threat, which left her unable to utter a sound as the door closed behind him.

CHAPTER EIGHT

With a worried frown, Maureen laid down the book she had been trying to read for the last half hour, and walked once again to the large picture window, which looked out over the long, curving drive. Pulling back a corner of the gold velvet draperies, she stared out into the emptiness of the night, tensing herself as she waited in vain for lights to pierce the darkness, or the sound of a car engine to break the uncanny stillness.

Biting her lip in despair, Maureen turned into the room once more, the curtain falling disconsolately from her trembling fingers. Her eyes gazed unseeingly at the now familiar room, while her mind subconsciously registered its beauty. Delicate filigree metal sculptures adorned the walls, lending a serene elegance to their richly paneled surfaces. Maureen's favorite was a three-dimensional ship on the farthest wall. The rich mahogany panelling caught the shadows of the piece when the light of the crystal chandelier bounced off the glowing metal.

If only she had Gaye to talk to, isolated as she was on this vast estate, nearly a prisoner of Daniel's affluence. Sitting upon the white brocade couch, she grabbed a gold throw pillow, then cradled it to her breast and was comforted by its warmth. As she stared into the flames of the large marble fireplace before her she wondered what Gaye and Harry were doing, and how they liked living in Nevada.

Her eyes tracing the gold veins running through the white marble, she became lost in thoughts of the past. How quickly the time has gone, she mused, running her finger over the indented leaf pattern of the brocade, calmed by its continuity. It seemed her marriage to Daniel had caused a chain reaction, and now nothing was the same. It was as if the old Maurie was no more, as if everything that had made up her old life was wiped clean.

Grady and his wife had almost immediately left for Arizona, and Gaye and Harry were married two weeks following her own wedding. They became man and wife in a quiet courthouse ceremony, with her and Daniel the only witnesses. Within two weeks they, too, were gone, and the last letter she had received was full of the success of their new restaurant-club, which not only catered to diners but also had a small floor show and a series of rooms for a little select gambling. Maureen smiled as she remembered that letter, with Gaye sounding every inch the grand lady, stating that "her Harry" wouldn't have any one-arm bandits, alias slot machines, because he felt it lowered the class of their establishment!

Harry always had planned on going to Nevada when he and Gaye were married. He felt they could stand a better chance of attaining their dreams. He was to manage a casino for a friend who was a partner in a large conglomerate. Maureen hadn't understood the long talks between Harry and Daniel until about a month after their marriage, when all the pieces of the jigsaw fell together. A very excited Gaye had telephoned and told how Daniel had made all the arrangements and had loaned Harry the money he needed to buy his own club. She had also said something that had frozen Maureen into immobility, if Gaye had but known it.

Angrily she rose again to pace the large room, her steps muffled in the sumptuous gold carpeting. Gaye had told her Harry had decided against going to Nevada, for he felt the promised job wasn't all that secure. They'd decided they'd better stay in San Francisco, for the present anyway, where Harry had his job, and where Gaye could keep on singing in the club. It had been Daniel who had flown, unknown to Maureen, to Nevada, where he bought the restaurant outright for Harry. Thus her only real friends had left in a state of delirious happiness, with the deed to the club in their names, and a tentative agreement to begin paying Daniel back when they were able.

Yes, she thought, a bitter curve to her mouth, Daniel had planned well. Before she knew what hit her, he had installed them here, in a beautiful home, with acres of grassland and every luxury. There were tennis courts and an all-weather enclosed swimming pool with a roof that slid back to show the stars on a fine night, or to allow the sun's rays to penetrate when the weather was benevolent. Nonna had a small annex off one wing of the house, with her own kitchen, sitting room, bedroom, and a balcony for flowers and shrubs, which was her delight.

Katy . . . well, she was in her element. Daniel was more than generous with his time and his money. Nonna was ostensibly Katy's nurse, though Maureen knew her old friend was kept with them because of Daniel's fondness for her. Little wonder, she thought cynically, for Nonna openly shows her adoration of him. Katy adored "her Daniel," and it was small wonder at that, too. Daniel arranged his days so he could spend every available moment with Katy, and took her with him on little jaunts planned especially to appeal to a child.

Maureen sighed, for she hadn't been included in their expeditions lately. For the first couple of months after their wedding she and Daniel had seemed almost like friends, but little by little the strain was beginning to make itself felt. Daniel was becoming cold and distant all over again. He did make an attempt to appear loving in front of Katy, but the coldness was there in his eyes. How she hated her isolation, and the renewed nervousness she felt in his presence, but she hated those outwardly loving shows of affection even more.

She was very careful to hide the fact that they didn't share the same bed. A cynical twist came to her lips at the thought. She refused to hire the cook Daniel sent for her inspection, preferring to do the cooking herself, and other than the daily woman who came to clean, there was only

135

Blake and Nonna to worry about. When Daniel spent the night at home, Maureen was always careful to make his bed quickly as soon as he left the following day, and as he was invariably up early, so far she'd been lucky.

That was the key, for Daniel very rarely slept at home anymore, preferring the apartment close to work. Their estate was really like a small farm, located in the hills between what was called the Tri-Valley, comprising Dublin, San Ramon, and Pleasanton, and the Castro Valley, Hayward, and San Leandro area. It was quite a pleasant spot, with shops conveniently close, and she knew she was lucky to have all the material advantages Daniel had given them, but the price was too high. Slowly but surely, without her being aware it was even happening, Daniel had broken all her links with the past, even to the point of making it possible for Gaye and Harry to realize their dream, placing her miles away from Gaye's comforting presence.

She didn't begrudge them their happiness, she really didn't, but she couldn't stand this state of affairs much longer. In the three months of their marriage she had very rarely seen anyone but Katy and Nonna, except for the times she had gone shopping in town. Daniel couldn't be counted, for he seemed as distant as a stranger. The time he spent in their home he devoted almost exclusively to Katy, and more and more her little one was turning to him. It was remarkable the affinity that had grown between the stern, quiet man and the little girl with a mind like quicksilver. When Daniel was around, Katy had eyes for no one else. Maureen was grateful for this, because for the first time since Katy had become her sole responsibility, she knew her darling was truly safe, with a security she alone could never have given her. It was more than a financial security. Daniel had given Katy the emotional security of having a father figure, and for that she had to feel gratitude.

In a way I deserve to live in this lonely vacuum, she told herself with a degree of honesty she hadn't known she possessed. She had gotten exactly what she had asked for, after all. Hadn't she? With feet that felt weighted, she disconsolately walked down the long darkened hall and

136

entered the large family room. Automatically her eyes took in the decor that had so pleased her just a few weeks ago, for she had planned it herself.

It was difficult to capture that intensely satisfied pleasure she had when the decorators were finally finished. She sighed. She'd never before been in the position of not having to count the cost and for a while had been delighted at the novelty of being able to order whatever took her fancy. She tried consulting Daniel, but he curtly told her to use her own judgment; household matters were entirely her own province, he stated before leaving abruptly to close himself in his study. She had been surprised when his secretary, whom she'd detested even in the old days, called the next day to tell her she'd gotten a list of decorating firms and would set up appointments whenever it was convenient. Though hating the woman's patronizing attitude, she had capitulated. There hadn't been much else she could do, after all, and she had been itching to get started!

Turning to walk through the arched entry into the kitchen, Maureen, with a little surge of pleasure, let her eyes slowly roam the enormous room. She loved to cook, and this kitchen—truly a country kitchen—with its hardwood floors polished to glistening perfection, the oval Mexican throw rug in mellow earth tones, and its copper fitments glinting in the subdued lighting, was her favorite room in the whole house, which at times seemed to overshadow her with its immense austerity.

But her kitchen—her kitchen she had loved on sight, especially in the early morning when the sunlight danced through the large picture window taking up nearly the whole of the far wall, its sparkling glass expanse broken only by the cavernous rock fireplace at its center. At the other end of the long room was a sunken conversation nook, all warm amber carpeting and huge throw pillows, with a large glasshouse window beginning at floor level which overlooked a lush garden. The trees, shrubs, and graveled walkways were possessed of a wild beauty when all the lush flowers and beautiful rose borders were in bloom.

With a sigh Maureen poured herself a cup of coffee, and thoughtfully carried it back into the family room. Placing it on the pecan coffee table, she muttered under her breath when her trembling hands caused some of the hot beverage to slop over into the saucer. Groaning in exasperation, she switched on the television. The screen was set into the wall, giving the effect of a movie theater, though mercifully a small one. Panels slid, at the flick of a hidden switch, smoothly in front of the screen when the set wasn't in use. When the panels were in place, no one would guess it was there, they blended so perfectly with the rest of the pecan paneling. The paneling itself was a perfect contrast to the brown and gold foil wallpaper on the opposite wall, and the beamed cathedral ceilings inset with a skylight.

Her teeth biting the fullness of her lower lip, a nervous habit she'd acquired recently, Maureen switched off the television, unable to bear the thought of another lonely evening spent with its artificial stimulation. She sat down angrily, a frustrated tenseness invading her body, and slowly sipped her coffee, hoping the hot liquid would soothe her restlessness.

Suddenly she heard Katy's muffled crying coming through the intercom system. Relieved at the interruption, she climbed the curving staircase, her fingers automatically caressing the carved banister. Walking down the hall—her tread made soundless by the thick carpeting—she reached the end of the long expanse and pushed open the large double doors.

"What's the matter, darling, can't you sleep?" Maureen questioned the little figure sitting bolt upright in the small canopy bed topped by ruffled pink dimity curtains. The room was lit by a small night-light, the delicate figure of a little goose girl set atop a white and gold dresser next to the bed, and from its light she could see the tears glistening in Katy's eyes. The moonlight cas' soft shadows in the room, giving the walls a sinister quality. Maureen pulled the shade, thus blocking out the moonlight, and then walked back to the bed.

"Poor baby, did the light frighten you?" Maureen

crooned softly, lifting the bewildered little girl into her arms and carrying her small sleep-warmed body across the room. Sitting with Katy cuddled against her, she smoothed the damp baby curls from her forehead with her mouth. Sighing, Katy nestled deeper into her arms and the security they represented.

"Sing a Katy song, Maurie," she mumbled, already half asleep. With a smile Maureen complied, her voice husky and warm. Making up little "Katy songs" had delighted both of them, and she treasured these moments with Katy. Her voice fell sweetly on the ears of the now contented child. With a little sigh Katy once again fell asleep, this time soundly, unaware that her beloved Maurie held her long after.

As she gazed down into the little face she loved so much, the cheeks rosy from sleep, a little sob escaped her, and tears fell slowly from her eyes. Her little one was normally so independent and disdainful of being treated like a baby, and in such a hurry to grow up. "Slow down little one," she whispered, a wealth of sad entreaty in her voice. "Please don't be in such a rush to grow up . . . it hurts to be grown up." With sadness blocking her throat, Maureen rose and tucked Katy up in her bed with a last lingering kiss on her cheek.

Maureen decided to repair the ravages her tears had caused, and entered the bathroom leading off Katy's bedroom. Washing her face briskly, she felt ashamed of her sentimental weakening when she caught a glimpse of her woebegone face in the mirror. Shrugging her shoulders, she gave a last grimace at her reflection and left through the door leading into the playroom so as not to disturb the sleeping child. Pushing the red nose of the smiling clown on the wall to turn off the light, she walked quickly through the playroom, again marveling at its perfection.

A gaily painted Sleeping Beauty castle, perfect in every detail, sat in the center of the large room—ideal for a little girl to walk on, crawl through, slide down, and hide under. At intervals throughout the room were colorful shelves for toys and books, which nestled against walls painted in swirls of pastel colors. She remembered her surprise when the decorator had said, when complimented, that he was only carrying out the designs set out by Mr. Lord.

Thoughtful, Maureen closed the door on the bright room, and standing in the hall for a moment, she thought of the time and effort Daniel had spent, and sighed. She went down the hall to her own room, only hesitating a bit when she passed Daniel's bedroom door, then walking on and entering her own.

Taking little note of the sumptuous splendor of her own suite, she walked through her rose and cream sitting room and entered the bathroom. Maybe a warm shower would dispel her mood, and on impulse she quickly shed her beige silk lounging suit and stepped under the hot spray, which struck her body with stinging little blows.

Downstairs again, she curled up like a contented kitten on the soft velvet sofa. Her slightly damp hair spread around her like a cloud, she lay with eyes closed, pensively listening to the soft music coming from the stereo. Her body relaxed, and she was glad she'd showered away the tenseness. Mind floating pleasantly between sleep and wakefulness, she turned her thoughts briefly to Daniel. Confident that tonight too would find him away from home, she yawned and sleep overcame her. It was thus Daniel saw her as he entered the room.

Maureen's apricot silk dressing gown covered her body, her feet curled under the soft clinging folds. She reminded the grim-faced man of a child, curled on her side with one hand nestled trustingly under her cheek; but she was no child, and his cynical eyes roved the perfect curves of her body.

He strode to the bar in the corner and made himself a drink, tossing the whiskey down his throat and then fixing himself another, this time adding water. Turning, he seated himself in the large chair opposite the matching sofa.

He removed the coat to his cinnamon lounging suit and threw it carelessly over the arm of the chair. His tie, angrily ripped off, landed on an end table, its amber lamp casting a mellow pool of shadows over the dark brown material heaped beside it. Taking another long drink, the smooth tanned column of his throat rippling, Daniel slowly unbuttoned his shirt nearly to his waist and ran his hand over the fine hairs of his chest, his eyes never leaving the reclining body of his wife.

My wife, he thought cynically, molding his chiseled lips into a sneer. He'd seen less of Maurie since their marriage than before. He spent most of his evenings at his apartment, after working late into the night, tired enough physically then to sleep. Even then—the mocking thought crossed his mind—he had been unable to entirely block out thoughts of this black-haired little witch. God, he thought agonizingly, how many times have I imagined her just like this, like a sexy little cat curled up complacently, waiting for me?

The strain of their relationship was telling on him, for he slept badly, unable to keep her out of his dreams, and there were tiny lines around his eyes that hadn't been there before. His face, never fleshy, was now lean, the prominence of his high cheekbones more apparent. The forbidding harshness of his mouth—softened only by the full, sensual lower lip—and the bleak hardness of his piercing gray eyes made that face a mask hiding his thoughts. Blake was disturbed by the situation, as was Nonna, but both kept their own counsel, their attitude only apparent in the reproachful looks they often sent his way. It seemed that, no matter what their thoughts on the subject, they preferred to let the "lovers" work out their own salvation. Well, he'd do something about that tonight. He laughed harshly.

The sound penetrating her consciousness, Maureen, bewildered, opened her eyes. Seeing Daniel seated there in the shadows, long legs spread indolently in front of him and his strangely glittering eyes piercing her, Maureen sat upright with a jerk, her hand going convulsively to cover the little pulse jerking in her throat.

"Daniel, you frightened me," she gasped, her mind in a whirl. She had been sure Daniel wasn't intending to come home tonight, and had felt safe in the knowledge. Normally she would have had enough warning of his approaching car to slip upstairs, but the lateness of the hour had lulled her into a false sense of security.

"Who did you think it was . . . Jack?"

Ignoring the ominous quietness of his voice, Maureen lashed out indignantly, uncaring of the consequences: "What are you implying?"

"Implying, Maurie?" Daniel's voice mocked her.

"Yes, damn you. What did you mean by that remark, Daniel?"

"Did I mean anything?"

"Don't play games with me, Daniel," she replied, running a hand over her hair.

Seeing her shaking fingers, Daniel abandoned his indolent pose. His control, weakened by his earlier thoughts, snapped. The muscles of his body tightening, he too lashed out, "What were you doing lunching with him?"

"Just that, having lunch."

"How often are you seeing him?" Daniel questioned, the muscle pulsing in his cheek indicating fury barely held in check.

"What do you care? You're busy every night with your so efficient secretary, aren't you?" Maureen ignored the warning signs in his face.

She'd been shopping in San Francisco the day before and had met Jack in Maiden Lane quite by chance. Over lunch he told her about his new girl friend, and she had wished him well. She had been fully aware of his growing interest in her before her marriage, and the disillusionment he suffered over her relationship with Daniel, and she was glad he'd found someone who was free to return his affection, as she'd been sure he would.

After lunch they strolled down Maiden Lane, entering the tasteful shops to look for a gift for his friend, Christy. After finding the perfect gift, a beautiful filigree music box, Jack had talked her into spending the rest of the afternoon sight-seeing. Hungry for a friend, she had agreed and been absolutely amazed at Jack's knowledge about his beloved city.

Walking down Maiden Lane, with its terraced walk-ways, he told her about the annual Daffodil Festival held there in the spring.

"It's two blocks long, Maurie, with the merchants blocking off traffic, and the street filled with flowers."

"It sounds beautiful, Jack," she said, smiling at his boyish enthusiasm. She could picture the beauty and excitement of the scene Jack described, with lovely flowers everywhere and crowds of people with cameras at the ready.

Jack's voice had interrupted her thoughts.

"In the old days of the Barbary Coast," he said, "this was known as Morton Street. It was supposedly the worst part of San Francisco's 'red-light district,' and contained the worst cribs in the city."

"Cribs?" Maureen questioned, puzzled at the unfamiliar word.

"You know, Maurie. Houses of ill repute," he smiled.

"Oh!" Maureen had laughed, flushing foolishly.

As Jack talked, the past came alive for her. Strange, she mused, how a city changes. After the 1906 earthquake and fire Maiden Lane arose from the ashes, a street of flowers instead of whores.

She had made sure they avoided Montgomery Street, where Daniel occupied offices. Called the Wall Street of the West, it served as the nervous system of most of Western America and a good portion of the Pacific Far East and was the center of power in the city. She'd been there many times before and always felt that sense of intense vitality that radiated from the surging populace and the imposing buildings.

Instead, Jack had taken her to the St. Francis, still one of the city's most fashionable hostelries. They'd rested their aching feet in the bar, and Jack had made her laugh by telling her that in the old days the St. Francis's reputation came from its being the first one in the city to put sheets on its beds.

They had ended up in Union Square, a moderately quiet oasis in the downtown shopping area, where they sat on a bench and watched the children playing on the lawns. There were flower festivals held here the year round, and she remembered seeing one with her parents. They'd brought her there when she was little older than Katy. It had been Christmastime, she told Jack, and there was a huge tree and elaborate decorations, which made the little girl she was then breathless with their beauty. Their talk had then automatically turned to Christmas, which was little more than a month away, and Jack blushingly told her of his plans to give Christy an engagement ring on Christmas Eve, turning even redder when she teased him about his sentimental streak.

All in all her afternoon with Jack had been an innocent day of sunshine and laughter, and it sickened her that Daniel should make something cheap and tawdry out of it. She could just bet who his informant was. Earlier, she thought she'd caught a glimpse of Daniel's elegant secretary, and now she was sure of it. The woman had obviously been in love with Daniel, or his money, for years. During their wedding reception she had disgusted Maureen with her cloying sweetness, all the while making innuendoes about Daniel and their long-standing relationship, and sending him private messages with her eyes. Her greedy hands with their bronze-tipped nails had used any excuse to touch him, and whenever he looked away, her eyes glinted at Maureen as if telling her their marriage would make no difference to the relationship she had with Daniel . . . her glances implying it was a very, very intimate one!

Now Daniel watched the play of emotions crossing Maureen's face during her reveries, and with a savage oath he jerked out of the chair. Before she had a chance to move he was beside her, and her startled glance locked with his. She felt a small whimper escape her. Dear God, he looks as if he wants to kill me, she thought, her eyes dilating in fear, and with a strangled cry she tried to push herself away from him.

"Daniel, let me explain," she gasped, her whole body shaking. Quickly she poured out the story of the accidental meeting with Jack, eager to get out of the situation she found herself in. God, why was I so sarcastic, why

144

didn't I tell Daniel the truth in the first place? I should have known better! As her explanation came to a stammering close she used the excuse of loneliness for her afternoon with Jack, hoping Daniel would calm down if he felt guilt at his neglect of her.

She realized her mistake almost at once. The anger in his eyes was slowly replaced by another look, one that burned into her with the searing force of a branding iron.

"So my little bride doesn't like the bargain she made," he whispered suggestively, his eyes caressing her cringing figure.

Words of denial froze unuttered on her lips as she gazed into his glittering eyes mesmerized, knowing those words would be lies.

Sitting beside her, his arms on either side of her effectively preventing escape, Daniel leaned closer, his breath warm on her averted cheek.

"You don't have to be lonely, Maurie," his voice seduced. "You obviously need a man's company, so why not your husband's?"

While he spoke his lips found the lobe of her ear, his circling tongue causing tremors to shoot through her body. Why am I such a weakling as soon as he touches me? She shivered at the sparks his caressing mouth was sending through her. He knows what it does to me . . . why can't he play fair? Tears glistened in her eyes, tears of defeat. She felt the weakening inside her, brought on by the terrible barrenness of their marriage to date. Their marriage was everything she had demanded it should be, and she hated it! There was no future and no past, just the reality of Daniel's hard body pressing her down into the softness of the sofa, the clean male scent of his moist skin in her nostrils.

"Daniel," she whispered. She turned her head, her eyes melting in his gaze. He could read the yearning message deep inside her, the message that she wanted him as much as he wanted her.

Daniel looked down at the girl in his arms and felt remorse for his accusations. God, he'd had proof enough of her innocence. If he was truthful with himself, he would admit his anger with her tonight had been prompted by one thing and one thing only—raging jealousy. To lose himself forever in those eyes, to possess this slim golden body—these thoughts obsessed him to the point of madness!

"God! Maurie . . . please," he groaned, forgetting his pride, and this firmed her capitulation as nothing else could have. She knew her eyes were reflecting the hunger she could see in his, but she was beyond caring. Trembling, she raised her face to his. She could feel the warmth of his mouth on hers, could feel his swift intake of breath as her lips parted in response, willingly, eagerly, giving as well as taking.

When his mouth lifted abruptly from hers, she almost cried aloud, muffling the protest in the tautened cords of his neck. She barely felt him lifting her in his arms, unaware of being carried until he laid her gently down on the soft carpet in the darkened living room.

She felt the warmth from the fireplace. The soft flicker of the flames provided the only illumination. She wantonly caressed the hair at the back of his head as his mouth on her face and neck sent tremors of desire through her body.

His hands drew apart the silken folds of her robe, and she could make no move to stop him, her shyness forgotten in her eagerness to get closer to him, past the barriers dulling the contact of flesh upon flesh. She shivered as the air touched her heated skin. With a surge of pleasure she felt him stiffen as his eyes roamed her body, for she was suddenly conscious of being glad he found her beautiful. She had never imagined she could feel so unselfconscious, and was amazed at how right it felt to have Daniel's eyes on her nakedness. She drew him down to her gently, and felt her pleasure intensify as he began to tremble in her arms.

Groaning deep in his throat, he sought out the softness of her neck with his mouth, forcing her head back over his arm, but she needed no urging to arch her body against the responsive hardness of his. She could feel the muscles of his thighs flexing against her own, the rhythmic

146

movements sending through her awakened body a message as old as time.

He cupped her breast in his hand, and she gasped as she felt the flesh swell and firm, the nipple hardening at his touch. Closing her eyes, she grasped the back of his head, delighting in the feel of the thick, rich-textured hair between her fingers, wanting the sensations his hand was causing to go on forever. Suddenly she could bear it no longer, and with a gasp she pulled his head toward hers and nearly moaned aloud at the added sensation as his mouth parted hers. Breath mingling, he ran his hand from her breast to her waist, and downward, and she felt the flesh of her stomach knotting beneath his probing fingers.

Quickly shedding the restricting confines of his clothes, his impatience was apparent in the shaking of his hands. Bending over her once again, his mouth sending trails of fire down her body, he heard the sound that told him her passion equaled his own—and the moaning chant she was unaware of making.

"Daniel, please. Oh, God, please, please!" He heard her soft pleadings, but for him they weren't enough. Lifting his mouth from the scented valley between her breasts, he captured her chin in his hand, forcing her thrashing head into stillness.

"Do you want me?" he whispered.

"Yes, oh, please," she gasped, feeling as if her body was burning from the inside outward.

"Say you love me, Maurie. Say it!" Daniel demanded, running his tongue lightly over her lips swollen from his kisses.

"Oh, God. I love you, I've always loved you," she cried, and her words let loose a torrent of passion in them both, at the same time making him more tender as if to reward her for saying at last what she had so vehemently denied.

As her passion rose she felt as if there were only these moments, only Daniel's body, with his maleness apparent, pressing hers down so pleasurably. Her mind whirling, her gasping breath mingling with the harsh grating of his, she forgot everything except the thought that now was all that really mattered. The past was done and couldn't be undone, but now they could make a new beginning, and maybe someday he would love her. For now only the present mattered, the sweetness of Daniel's body warming hers, the sound of his whispered words urging her on to undreamed-of heights. Soon even those thoughts were lost as she gave herself over completely to Daniel, her own body lost in a vortex of sensation.

CHAPTER NINE

Maureen listlessly strummed her guitar, sitting cross-legged while she looked out the greenhouse window at Katy playing in the garden. Her playmate was a new acquisition, a Labrador puppy Daniel had presented her for her third birthday. She'd named him Snuffles, a rather unlikely name for a pedigreed Lab, but Snuffles didn't seem to object. Katy adored her new pet, and Snuffles followed her around devotedly. There he is with his nose to the ground again, she thought with a smile. Snuffles was a good name for him after all! She should have known they could trust Katy's judgment.

"Oh, Nonna, come quick!" Maureen exclaimed, laughter choking her voice.

The old woman laid down the silver she was polishing, and, dusting off her hands, hurried over to join Maureen. Nonna's body shook with laughter when her eyes followed Maureen's pointing finger.

"Ah . . . that little one. She is *loco*, no?" Nonna choked, laughter still quivering in her voice as she wiped her eyes with her apron.

"She's *loco*, yes!" Maureen exclaimed, and indeed so Katy truly appeared to be, for there she was on hands and knees, trailing around after Snuffles with her nose to the ground.

As the two women watched the antics of the child and

pup their faces were wreathed in smiles, love and pride in the adorable little girl written clearly on them. Suddenly their expressions turned to incredulous dismay as Snuffles lifted his leg and proceeded to answer nature's call. With a muffled gasp Maureen jumped up and ran through the kitchen and into the family room, to throw open the sliding glass doors leading to the garden.

"Kathryn, don't you dare!" she shrieked, but as she approached Katy, her experienced eyes could see she was much, much too late as they traveled over the betraying moisture staining the child's overalls.

"But, Maurie, Snuffles does it." Katy's bewildered eyes traveled to her pet, and a mutinous pout formed on her mouth as she looked from the dry dog down at her uncomfortably wet pants. Before Maureen could remonstrate with her about dogs and people, Katy solved the problem herself.

"Snuffy, you cheated," she exclaimed, her hands clenched into fists, anger in every line of her small body. "You don't gots your pants on!" Glaring up at Maureen, Katy stalked indignantly toward the house, a very abject Snuffles following behind. Maureen had just barely managed to control the laughter bubbling inside her, but she lost the fight completely when she heard Katy tell the mournful little dog, "You just wait till Nonna sees the mess you made, are you gonna get it!"

Still chuckling, she heard Nonna's voice muttering imprecations in a mixture of Spanish and English, her voice fading as she marched the protesting child up the stairs. With a smile still dimpling her cheeks, Maureen closed the door left open by the furious little tornado and, turning, decided to walk in the garden. Thoughts of Katy still foremost in her mind, she was sorry Daniel hadn't been here to see the little drama just enacted.

Inevitably the thought of Daniel sobered her. She missed him more than she thought possible, and even though he called regularly, he always sounded so abrupt and stilted on the phone. She wished he hadn't had to leave for Europe so unexpectedly. She remembered the dismay she had felt when he'd called from the office, explaining he

150

had no alternative. Maureen hadn't seen him again, for he had to catch a plane almost immediately, but she had felt slightly happier when flowers arrived for her. There was no note, but a beautiful bouquet of daffodils told their own story. She had been delighted at the secret message she alone would understand.

She walked steadily away from the formal paths of the garden. Her mood was too chaotic to appreciate the orderly rows of shrubs and late-blooming flowers. Walking briskly to ward off the early December breeze, she crossed her arms one over the other, trying unsuccessfully to keep the cold from biting through her gray wool pantsuit. The sound of the wind blowing through the trees overhead had a mournful sound that especially fitted her present mood, and the smell of the ground cover, still wet from recent rains, drifted upward. A sudden gust of wind, stronger than the others, whipped her hair into wild disorder, and she brushed it from her face impatiently.

This little copse was one of her favorite walks, for she appreciated the untamed naturalness of the trees far more than the esthetically pleasing but almost too formal garden. They were, in her opinion, far more beautiful, and also served the useful purpose of being an effective windbreak for the house and grounds.

She turned abruptly, suddenly disgusted at her own moodiness. Mooning around feeling sorry for herself wasn't going to help the situation any, and she had been doing just that for much too long. Physical activity was the answer, and with a more characteristic determination she walked quickly back to the house.

Feeling an almost desperate need for company, she ran up the stairs calling for Nonna. Her breath rasping, she deliberately slowed her steps in an attempt to still her ragged breathing.

"Here, Niña." Nonna's voice called her from Katy's room. Entering the bedroom, Maureen smiled at the cosy scene. There was Katy, sitting bolt upright in the middle of her bed, black curls tousled from her recent bath and shining face cherubic. Nonna briskly gathered the child's

151

soiled clothes and, with a conspiratorial smile for Maureen, left the room.

"Maurie, I don't wants to take a nap." Katy pouted.

"I don't *want* to take a nap," Maureen automatically corrected, lifting Katy to her feet and turning back the covers of the bed.

"You don't wants to either?" Katy questioned, eyes opening wide.

"No—I mean yes—I. Oh, never mind!" Maureen stuttered, mouth quirked in exasperation as she turned to give Katy a swift hug.

"I don't wants Snuffy to sleep with me anymore," Katy told Maureen, turning to glare at the little dog curled in a wicker basket by her bed.

"But, darling, you begged to have Snuffles with you. I thought you and Snuffy were best friends?"

"Snuffy made me gots a spanking, so now I don't like him anymore," she said, glaring down at her dog once again.

"Katy, Snuffles was behaving like a good little dog. He didn't do anything wrong, sweetheart," Maureen coaxed. "Why don't you kiss and make up, hmm?"

"No!"

"Sweetheart, when you've been naughty we don't stop loving you, so do you think you're being fair to poor old Snuff?" Maureen questioned softly.

Head tilted to one side, Katy considered Maureen's words, her expressive face mirroring her thoughts. As she looked down at her abject dog who lay mournfully looking up at her, head on his paws, she suddenly relented. Face wreathed in smiles, she wholeheartedly threw her chubby arms around the puppy's neck. Katy's friend immediately responded, tail wagging furiously as he adoringly licked the now giggling little girl.

Finally settling the happy duo down, Maureen lifted the yawning child into her bed. Tucking the covers around the nestling body, she bent and placed a kiss on her pert nose. She gently pulled the window shade, blocking out as much as she could of the sunlight. Tiptoeing to the door, she whispered, "God bless, baby."

"Say 'God bless' to Snuffy, too!" Katy demanded drowsily.

"God bless, Snuffy." She complied with a smile, giving a small chuckle as she glimpsed the slowly wagging tail before closing the door softly.

Strange how a child can lighten your mood, she thought. Here she had been depressed just a short while ago, and now she felt almost happy again. She would take a bath, she decided on impulse, and soak away any remaining tenseness. Her quick steps took her through her sitting room and into the bedroom. Quickly shedding her clothes and sending them sailing down the laundry chute, she didn't bother with her robe but walked directly into the bathroom.

Humming softly under her breath, she adjusted the flow of the water, and soon steam drifted softly upward. Lavishly adding bath crystals, she moved over to the dressing room alcove, her body reflected and re-reflected in the mirrored walls. This room used to embarrass her, she remembered with a smile. For a long time she hadn't been able to bring herself to relax, because everywhere she had turned there seemed to be another person in here with her. Chuckling at the memory, she could understand her feelings somewhat, for she had never been used to seeing her naked body full view, and one could hardly avoid it in here.

Sitting down at the dressing table, Maureen quickly piled her hair on top of her head and secured it with pins. Rising, she walked back to the bath and turned off the silver taps. As she stepped down into the water she gave a muffled gasp, for the fragrantly perfumed liquid, with its abundance of bubbles, was extremely hot. She slowly eased herself downward until she was completely submerged in the depths of the sunken tub, a sigh of contentment escaping her as she laid her head back against the black shiny porcelain and stretched her legs sensuously.

Talking of sensuous, she thought, her eyes raking the splendor around her. She had always loved to bathe as a child, playing with her toys or pretending she was swimming, so to her a bathroom should be more than just functional. This one certainly was that, for it was a miracle in black and silver. As her mind drifted pleasurably all the tenseness seemed to flow out of her body.

"Well, what have we here?" a deep voice drawled.

Gasping, Maureen whirled around, her arms crossing instinctively over her breasts. "Daniel." A sudden light glowed in the beautiful darkness of her eyes, eagerness tensing every line of her glistening body. Gazing at the lean masculine form leaning against the door frame, Maureen felt her breath begin to quicken and a weakness invade her limbs. She stared at him as if mesmerized. His lids lowered to hide the sudden gleam in his eyes, which were no longer content to stare into her face, but roamed over her exposed skin, their darkening gray depths trying in vain to pierce the water. In response her breath caught in a small gasp, and a fiery blush tinged her skin.

Returning to her face, Daniel's eyes once more locked with hers. Straightening his body, he slowly entered the room, closing and locking the door behind him.

"I was going to take a shower, but this is a better idea," he whispered mockingly as he began slowly unbuttoning his shirt, his eyes never leaving hers. Moistening lips suddenly dry, Maureen tried to speak, but no words could get past her tense throat.

Daniel walked across the room toward her, muscles rippling under bronzed skin, his stirring masculinity leaving her in no doubt as to his thoughts. Stopping abruptly beside her, he rasped over her taut nerves, the words cutting through her, "For God's sake, don't sit there as if expecting rape! I've been traveling for a damn sight too many hours to be interested." His mouth thinning in disgust, he grabbed a towel off the silver rack opposite and, turning, walked quickly through to the dressing room.

The noise of the shower penetrated her consciousness, the ordinary sound waking her out of incredulity. What had happened to Daniel? He had looked as if he hated her! Shivering from more than the rapidly cooling water, she quickly stepped out of the tub. Drying herself automatically, she tried to make some sense of her jumbled thoughts, fighting the urge to cry. Of course he's tired—her thoughts rambled, considering any excuse possible. Traveling for hours, probably overworking himself in the last few weeks so he could hurry home. With no one to greet him when he finally arrives, of course, he's bound to be annoyed! She knew she was grasping at straws, but there had to be an explanation, there just had to be! He'd been like the old Daniel, stepping on her feelings, uncaring of her emotions, as if what they had shared had meant less than nothing to him. No, she thought determinedly. There was an explanation and she must find it, for remembering that night she refused to believe he had felt less than she. He had trembled in her arms, calling her name, and at the peak of their pleasure he had kissed her and she had tasted tears, and she was sure they hadn't just been her own.

Of course, he hadn't stayed with her. The insidiously disturbing thought came unbidden. Looking back now, she realized that should have been significant, but in the drowsy aftermath of their lovemaking she had felt he was being considerate of her extreme tiredness, and possibly overprotective. His arms had been so warm and gentle as he had carried her upstairs and laid her on her bed. When he had risen to leave her, she had protested sleepily, she remembered now with a blush. As he tucked the blanket around her he had been preoccupied, but his husky good-night had been reassuring.

The cessation of running water sent her hurrying into the bedroom. Scrambling through her clothes, she automatically grabbed a sweater and slacks combination but, with a look of distaste, placed them back on their hangers. Hands shaking, she caressed a fold of material hidden deep in the corner of the cavernous wardrobe. She pulled the lovely fabric off the hanger, stepping into it before she could change her mind. How mutinous she had been that day in the small but exclusive dress salon. Smiling at the memory, she stroked the cool silk down over her hips. She had resented Daniel's presence, and was she

155

ever furious at his insistence that they buy the glowing red lounging pajamas. Privately she had made up her mind never to wear them!

How stupid her attitude had been, she realized that now. She had acted like a child instead of the woman she was supposed to be. It had been safer to nurture her hatred and resentment, safer than letting herself care again! Maybe if she had behaved more like a woman all those years ago, and less like a confused child, just maybe Daniel wouldn't have turned from her. She was horrified as the thought struck her . . . she had nearly made the same mistake again tonight. Her shyness had again been misinterpreted. To him it must have appeared to be revulsion!

Turning to sit at the mirrored dresser, Maureen unpinned her hair, darkly shimmering folds cascading down her back. Her eyes gazed at her image, which was strange even to herself. The lounging outfit was deceptively simple while at the same time managing to be decidedly sexy. Back was covered; arms were covered; legs in the wide folds of the harem pants were more than covered—they were totally disguised! There was only one little detail that had been unacceptable to her, making her horribly embarrassed when she had been led by an exuberant saleswoman to stand in front of a smirking Daniel. The deep vee neckline plunged nearly to her waist!

Daniel had looked her over very thoroughly, and seeing the rebellion in her eyes, he mockingly overrode her protests. When the clothes ordered that day were delivered, she had been tempted to destroy the sensuous red silk. She had wanted nothing more than to rip the lovely folds end to end, but something stayed her hand, she remembered. At the time, all the clothes seemed to represent her relationship with Daniel, for wasn't she his thing, his possession to dress as he saw fit? How inane that all seemed now, when all she could remember was the look in Daniel's eyes when she first appeared before him dressed as she was now. He wanted her, it had been written there in his eyes, which had scorched her with their look before his lashes had blocked out the fire of his gaze.

Stroking the brush over her hair until it crackled and shone with blue-black fire, she could finally admit to herself why she hadn't destroyed these clothes. While she tried to subdue her sexuality, deep inside her she had really wanted to revel in it. Wasn't that the truth? Yes, there was no point lying to herself anymore, and with bravado she reached for the perfume Daniel had bought her in Paris, and sprayed it on lavishly. He had brought her sensual nature to the surface, and like the scared young fool she had been, she had blamed him solely for the results. His own masculinity had acted like flame to dry tinder, but how had she been blind enough to blame him entirely? She was as much to blame as he, and now was the time to be woman enough to admit it!

A tiny smile dimpled her mouth, needing no lipstick to enhance their natural rose color. Her eyes looked back at her with new knowledge before her thick dark lashes obscured their gleam. She gave a sigh and realized it was a sigh of freedom, freedom from fear, from the Maureen who haunted her past, and, more important . . . freedom from shame. No longer would she fear Daniel's lack of love, for he wanted her and that would have to be enough for now. Let the future take care of itself. Let there be no more fear of her own powers as a woman. Daniel thought her beautiful. He had proved his desire for her transcended even what he was willing to allow. Hadn't he married her despite all the other women in his past? She would fight fire with fire, for she was woman enough now to match his desire, and maybe if she finally fought with a woman's weapons, just maybe she would emerge victorious. What did she have to lose, after all? Self-respect didn't keep you warm at night. The words of the marriage service came back to her, words she hadn't been aware of until this moment. To love, honor, and obey . . . where was the self in that? The love she had, but honor and obey? There can be very little self in a true marriage, she saw that now. What was love but a mutual

157

giving of oneself, in every respect, when all is said and done?

The sound of the bathroom door opening roused Maureen from her reveries, and with a proud tilt to her head, revealing the lovely lines of her neck to the startled gaze of the man standing behind her, she rose and slowly turned. Shoulders held back, breath erratic, she stared silently at Daniel, who appeared to be rooted to the spot, towel draped around slim hips.

Ignoring the mocking smile curving his mouth, Maureen walked slowly toward him. The tanned and rugged planes of his face began to harden—the mockery wiped off as if it had never been there—as his body tautened. Ah . . . Her eyes raking his body obviously did the same thing to his metabolism as it did to hers when the situations were reversed. She smiled at the thought. That's one up for me! Raising her face to meet his gaze and smiling softly once again, she was encouraged by the sudden pulsing in his cheek. She knew him well enough to understand she was getting under his skin, but was she being too confident of her attraction for him? Oh, Lord . . . this is no time to be having second thoughts! Taking a shaking breath, she slowly reached out to timidly caress the dark curling hair of his chest. When he didn't move either to encourage or to repress her touch, her small hand boldly traced the line of hair from his chest to his navel, fingers curling sensually in the curly matted surface.

"I missed you, Daniel," she told him softly.

"Did you, baby?" Daniel's voice was harsh, his breathing deepening as he looked down at her hand against his skin.

"What's wrong, Daniel?"

His eyes closed convulsively, and she could feel the deeply ragged breath he drew beneath her caressing hand. As she gazed with a troubled frown at the chiseled lines of his face, a sigh escaped her.

"Daniel, can't you tell me what's wrong?" Maureen knew she was begging, but she felt desperate. There were elements here she didn't understand, and she was suddenly frightened. Why didn't Daniel speak? Couldn't he tell his silence was unnerving?

"What could be wrong, Maurie? Haven't I everything a man could want?"

Maureen didn't like the mocking quality in his voice, nor the almost sneering tones.

"Yes," he continued. "I have money, a beautiful home, and last but not least . . . a loving, virtuous, honest little wife. What the hell more could I expect?" This last was said under his breath, in tones of self-reproach—almost as if he were regretting something deeply, but for the life of her she couldn't think what he had to reproach himself for.

Maureen was conscious of his hands caressing her arms, almost without his volition—as if he were holding himself under intense restraint. The movements of his hands gliding over the smooth silk of her sleeves sent shivers of awareness through her, and as his hands moved upwards to probe the sensitive skin beneath her ears, she shivered. Still, she was unable to give herself over entirely to her emotions as he molded her body to his, his mouth following the trail blazed by his hands. This wasn't like before. There was no joy, no spontaneous emotion.

She was suddenly horrified as it occurred to her that Daniel had surely been convinced if not of her hatred, at least of her contempt of him. Hadn't she spent the whole of their marriage—yes . . . and before—convincing him of that? In self-reproach she thought how he must have construed that night two weeks ago, and the idea appalled her. It was true their lovemaking had begun with anger and bitter accusations, but their consummation had ended in intense joy as far as she was concerned. But had Daniel felt the same? The thought tortured her with its implications. Could his reproach be for her, and not himself? Dear God, is Daniel seeing my surrender as cheap, my words of love as a lie? Just like four years ago, her inner self whispered. Just like the night he had hurled those degrading, hateful, shaming words at her.

God in Heaven, how could I forget? Her head was tossing from side to side in a silent scream of protest.

159

She wasn't aware of being laid upon the bed, her thoughts had made her oblivious to everything else, even the weight of his body on hers. She had truly forgotten the past in a healing surge of love, but Daniel had no way of knowing that. She thought her actions that night were telling him she loved him, as well as her words, but obviously both had been misconstrued. Of course he would think me a cheap little tramp, she thought, shame washing over her, moistening her body with waves of heat. Hadn't she responded to every command of his hands and lips? Disgusted, she saw a picture of herself that night, abandoned, clinging, responding without restraint to every movement of his body. She had even begged, she remembered, and if at the time it had seemed natural to verbalize the craving for his body, now the memory had the power to shock. Tonight could have only strengthened his disgust of her!

Memory of her deliberate attempt at seduction returned to haunt her. After all her preaching, after the principles she had so often spouted to him, her sudden changeover to passion as scorchingly intense as his own must have made him feel disgust for her. That's why his voice was sneering when he mentioned having a loving, virtuous, honest wife. He didn't believe she loved him, just lusted after him, and how could he believe her to be either honest or virtuous? Suddenly her eyes smarted with tears of self-pity, tears she had desperately been trying to hold back. It was all right for Daniel to feel only lust, but never for the woman he chose to be his wife! He regretted their lovemaking!

The thought struck her with white-hot fire, and with it, all her anger and bitterness returned.

"No, don't touch me!" Her scream rent the air, slicing the tension in the room like a knife through butter.

"What the hell do you mean? You want it as much as I do," he mocked, his tongue circling her ear. "Maybe more!"

"That's not true," she sobbed, her tears flowing in earnest.

Lifting himself to lean over her, Daniel cynically surveyed the tears coursing down her cheeks. Angry, he grabbed her chin in his hand, forcing her face around to look directly at him.

"You know damn good and well it's true, Maurie. You obviously have more than a small taste for sexual pleasure, and having tasted, you want more." He lowered his head and his mouth covered hers in a punishingly brutal kiss, his lips coaxing a response. Feeling that involuntary response as her body moved against his, he didn't bother to follow his advantage. A wry smile curving his hard mouth, he again lifted his head to look into her eyes.

"You see, Maurie? Your lips say one thing but your body says something quite different." His whispered words were followed by the continued movements of his hands on her body, arching her effortlessly to his own masculine form.

"Please, not this way, you don't understand!" Maureen cringed at the abject pleading in her voice, which sounded like a stranger's. "Let me explain, Daniel. I don't want—"

"Your little seduction scene left me in no doubt as to what you wanted, Maurie. Do you want me to be blunt? Do you want a step-by-step description of exactly what you do want . . . is that how you get your kicks?"

"No!" Maureen's horrified exclamation was torn from her as she stared in dread into his angry face.

"Then shut up and listen." He ground out the words between clenched teeth. "From now on I won't deny myself my pleasures, so you don't have to be afraid of being neglected." This last was said with a cruel laugh, which wiped away the last vestiges of her self-respect.

His words went on, and with them went any hope for love from this man. She had felt pain before at his hands but nothing like this torment! It was a nightmare, as four years ago was a nightmare; but now there was the added agony of knowing her love had deepened and matured, that she would never be free of loving him no matter what pain he inflicted on her. When she was seventeen she thought she could forget him, but as much as she tried, she hadn't been able to oust his image from her mind. What she thought of as hate had only served to foster his memory. Now that her emotions had grown, there was no hope in her bruised heart for happiness in a future away from him. Indeed, without him there would be no future.

Dear God, help me to bear it, she prayed silently as Daniel's passion erupted completely. Her body was responding to the touch of his hands, for he was experienced enough to know all the secret places, all the most sensitive areas of her body. The Lord knows, he has enough experience, she thought cynically. But there was no joy and no spontaneous love vibrating between them. This was ravishment of her body and soul, and the loving was bitter and cruel. Each whispered love word that should have been spoken remained unsaid. Each cry of rapture remained muffled.

When all emotion was spent, Daniel lifted his sweat-slickened body away from her, and she turned her head to meet his look. This time there was no reproach for him in her eyes, which remained curiously blank. For just a moment, Maureen saw a look of regret in his eyes again, and the pain of his glance caused her to close her eyes in agony. With a muttered curse Daniel rose to his feet. Her eyes flew open at the controlled slam of the door.

The tears she'd forced back suddenliy found the freedom to flow, but the release of pent-up emotions caused her stomach to churn sickeningly. With a sob she reached the bathroom on unsteady legs, crouching there in abject misery until her stomach had emptied itself. Maureen bathed her face and, with a grimace at her appearance, began to repair the ravages of the last hour. She did what she could to regain at least an appearance of normalcy.

Maureen reached for fresh clothes and quickly dressed. Going to the shoe rack at the other end of the large wardrobe, she automatically reached for brown low-heeled wedgies to complement her brown plaid skirt and cotton blouse of lemon yellow. This outfit was Daniel's least favorite, she remembered, her smile strained in the whiteness of her face. She knew wearing it was more a defense mechanism than anything else, but she was past caring. After today she never wanted him to find her attractive again, and at least she would feel a little more confident when she had to face him. Closing the door quietly behind her, she walked down the stairs before her courage deserted her.

After a subdued greeting for Nonna, Maureen felt a strong need of fresh air. Letting herself out the front door, she walked down the long graveled drive. Absently she noticed the gardeners had finally been to clear the copse of the deep-rooted manzanita that had taken over, making it impossible for any other growth to flourish. It took a few minutes for her to register the wetness on her cheeks as the beginnings of rain and not tears, and with a sigh she turned her steps back toward the house. Even the weather is against me today, she thought in self-pity while quickening her steps.

The rain was coming down in earnest when she heard a frenzied barking coming from the copse she had been inspecting earlier. No, she had to be mistaken, for there were no other dogs within miles of them. She saw a small frenzied ball of golden fur running toward her, and suddenly a cold fear clutched her heart. Running toward the copse for all she was worth, the rain letting go in a torrent, she was half blinded as she ran. A small, distrait dog was jumping at her running feet, nearly tripping her before running back the way it had come. Oh, God, there's something wrong! Katy must have sneaked out of her room to play, for Snuffles couldn't have gotten out of the room otherwise, she thought frantically, searching the bushes and trees surrounding her.

"Katy, where are you? Katy!" Maureen's screams echoed around her as she stumbled in terror toward the small creek at the back of the copse. If she had fallen, hit her head! People have drowned in a few inches of water, she thought, her sobbing breath coming from strained lungs, as she ran as fast as she could through the dense underbrush. Please answer, oh, baby, please answer! she prayed. Only silence met her calls.

Why hadn't she kept Snuffles in sight, how could she have been so stupid? She reproached herself as she checked the small area of the creek. There was no sign of Katy. Was it possible that Snuffles had gotten out on his own? Perhaps Daniel had opened the door to look at Katy and the pup had been able to sneak past. Dear God, please let her be in her room! She was grasping at straws, but it was possible. Maybe Katy hadn't answered her calls because she was afraid of being punished for leaving her room. She would have to keep looking, for if the child was out here hiding from her, she could end up with pneumonia. Some of the fear slowly drained away from her—at least she hadn't found her lying in the creek. Suddenly she stood rooted to the spot as she listened to a keening wail coming from a few remaining clumps of manzanita to the left of where she was standing, about a yard away. Fighting her way through the thick growth, she wasn't conscious of the gnarled plant tearing at her flesh, for she knew now for certain Katy was there somewhere, and from the sound of Snuffles's howling, something was terribly wrong. She had never heard the animal howl now assaulting her ears; it was unlike anything she had ever imagined, even from the depths of a nightmare. Its eerie keening seemed to freeze the blood in her veins.

She stood for what seemed to be precious minutes, but which in reality were only seconds, before, with a muffled groan, she knelt beside the tiny prostrate body. It was obvious Katy had fallen on an upturned hoe, but God alone knew how long she had been lying here. Her hands worked swiftly and automatically, tearing strips of the yellow cotton from her blouse to form a tourniquet above the nasty gash in the child's leg, from whence the blood gushed alarmingly. Tears mingling with the rain streaming down her face, she lovingly cradled Katy in her arms and ran for all she was worth toward the house. Screams were locked in her throat, but it was doubtful if they would be heard anyway above the frantic barking of the little dog, who at least had the sense to keep from under her running feet.

Dear God, she's so little, she's just a baby. "Please God, let her live." Maureen wasn't aware of saying the words aloud, conscious only of the precious bundle so still in her arms. She reached the door and opened it automatically, stumbling through the opening. She had no more strength left, and the scream couldn't be made to pass her throat as she stood with the child . . . like a piteous ghost risen from the sea, shock apparent as she stood facing Daniel and Nonna. Daniel gently took Katy into his arms, having to exert a little pressure, for Maureen's arms seemed frozen around her pathetic little burden.

"Maurie, we must stop the bleeding and get her to the hospital," he whispered urgently, as Maureen's arms still refused to release Katy to him. Gazing down at the long lashes fanning the whiteness of cheeks once pink, her eyes traveled down to Katy's small leg, and what she saw there made her gasp. Daniel was right. The gash was still bleeding, though not as profusely as before, and the realization seemed to jolt her out of her stunned immobility. Giving the child up to Daniel, she watched as he laid her down gently and then ran for the first-aid box. With Nonna's help he wrapped gauze tightly over an improvised pad.

If only I could live this day over again, she thought in an agony of remorse, holding the blanket-wrapped child tightly in her arms as Daniel sped on the freeway toward the Valley Hospital.

"Thank God, the rain has stopped," he muttered, sending a quick glance toward the still figure in Maureen's arms.

The sky had darkened into a night as black as pitch, there was no moon to relieve the severity of the darkness, and any stars were swallowed up by black storm clouds. It was as if they were traveling through a tunnel lit with streetlights from within, an infinity of emptiness without. At any moment that great yawning pit might snatch her beloved baby from her, to leave her forever searching for a glimpse of a laughing mouth calling her name while warm baby arms encircled her neck. Dear God, don't make her suffer for my sins. She's so little, and she loves life so. Please, God, punish me, but not this way . . . not through my baby! The prayer went round and round in her brain but brought her no ease, for Katy was so still, her pulse so weak. There had to be a chance for her! But how much blood could a little child lose, and still survive? Had she reached her in time? "Please God," she whispered. "Let us be in time." The squeal of the tires as the car approached the hospital sent a nervous tremor through her.

White-coated figures ran toward them from the emergency entrance and, literally snatching the unconscious child from her arms, quickly and efficiently strapped her to a gurney, her small shape nearly lost among the whiteness of the bedlike surface. Their running steps sent a wet spray from the puddles beneath their feet as they entered the large double glass doors. Maureen and Daniel ran behind the orderlies, but the gurney was propelled through large doors with a sign stating that entry to the area was restricted to hospital personnel only. As the doors closed behind them, Maureen stood staring in disbelief, Daniel's hand firmly holding her back.

A dam burst inside her, released the screams held inside her since she had first seen Katy's bloodstained body lying amid the damp undergrowth like an offering to the cruel gods of a pagan past.

The last glimpse she had was of two nurses running toward her and Daniel's arms reaching out to her as the lights whirled crazily above her head. Gasping, her hands clutching at Daniel, she felt herself whirling away into a black yawning pit of emptiness where she searched in vain. Her Katy was running farther away from her, ever farther into the blackness, and her own feet were too heavy to keep up. The child turned, her face alight with mischievous laughter, dusky curls bouncing on fat cheeks. Maureen could barely see her now, as she floated unwillingly backward, away from Katy. Trying frantically to pierce the dark, she saw Katy raise her small arm in a wave.

"Katy, come back! Please don't leave me." Maureen's screams seemed to be swallowed up by the dark. From far, far away, in a distance so vast as to seem infinite, came a whisper. "Maurie, I love you," and then there was nothing, as she seemed to fall crying into that terrifying black pit, farther and farther away from her precious Katy.

CHAPTER TEN

Silver speckles of light danced riotously behind her eyelids, and an acrid smell filled her nostrils. She tried turning her head to escape the terrible smell, but her head was held in a vise of steel. Lifting her weighted eyelids, she glanced around the bare, antiseptic room, her mind foggy. Her eyes finally focused on a woman's ample figure. From her movements the woman appeared to be returning a small bottle to the shelf above her head.

Maureen sat up with a jerk, as full memory returned. With memory came that surge of blinding fear. Startled, the woman turned, and Maureen saw the nurse's uniform with a sense of relief.

"Now, girlie, are you feeling more the thing?" the woman questioned gently. "I'm Nurse Carruthers." Smiling, she walked over to Maureen and grasped her wrist between cool fingers.

"Where's Katy? Where's my baby?" Maureen moaned, eyes enormous in her pale face, as she glanced beseechingly into the sympathetic face above her.

"Don't you be worrying, girlie. The little one is safe, and the doctors are taking excellent care of her." Smiling in satisfaction at the much slower pulse rate, Nurse Carruthers gently released Maureen's wrist and clasped her hand reassuringly.

"You're lying to me!" Maureen was hardly conscious

of the words passing her lips, until Nurse Carruthers frowned in reaction, tightening her grip on Maureen's shaking hands.

"Now, now . . . don't you go upsetting yourself again after all the work I've put into calming you," she said with a smile. "I can hardly blame you, for I'm a stranger, and why should you believe me? Maybe that handsome husband of yours can convince you. He's waiting outside with the doctor." Before Maureen could utter a word, Nurse Carruthers bustled from the room, her orthopedic shoes squelching as she disappeared through the door. She stared at the door as it slowly closed, and watched, hands clenched, as it just as slowly swung open again.

"Mrs. Lord, I'm Dr. Bradley. Do you feel up to answering a few questions for us?"

Licking lips suddenly dry, she nodded, looking at Daniel with a question burning in her haunted eyes. Quickly he sat beside her and laid one firm hand over her clenched ones. Searching his face, Maureen realized this horrible day had left its mark of suffering upon him also, for he seemed to have aged since she saw him last. As she felt the warmth of his hand over hers, she knew he was trying to impart some of his strength to her, and, strangely enough, she did feel a new surge of hopefulness enter her. Relaxing her hands with conscious effort, she faced the doctor.

"I'll tell you anything I can, Dr. Bradley, but please tell me how Katy is."

"I'm not going to lie to you or your husband, Mrs. Lord. It was a nasty gash, and the child lost a lot of blood."

"But surely blood can be replaced, Dr. Bradley."

Tiredly the doctor perched on a nearby chair, leaning forward with his arms resting across his knees.

"Of course blood can be replaced, Mrs. Lord, but we've run into a problem. Katy is of an extremely rare blood grouping and a fresh supply is being flown in. We have her on a treatment to prevent shock, but in her case time is of the essence."

"But surely I—"

"Mrs. Lord," Dr. Bradley cut in firmly. "The first thing we did was take a sample of your blood, and though it's compatible with your sister's, it shows traces of anemia, which makes it too risky to contemplate using."

Shock registered on Maureen's face as the doctor's words penetrated her numbed mind. Dear God, Katy needs blood and I'm unable to give it to her. Tears hovered in the back of her eyes, and with a moan she covered her face. She remembered when she had developed the anemia, and ironically Daniel had been the cause, for after they parted she had endured months of torment and loneliness. Oh, God . . . why should Katy have to pay? Daniel and I are the ones who are guilty. Daniel . . .

Lifting her chin, she stared into the doctor's kindly face, no hesitation marring the flow of her thoughts. This was no time to worry about anything but Katy's life, and no matter what the consequences to herself, she must speak.

"Dr. Bradley, I don't think you quite understand the situation. Nor, I'm afraid, does my husband." She spoke softly but clearly, wiping the moisture from her palms against the material of her skirt. Drawing in a shaky breath, she continued, avoiding Daniel's gaze.

"Y—you see, Katy isn't my sister, Dr. Bradley. Katy is my daughter." This last was said almost defiantly, and hearing the tone of her own voice, sounding more confident than she felt, she knew a strong sense of release. No matter what happens now, she thought, there will be no more deception.

"Mrs. Lord." Dr. Bradley's voice was uncomfortable as he too avoided Daniel's eyes. "I understand your reasons for telling me this, especially with your little girl lying critically ill, but I don't see that, considering your inability to give your blood, it serves any purpose, except for the hospital records."

"Doctor," she interrupted firmly. "Couldn't the father's blood be used?"

"Mrs. Lord, can you contact the child's natural father? There's just a chance, of course, and time is our biggest enemy, but if the father is close and is willing to . . ."

Gathering her courage, Maureen looked at Daniel. He was sitting quite still, his face harsh and cold, a forbidding cast to his mouth. For a moment, meeting the accusing coldness of his eyes, her courage almost failed her, but an image of Katy, laughing and full of life, superimposed itself on his face.

Her voice just a thread of sound, her eyes never leaving Daniel's, she continued: "Yes, Doctor. Katy's father is close, and I'm sure he would be more than willing to give his blood for his child."

Daniel's lips curled cynically as she spoke, the bitterness on his face unmistakable. Maureen could understand, and she couldn't blame him. How he must hate her now! After all, she had lied and deceived him right along. How stupid she had been, from the very beginning of their relationship, and now it was time for her to pay for her mistakes. Yes, she thought, her lips trembling as she tore her eyes away from his. She would pay willingly, as long as Katy didn't have to. Katy would have her life, and Daniel would see to it she never suffered.

"You see, Dr. Bradley"—Maureen spoke almost pleadingly—"he doesn't know, has never known he was a father." She rose and teetered across the room to look out the small window on the far wall. Wrapping her arms defensively around her shivering body, a sigh welled up and escaped from deep within her. Turning to face the doctor, she said, "May we have just a few minutes alone?"

"Of course, Mrs. Lord. I'll be waiting at the nurses' station." The doctor rose and left the room, and as the door closed behind the white-coated figure she felt the tension in the room. Glancing at Daniel in trepidation, she started to speak, but he erupted from the couch, rage in every line of his body.

"What the hell is going on?" The question was ground out between clenched teeth while he grabbed her upper arms with a grip that bit into her flesh.

"Please, you're hurting me."

"Hurting you? I find out you're Katy's mother . . . not her sister, and as if that isn't enough, you've got

172

her 'natural father' somewhere conveniently close. You've lied to me right along, played me for a sucker out of some childish urge for revenge, and you have the nerve to say I hurt you!"

As he spoke Daniel began shaking her. When he saw her face whiten, contrition smote him, and with an effort he removed his hands.

"I'm sorry, I didn't mean to do that," he groaned, lighting a cigarette with shaking hands.

"I know you didn't, Daniel." She closed her eyes in silent prayer, blotting out the sight of his muscular back and the hair falling in waves over the back of his tautly held head.

"I agree we have to contact this guy, Maurie, but I want one thing clear." His voice, like ice, sent shafts of pain darting through her. "Katy's mine, and if this joker decides he wants to play father, he can just think again. After she's well, I intend to legally adopt her, and neither you or your lover are going to stop me!"

"There's no need," she told him quietly. "Please, don't interrupt," she asked, raising one small hand in a gesture partly supplicating, partly defensive. "Don't make this any harder for me than it already is." Maureen turned away from him and stared out of the window, marshaling her thoughts.

"Let me tell you what I have to . . . Explanations can come later." Biting her lower lip, she once again hugged her shaking body.

"Daniel, you're Katy's father!" The words came out baldly, and she drew a sharp breath before she was able to continue, Daniel's gasp resounding in her ears. "I— I realize I was wrong not telling you, but I . . ."

"God, you really do take me for a sucker. Are you trying to tell me I fathered a child and don't even remember?"

Maureen had expected a lot of things but not this. Turning jerkily, she taunted, "Don't you remember, Daniel? Don't you really?"

Looking into her eyes, he saw the truth there, overlying the anger in her voice.

"That last night, when you ran out on me?"

Daniel's eyes widened in horror. Dear God, it makes sense. He remembered holding her in his arms. He had been drunk but apparently not that drunk. Running a hand through his hair, he remembered falling, and the pieces of the puzzle fell together.

"Maurie, I . . ."

"No, no more needs to be said. I—we'll talk later, but for God's sake, help Katy, Daniel. She needs you now . . . please." Ignoring her tears now freely flowing, she clutched at his sleeve in desperation. He hesitated, opening his mouth to speak, but the words remained unsaid.

"Daniel, hurry . . . please. Oh, Daniel, don't let our baby die," she sobbed.

"Will you be all right?" His voice was gruff, choked by emotion.

"Yes, don't worry. Please, go now!"

"Of course," he said, already halfway across the room. Turning at the door, he reassured her: "Don't worry, she'll be fine, there's plenty of time now that we don't have to wait for that damn plane."

Smiling through her tears, she whispered, "I know, Daniel. She will be fine now!"

As the door closed on his striding figure she turned and leaned her hot forehead against the cool glass of the window. She heard footsteps behind her but was too drained emotionally to care.

"There, dearie, you're to come with me. We'll get you to a comfortable place to wait for news, and get some hot coffee inside you."

Maureen began to protest, to no avail, and found herself being led meekly out of the dismal room. Following Nurse Carruthers's robust figure down the long corridor was exhausting in itself. As she looked at the hurrying figure ahead of her, short legs carrying it quickly along, red hair peeping out from around the nurse's cap and showing streaks of gray, Maureen marveled at the woman's vitality. Nurse Carruthers was obviously old enough to be her mother, but as far as energy and youthfulness went, she couldn't help feeling she was about a hundred years older than the kindly woman.

Nurse Carruthers led her to a little alcove set at the end of the long corridor. After fetching her some coffee, she left her with a few reassuring words and a promise to let her know as soon as there was any news. Maureen sighed as she watched the retreating figure. Part of her wanted to be alone, but a more cowardly part wanted the comfort of people around her.

She sipped the revitalizing beverage absentmindedly, cupping her cold hands around the chipped enamel mug and savoring its warmth. Emptying the cup, she laid it down on a plastic-topped table. Unable to sit still, she rose, her feet beating out a desolate pattern on the battered floral carpet. Looking for the thousandth time, or so it seemed, at the black-and-white face of the clock glaring from the wall like an enemy, she ran a shaking hand through her tousled hair. She was so preoccupied she was not aware of the sympathetic glances coming from the passing hospital staff; nor did she realize that her huge eyes, set in a face drained of all color, and the striking contrast of black hair and brows gave her the appearance of a forlorn and tragic Madonna.

Dear God, how long will it take before I know, she thought in an agony of suspense. She knew she was indulging in self-pity, but this waiting was intolerable. Each minute seemed like an hour, and the ticking of the clock was overloud in the small alcove. Rubbing tired eyes with hands that she couldn't seem to stop from shaking, she sighed. How can this be taking so long? There must be complications. Oh, why doesn't someone tell me something before I go mad! Again she turned to look hopelessly at the clock, all the while knowing the dark pointing fingers had barely moved.

"Mrs. Lord?"

With a gasp she turned, seeing Dr. Bradley's weary white-coated figure standing there like a mirage in front of her. Swaying, Maureen felt the doctor's firm hand clutching her arm, as he assisted her to the low divan in the corner.

175

"Katy?" Maureen's voice was a frightened thread of sound. Hearing the underlying hysteria in her voice, Dr. Bradley quickly sat beside her and clasped her hands firmly.

"She will be just fine, Mrs. Lord. Mr. Lord's blood was completely compatible; in fact, it was from her father she inherited her blood type." He smiled. "The child is now completely out of danger."

"You're sure? Y—you wouldn't lie to me?"

"No . . . I wouldn't lie to you, Mrs. Lord. Katy will be fine, there's no more need for concern," he reassured her kindly, giving her hands a tight squeeze before releasing them.

"Thank God!" Maureen closed her eyes in relief, opening them again to question: "There were no complications?" She seemed unable to grasp the fact that the nightmare was over.

"None whatsoever, Mrs. Lord. This kind of transference takes time, of course. I know the waiting was difficult for you."

"Daniel—is Daniel all right?"

"Fine, although he gave more blood than we would normally accept from one donor."

"But he will be okay? There won't be any unpleasant after effects for him?"

"Not at all, though under the circumstances he is rather weak, and we'll be keeping him in the hospital tonight. He'll be fine by morning, though he should take it easy for a few days. We'll let you look in on Katy and your husband for a moment, just to reassure yourself of their well-being, but then you should go home and get some rest before we have to find a bed for you, too," he advised jokingly.

Smiling in response, even if it was a feeble effort, did her a world of good, she realized. Thank you, God. Oh, thank you! Maureen's thoughts centered on little else but her gratefulness. The two people she loved most in the world were safe, and that was all that mattered.

Later, after a quick call to Nonna to tell her the news, Maureen followed Nurse Carruthers down the long corridor, the sound of Nonna's thankful sobs ringing in her ears. Poor Nonna! Here she had been feeling sorry for herself, waiting and praying. How much worse it must have been for Nonna, left at home, to bear the waiting in a large house that must have echoed with the remembered sounds of Katy's laughter. Tears coming at the thought of what Nonna must have suffered, she felt ashamed. Nonna had called the hospital as Daniel had ordered, to prepare them for their arrival, and then had been left alone with barely a thought of what she would go through. She knew it was no use looking back—how well she knew it, but how sorry she was now that they'd not thought to take Nonna with them. It was thoughtlessness that could have been hurtful to anyone else, but when Maureen had stammered her remorse, Nonna had stopped crying long enough to scold her. She had told Maureen that she needed her man beside her at such a time, and no one else . . . but she doubted if Nonna knew just how true those words were!

Suddenly they arrived at a door like all the other doors along that endless corridor, impersonal and uniform, but behind it lay the one man in the world she could ever love.

"I'll wait outside, dearie. You'll want to be alone for a while," Nurse Carruthers said with a smile. "But don't you stay too long, mind . . . the lad needs to rest."

"N—no, I promise to hurry."

"Yes, I'm sure you won't be wanting to disturb him for too long. Why, it's as plain as the nose on your face how much you adore that man. All the young nurses are jealous of you!"

Startled, Maureen searched Nurse Carruthers's face. Were her feelings for Daniel that apparent, then? Seeing the expression on the homely, kindly face before her, she read the answer there and flushed a dusky red.

"Humph! With a gorgeous hunk of man like that coming home to me every night, I'd blush too!" The grinning nurse, eyes twinkling, gently pushed Maureen through the door.

Her softly flushed face, a smile still on her trembling

lips from the nurse's parting words, made her seem lovelier than ever to the man lying there beneath the whitely antiseptic confines of the narrow bed. His eyes drank in her face as she walked toward him slowly, and he saw her hesitate, unsure of her welcome. The tentative smile faltered and then disappeared as she saw his mouth firm into a white line. Glancing at him, at the set mouth, she longed to smooth the harsh lines away with her lips, to brush back the unruly lock of black and silver hair that had fallen across his moist forehead.

"How are you feeling, Daniel?" She could have kicked herself for saying those conventional and stilted words, when she wanted with all her heart to throw herself into his arms.

"How's Katy? Is she okay, Maurie?" How abrupt and cold he sounded! Forlorn at his tone of voice, Maureen lowered her eyes from the piercing scrutiny of his.

"They said she'll be fine." Gulping, she stood fighting sudden tears. Forcing herself to look at him again, she feigned an air of calm. "Daniel . . . how can I ever thank you?"

"Thank me?" Daniel retorted savagely between clenched teeth. "Why in hell should you thank me for helping my own daughter, Maurie?" Shrugging himself impatiently into a sitting position, he angrily brushed away her restraining hand. "I still can't believe she is my daughter, my own flesh and blood," he whispered, his hand brushing that errant lock of hair from his forehead. "From the beginning I felt strangely drawn to her," he continued thoughtfully, "but I never imagined—I always thought it was because—" His voice halted on a thread of sound, and his expression hardened again as a new thought, obviously unpleasant, crossed his mind.

"What do you mean by 'they said,' she'll be okay, Maurie? Haven't you seen her?"

The accusation in his voice almost stopped her breath, coming as it did after all the strain of the last few hours.

"Daniel, I—" He didn't let her finish her words, cutting across them with rapier swiftness.

"What can you explain?" He gripped her wrist. "Can

you explain why you have denied being her mother all these years? Or maybe you would like to explain why you neglected to tell me she was mine?"

The possessiveness in his voice when he said "mine" told Maureen that what she had feared had come to pass; but strangely enough, it no longer seemed to matter. Daniel is a possessive man, she thought. She had known that in the beginning and loved him in spite of it. In all fairness, how could she expect anything different from him now, especially since now he had every reason to be possessive of his newfound daughter? Funny how she had shied away from that thought, even in her own mind. Now, though, she could face the idea head-on, with all its implications for herself. His daughter! She knew Katy could never be shared between them, could never be "ours." Hadn't that been the reason why she had been afraid of telling him? Oh, she had told herself it was because he would use Katy as a lever, but had she really believed that after seeing them together? No, she thought in disgust. She had been the one to use her baby as a lever. As soon as she realized that Daniel had never received her message telling him she had to see him, that was when she should have told him about the baby. Why hadn't she? Because she felt he wouldn't believe her? Or if he did, was she afraid he would try to take Katy . . . and not her? Was it resentment at the way he once again was forcing her to his will? Of being rejected once again? God, the list is endless!

No, it had been her damn pride . . . but that wasn't true and she knew it! The sordid truth was she wanted to hurt Daniel as she had been hurt, and as she saw the love he felt for Katy growing, the secret locked inside her gave her a kind of warped satisfaction. Facing the truth at last, she felt sick. God, how could she have hurt them like that? Not just Daniel, but Katy too. What kind of a mother was she, to keep the fact that "her Daniel" was really her father from a defenseless little girl, who would have been overjoyed at the truth. Katy knew she was her mother, but she had always called her Maurie, because it was what she heard others call her . . . even

179

though she had tried to get her to say Mommy—the two were enough alike to be confused.

Had the deception started as revenge and gone on to jealousy? Yes, she thought, her body stiffening in rejection of her thoughts. Yet the need for revenge had been short-lived, and looking back over the past few months made her realize how completely her motivation had changed. Because she hadn't told him the truth from the very beginning, she was then afraid to tell him later, too much of a coward to chance his rejection! By keeping silent, she tried to gain time, to make herself necessary to him, so that when he learned the truth he wouldn't leave her!

Feeling her body stiffen under his touch, Daniel tore his hand away. Closing his eyes, he sank back against the pillow, his whole being understanding her rejection, not knowing it was her anguished thoughts she was recoiling from. Tiredly he opened his eyes and, turning his head, looked away from her.

"Go and get some rest, we'll talk later. Not that it'll do any good," she heard him mutter under his breath. Seeing his eyes close again, she turned without another word and, with lips pressed tightly together to prevent a cry of pain, walked to the door. Looking back at him was agonizing, but Maureen couldn't prevent her hungry eyes from turning in his direction. He opened his eyes, and their glances locked for precious moments.

"Good-bye," she whispered, leaving the room quietly. As the door closed behind her, she walked quickly away, failing to hear the cry from the room as she left.

Walking through to the nurses' station, Maureen slowed her steps as she faced Nurse Carruthers once again.

"Please, I'd like to see my daughter now!" She knew her voice sounded cold to the woman who had been so kind to her, but for the life of her she couldn't seem to infuse any warmth into either her tone of voice or her carefully controlled features. How could she when she had finally decided what she must do?

Doing the right thing was going to be hard, but not as difficult as hurting Daniel and Katy any further than

180

she had already. The decision made, her heart felt like a dead thing in her breast, and she felt as if she would never be able to feel enough happiness ever again to lend warmth to her life.

Leading the way toward the pediatrics unit, Aggie Carruthers was intuitive enough to forgive the coldness in the little lassie, for in her career she had seen more than her share of pain and suffering. It puzzled her, though! Why, now that the little girl was safe and out of danger, should her mother have that look about her—a look she had seen many times before on the faces of patients and relatives who had been told there was no hope for loved ones? A kind of resigned despair? No one so healthy and beautiful as this young girl should look like that, she thought compassionately.

"Dearie, I don't want to be interfering in your business." She spoke to Maureen gently, laying a hand on her arm as they reached the door to Katy's room. "But if you need someone to talk to . . . if I could help in any way . . . ?"

Raising her head with quiet dignity, which brought a gleam of admiration to the other woman's eyes, Maureen replied, "Thank you! I—I'll always remember your kindness to me, and may God bless you for it." Turning staunchly, Maureen disappeared through the door.

Standing very still after Maureen had left her, the usually cheerful Nurse Carruthers felt a terrible depression as a feeling of helplessness settled over her. With a pitying shake of her head she turned and slowly walked away.

Maureen stood beside the crib with its metal bars slotted high around the tiny sleeping figure, and smiled while tears coursed down her face. As she noted the color flushing Katy's cheeks a soft pink, and the dusky curls clustering around her small head, she felt a great tenderness deep inside herself. Closing her eyes, she moved her lips in a quiet prayer of thankfulness, and a heavy burden carried too long seemed to have been lifted from her in those few quiet moments.

Reaching between the enclosing bars of the crib, her

fingers felt the warmth of the small hand under her own, and she gently caressed its tiny fingers. How many times had she gone in to tuck Katy in for the night and performed this same loving gesture—stroking the little hands before placing them gently under the warmth of the blankets?

"Never enough times, my darling," she whispered, her other hand brushing the soft curls from Katy's forehead. Sobbing, she pressed against the coolness of the metal bars. Dear God, it's so hard, she thought, desperately trying to memorize every beloved feature of the small face lying there.

"Be happy!" Her choked whisper echoed around the silent room, and with a moan she stumbled away from the bed.

Later, she did not remember calling the taxi, or even the fifteen-minute ride home through the quiet of the rain-washed night. Folding the last of her clothes in the suitcase automatically, she was amazed to realize she didn't even know if it had still been raining. Not that it mattered, she thought tiredly, her heart like a lead weight within her. The only consolation she had was being able to picture Daniel and Katy happy. If she stayed, all the loving would be on her part, and she had already had enough examples of the futility of that. After what she had done to Daniel, she could only pray that someday he would be able to forgive her and maybe think of her with a little kindness.

Walking quietly down the empty hallway and descending the stairs, she left her cases standing in front of the door in the entry hall and, turning in the opposite direction, entered Daniel's study.

Reaching out, she switched on the light. The room was bathed in a gentle radiance from recessed lighting set high in the ceiling. Walking over to his large desk, and taking out writing paper and pen from the middle drawer, she felt like an interloper. This was Daniel's private sanctum, his holy of holies, the one room in the house he reserved strictly for his own use. She had to force herself to sit in the encompassing softness of the large swivel chair and was cynically amused at her reluctance.

After many attempts the letter was finished, but she sat on dejectedly. Her gaze noted the bookshelves, their rich brown wood contrasting with the muted orange-toned walls broken only by the large fireplace, with its antique mahogany mantel and mirror, nestling warmly against the wall and setting a perfect focal point for the room.

Maureen felt the thick softness of the orange and brown carpet beneath her feet, as she moved to stand in front of the mantel, caressing its exquisite carvings with a loving hand. Daniel loved beautiful things. Had his hand caressed the satiny texture of the wood just as hers was doing? His presence seemed to emanate from this room as in none other, but then the room was like him, she thought, amazed at her own intuitiveness. Strongly masculine, even slightly forbidding, but with a warmth underlying the whole. Why, oh, why hadn't she seen that before it was too late? It would be impossible not to love this room, as impossible as it had been for her not to love Daniel. Though she knew she must leave its sheltering peace soon, she was strangely reluctant to do so. With a determined lift to her shoulders she turned to leave, only to fall back with a gasp, her fingers unconsciously gouging the mantel's carved posts.

"Daniel!" Her gasp seemed to echo unendingly as she stared at the man standing there so quietly, his back to the door. She had been so preoccupied with her thoughts she hadn't heard him enter. No wonder I felt his presence so strongly, she thought, forcefully subduing the hysterical laughter threatening to bubble from her throat.

"Running away again, Maurie?" Daniel's tones, though quiet, demanded an answer.

"Do you blame me, Daniel?" she said, her tone equally bitter.

"No!" The single word, spoken as if forced from him, caused her to stare at him in silent stupefaction.

He walked toward her, and though she longed to retreat, she stood her ground, her running days over. Stopping a few feet short of her, he began once again to speak, and she looked down at her clenched hands rather than at him.

"Maurie, when you left me at the hospital, the way you said good-bye kept going around and around in my mind. Then, when Nurse Carruthers came—"

"She had no right!" she interrupted hotly, feeling oddly betrayed.

"Please, let me finish," he said quietly, strain evident in his voice. "Anyway, after putting two and two together, I guessed you'd try something like this, so here I am."

"Why bother, Daniel? You're not going to stop me!"

"Katy needs both her parents, Maurie."

"No, Daniel!" Maureen swallowed jerkily, gathering what little courage she had left. "Eventually the lack of love between us would erupt into bitterness, as it did yesterday, and we would tear her apart, as well as each other," she said, raising pleading eyes to his, silently begging for his understanding.

Hopeless, Daniel turned, leaning dejectedly against the mantel, one arm stretched out with muscles taut.

"I don't blame you, Maurie." He spoke gratingly through clenched teeth, a muscle jumping in the chiseled contours of his cheek. "You couldn't despise me more than I do myself!"

"I—" she began, to be stopped abruptly by the savage movement of his hand. At the sight of her body flinching away from the sudden gesture, something inside him seemed to snap, and with a groan he pulled her body into his arms.

As his mouth closed over hers all resistance left her for a few blissful moments, and her thoughts became a mass of chaotic sensations. His lips, at first gently probing the throbbing sensitivity of hers, suddenly hardened into passionate life. When he pulled away abruptly, she felt bereft, though his strong arms still cradled her body. Hurt beyond bearing, she was at first unaware of the meaning of the words muffled against the silky softness of her hair, but as their significance erupted into her consciousness she felt a delirious joy, its warmth melting forever the hurt and bitterness of the last years.

"Maurie," he whispered. "I won't take Katy from you! My God, you've got to let me take care of you both, or I'll go out of my mind," he begged, his voice choked with emotion. Feeling her body become quiet and tense in his arms, he tightened his hold.

"Maurie, I can't ask you to forgive . . . no woman could be expected to forgive rape . . . especially twice," he groaned. "If it's any consolation to you, yesterday happened because I love you so much I was eaten up with jealousy!" Daniel moved abruptly from her to the other side of the room, as if he couldn't bear contact with her body. Perching on his desk, one muscular leg braced against the floor, he tiredly rubbed his hand against the side of his face. Maureen watched him, silently willing him to look at her, but his gaze remained averted.

His harsh laugh rang out in the stillness. "It's bloody ironic . . . a man being jealous of himself!"

"I don't understand."

"That last trip I took—I didn't have to go, but I needed time to think, Maurie. I knew when I was away how much you meant to me. I couldn't sleep thinking of the way we made love that night, how lovely you were lying beneath me, the firelight flickering over your body. God, the agony I went through thinking of the other man you had been with . . . I wanted to kill him, and you too for acting virginal before we were married, and even after. You had led me to believe—it was the lying I couldn't take," he spat out savagely.

"There was never another man, Daniel," she told him steadily. "That's why Katy became my sister, I was afraid men would see me as easy game if I . . . Anyway, I wanted nothing to do with men."

"Don't you think I know that? God, after the way you've suffered at my hands, you must have wished you never had to see another man again!"

Daniel had more than come halfway, now it was up to her, and she trembled at the thought. As she moved toward him quietly, she realized he was so tortured by his own thoughts, he was unaware of her approach. The night Katy was conceived had been as much her fault as his, she thought with honesty. He could be forgiven for taking her by force, because her initial response to his lovemaking seemed to prove him right in his original poor opinion of her morals—that she was literally selling her virginity for her father. In her innocence she had led him on, and when she had taken fright it had been much too late for him to resume control, especially since he had been drinking. True, he had later hurled terrible accusations at her, but now she tended to believe his anger had been less at her, and more in disgust upon finding himself capable of such actions. Knowing he loved her now, the past no longer mattered, for maybe he had unknowingly loved her then too—she would like to think so.

Reaching his side, Maureen moved around in front of him, placing her hands on his tensed shoulders as she levered her body close between his outstretched thighs.

"Maurie!" His voice was a hoarse groan, aroused unbearably at her closeness. The last few tormenting moments of contemplating the bleakness of a life without her had sapped what little control he had left. Closing his eyes, he gritted his teeth, needing nearly superhuman endurance to stop himself from crushing her in his arms . . . afraid of reacting like the animal she must think him.

As she heard him say her name so achingly she smiled. She could afford to be generous, for hadn't she gained the love of the only man she had ever cared about? To love meant to want to protect and soothe the loved one, and only she could wipe out forever the horror of self-blame he was suffering. Moving her hands to cradle his face, she spoke softly, letting him see the love she felt for him.

"Darling . . . that night I wanted you to love me, but I was young and frightened," she said earnestly. "It was my own guilt and immaturity that spoiled our lovemaking that night, because no one could have been more tender."

"Maurie, is that true?" Daniel's question was tormented; he was afraid to let himself believe the burden of guilt could be lifted. Her smile and assenting nod were his answer, but still he wasn't convinced.

"Even so, yesterday I forced——"

She placed caressing fingers over his firm lips to quiet his self-denigration.

"Darling, if you remember, I started it!" Maureen chuckled out loud. "I wanted you to love me, Daniel. I only fought you at the end because I thought you didn't —that you regretted our lovemaking. In fact, for the very reasons I ran away from you four years ago!"

Her nearly incoherent explanation was silenced by his mouth. As her lips parted beneath the lovingly gentle caress she felt him tremble against her. With a murmur he lifted her high in his arms, and as she nestled her head lovingly against his warm chest she knew without doubt the bitterness of the past was truly gone. For them there was only the present, and the joy of a future shared.

ANNE N. REISSER
The Face Of Love

CHAPTER ONE

If she kept her eyes fixed only on Johnny's face, she was almost able to pretend the head table didn't exist, to ignore the voluptuous redhead, who so determinedly pressed her cushiony breasts into the obliging arm of her table companion. Johnny looked at the frozen blankness of her face and realized the depth of the mistake he had made when he persuaded her to come to the party with him. He hadn't realized that it would affect her so badly.

"Would you prefer to go home now, Andy?" he asked softly. "There's no need to sit here and be tortured. I'm sorry, my dear. I didn't know it would be like this. I wouldn't have made you come with me if I'd realized . . ." His voice trailed off helplessly.

The blank eyes came up to focus on his, their normal soft gray shining with a steely glitter. "It's always like this." There was a shocking wealth of bitterness and hopeless pain in the husky voice. "She's not the first, and she's nowhere near the last. Others pay for the pain he causes, and I curse the ties that bind me to him. Husband, father . . . lecher! How can a woman know him for what he is and love him still? You tell me, Johnny. What qualities has such a man that he can command such devotion from a woman, any woman?"

7

Two fat tears sparkled in the inner corners of her eyes, and he pressed comforting hands over her small clenched fists, which pounded softly on the table between them in rhythmic agony as she talked. Fortunately the others at their table were already dancing, so they had relative privacy, but he knew that sooner or later someone would notice. He had to get her out and away before her control snapped absolutely.

"Andrea!" He spoke sharply, hoping to break through the low-voiced monotone. "Andy, stop it! I'll take you home. Pick up your purse, dear. We'll go home."

He made a move to rise, but she restrained him, laying a pinioning hand on his arm while she made a massive, visible effort to control herself. She fought and won her battle and then smiled shakily at him.

"I'm sorry, Johnny." Her smile was penitent and sincere. "I usually handle it better than this, but I stopped by the nursing home before we came here and the contrast was bitter. She is so frail and in so much pain and so damned *brave* about it all, and she loves the bas—" Johnny's fingers smothered the expletive gently but firmly.

"He's your father, Andy," he reminded her sternly.

"That doesn't change what he is, Johnny," she retorted hotly. "My mother lies dying by inches in a nursing home, twisted in agony, and my *father*"— the bitter scorn she packed into that word appalled him—"my father sits cosily beside his latest mistress, unsubtly disguised as his secretary, laughing and enjoying himself. And make no mistake, it's no pose hiding a tortured heart. He really is enjoying himself.

He visits Mother once or twice a week, professes love, and returns to the hot arms of his latest whore."

She looked at Johnny's white face and a caricature of a smile twisted her mouth. "Pretty, isn't it? And believe me, Johnny, dear friend that you are, you couldn't begin to guess the half of it. Maybe someday, after my mother dies, if you get me drunk and maudlin, I'll tell you the sordid whole."

This time her smile was dreamy, as if the dream were a nightmare. "The whole is beyond your wildest imaginings, my innocent friend. The unexpurgated saga of Devlin Thomas, stalwart husband and father. Oh, hell, dance with me, Johnny! The storm has blown itself out. I'll be a good girl now, and I won't even spit in his eye if we happen to come face to face with him on the dance floor."

Her smile now was tight but natural, and he stood, pulling her chair back to free her from the constricted space. She came to his arms gracefully, with that lithe economy of motion that characterized all her movements. If she were not a painter, she would have been a dancer, and the controlled elegance of her shapely body drew many an appreciative masculine eye.

It drew the eyes of two men at the head table, speculative gray and Viking blue. Gray-sprinkled black head and dark blond swiveled to trace the course of the dancing couple and the ignored redhead seated between them seethed, silently at first, but when pique overcame caution, audibly.

"Devlin," the voice grated shrilly and inappositely from such a pouted mouth. "Devlin, I want to dance now." She tugged at the arm she leaned against to command his attention. When his eyes came reluctantly to hers, she fluttered mascaraed lashes invitingly.

"We've only danced once tonight, Devlin," she reminded him and leaned forward slightly, allowing her décolletage to gape explicitly. Since she wore no bra, it was more explicit than might have been expected, and the man who raked her with jaded gray eyes was not yet proof against that invitation.

"Of course, Marta, my dear. Excuse us please, Breck," he said courteously to their companion.

"Certainly," came the smooth reply. "But before you go, do you know the man dancing with the black-haired woman in the blue dress? Does he work for the company or does she?"

"I know them both," was the curiously curt reply. "Shall I bring them to the table for an introduction?"

"Yes."

Royal command could not have been more sure of obedience, and blue eyes dismissed the standing couple to return to the swirling couples on the dance floor. It took a moment to locate the blue dress again, but once found, the blue eyes tenaciously kept the flash of color in view until, and after, the music blared its last drum-heavy note.

The eyes noted the approach of the older couple, redhead clinging limpetlike to the suited arm of her escort; saw the stiffening of the supple blue figure and the instinctive, abortive motion away from the speaking man; saw, narrow-eyed, the supportive, protective arm of the brown-haired escort go around the waist of the blue-dressed figure as the group of four turned to approach the head table.

The gold-haired giant rose as the two couples neared, and Andrea's stormy gray eyes traveled up the looming monolith to meet bright blue eyes under

10

hooded lids. Had it not been for Johnny, she would have had no compunction about refusing her father's request—huh, command described it better—to meet the new, or rather soon-to-be, owner of the company. As an executive vice-president, standing in for a stroke-felled president, her father played the part of host tonight. Johnny, lowly on the rungs of power, was vulnerable to any overt insult she might vent upon her revered parent.

Besides, Andrea had given her promise not to spit in his eye, overwhelming though the temptation might be. The memory of her mother's twisted, pain-tense body, which even merciful drugs could not make flaccid, churned bitter gall in the back of her throat, envenoming any words she could choke past that sharp-edged lump in her throat.

She barely listened to the smoothly practiced charm of her father's voice as he embarked on the introductions, but she did not miss the almost imperceptible start of surprise on the part of the giant when her father, oozing saccharine pride, announced their relationship.

"Ah, Breck, allow me to present my lovely daughter, Andrea, and her escort for the evening, one of our very bright young men, John McKay. Andrea, John, this is Breck Carson, soon to be your boss and mine, John."

Andrea was alerted to some undefined, strained inflection in her father's voice . . . she knew every lying intonation so well . . . but before she could analyze it, her automatically outstretched hand was taken in an engulfing clasp and her attention was captured by the voice that matched its hard strength so well.

"Miss Thomas," he acknowledged. "How remiss

11

of your father not to assure you and your escort a place at the head table."

He did not miss the steely flash in her level gray eyes and the sardonic curl of her full lips, nor the underlying chill in her husky contralto as she answered him politely but firmly.

"My father knows I prefer not to be on view at the head table, Mr. Carson, and I am sure he is surprised to see me here tonight. I do not usually appear at these functions and have done so tonight only at Johnny's behest."

She withdrew her hand from his clasp and tucked it back through Johnny's arm. "I have no connection with the company and am here only as Johnny's guest. I am not my father's hostess. Many others fill that role willingly."

Her voice was now a soft drawl and her gaze flickered dismissively over the redhead, who glared venomously at her. Andrea met her glare levelly, and Breck was interested to note that the redhead's green eyes fell before the contemptuous gray ones. He was even more interested to observe the dark flush that stained the face of her father, the father she so pointedly ignored with half-turned shoulder and averted face.

Was the girl condemnatory because of the obvious relationship between the father and his secretary? A daughter's jealousy over a diversion of attention away from herself, or deeper moral scruples? With a face and figure like hers, she certainly would not lack masculine attention herself, and latent fire burned beneath that icy glaze that so effectively cooled what he surmised would normally be dove-soft gray eyes. He came to a decision.

"McKay, I hope you'll allow me the pleasure of a dance with your charming date?"

It was phrased as a request, but rock-hard command underlay the smooth words. Even so, Johnny looked down questioningly at Andrea, and only after her tiny nod of acquiescence did he answer graciously, "Of course, Mr. Carson."

He relinquished Andrea's hand once more into Breck's keeping and smiled down at her. "I'll wait for you at our table, my dear. A pleasure to meet you, Mr. Carson." His smile to Breck was genuine, but his nod and "Mr. Thomas, Miss Stringer . . ." was perfunctory and just within the bounds of politeness.

Still never looking at her father, Andrea moved with economical grace to stand beside Breck, tilting her head back to meet his bright blue eyes. Her face was a perfect social mask, and he felt a violent impulse to force her response to him as a man. He already knew what he wanted from this woman, would have from this woman. Only the timing was at issue. Perhaps his own social mask was not impervious to her, because she went suddenly rigid and pulled her hand free of his.

"I believe you wished to dance, Mr. Carson?" she questioned him, lambent sparks flickering deep behind those gray eyes, which had suddenly gone depthless and impenetrable.

Andrea had read nothing in Breck's face. She had simply been overcome with a desire to go home, put her head down on her pillow, and cry. The accumulated stresses of the daily visits to her mother were wearing her down, and the confrontation with her father and his latest woman was nearly the final straw in a long and painful series of burdening straws. She saw Breck merely as a duty dance, to be

13

endured and, when done with, forgotte... She had not yet registered him as a man, a personality, only as piercing blue eyes and looming height. Her artist's eye would have enabled her to sketch him from swift memory, but only as the shell of a face, the personality behind it as yet undiscovered.

He led her onto the floor, and she automatically came into his arms. Her body was graceful and quick to follow his lead, but for all the sensual awareness she had of him, he might as well have been his own grandfather. Breck knew it and the realization stung.

He was determined to make her aware of him, to shock her awake if necessary. Was she in love with her escort? The thought was disturbingly unpalatable. What was the source of the all too obvious tension between father and daughter?

Breck was used to thinking on several levels at once, and while one portion of his mind considered the girl in his arms, another pondered the implications of the situation as it might affect one of the key executives of the company he was about to acquire. He needed more information. He had to untangle the twisted skeins of human relationships and lie them straight for his understanding.

Vigorous and ambitious, Breck Carson had come from nowhere with nothing. He used his body to win a sports scholarship and his brain to make the best use of the facilities the university offered. He had worked nights and studied days, and only an abundant vitality and the legacy of a splendidly healthy body kept him from burning himself to a cinder from the pace he maintained. He went after what he wanted and, thus far, whether it were a company or a woman, had gotten it.

Arrogant, ruthless, merciless . . . his enemies used

them all. Honest, brilliant, able . . . his friends and admirers retorted. None said gentle or benign.

They had danced in silence, bodies smoothly fitted together in the harmony of the music. Given the extra inches by her shoes, Andrea's head came just below the level of Breck's chin, and the faint fragrance of her hair had tantalized him ever since she had come obediently to his clasp. He could feel the silky softness of the blue-black shining cap of waves and curls . . . soft, not coarse. There was *nothing* coarse about the fine-boned elegance of this girl. Something sad and angry and hurt perhaps, but never gross or coarse.

"You said you had no connection with the company," he began probingly. "Are you still at school, then? Or do you occupy your days with Junior League and good works?"

"I visit the sick," she retorted with savage bitterness, betrayed by the memory of the afternoon she had spent, helpless and agonized, beside her mother's bed, parrying questions about the whereabouts of her father.

"I'm sorry!" she apologized immediately. "That was inexcusable." She continued in a forcedly normal tone. "Actually, I'm a commercial artist. I freelance, do book covers and illustrations, and when I have the time and energy, manage to dabble in oils and portraiture for the good of my artistic soul." She smiled whimsically up at him. "Art for art's sake may be good for the soul, but it tends to rubberize the checks you write for groceries and rent. Hence the descent into the mundane commercial world."

He probed further and hit a nerve.

"Are your oils good?"

"Yes," she admitted with simple candor.

"Well, surely your father could subsidize you until you—" He broke off abruptly as she lifted icy pale eyes to scan his face. No woman had ever looked at him with such chill contempt.

"I left my father's house when I was eighteen. I took nothing he had given me when I left and I take nothing from him now. I cannot help the blood that flows in my veins, and someday I shall change the name I bear. I am as polite as I am able when I am forced to endure his company, which is as infrequently as I can make it. The rest of the time I assiduously avoid seeing or thinking about him. Is there anything else you wish to know about the relationship between my father and myself?" She gave him no chance to answer, continuing in level, precise tones. "No? Good. The dance is ending. Please escort me to my table."

She slipped out of his arms as the music ended and turned toward the table where Johnny waited. Breck grasped her elbow firmly, intending to detain her, and swung her back to face him.

"Don't walk away from me, Andrea," he ordered harshly.

She looked down at the hand that was clamped above her elbow and then back up to meet his blue eyes squarely. "Then walk beside me. I do not care to dance again, and I wish to return to my date. I'm very tired, and he'll take me home. It was a mistake for me to come. I knew better . . . I won't make this mistake ever again."

"I'll take you home."

They started threading their way slowly through the dancers who remained on the floor. Andrea was at the end of her tether, and she knew if she didn't go home soon, she'd lose what thin shreds of control

16

still remained within her. Breck Carson, with his probing and prodding, had lifted the thin scabs of her wounds, and the poison that festered beneath was oozing irresistibly forth. The reserve she had so painfully cultivated these past three years seemed easily shattered by this dynamic, imperious man. Instead of ignoring his questions, she flew at him in rage, exposing her vulnerability with hasty, anguished words.

She was so tired. She had been working against a deadline for the past week, and the late nights and tension had taken a heavy toll. The visits to her mother every afternoon battered her emotionally and also forced her to work long, late hours to make up the time lost at the nursing home.

Then, this morning, she had mailed off the completed work, accepting the registered mail receipt from the mail clerk with a dazzling smile and a gay quip. As she reentered her apartment her phone had begun to ring. Johnny caught her in a mood to celebrate. He offered dinner and dancing, and not until they were in the car had he disclosed that the price she would pay for her evening out was to attend a company party given in honor of the new owner.

She had remonstrated, but the lateness of the hour and Johnny's imperative need to make an appearance for form's sake overrode her well-founded objections. It wasn't really Johnny's fault, Andrea admitted fairly to herself. He knew of the estrangement, but not of its depth and breadth. He was new to the company, though an old friend from her high school days, and had been away at college at the time she moved out and her mother entered the nursing home.

Rumor had informed Johnny of the liaison between Devlin Thomas and his lush secretary, but he

17

had not expected the blatancy of their association and the subsequent effect it was to have on Andy's nerves. Now he wished with all his heart that he had resisted temptation and been content to take Andy out for dinner another night. But she'd been so busy lately. . . .

He watched glumly as Andrea swirled and circled in the arms of his new boss. That was another thing. He didn't like the way Breck looked at her. He was attracted, but then most men were. When she was happy, Andy sparkled. Even strained and subdued she was a beautiful challenge, with a remote reserve appealing to both the predatory and protective instincts. Breck Carson was a man who took what he wanted, and Johnny hoped he didn't decide that he wanted Andy.

Breck's assured statement that he would take Andrea home would have in no way reassured the anxious Johnny. Andrea did not slow her steady exit from the dance floor, but she did answer back over her shoulder.

"You're the guest of honor," she reminded him, determined to be polite.

"I'm also the boss," was his retort. "If I want to leave, who's going to tell me to stay?"

"I will," Andrea flared again, "if you're only planning to leave because you want to take me home. I came with Johnny, and I'll leave with Johnny."

He tested her. "I'm Johnny's boss too."

At that she whirled, eyes no longer icily chill. Burning anger blazed in eyes gone dark with fury, and a hot flush flagged her high cheekbones. "Let's get something straight, Mr. Carson. First, you're not *my* boss and second, I don't blackmail." She looked closely at his impassive face, surprised to see no signs of anger. She continued with less heat. "And third, you wouldn't use your position as owner of this company to try to take another man's girl away. It's not your style."

"Are you his girl?"

"I'm his date. I'm no man's girl."

He gave a satisfied nod. "Good. I'll return you to your date. Just remember, when you're my date, I'll expect the same standard of loyalty."

If he had hoped to achieve a reaction to this pronouncement, he was disappointed. Andrea was exhausted and had the beginnings of a throbbing headache behind her right eye. The smoke and noise and blaring music completed the job the evening's events began, and now her dearest wish was to go home and sleep.

She forged steadily through the obstructing couples until she came to the table where Johnny stood waiting. With a polite half smile she mouthed the conventional phrases to Breck and then laid a beseeching hand on Johnny's arm.

"Johnny, dear, I'd like to go home now. May we leave, please?"

Johnny looked tenderly down at the weary, shadow-smudged face and agreed instantly. Both men watched as she gathered her purse from the table, and Johnny sprang forward with eager hands to help her into her lightweight jacket, which he lifted from the back of her chair. She thanked him with a small smile and tucked her hand into the crook of his bent elbow.

Breck watched them leave, not returning to the head table until they had actually left the room. He ignored all the speculative looks cast his way. Whatever he did would be food for gossip, and rumor

19

would swiftly make the most of his singling out Andrea. He had danced with no woman the whole evening, not even the all too willing Marta, nor had he planned to dance until he had seen Andrea across the room.

Social conventions had never overly concerned him. He used them when they had value to him and ignored them the rest of the time. He feared no man's censure nor cared for anyone's good opinion of him save his own. His business reputation was impeccable. He was acknowledged to be ruthless, shrewd, and possessed of an almost uncanny ability to acquire and reanimate faltering companies. Some he kept and some he sold, once they were healthy again, at no small profit for himself. Only two men had ever tried to cheat him. He broke them both. His own word was his bond, but he was known to keep some of the finest available legal minds on yearly retainer.

Of his personal life little was known except that there was one. No man with such a physical presence and cynically knowing eyes could be supposed not to have one, but even his most assiduous detractors could find no leverage in his personal life. He had escorted many attractive women, but was linked with none. Gossip columnists found him poor fare and, moreover, dangerous fare, as one unwary columnist discovered after an unsuccessfully defended suit for slander beggared him and disastrously affected the balance sheet of a newspaper that had once employed him. If Breck's name appeared in the columns now, it was as a mere passing reference. H̄ was ferociously discreet and willing to go to so lengths to remain so.

The sooner she could forget the evening's events,

the better. Andrea laid her head wearily back against the head rest of the seat in Johnny's car. She acknowledged that she needed a holiday, but knew she couldn't take one. Her mother depended heavily on her daily visits, and after her discussion with the doctor today, she accepted the fact that all too soon she would be free to go where she would and do as she pleased. There would be nothing more to hold her to this place.

Three years of faithful daily visits, of searching the stores for amusing and distracting presents. It was fortunate that she had been successful as a commercial artist. Out of season fruit to tempt a laggard appetite and out of season flowers to interest and brighten four monotonous walls don't come cheaply. She never went to see her mother without some small offering . . . a new book, a puzzle or new music cassette, or perhaps a wickedly drawn cartoon to illustrate an amusing story she would relate to her mother. Love and pity made her endlessly inventive, and the room that was her mother's prison had the character of a home, insofar as such a room can.

Andrea had prevailed upon the proprietors of the nursing home to allow her to replace the usual curtains and bed cover with ones she herself supplied. Those she changed often to give her mother a variation in surroundings. Textures, colors, hand painted fabrics . . . she utilized them all to broaden the constricted environment her mother was condemned to endure.

The nurses admired and adopted her ideas where they could so other long-term patients benefited from Andrea's determined refusal to allow shackling pain to narrow her mother's life to days of dreary sameness. When she changed the curtains and bedspread, she passed the discarded ones on to some other long-resident sufferer. Books and bibelots made the rounds of rooms, and her lightning fast cartoons and caricatures could generally draw a smile from the dourest of patients.

The price Andrea paid was not in hard-earned money alone. She paid in time, in late nights racing to meet deadlines. She paid in smiles and cheerful words while her heart was dripping bloody tears. Her eyes were sad and wise before their time . . . to watch the anguish of a loved one is often harder than to experience the physical torment oneself.

And now . . . her long vigil was drawing inexorably to a close. The doctor had been blunt this afternoon. The dosages of merciful opiate had been increased again. It was the beginning of that long, final slide to surcease from all pain, forerunner to the time of release from the days of purgatory for her mother . . . and not only the purgatory of physical pain.

As much as she could Andrea had avoided an overlap of visiting time with her father. Her mother knew her feelings toward her father. When and while he made his duty visits, Andrea left. She was polite, as to a stranger newly met. More she could not be, even for her mother's ease. Infinite forgiveness was beyond her. Her mother was a saint, purified by love and pain. Andrea was human and she hated.

"I am sorry, Andy." Johnny apologized again, breaking into her train of thought.

"It's okay, Johnny," she assured him. "You couldn't have known. It's not something one talks about . . . the fact that one despises one's father."

The light from the streetlamps that flickered past aged and harshened the contours of her bone structure. In the glances he could spare from concentration on the road, Johnny didn't miss the grim set of her mouth or the controlled tenseness in the clear line of her jaw.

She was much changed. Even in high school she had been oddly mature, never giggly or gawky. There had been an innate air of reserve to set her apart from the common run of girls, but in spite of, or perhaps because of, this same reserve, she was one of the most popular people in her class. Cheerleader, homecoming princess, student council officer . . . all had been hers without her seeking them.

But now? No flashes of impish humor brightened the grave, level gaze. Control, not serenity, sculpted the planes of her face. Johnny longed to probe, but there was a daunting impenetrability about her that even an old friend hesitated to confront. Even with his extra years he felt a youth yet to her maturity.

Andrea hoped that he would be content to take her home and leave her there. By clock hours it was still early, but her day had been years long. When he parked in front of the building that housed her apartment, she made the small but unmistakable preparations for imminent departure that told him he wouldn't be wise to attempt to detain her.

Sensitive to nuances and withal no fool, he promptly got out of the car and walked around to help her out. They shared the noisy elevator to the top floor in silence and traversed the short hall to her door. She had her key ready, and it slid smoothly into the lock.

"May I call you in a few days, Andy?" His question was diffident.

"Of course, Johnny, dear. Please do." She tried to inject as much warmth as possible into the permission, but exhaustion made it ring flat. Just now she didn't care whether she ever saw him again or not. Any emotion, even that of friendship, seemed to require too great an effort.

Obediently Johnny kept his good-night kiss brief and as nearly passionless as he could manage, and after bidding her not to watch him to the elevator, he left her. Andrea took him at his word and went directly into her apartment and locked the door behind her.

As the dead bolt snicked home she sagged back against the door, head bowed, shoulders drooping. She stayed that way for a long moment and then, with a thrust of her shoulders, levered herself away from the door. Her footsteps clicked a dispirited rhythm across the polished wooden floor, muffled momentarily when she cut across the corner of the area rug near the couch, heading toward the rectangle of light that spilled toward her from the bedroom door.

As she entered her bedroom she tossed her purse on the single bed and went directly to the wall-to-wall, ceiling-to-floor, flower graphic decorated curtain, which matched the bedspread and the curtains at the window. When she had supervised the partitioning of the expansive open space of this building's top floor into rooms, there were no closets. With typical ingenuity she hung poles on chains attached to eye bolts driven into the ceiling beams and masked the contrivance with the false wall of the curtain. The fabric was hand printed with her own designs, as were the matching spread and curtains. She had painted the fabric herself, and a very talented friend transformed the lengths of cloth into a quilted spread and drapes.

For the first year after she had left her father's

house Andrea had lived frugally in a small, very cramped furnished apartment. Then, as she began to find a larger measure of financial ease—she was really very talented—she started to look for something more spacious. By chance she heard of a building, once derelict offices, that some enterprising young people were renovating and turning into apartments.

She had investigated and found the terms agreeable and the top floor space ideal. It had large windows and a good exposure in the area she decided to make her studio, and when the owners promised to install a bathroom, kitchen, and room partitions at her direction, she signed the lease without a qualm.

She had never regretted it. She had privacy and space and if not much furniture, each piece she had was good, lovingly chosen after much searching. The partitions between the rooms were thin, but with only herself to consider . . . there was only one apartment per floor . . . the lack of soundproofing was no drawback. Color made the apartment cheery where lack of furniture might have chilled and emptied it. And it was hers alone, her citadel from which she issued forth, her refuge where she retreated to gather strength for the next day.

Andrea hung up her jacket and dress, lined her shoes neatly on the floor, and headed naked toward the bathroom to wash her face free of the light makeup she wore and to brush her teeth. She tossed her underclothes into the wicker basket that was her clothes hamper, creamed and cleansed her face, and grimaced unconsciously at the minty bite of the toothpaste she was currently using.

Just before she slid between the smooth sheets, she shoved a cassette into her portable tape recorder, which lay on the floor beside the head of her bed. She had no formal religious alliances, but at times found the sonorous rhythms of stately Gregorian chants calming and soothing. As the blended male voices began to drone softly into the stillness of the room, she burrowed into the sheets and waited for her body warmth to drive away the chill from her nest of covers. By the time the tape had wound its way to the end and shut off automatically, she was deeply asleep, curled tightly in a defensive ball, which relaxed only slightly as the night progressed toward the dawn.

She lay abed the next morning past a leisurely eight o'clock. When she raced a deadline, she generally rose at first light to begin work, but all her current commissions, except the one she had just completed, had no time limits save that of her need for the money they would bring. Her bank account was comfortably red-blooded, preserved from anemia by the infusion of checks for three recently completed assignments and the soon to be due check for the material she had sent off yesterday.

She showered, shampooed, and blew dry her glossy black cap of curls and dressed for the day. Since today was not to be a working day, she chose a simple cotton knit top, teamed with a gaily patterned skirt. She always wore vivid colors when she went on her visits to her mother, and today would be no exception. It was fortunate that she had the coloring to carry off the dramatic colors.

When she investigated the contents of her refrigerator, she realized what her morning's activities would have to be. She cubed some leftover steak and added it to the last two eggs, which were scrambling in the skillet. There was no bread, not even a stale heel, and she remembered she had used both heels at noon the day before yesterday for a hasty peanut butter and jelly sandwich.

She checked the freezer and the cupboard she laughingly dubbed the pantry. Not too bad . . . not a complete restock, then. She just needed the perishables and a nibbler's supply of fruit, oh, and another jar of peanut butter. Never run out of peanut butter, she admonished herself silently. It's stood between you and starvation many a time during a rushed assignment.

Just before she left on her shopping expedition, she called the nursing home to bid her mother good morning and ask, as always, if there was anything special she could get before she came for her afternoon visit. And sadly, as always, the reply was, "Nothing, dear."

No, there was indeed nothing. What her mother needed most of all, a faithful husband and legs that walked, was beyond Andrea's power to give her.

Determined not to be enmeshed in a black mood, she made a hasty exit from the apartment. As she headed for the fire stairs she heard the muted burr of the phone and debated for a moment whether to return and answer it. It would not be her mother, but it might possibly be her father, calling to take her to task for her behavior last night. Perhaps he wished to protect his image before his new boss.

That thought made her decide. She entered the stairwell, and as the fire door closed behind her the phone sounds were cut in mid-ring. She usually walked down the stairs and quite frequently up them as well unless burdened by packages. Her life was far more sedentary than she would have liked, and it was a small way of exercising.

27

Just before lunch time she returned, riding up in the elevator in deference to the two heavy bags of groceries she was balancing precariously in her arms. She knew she should have brought them up one at a time, but was loath to make two trips when one would do. It took some rather involved contortions, balancing one bag on an uplifted knee, steadied by her arm, to allow her to reach the sixth floor button, but the elevator began to rise with the bags still safely intact.

She negotiated the short hall to her front door rather quickly, because she could feel an ominous tear beginning at the side of the bag where a damp patch had weakened the paper. It was her preoccupation with the sacks she carried that caused her to miss seeing the flowers immediately.

They were certainly lovely enough to command attention, and the vibrant crimson of the topmost buds soon caught the corner of her eye. She knelt before her door and eased the grocery bags gingerly to the floor. From that position she was nearly nose to nose with a glorious arrangement of roses, all half-opened buds, shading in color from a pure virgin white to pale then deeper pink, and on through a spectrum ending in a clear, passion-dark crimson.

It should have been ostentatious, but instead it was breathtaking. A chaste cream envelope was tucked amid the glossy green foliage, but she left it where it was for the moment. The groceries were her first priority, and if she didn't get that one bag inside, she'd be chasing oranges down the hall.

After attending to the groceries, she carefully carried the vase of flowers inside, setting it on the dining table. Some water had slopped over, so she mopped it up and slid a protective plate beneath the vase lest it leave a ring on the table. Only then did she take out the envelope and open it to withdraw the card.

An aggressive black scrawl slashed across the flat card and she deciphered the message curiously: "I'll pick you up for dinner at seven p.m. Friday night. Wear a long dress."

It was signed with the initials B.C. Who the devil was B.C., and what the hell did he mean by sending her such an outrageous message? She had met a new doctor at the nursing home, and she could tell he'd like to ask her out. His name was Robert Culhane, but he was rather shy and this—she snapped the card with an irritated fingernail—didn't seem at all his style.

Her forehead creased in perplexed thought, and she tapped the edge of the card meditatively against her front teeth. Was it perhaps Johnny's idea of an amende honorable for the debacle of last night? She dismissed that idea almost before it had a chance to form. Johnny would have to forgo all his lunches for a month to come up with the wherewithal for such an expensive invitation to dinner. And . . . not his style either. If he gave her flowers, they would probably be filched from his mother's garden and all she ever managed to grow were zinnias!

Style. That struck a chord somewhere. Someone aggressive and blunt, used to taking what he wanted. Two bright blue eyes floated into her inner vision. Good God! Breck Carson, the new boss man.

Her first thought was, What arrogant nerve! Her second, He can't be serious! and her third, as she looked at the decisive black writing again and from the card to the flowers, He is serious. Do I want to go?

She hesitated, then walked over to the telephone.

She flipped through the phone book, ran a slim forefinger down a line of listings, and then dialed. When the switchboard answered, she said crisply, "Connect me with Mr. Carson's office, please."

She waited, drumming suddenly agitated fingers on the table while the receiver spat forth a series of clicks and buzzes, and when another female voice informed her that she now spoke to Mr. Carson's secretary, Andrea drew in a deep breath and said, "This is Andrea Thomas. I wish to speak with Mr. Carson, please."

The impersonal businesslike tones underwent a dramatic change. "Oh, Miss Thomas. I'm Miss Jenkins. Mr. Carson told me to expect your call. He told me to assure you that he would indeed be back by Friday." The secretary assumed a chatty, confiding tone and continued, "He called me from the airport just before his plane took off, and gave me my instructions. I've just received confirmation, in fact, that tickets for the opening night will be waiting at the box office for you and Mr. Carson." Her voice held distinct tones of awe. "The tickets are coming directly from Devon Harmon, you know. Isn't he just super? Mr. Carson is a personal friend of his, and to think that he'll be at the opening night party afterward . . ." Her voice trailed off in near ecstasy.

Andrea fought the impulse to break into hysterical giggles. The voice chattered relentlessly onward. "Was there anything else, Miss Thomas? Mr. Carson gave me strict instructions that if there was anything you needed, I was to put myself at your disposal." Her voice fairly quivered with eagerness to please.

"No. Thank you, Miss Jenkins," Andrea responded dryly. "I believe that just about covers everything.

You're sure Mr. Carson won't be back before Friday?"

This unleashed another spate of words. "Oh, no, Miss Thomas. In fact, he had been scheduled to be gone the full two weeks, but I was able to clear his reservation to return late Sunday night without too much trouble, and he said he would take care of coming in on Friday himself."

There was nothing left to say. Andrea extricated herself from the conversation before Miss Jenkins swept them both away on another floodtide of eloquence. She rather hoped the woman had good dictation and typing speeds as part of her qualifications because discretion did not seem to be one of her secretarial skills. Andrea had a feeling that Miss Jenkins would not long reign as Breck Carson's confidential secretary. Confiding she was. Confidential she was not!

Mechanically she began to put the groceries away, moving between the counter and the refrigerator as she pondered all that the voluble Miss Jenkins had disclosed. Somehow Breck had managed to arrange for tickets for the new, highly touted Devon Harmon play, and the opening night performance at that. The play had been sold out for the entire first month's run for the past six weeks and tickets for later performances were devilishly hard to get. Even the scalpers weren't able to find tickets for the early performances, but Breck had managed to do so between the time Andrea left him at the party and before his plane took off.

She shivered slightly. The man wielded power.

While she ate a small chef's salad Andrea tried to call Breck's features to mind. She could see only piercing blue eyes. She went into her studio and came

31

back out with a block of sketch paper and an artist's pencil. If her mind could not tell her, her fingers would. She began to slash swift, dramatic strokes on the paper, her salad forgotten.

When she was done, she ripped off the top sheet of paper and propped it against the vase of flowers. The crisp, aggressive lines of the portrait contrasted sharply with the sensuous softness of the flowers. A very disturbing man looked back at her.

It was a direct gaze, clear and uncompromising. If there was any softness in this man, it was buried too deeply for her fingers to find. He liked his own way and knew how to get it. Possessive . . . what I have, I hold . . . it was there in the thrust of the squared-off chin. The mouth was firm, controlled, but yet she knew, almost as though she had seen and felt it, the lips could soften into sensuality and spark wild hunger where they touched.

Handsome? No, too strong a face for that sleek descriptive. Some Viking ancestor had left his seed behind when he came a-raiding, to reincarnate in bone and blood in these modern times. An imperious nose to match an imaginary winged helm and springing dark gold hair, worn slightly long, but burnished with an almost metallic sheen.

Disturbing and . . . dangerous. A warrior who would take a captive or a concubine and leave her behind without a qualm when it was time for the next foray. Her hand went out to crush the sketch and then drew back slowly. What the hand had seen, the mind should remember. She would keep the sketch as a reminder.

CHAPTER TWO

Her mother was much the same, soft brown eyes faded and sunken, the color leeched away by constant pain. Her hair, once a thick, rich auburn, was gray and sparsely lank. Andrea had arranged for a hairdresser to come twice a week to condition and style it, but when the body's vitality is gone, no skill can keep the hair from reflecting the truth. Her skin was crumpled, not with the soft lines of graceful age but sharply grooved and scored, as though a stiff piece of paper had been twisted between two hands and only roughly flattened out again, leaving sharp corners and deep creases to mar its once smooth surface.

The wasted, twisted body was shielded from sight by a softly shirred nightgown and matching bed jacket, but the stick-thin arms with ropy blue veins and fleshless fingers told the tale. Her mother was forty-seven years old. Her hands belonged to a crone of double her years.

Andrea's heart wept but her face smiled as she bent to kiss her mother's withered cheek. She rummaged in her purse and pulled forth a brightly papered package, tied with a broad velvet ribbon which needed only a tug to release itself. Her mother loved the feel of soft-napped fabrics and could stroke the rich blue width as though it were an Angora-soft pet.

When the paper was laid back, a spring-flowered muslin sachet bag was revealed and the evocative scent of old lavender drifted up to tease the nostrils. Jeanne Thomas lifted the bag in tremulous hands, the better to inhale the memory-rich scent. Small pleasures alone were left her and scent enjoyment was one. Her old, accustomed perfumes turned acid sour on her skin now, but Andrea insured that her soaps and lotions had pleasing fragrances and that her bedwear hung in scented proximity to pomander balls until it lay soft and aromatic against her sere skin.

"We'll pin the bag to your pillow so that you need only turn your head to catch the scent easily," Andrea assured her and suited actions to words. The pin she used to anchor the bag in place was an enameled purple and gold pansy face, a charming little frippery which did the job as well as the utilitarian safety pin another might have used. A small touch, but small touches lifted the spirit, and when one's whole existence is bound within four sterile walls, small touches and small irritations assume magnified importance.

"Thank you, darling." Jeanne thanked her daughter for more than the sachet. "I'll enjoy it in the night."

Andrea's heart twisted. The wakeful dark nights when her mother twisted on the rack of pain and fought the silent losing battle. Even the ever stronger doses of mercy could not totally cage the sharp-clawed tiger which gnawed her spine.

"How is the painting you're working on now coming along?" Jeanne asked. When a painting was finished, Andrea always brought it to show to her mother and, if Jeanne desired, arranged to hang it for several days so that she might enjoy it before it went to those who commissioned it or had bought it. Her oils always sold well, but the commercial assignments took less time and paid much better for the time involved.

Time was subjective but not elastic, and since she never skimped on her visits to her mother, the time must come from that allotted to serious painting. Consequently there was a backlog of commissions that she worked on as she was able, or when the prodding from impatient clients was more importunate than usual.

"It's almost finished. I should be able to bring it for you to see sometime next week. I'm very pleased with it. Sylvia Carrington saw it in embryo and paid a deposit on the spot. She's been amazingly, for her, patient, especially since she plans to make it the focal point for her living room and is holding the decorator off until I've completed it. She only calls me once a week. When I was working on the one she has hanging in her guest room, she called me twice a week until I threatened to wipe the whole thing out with turpentine." Andrea grinned. "That scared her so badly that I didn't hear from her again until I called her to come pick it up. You remember that one, don't you? The field of wild flowers with the single bleached tree in the left foreground? You liked it so much, we left it hanging for a week and a half."

"Oh, yes. That was one of my favorites. You could almost see the flowers move as the wind passed by. You brought me a bouquet of the same kind of flowers that week. I remember it well. I held them in my hands and imagined I had just picked them from the

35

field. I even felt the texture of that dried, dead tree
. . . the smooth peeled places and the patches of
rough bark. It was a very good painting, Andrea."
Her voice was quiet and dreaming, perhaps back in
time when she could have indeed walked in the field
and touched the tree.

Andrea half turned her head, looking out the window. Her voice was steady but her eyes were moist.
"I'm glad it gave you pleasure, Mother. Would you
like to see it again? I can borrow it from Sylvia for
as long as you like."

"Yes, I think I would." Jeanne's voice still had
that reminiscent tone.

"I'll bring it with me tomorrow, Mother," Andrea
promised.

They talked of other things. Andrea read the
newspaper to her mother and then several chapters
of a current best seller. There was a rack to hold the
book at a comfortable angle so that Jeanne need only
turn the pages, but she loved the sound of her daughter's voice, husky and musical, so Andrea read aloud
whenever and from whatever Jeanne requested.

Soft-footed and smiling, a nurse came in to give
the early evening shot and pills, the signal for Andrea
to prepare to leave. While the drugs held greatest
potency her mother could sleep, recouping somewhat the strength pain drained away, but the credit
and debit sides never balanced out. Always the slow,
remorseless seepage. The cup never filled again to the
same level, but ever lower. One day the ebb would
turn no more.

Andrea bent to kiss the proffered cheek farewell as
she did in greeting, but her mother's attention was
fixed on the brief oblivion the nurse held in capable
hands. Her good-bye was preoccupied, almost curt,

and Andrea smiled sadly at the waiting nurse, receiving knowing commiseration in return. They came, they went, but the pain stayed. To drive it back for even a short time was a boon she would not delay or deny her mother for an instant.

The days before Friday were busy. Several new assignments came in, the flowers on her dining table opened to full glory and then blown, began to drop their petals. Andrea obtained the loan of the picture she had promised her mother by agreeing to hurry completion of Sylvia's new picture. She shopped, she visited her mother, and sometimes in the solitude of her apartment she wondered how long she could keep the pace.

On Thursday she decided to treat herself to a dress worthy of a Devon Harmon opening night. The check for the commission she had mailed off the day she met Breck arrived in the morning's mail and with uncharacteristic extravagance she decided it would be symbolically meet to use most of it to outfit herself appropriately. The dress she chose did indeed consume a goodly portion of the check and was worth every paint-spattered penny.

It was black and anything but basic. She took it with her when she went to see her mother and even slipped it on to model it. Several of the nurses came in to "ooh" and "aah" and to comment enviously about her good fortune in getting to see Devon Harmon. When her mother proudly announced that Andrea was going to the opening night cast party as well, the exclamations redoubled in force. Andrea was adjured to remember Devon Harmon's every word and facial expression to enable her to render a faithful accounting the next day.

Friday came and, although the week could not be said to have dragged, she greeted the morning with almost a sigh of relief. She was, she admitted honestly, looking forward to the evening. Though she was not particularly overawed by the Devon Harmon mystique, he was a fine actor. The story line of the play was intriguing and, after all, a first night is a first night!

She put in a short morning at work, finishing Sylvia's picture. With proper precautions she could take it for her mother to see and enjoy over the weekend before delivering it to Sylvia early next week. A day to dry, and she'd hang it for her mother, unframed, tomorrow.

Precisely at seven that night an imperative knock rapped twice on the front door. Andrea opened the door and stepped back, inviting him in by a gesture with her left hand.

He really was magnificently male! Her fingers had not lied. The severe elegance of his evening attire fitted the massively broad shoulders and narrow waist without a wrinkle. No off-the-peg rental tux would fit him, and he wore the formal clothes with an accustomed ease speaking of casual familiarity.

He stepped into the apartment and she closed the door behind him. She turned back to face him and discovered he had not taken his eyes from her. His face was inscrutable, but his eyes were a bright, dark-pupiled blue. His intense gaze made her nervous.

"G-good evening, Breck." Not knowing what else to do, she held out a shy hand to him.

In a totally unexpected maneuver he used her outstretched hand to pull her gently near and dropped a petal-soft kiss directly on her surprised mouth, for all the world as though they were old friends meeting again after an absence of months.

While she gaped speechlessly at him he said in satisfaction, "I knew I'd remembered."

"Remembered? Remembered what?" she asked faintly.

"How beautiful you are . . . and how much I was looking forward to kissing you. Although," he considered judiciously, "that really wasn't much of a kiss. Care to try again?"

She moved hastily backward. He grinned suddenly and remarked, "Pity. You've made it very difficult for me to concentrate on anything else this past week."

Before she could respond he turned to survey the room, and she was sure not an item escaped that incisive gaze. "Very nice. Your own work?" He had moved to stand before the focal point of the living room, a fantasy underseascape of swirling blues and greens interspersed with streaks of yellow, red, and orange, which coalesced into fantastic coral shapes as one looked. He peered closely at the upper right corner and she smiled quietly. He'd seen the mermaid's face, her own, which had the disconcerting habit of becoming visible, only to vanish in a clever optical illusion. The face was attatched to the faithful rendering of her own nicely curved upper body, which was in turn melded into a sinuous fish's tail.

It was really quite a modest work, because it was impossible to hold the focus of the eyes long enough to make out much specific detail. One blink and the mermaid coyly dissolved again into blue-green formless mist.

He chuckled. "She's quite a tease." He looked Andrea up and down as though considering just how faithful the rendering of the mermaid had been. "You were much too modest."

Andrea stiffened and her eyes sparked with incipient ire.

"You told me your oils were merely good," he continued smoothly, leaving her to wonder if he had indeed meant the double entendre. "You are extremely talented. Have you many completed canvases ready? Enough for a small show?"

"I'm afraid not," she said a trifle coolly, more than a little suspicious of his bland innocence. "Almost all of my canvases are commissioned and those that aren't sell too rapidly for me to build up enough material for a full-scale show. The only ones I have on hand are a few personal ones which are for my own pleasure and are not for sale. I do have one I've just completed, but it's been sold too. I'm to deliver it next week, but you may see it now if you'd like."

She took him into the studio and flicked on the overhead lights. She had used a variation of the technique which had achieved the mermaid's elusive qualities to impart a sense of breeze-directed movement to the peaceful woodland glade. No animal life was visible, but one felt that only seconds before, the open space had teemed with motion. The viewer, an intruder, had just sent the glade's inhabitants scurrying for cover and even now eyes peered, hidden in the dappled, shifting shadows, waiting for the alien presence to leave so that a normal routine could resume. The ear was tricked into listening for the rustle of leaves, depending on the message from the eyes that the leaves had just moved.

He moved to view the painting from several angles, shook his head, and stepped back to her side again. "Amazing. The textures of the bark and leaves, the shifting light and shade . . . add scent and sound and we're there." He looked sternly down at her. "You waste time on commercial art when you are capable of this?" He waved an expressive hand at the painting.

"This," she in turn waved toward the painting, "is not done in a day, nor yet a week. Some day, perhaps . . . but for now, I have to eat and I have other obligations." None of which are your business, her tone implied.

"And I think I'd better feed you." He smiled down at her. "You're obviously hungry."

And you're obviously a master of the innuendo, she thought rather sourly, implying my temper and perhaps my manners suffer when I'm hungry. Well, Mr. Carson, if I'm ungracious, you're nosy, and she firmly flicked the lights in the studio off as they left the room.

She gathered her wrap and purse and switched off all the lights except one small one by the couch. The diffuse illumination made a dark mystery of the sea scene, heightening the illusion of restless waters, and Breck shook his head in admiring bewilderment.

"I'll be damned if I see how you achieve that effect. If I touched the painting, I'd expect my fingers to come away wet."

She stood by the door, the key for the dead bolt in her hand. "There's a small one in my bedroom in which a school of fish appear and then disappear. That one took me two months, off and on. It was the first one that really achieved the effect I was after." Her face shadowed. "I was seventeen when I finished it."

She locked the door behind them and dropped the key into her purse. She headed automatically for the stairwell and then caught herself. "Sorry. I usually go up and down the stairs. It's my one regular form of exercise; but not"—she grinned—"when I'm all gussied up."

When they were in the car and driving toward wherever he was taking her to dinner—he hadn't said and she didn't ask—he returned to the subject of the painting she had just completed. He wanted to know to whom she had sold it and she told him, explaining that Sylvia also had another one of her paintings. She wondered why he had wanted to know, so she asked him.

"Because I want to buy it from her," he admitted bluntly.

"Oh," she responded, rather blankly. She supposed it was flattering that he liked her work so well, but she was reminded of the ruthless determination which had appeared so clearly in the sketch she'd done of him and she was uneasy. Her work was a part of her, a piece of her thoughts and skills, and she wasn't sure she wanted him to own any part of her, even a painting.

"I don't think you'll be able to convince Sylvia to sell," she advised him. "She's waited several months for this particular painting, and she's planning to redecorate her living room around it."

He merely smiled slightly and began to talk of other things. She followed his lead obediently and they talked amiably and volubly through an excellent dinner, right up until the curtain rose on the first act.

Andrea discovered that Breck had a dry, incisive wit, when he cared to display it, and a keen, exciting mind. They argued, agreed, and argued again on a broad range of subjects, and while she could not match him for depth of knowledge in all areas, she knew she gave a good account of herself.

She didn't bore him and more than once his deep chuckle rumbled forth as she scored with some sally. Halfway through dinner she realized, with some amusement, that he had deftly put her at ease. Her initial wariness had melted away beneath the balm of his charm. She was truly enjoying herself, more so than she could ever remember, and it wasn't just the delicious dinner and the prospect of a first-rate play. It was the man himself.

When they left the restaurant, she made no demur when he tucked her hand beneath his arm, covering it possessively with his own large hand as they strolled to the theater, which was only a block away.

The timing was perfect. The tickets were waiting and they were escorted to their superb seats with unhurried leisure. There was time to settle comfortably and to scan the program and then, almost as if at their specific command, the house lights dimmed, the curtain rose, and the play began.

Andrea smiled. She laughed and then she cried. She pulled herself away from the world the actors had created with an effort when intermission came, and as if he understood and was giving her time to readjust to reality, Breck led her silently out into the foyer, tucked her securely behind some scruffy potted nameless plant, and left her. He seemed hardly gone a minute before he materialized again, confronting her with two brimming champagne glasses carried steadily in his hands. She accepted one readily and sipped, cocking an eyebrow at him in surprise at its quality.

His answering grin was oddly boyish. "Private stock," he explained with a chuckle. "Devon arranged to have a bottle left for me in the theater manager's office."

"Beats waiting in line," she murmured. A thought struck her. "Are you, what's the term, an angel?"

"Not for this play," he denied, "but I have backed a couple of his plays before. He hopes I will again in the future." A faint lacing of cynicism threaded his voice, and he sipped the champagne as though it had suddenly soured slightly.

"You might have missed out on a good investment," she said lightly and led the conversation into a discussion of the play so far. Her diversionary tactics were successful and carried them through another glass of champagne and the return to their seats, where he possessed himself of her hand and refused to release it for the remainder of the play.

When the last bow had been taken, they waited calmly in their seats as the crowd cleared the aisles, and she turned to him with a smile. "Whew! I've really been wrung out. Quite a catharsis, and I enjoyed every moment of it. Thank you for the loan of your handkerchief. A Kleenex may be disposably sanitary, but a handkerchief is much more satisfying to weep into. You know," she added thoughtfully, "a good cry under artistic stimulation is really remarkably invigorating."

"Good," he responded. "Then I won't have to warn you to brace yourself. First-night parties are invariably raucous and exhausting. The suspense is over and everyone treats him or herself to one hearty blowout before settling down, they hope, to the grind of a long-term run. Devon's parties," he finished dryly, "have a tendency to be more so than most."

She looked at him curiously. "You don't sound much enamored of cast parties."

"I'm generally not much of a social animal," he explained carefully. "Large groups of drunks irritate me, and I prefer to entertain on a more intimate basis." He gave her a wicked smile and laughed at her involuntarily shocked expression.

She regathered her composure and said as repressively as possible, "Then why are we going to this one?"

"Because I thought you might enjoy it," he said simply. She was immediately disarmed, all her resurgent wariness quashed by the sincerity of his words. He continued, "I thought you'd like to meet Devon and some of the other members of the cast, and I believe the playwright will be there too. He comes to first-nights but refuses to appear and take public bows. But it's up to you. If you'd rather, we can go dancing. . . ."

"Oh, no," she broke in hastily. "I'd really like to go to the party. I've admired Devon Harmon as an actor for quite a while."

He was very astute. "But not as a man?" he queried perceptively.

"Well . . ." She hesitated, but whether Devon was his friend or not she could only answer candidly. "No, I don't admire him as a man. I don't think much of men who prove their virility and masculinity by the number of women they take to bed. That should be a special relationship between a man and a woman, not a numbers contest. Unless his reputation is a total fabrication, he has more notches on his bedpost than Baron von Richthofen had air kills."

Breck surprised her. "Good!" he said with obvious satisfaction. "If you don't like him as a man, I won't have to warn him to keep away from you. Devon does have an abiding weakness for lovely women,

45

and I wouldn't want to put his dresser to the trouble of having to disguise two black eyes for his stage appearances."

She thought he must be joking. He wasn't. She had only to look at the hard jut of his chin to realize he was perfectly serious. What was his, was his, and he didn't share.

The crowd had thinned and he guided her backstage. Quite a number of people greeted Breck cordially and he responded casually, congratulating them on the quality of the play. Andrea found it all fascinating and as they chatted with the second male lead while waiting for Devon to finish changing, she mused thoughtfully on the interesting process of metamorphosis the actors all underwent, from larger than life characters back into real-life human beings.

Breck duly introduced Devon before they all left to go to the hotel where the party was to be held. Andrea found him a most handsome animal, physically magnetic, but the use of her artist's fingers was not needed to lay bare his character. His eyes were dark and ardent, but his mouth had a lurking weakness. His charm was too well practiced and as a man he left her cold.

Breck must have been able to sense her perceptive summation of Devon, for, after watching their initial meeting with narrowed eyes, he suddenly relaxed and regarded the casually chatting pair amiably. Andrea was more than capable of keeping Devon in what Breck considered his place, and he seemed well content to let her do it. He did, however, tuck her hand in his arm once more, with a casually proprietorial air, when they all began to disperse before meeting again at the site of the party.

Devon watched this small byplay with an amused

and slightly rueful eye. Breck had found himself a real beauty, and it would have been interesting to have had a go at breaking through that intriguing air of reserve she wore like a cloak. A very tasty morsel, and he envied Breck first bite. He shrugged. His current leading lady was meal enough for any man.

Breck had been guilty of understatement, Andrea admitted silently. Devon's parties, if this were a representative sample, *were* more so than most. It seemed to be composed of a large number of wildly gesticulating, loudly talking people determined to consume tremendous amounts of liquor and very little else. The noise was just short of deafening, the haze of cigarette smoke steadily thickening, and the heat from the large number of bodies nearly stifled her. She had had enough.

Breck had been watching her closely and no sooner had she reached that conclusion than he bent to her and said quietly, "Had enough?"

She gave him a grateful smile. "Yes, please," she responded politely, a well brought up child. "It's gotten rather hot and noisy, hasn't it?"

"Yes, it has," he agreed smoothly. "We'll go somewhere quieter."

It wasn't what he said, and she really couldn't fault the way he said it, but suddenly Andrea had a flashing image of him as a Viking again, about to toss his spoils of war over his shoulder. Perhaps it was the way he had fended off the men who had tried to flirt with her, and there had been a considerable number of them.

She was an anomaly in this rather jaded, world-weary group, and she had drawn men's eyes like a magnet. Her serene reserve allied with her so obviously innocent enjoyment was irresistible, and a number of would-be gallants had tried their luck. At first Breck had seemed amused, content to allow Andrea to gently discourage without offense, but as the party had gotten louder and the advances more insistent, he had once again moved to make his claim obvious with a possessive arm about her waist.

No man with the smallest sense of self-preservation tries to take a juicy bone away from Cerberus, Andrea thought with amusement as the advances abruptly stopped.

There had been overtures toward Breck as well from the female segment of the party, but he had quickly, and in several instances rather brutally, made it clear that his only interest was in the woman who stood at his side. Even the leading lady, who was indeed a banquet to satisfy any man, received short shrift. She attempted to fling her arms around Breck's neck in exuberant greeting when she arrived on Devon's arm at the party, but was stopped by the firm grip of Breck's hands on her upper arms, which held her immobile several feet apart from him.

From the venomous look she shot at Andrea it was clear that she would not soon forget Andrea's witness of her humiliation, and several times during the evening Andrea intercepted seething glances directed her way. Breck had intercepted one of the glances and his face had become a hard mask.

It hadn't bothered Andrea in the least. She'd probably never see the woman again on a social basis, and her heavy-handed advances toward Breck had not touched Andrea at all. She was enjoying Breck's company, and it is never·pleasant when one's escort for the evening pays marked attention to another woman, but she felt no deeply possessive instincts toward him.

Andrea was, if anything, rather leery of becoming closely involved with any man. The legacy of distrust, an inheritance from her father's behavior, made her chary of bestowing trust, and for her, where there was no trust, there could be no relationship closer and deeper than mild friendship, or so she told herself. The real truth was that no man had yet laid seige to her emotions. At a time when other girls were trying out their fledgling powers of fascination, she was earning a living and sitting beside her mother's rack of agony.

For the first two years after her mother's accident, she had dated no one. Too raw from grief and guilt, too tired from her hectic work schedule, she had hoarded her small amount of free time like a miser, using it to put her emotional house back in order. For a long time she had shunned men, tarring them with her father's brush, but finally her natural common sense and sturdy emotional balance had reasserted itself and she began to date again. With a wry mental smile she had told herself that men were people too, some good, some bad, and all to be taken on an individual basis, judged on their own special merits, not prejudged through the screen of her hatred of her father. Her emotional maturity was just about to catch up with her physical maturity. She was ripe . . . and very vulnerable.

Devon started to object when he saw them preparing to leave the party early, but one level-eyed look from Breck's blue eyes choked the words unsaid in his throat. No sneering insinuations blurted forth either. Breck was capable of ramming unwise words back down the unfortunate throats of those who uttered them and his markedly possessive air was warning enough that the lady was *his* lady.

The byplay went totally over Andrea's head. The smoke and the noise had given her a headache that fresh air would cure, but while it lasted, nuances were beyond her. She appreciated Breck's immediate response to her unvoiced desire to leave but considered no implications. Since he had made it perfectly clear that the party was for her delectation, it was logical that they leave as soon as it ceased to be fun for her. She really didn't consider the insight that allowed him to know the instant she stopped enjoying herself. A more experienced woman would have.

The walk to the car cleared her head, blowing away the cobwebs of headache. She drew in deep lungfuls of crisp air and a sudden excess of joie de vivre overcame her natural dignity. She gave an impulsive skip, like a lamb gamboling in a spring meadow.

While Breck regarded her with almost paternal benevolence she tucked her arm confidingly through his and said with all the guileless candor of a child, "Thank you so much, Breck. The dinner was delicious, the play excellent, and the party a real experience. I enjoyed myself immensely." She smiled teasingly up at him before continuing in mock sorrowful tones, "And to think that I almost didn't come."

"And why didn't you almost come?" he asked indulgently, enjoying the play of the streetlights over her superb bone structure.

"Because I like to be asked, not told, even with such beautiful messengers," she responded, momentarily serious.

"Ah, but I only ask when I'm sure I'm going to get the answer I want. When I'm not sure the response will be favorable, I tell, not ask. It saves time."

"And when you tell, people do?" Her voice was still bantering, expecting him to laugh at the absurdity of a man *always* getting his own way.

"Yes, they do, little one."

She wrinkled her nose at him, still refusing to take him seriously. "Shall I tug my forelock, my lord, and sweep a humble curtsy?"

He chuckled at that. "You curtsy, men tug their forelocks. And then I sweep you up on my war-horse and carry you off to exercise my droit de seigneur, the fate of all lovely maidens who catch the eye of the lord of the manor."

"You're no lord of the manor. You're a Viking," she blurted out.

"That won't save you. Same fate, different surroundings. You're not prone to seasickness, are you?"

"Horribly!"

"Impossible. No mermaid was ever seasick. You can't escape your fate, my little siren of the sea."

Andrea was glad that they had reached the car. Breck helped her in and watched while she buckled her seat belt. He then locked and closed her door and went around to his own side of the car. She stretched over and unlocked his door before he could insert the key, and as he slid into his seat behind the wheel, she felt a sudden constriction in her throat. He was *so* big, so vitally masculine. She, unexpectedly and for the first time in her life, was sharply conscious of a man as a *man* in relation to herself as a *woman*.

Perhaps it was the conversation, lighthearted as it had been. In spite of dubbing him Viking, she suddenly had no trouble visualizing him as a blond Saxon/Norman amalgam, taking his pleasure from a village serf girl who caught his eye as he rode on tour of his demesne. Imperious Norman nose and clean-skinned jaw, blue-eyed, blond-haired Saxon coloring, and all the vigor of a hybrid.

She felt curiously flushed and hot, a warmth tingling through her veins. Perhaps it was the wine she'd drunk at dinner and at the party. She'd only had two glasses with dinner and another one at the party, holding it more for form's sake, but unconsciously sipping at it from time to time.

"Home?" he questioned her, breaking her train of thought into a million brittle slivers.

Her mouth opened, but the flippant "Home, James" wouldn't come. There was a sudden crackling tension between them. Home and . . . what? A chaste good-night kiss at the door? Suddenly she was as absurdly nervous as a girl on her first date. Will he or won't he, and if he does, what will I do?

Perhaps he took her silence for consent, or, in the dimness of the car, thought she had nodded acquiescence. He started the car and soon they were nearing familiar streets.

He parked the car and with unhurried smoothness got out and was around by her side, waiting for her to unlock her door. She did so and he helped her from the low seat, the warmth of his hand beneath her elbow a brand burning through the cloth to imprint the skin of her forearm with the length and strength of his fingers.

He slid an arm around her waist and they entered the elevator together, riding the clanking monster up and up. By the time they reached the sixth floor Andrea's throat was dry and she licked her lips nervously, once, twice.

What in the world was wrong with her? If Breck kissed her good night, what of it? Johnny had kissed her good night last week and would again when she went out with him. But Johnny is a boy, her mind whispered. Breck is a man and . . . they had reached her front door.

"Would—would you like some coffee?" she stammered. FOOL! her mind shrieked.

Breck smiled down at her. Her eyes were huge and uncertain and her lower lip trembled just a little. "I don't think I'd better," he responded dryly.

Her eyes grew larger, if that were possible. Disappointment and relief were inextricably mingled in eyes gone smoke soft and dark gray. "I—I—" she began.

"Little fool," he said with soft violence. "If I come in with you, I won't leave tonight, and you're not ready for that . . . yet."

Andrea gasped, as though she had just received two stiff fingers into her solar plexus. Shock, inexplicable excitement, relief, regret . . . she was a maelstrom of conflicting emotions and desires, and when Breck pulled her into his arms as though he couldn't help himself, she fell pliantly against him, trusting his powerful arms to be her support because her legs seemed suddenly jellyfish boneless.

She had never been in such intimate contact with the length of a male body. It was like leaning against a rock, hard, unyielding, yet burning with a heat which spoke of a molten core. Her warmly fleshed frame molded to his with the instinct of one piece of a jigsaw fitting into another.

He had no need to tilt her face up to meet his. Andrea's face lifted as the sunflower lifts to follow the god Apollo in his daily race across the sky. Her lips were closed but they parted beneath the touch of his, opening a gateway of exploration and delight.

Her arms crept up across his shoulders to wind around his neck, while his hands shaped and molded her, lying across the swell of her hips to pull her firmly against his lower body. She was only vaguely conscious of the intimacy of such contact because her attention was focused on the invasion of his mouth. She had known she was inexperienced, but he showed her just how much she had to learn.

She couldn't help herself. She responded to him with an untutored intensity that was to cost her a sleep-short night. If he had plundered, she had submitted, and even when she later castigated herself as all manner of idiot after he had gone, she could not lay the charge against him that he took what she was unwilling to give. Self-deception was not one of her faults, and she would not be able to excuse herself on those grounds. She had been a most willing participant, and if he had not allowed time for panic to set in, she would have agreed to . . . no, *urged!* . . . the final and complete ravishment of her senses.

As she lay in bed later that night, she went cold and shaking at the thought. She had been smug, strongly armored against overwhelming passion by her father's example. No man would enslave *her* as her mother had been enslaved, prisoner to a man's mastery of her desire. Andrea's passions would be closely reined, harnessed in the context of marriage, to a man she could trust. How bitter to learn she was human after all!

Breck had freed her mouth only to chase chills down the side of her neck to the soft hollows of her shoulder bones. In her dazed state it took awhile for the words he had whispered as his mouth trailed past her ear to form themselves into coherency.

"Perhaps I was mistaken," he had muttered. "Shall I indeed come inside with you?"

Passion shut off like a light switch clicking. Had he not spoken, had he just swept her into his arms and carried her into the dimly lit apartment, continuing to kiss and caress her with shattering, reason-blocking expertise, she might not now be lying in this bed, shivering and blessedly alone.

At her strangled "No!" he had paused, lifted his lips from the angle of her neck and shoulder for a moment, and then began to trail kisses back up the path he had just traced downward, intending to recapture her mouth and repair the damage his muttered words had torn in the fabric of sensual enchantment he was weaving around her.

To prevent the capture of her lips he so obviously intended, she buried her face in his shoulder, rolling her forehead back and forth against his collarbone in negation. He was too wise to force her head up. The strands of bewitchment are delicate and what begins as a small rift can rend the fabric beyond repair if too heavy a hand is used to mend it.

His hands began to stroke her back, gentling and soothing her, coaxing, not demanding. When she relaxed slightly, he eased her away from him and tilted her chin up to let her eyes meet his. He could not quite subdue the rueful twist to his smile, but it was a creditable effort nonetheless.

"Coffee would keep me awake all night and I have an important meeting to go to early tomorrow. Will you have dinner with me tomorrow night?"

Her instincts had urged an immediate and resounding "No!" but the husky "Yes" popped out instead. He had asked, not told, but the result was the same. He had given her no chance to back out.

55

At his gesture she had handed him the key and he had unlocked the door. He gave her back the key and, grasping her shoulders gently, he dropped a kiss on her forehead, turned her about, and propelled her inescapably into her living room. His voice came softly over her shoulder, but she could tell he had not entered after her.

"I'll pick you up tomorrow night at seven. Lock the door behind me."

The door clicked shut behind him, but he didn't move away at once. When she made no move to obey him, he tapped softly on the door and reiterated through the panels, "Lock it, Andrea."

She hastily obeyed and he moved away, his firm footsteps echoing down the hall. Andrea fled to her bedroom before the elevator began its descent.

Now she lay in bed, her eyes riveted to the sketch, trying to pull from it the answers she wanted from its living model. She put it down, picked up her sketch block, and drew another. Perhaps she could now see deeper into the complexities of his personality.

The second sketch was done. She held the two up to compare them. There were differences, to be sure. More humor glinted in the eyes, but to her dismay, more ruthless purpose firmed the lines of the face of her second sketch. This man looked at what he wanted and was prepared to take it. Patience, a quality she had overlooked before, was there, but when patience was ended and still his will was thwarted, he would take. More of the primitive sensuality showed than in the previous sketch, but perhaps that was because she came fresh from its experience. It had always been implicit.

It was the portrait of the Viking still, making no

commitments save those of the flesh, ready to go a-roving after lust was assuaged. In modern terms, her mouth quirked wryly, a man for affairs, not binding commitments.

How ironic! How sadly similar . . . she and her mother. Had she learned nothing from that bitter lesson, that she would so easily fall into the arms of a man who would take and take and never give her anything but passion?

When the body craves and the mind denies, the resultant conflict can be fierce and prolonged. Andrea's body, newly wakened to passion, was not prone to go meekly back to innocence. Impossible to spit out the bite from the fruit of the tree of knowledge . . . the flavor lingers seductively on the taste buds. But in the end the weight of experience, her mother's experience, told. Her mind mastered her rebellious body. She would go to dinner with Breck tomorrow night, but no more. She was achingly aware of her vulnerability where Breck was concerned, and she was not too proud to find safety in flight. No charge of cowardice, no sweet persuasion would move her. Three years of discipline and many more of watching the pain a faithless husband can inflict had done their job. Her body would obey her mind in this matter!

The next morning she resumed her routine. If her face was a little drawn and her eyes held more than a touch of frosty bleakness, it could be laid to a late night partying. Her mind might have won, but the body wasn't going to yield a bloodless victory. She had slept badly and had woken more than once, twisted in the sheets and hugging her pillow in a death grip.

She checked the painting and found it dry enough

to transport if she was careful. She inspected it critically and even her currently captious eye could find no fault. Andrea had achieved exactly the effect she had striven for and just now that achievement was made savorless by the deep longing for the taste of one man's mouth and the hard strength of that one man's arms . . . a man she should not, would not have.

She took the painting with her that afternoon and the delight in her mother's face was reward enough.

"It's the best you've ever done, Andrea, dear," Jeanne's thin voice said quietly. "I can smell the fresh earth and hear the breeze rustle the leaves. When I look at it, I am free from this prison of a room and body for a while. Remember the long walks we used to take when you were a little girl and that grassy little hill that we always stopped on to eat our picnic lunch? When we were finished, you used to roll down the hill, over and over."

Andrea laughed gently, falling deliberately into the mood of drowsy reminiscence. More and more her mother seemed to escape her current dreary life into the happier, pain-free past. "I remember," she agreed softly. "And remember the one time you decided to roll down the hill yourself? Those two prim school teachers and their nature class came along and caught you. So disapproving and sour . . . I bet they were just jealous because they were too inhibited to try it themselves."

Jeanne grew suddenly serious. She looked at her daughter as she sat beside the high hospital bed. She stretched out a fleshless hand and Andrea grasped it warmly with her young, supple, clever fingers. Jeanne's hand was dry and cold, unable to grasp anything strongly anymore, even to hold on to her life, which was slipping relentlessly through her strengthless fingers.

"Andrea, my very dear daughter. The best thing that ever came into my life was given to me when I flouted a convention the world cherishes. I have never regretted what I did. I want you to know that." She paused, seeming to search for words and strength.

"I know this has been cruelly hard on you, darling. Your father . . ." Andrea's face assumed a masklike rigidity, but her mother pressed on, rather desperately. "Your father is not an easy man to love. I know his faults . . . who better . . . but the habit of love is strong, and I have loved him from the time he was the boy next door. Perhaps, if at the first I had acted differently, our lives might all have taken a better path, but by the time you came along the pattern was set and he and I were locked into our assigned roles. You were my small miracle, you know. I loved you from the first time I held your warm tiny body next to my heart, and you washed away the bitterness that lurked, corroding, in my heart. I forgave him much when he gave me you."

"Oh, Mother, please don't!" Andrea's voice was muffled, her face buried in the bedside. "I can't bear what he's done to you. I cannot love him, even for your sake."

Jeanne patted and stroked her daughter's bent head. "I know, my dear." Her voice was sad. "Through his own willful, weak actions he lost one of the greatest gifts life offers us, the unstinting love of his child. If you could have known him as a child . . . you were very like him, bright, eager for life . . . he didn't always content himself with the dross."

She rested for a moment and then continued, "I

have loved him for so long . . . Andrea, listen to me. He does not hurt me anymore. I . . . I pity him now. I've paid and learned from my mistakes, but he is still the greedy child, grabbing at pleasure and watching it melt, insubstantial and unfulfilling, through his hands. If you cannot love him, at least don't hate him anymore, for your own sake. Pity him instead. To hate him will only hurt *you*. It will warp you. Hate corrodes and twists the one who carries it within him like a cancer. You can't accept joy if you are filled with hatred. Learn from your father's and my mistakes, my very dear. Don't let our example make you afraid to love, to trust. You may get hurt . . . life is painful . . . but you will also find joy. I want that for you, Andrea. I want it very badly."

Andrea was sobbing softly. She wasn't a small child anymore, able to take her small tragedies to her mother and have them all made well. Her tragedies were big ones now and there was no one to take them to. Somewhere, somehow, she had to find the inner strength to bear them herself and to justify this woman's faith in her. They were silent for a long while after that, the woman who was at the end of her life and the young girl just beginning hers.

Finally Andrea was able to raise her head. Jeanne was looking peacefully at the picture Andrea had brought and hung, for the moment all tension and suffering in abeyance. She turned her head and smiled sweetly, a glimpse of her old beauty flickering into life. "And now, Andrea, dear, tell me about your evening last night. How was the play, and is Devon Harmon really as handsome as he seems from his pictures? Do you like this Breck Carson and—"

"Stop! Halt! Cease and desist!" Andrea was laughing at the sudden flood of questions. "I've already forgotten what the first question was. One at a time, please, if you really want them answered."

She went on to describe the play and party in detail, what the various personalities she had met had said and done (some of it) and her impressions of some of the great and near-great when met in the flesh. She talked determinedly of everyone and everything except Breck.

She should have known her perceptive mother would not let such blatant evasion pass. The quiet "And what of Breck Carson, Andrea? Do you like him?" jolted her eloquence to a halt in midspate.

Andrea thought faster than she ever had in her life. This had to be done just right. She allowed a smile to crinkle the corners of her eyes. "Well, that's sort of hard to say. Breck is too dynamic a person to say you merely like him. I enjoyed my evening and he was a most attentive escort, but I think a steady diet of him would be . . . ah . . . overwhelming. He's rather exhausting." She continued carefully. "I *am* having dinner with him tonight, but then he's flying off to some big meeting and I don't imagine I'll see much of him for a while after that."

There, not a lie in the bunch. Her mother had an uncanny ear for the lie. She always had, probably from listening to so many of her husband's, Andrea thought cynically.

The rest of the visit went smoothly. Andrea left a bit earlier than usual because her mother was very tired, and she knew she could make good use of the time, preparing herself for the evening. There was no anticipation, only dread. If she could, she would like to sleep through the whole thing and wake up the next morning with it all behind her, like some nightmare that would eventually fade with the dawn and full awakening. Breck wasn't going to be easy to get over, but the sooner she started, the better for her.

CHAPTER THREE

Promptly at seven that imperious double knock echoed through the door. As before, she opened the door and gestured him inside, but this time she didn't offer him her hand, nor did she stand where he could pull her into his embrace. He noted her caution and his mouth twitched while a glint appeared in his eyes.

"There's no need to stand so far away, Andrea. It won't make any difference. If I decide to kiss you, I'll just come get you." He grinned, but she could see he wasn't joking.

She decided it would be more dignified to ignore that sally, and besides, she couldn't think of a good comeback. "Would you like a drink before we go?" She was the poised hostess, and his mouth twitched again.

"Yes, I believe I would," he answered her quietly.

She started to move toward and past him to the kitchen, where she kept the few bottles of liquor for her occasional guests and the wine she herself preferred when she infrequently drank. "What would you care for?" she began to say.

As she came level with him, he swept her into his arms and chuckled, "You! How obliging of you to come to me. It saved me the trouble of coming to get you." He kissed her with leisurely thoroughness.

When he released her, Andrea could only sputter, "You said you wanted a drink!"

He laughed, the first one she'd ever heard from him. It was a very nice laugh, she thought wistfully, deep and rumbling and uninhibited but not booming. "You're the only thing intoxicating I need, honey. Come on, it's time to go if you expect to go out for dinner tonight. I'd just as soon stay here, but I did promise to feed you."

They had dinner at a different restaurant from the one they had gone to the night before, but the food and service were equally good. It seemed that Breck had only to lift an eyebrow and a waiter would materialize at his elbow. He seemed intent on plying her with wine and Kobe beef until she wondered aloud if he were trying to get her either too drunk or too stuffed with food to move when he made advances.

That marvelous laugh rang out again and the look he gave her warned that she trod on dangerous ground. Such suggestive bandying opened avenues of speculation she must keep closed, although, she mused, it wasn't necessary to put ideas in his head. Every look he gave her told her that they were already there.

After they had chosen their dinner menu and selected personally which of the superb thick steaks were to be grilled to perfection, he didn't really take his eyes off of her for the rest of the evening. When a waiter appeared, ready to carry out his slightest command, he gave his orders without shifting his attention from her face.

For all her dread of the scene that was bound to ensue at the conclusion of the evening, Andrea found him easy to talk to. He had definite opinions on a wide range of subjects without being opinionated. He could make her laugh, and did, and he held her spellbound with stories of his summers at lumber camps.

Deserted by his parents when he was a young boy, Breck had gone through a very rebellious period, passing through a series of foster homes so quickly "they barely had time to learn my name. I escaped being remanded to custody of the local reform school only because I finally ran up against a foster parent who was bigger than I was. He literally walloped the daylights out of the seat of my pants. Then he sat me down and told me that if my eventual destination was to be state prison, I was well started. If, however, I wanted to make something of myself and prove that I wasn't as worthless as the parents who had abandoned me, he'd show me the way."

Breck's voice was sad. "He's dead now, but before he died, he convinced me to buckle down to studying. Then he arranged summer jobs where I could use my strength and work off some of the normal frustrations any teen-age boy has with hard, grinding labor. It was just what I needed. In the lumber camps nobody cared about my background. They accepted me for what I was and the work I could do. I earned my place among them by the sweat of my brow, literally."

When he began to tell her about his background, Andrea had writhed inside. Don't, she had wanted to say. Please don't. What good will it do me to see behind the outer skin, to know why you are the way you are today? Will it change the way I feel about you or only deepen my feelings, make it that much harder to forget you, as I must?

She could have wept for that little boy who

65

thought himself worthless because his parents had abandoned him, and would have proved it to the world if a wise, practical man had not shown him another way. She would weep later for the strong man as she strove to cut him from her life, severing with surgical brutality all the emotions and longings that already bound the image of him in her heart.

He had captured her hand across the table and was stroking the back of her palm with his thumb, distractingly, as he talked. "I finally evolved a workable philosophy from all that," he concluded. "Your parents, whoever and whatever they are, give you life and, if you're lucky, a good base to start out from, but what you make of yourself, in the final analysis, depends at last on your own abilities and the use you make of them. If you have rotten parents, you start out with a handicap, but one that can be overcome."

The look he gave her was somehow significant, but Andrea was unwilling to decipher it, so concerned was she with combating this man's heady and growing attraction. She turned the conversation to less personal topics and he followed her lead, but a shade of disappointment flashed across his face so swiftly, she wasn't even sure she had seen it.

When the leisurely dinner was finished, they sat for a while over coffee, engrossed in conversation. Andrea was enjoying herself thoroughly, living for the moment, forgetting what was to come, but when Breck began to probe again, as he had the night they had met, she snapped back into her defensive shell.

"I don't talk or think about my father, Breck, if I can possibly avoid it." Her eyes had lost their gray-velvet softness and paled with an icy sheen. "What he is and what he does now cannot affect me anymore. What damage he can do has been done and is

66

past mending. His business life was never my concern, and his personal life doesn't interest me in the least. He'll find his own damnation, and those he'd have taken with him are free of him now."

He was taken aback by her vehemence. He had known there was no love lost on her part, but this depth of feeling went beyond simple jealousy or moral outrage. He'd not yet received the complete dossier on Thomas, but he'd have it by tomorrow to take with him for study, or someone's head would roll.

"All right, Andrea," he agreed peaceably, but the damage was already done. She was tense and nervy again, all accord between them disrupted. When she requested that he take her home, he agreed. He had the feeling that she would be capable of taking a taxi alone if he didn't, and while he wouldn't have let her do it, he didn't fancy having to sling her over his shoulder to prevent it either. There was plenty of time to find the key to her behavior. It obviously lay somewhere in the relationship between Thomas and herself, and once armed with more facts about Devlin Thomas, he'd know the best way to approach her without perpetually running afoul of the minefields which guarded the subject.

He didn't try to touch her as they walked back to the car, wisely, because Andrea was ready to react to his slightest advance with the ferocity of a young wildcat. Any mention of her father had a deleterious effect on her temper and had only reinforced her decision to break off her developing relationship with Breck. Her mind was in full ascendancy and she used the weapon—her father, and Breck's probing about him—to augment her determination to subdue her treacherous body's yearnings and awakened hungers.

As before, they stood outside her door, but this time Breck didn't try to kiss her. He waited until she unlocked the door, and as she turned back to thank him for the meal, he forestalled her words.

"Don't say good night yet, Andrea. I'm coming in for that cup of coffee, and there's something inside that belongs to me."

She looked closely at him, trying to fathom what was behind his words. If he was giving her fair warning that he intended to seduce her, she might have a nasty surprise for him. Right now she was proof against his lovemaking, and the only way she'd succumb to him tonight would be if he raped her, and *that* wasn't his style.

"All right, Breck. A cup of coffee it is."

Now it was his turn to eye her closely. She had agreed easily, but he suddenly realized that somehow she was completely impervious to him. She had moved to some remote distance, though her body was still enticingly close and he could smell the delicious scent of her. It was the same feeling he'd had when he danced with her the first time. She had deliberately cut off all sensual awareness of him as a man. It irritated him, because he had held her in his arms and knew she was alive and warm, exciting to him as no other woman had ever been.

Andrea left him in the living room, standing before the painting, marveling again at the technique that had made the coy mermaid come to life. When she came back, bearing the coffee and impedimenta on a tray, he was still in the same position.

She smiled slightly and remarked, "If you try too hard, your eyes will start to cross from eyestrain.

Mermaids are elusive creatures at best. Let the poor girl swim away to the depths where she's happiest, Breck. Your coffee's poured and getting cold."

"Mermaids are trappable," he responded as he obediently picked up his cup and sat down on the couch. "It just takes the right kind of bait."

Andrea kicked off her shoes and tucked her feet up under herself as she sat on the couch. She regarded him thoughtfully over the rim of her own cup. "And just what bait would you use to trap a mermaid? Jewels, pieces of eight?" she scoffed gently. "She can get those herself from the bottom of the ocean floor. I think it would have to be very special bait to tempt a mermaid, to make her endure the pain of breathing air like sharp knives through her gills and walk slowly and painfully on dry land after she had been able to glide through silken waters with the freedom of a bird on air. Mermaids know their fate on dry land, you know. Word got passed around after the Little Mermaid came to grief. Mermaids were never too proud to learn from another's experience, and they have long memories as a breed."

Her face was bitter and sad as she looked down some dark memory of her own. He would have given much just then to be able to read her mind. She was warning him off. It was unmistakable, and the memory that lay sad shadows over her face held the key he needed.

"I won't tell you what bait I plan to use. You might warn the mermaid, and then she'd get away from me. I don't intend for that to happen. I've wanted her from the moment I laid eyes on her, and I'll have her." He kept to the metaphor they both employed to cloak the direct meaning and watched her face grow grave.

69

"Have you thought about the mermaid at all? How she feels, I mean? You're prepared to take her from her natural element, to force new experiences on her that she may not want." She looked directly at him for the first time, her gray eyes questioning and pleading. "Trophy fishing is a cruel sport, Breck. A mermaid deserves a better fate than to be a dusty symbol hung up on some hunter's game room wall."

It was the only appeal she would ever make to him and she knew before she made it that it was useless. Futile to hope for mercy to soften that warrior's face. Her fingers had not lied. There was no compassion in those Viking-blue eyes, which met her own in silent battle.

Well, as you will, she thought dispiritedly. Let us play out the script to the black and bitter end.

"You said that there was something in this apartment that belonged to you, Breck. Would you like to tell me what it is now that you've had your coffee?" She put her cup down, half finished, and waited patiently for him to make the next move.

Her armor was back in place. For a moment she had let it drop and he had again glimpsed the woman, enchanting and desirable, and his determination to have her was intensified. She fired his blood and he was having a hard time keeping his hands off her. No man had ever had her. It was obvious—she might as well have worn a placard with VIRGIN splashed across it—and perhaps a good portion of her fears were directly attributable to that fact. That and a fastidious unwillingness to engage in casual affairs such as her father obviously cluttered his life with.

He grinned inwardly. The affair he had planned with her would have nothing *casual* about it! She'd be able to send a man mad with pleasure, and he'd damn well make sure to take her with him when he went. Oh, no! He'd have his mermaid yet, warm and willing in his bed, no trophy on a wall. Whatever had given her that idea in the first place? Did she think all he wanted from her was a one-night stand? Oh, little mermaid, how little you know of men and yourself, to think that a man could be satisfied to have you once and then forget you, walking away without a backward glance. I don't plan to leave you after just one night. I want more of you than that!

No sign of his inner musings appeared on his face, and when he spoke, she looked at him in surprise. He said, "What kind of frame had you planned to use on my picture?"

"*Your* picture?" Involuntarily she looked up at the sea scene on the wall behind them before looking at him in bewilderment. "Frame?"

"I told you I wanted it," he said patiently, but to her, obscurely. "I bought it this morning from Mrs. Carrington. Or, to be precise, I bought her right to buy it. I understand she had paid you a deposit but not the full price."

He half turned on the couch, felt in his back pocket, and pulled out his wallet. He opened it and took out a check, made out in her name, and handed it to her. She stared down at it blankly, then back up at him.

"Sylvia sold you her picture? This morning?" She couldn't seem to take it in. She would have sworn . . . He must have offered Sylvia an exorbitant amount of money.

"But you could have commissioned one for yourself if you liked my work so much. There was no need to let Sylvia hold you up. She wouldn't have let that picture go cheaply, and it isn't worth what I'm sure

71

you had to pay, including this." She gestured vaguely at the check, which lay in her lap.

"I set my own values," he responded with more than a touch of arrogance. "It's worth more than I paid and I wanted *that* painting. You price your work too cheaply, Andrea. Given the right exposure, you could command quadruple the price you ask now. You shouldn't sell piecemeal. Gather enough canvases for a showing, let a reputable gallery set up the show for you, and I guarantee that you'll more than cover the expenses the gallery will charge, as well as allow your private sales to skyrocket, both in demand and price."

"I don't have time to paint for a show. If I manage to turn out four or five canvases a year, I'm doing well. I earn my living, Breck. Right now serious painting has to take a backseat. I . . . I have other commitments."

"Commercial art!" His tone was contemptuous. "It's a crime against your talent. I'm certainly no expert, but even I can see the worth of what you can do."

She was getting angry now. She knew as well, no, better than he, that she should be painting seriously full-time, and she knew, as he did not, why she could not yet paint as she desired. Too soon, all too soon she would be free to paint, and the cost of her freedom brought tears to her eyes and a sharp lump to her throat. In her pain she struck out at him verbally.

"What I do is none of your concern, Breck. You can have your painting next week. I'll give you the name of the shop where I get my frames and you can pick out the one you like for yourself. I'll arrange it beforehand. Just tell Kevin which one you want and he'll frame it, no charge. It's included in the cost of the painting."

Andrea was being deliberately offensive, but she couldn't seem to stop. It was insanity to bait Breck this way, but the consequences didn't deter her. For too long, too many years, she had exercised unnatural control and she was reaching her limits at long last. With tremendous effort she looked directly at him, her face strained and masklike.

"The evening is over, Breck. Thank you for the dinner. I'd like you to leave now."

She rose from the couch and stood looking down at him, waiting for him to rise so that she could escort him to the door. The check had drifted to her feet, forgotten, and when she found it the next day, there was part of a footprint across it where one of them had trod upon it.

"I'd like to see my painting again before I go, since I can't have it until next week." Breck rose to his feet, and she had to tilt her head far back to meet his eyes, because she was barefooted, her shoes discarded by the couch.

"I'm sorry. That's not possible." She *was* sorry. If it would make him leave, she would have shown him anything.

His eyes narrowed. "Why isn't it possible? You said it was finished, and even if it's not dry enough to move, I won't be touching it. I just want to look at it." He started toward the studio door.

Her voice stopped him. "You can't see it now, because it's not here."

"Where is it, Andrea?" His voice was quietly dispassionate.

He never calls me Andy, she thought irrelevantly. I wonder why not? Aloud, she answered him precisely. "It's hanging on the wall facing my mother's bed, in her room at the Grayson Convalescent Home. I always leave my newest picture with her for a while after it's completed. It gives her something different to look at besides four hospital walls. I took it there today, as soon as it was dry enough to move. You can have it next week."

"Your mother? I thought your mother was dead. Your father—"

He found it hard to believe that such a bitter laugh could come from such a lovely mouth. "My father?" She finished the implied sentence. "No, my father doesn't advertise that his wife is still alive. But she is! My father will have to wait awhile to be totally free of her. But it's just a legal formality, after all . . . dust to dust and all that. She died to him a little over three years ago, and he plays the merry widower very well."

"Three years ago . . . when you were eighteen." Puzzle pieces were clicking into place rapidly now.

"One week after I was eighteen, to be precise. My mother was crippled in a car accident. After they'd done all they could for her in the hospital, she was moved to the nursing home and she's been there ever since, and will be . . ."

"And you left your father's house." He said it quietly, but it was a statement of fact, not a question.

"Yes."

"Was he driving?"

"No. But he drove her."

He considered that ambiguous statement and wondered if she'd enlarge on it. He looked at her face and knew she wouldn't.

"Is she paralyzed?" It seemed a reasonable question to him, but she flinched as though he had struck her across the face, and that biting, throat-tearing laugh, which was no laugh, ripped from her throat again.

"Paralyzed? No, she's not paralyzed. I wish to God she was! If she was, at least the pain would be gone. She can't walk, but she has feeling in her legs and torso. You can't imagine. I've heard her *screaming* from the feeling! Her spine was fractured beyond all mending, and they pulled her back from death to endure three years of living hell."

She had almost forgotten he was present. Three years of torment spewed forth in her husky voice. "I go every day. On her good days, we talk and I see the mute agony in her eyes and graven ever deeper in the lines of her face. On her bad days, I watch the tears that are forced from her eyes and listen to the moans that blurt from her lips, no matter how tightly she tries to close them."

Appalled, he said, "But there are drugs. Surely they can sedate her!"

Flatly she informed him, "Continued dosage strong enough to take away the pain, or even most of it, would kill her, and no doctor will take that responsibility. I would do it for her, if she asked me, but she will not. So they keep her balanced on the sharp razor edge, as they have for three years. Enough drugs to keep the pain from being totally unendurable, but not enough to release her. If she had been a weaker woman, she would have died long ago, but she is . . . was . . . strong and so she lingers."

"I'm sorry, Andrea. It's inadequate, but I'm sorry."

She looked right at him, but she didn't see him. "I hate my father, Breck. Before . . . before her accident I disliked him, but now I hate him. My mother tells

75

me not to hate him, but I do. He should be in that bed. Perhaps, when she is dead and at peace at last, I can forget him. Not forgive him, but forget him. Blot him out as though he never existed."

Long rolling shudders were shaking her slender body and her arms were wrapped tightly around her waist. She was still staring straight ahead, unseeing. He could see her face and her eyes were blazing hot and icy cold, but she was not crying. If her mother was in hell, had been for three years, Andrea had been right there with her. It was a crushing burden for such a slender back to bear.

He moved close to her and put his hands on her shoulders, intending to hold her close, to comfort her. She went board rigid and jerked away from him.

"No!" she gasped. Andrea knew she dared not accept comfort from him. She longed to, longed to let that broad chest block out the world and to have those muscular arms enfold her. She wanted desperately to be cradled and comforted. Breck had cracked her shell as only he seemed to be able to do at will, and she could not bring herself to trust him to give her only the human warmth of a body to lean against.

"Go away, Breck." Her eyes were pleading, piteous. "Go away and let me find what peace I can tonight. You've done enough damage to me with your prodding and poking. I've said things to you that I've never said aloud to another human being, and such things are better left unspoken. They do not purge or cleanse. They only sear the mouth that says them."

"Sit back down on the couch, Andrea. I'm not going to leave you while you're still upset. I won't touch you, but I'm going to get you a drink, a brandy if you have some, and I'm going to watch you drink it. And I'm going to have one myself," he finished twistedly.

There was no help for it. Andrea knew it now. The whole farce was going to be played out to the ghastly end. She had hoped to put it off until she had recovered from this devastating storm of emotion that had so recently raged through her, but he would not let her be. She would drink the brandy, which she loathed, regain her fragile calm, and then another storm was going to break over her achingly weary head.

Perhaps it was better this way, she thought as she moved to sit on the couch as he had directed. She leaned her head back against the wall and closed her eyes. Breck was opening and closing cabinet doors, looking for the store of liquor and the glasses. Let him. The longer it took him, the more time she had to pull herself back together. Perhaps it was cowardly to hope to put off the final confrontation, but it had to be done, so why not cap a perfectly awful day with a really massive explosion?

That was a rhetorical question if ever there was one. There was no way to put it off. Breck was adept at pushing her into corners. He'd been doing it ever since she'd danced with him . . . before even, because she knew he'd sent her father over to bring Johnny and her back to the head table. Her father would never have approached her like that in a public place, with one of his women in tow.

Devlin wouldn't trust her to preserve a polite facade. She'd never made a scene before, except for the time she had told him what she thought of him after her mother's accident. There had only been the two of them present at the house while she was packing to leave, but he'd never risk a confrontation like that one again.

Breck had found the brandy and glasses. Her glass was half full but his own was nearly brimming. It was the only indication that the scene a short while ago had affected him as well. His face was calm and a little remote; his eyes a darker blue than usual, perhaps. He handed her the glass, his fingers touching hers only briefly, releasing it as soon as he was sure she had a firm grasp.

He didn't take his eyes from her face, watching her as she sipped and made a face and sipped again. She really hated the taste of brandy. It hit her stomach with a dull thud and burned. She set the glass down half finished and said, "I'm calm now. I don't want any more brandy."

It was true. Resignation had made her calm. She supposed it must be akin to the feeling when sentence has been passed and the firing squad is inevitable. Resignation, dull acceptance, because the emotions have been wrung dry, and a readiness to have done with it. All hope gone and only grim determination to carry one through with some semblance of dignity.

"I have to fly back to New York tomorrow afternoon. I'll be gone a week." Breck's words were choppy, the sentences abrupt, spurting forth under pressure. "I have to go. Have lunch with me before I leave."

Here it was. She drew in a deep breath and let it out slowly, soundlessly. "No, Breck." Gentle but implacable. The refusal was for more than lunch, and they were both aware of it.

"Why?" His face was drawn, beginning to grow stern with anger. Two lines had appeared between nostril edge and the outer corners of his mouth, silent betrayal of the control he was exerting.

"I owe you no reasons, Breck." Her voice was still quiet and she met his blue eyes squarely.

"Don't you, Andrea?" His voice rasped slightly. His control did not equal hers. "Are you afraid of me? Or your own desires? You can't deny that kiss last night. You may be a coward, but you're not a liar."

"Thank you," she flared with heavy irony. "I'm not ashamed of it, Breck. You call me a coward and it's true. I'm attracted to you and I responded to you. I won't deny it." Her head lifted proudly and still she faced him eye to eye. "But it won't go any further than that, because I won't let it. It won't, and nothing you do or say will change that."

He started to speak, but she interrupted him ruthlessly. "Can you promise me that you would be content with a platonic relationship?" Her laugh held a touch of genuine amusement at the expression on his face. "No, I can see that idea holds no appeal for you."

She leaned forward, hands on knees. Determined to make herself perfectly understood, she spaced her words clearly and with chill precision. "I will not, will never have an affair with you. There are reasons you don't know and I don't propose to tell you that make me very sure of that. But you do attract me . . . see how honest I am being? An honest coward. I *don't* trust myself around you so I won't *be* around you. Call me coward, call me craven. You can't goad me and you won't change my mind. I have all the misery I can handle in my life right now and I am not about to deliberately set myself up for more. I am a coward, but I'm not suicidal."

She stood and faced him bravely. "Please go now, Breck." Her words were little more than a husky whisper. She was at the end of her strength. "Throw the mermaid back. Take her off that cruel hook and let her swim away to her safe, dark depths."

It was an appeal that should have cracked a stone. Not a muscle flickered in the mask of his face. Had she sketched him just then, there would have been nothing but a cruel, blank mask, no feelings exposed, no pity. Only his eyes were alive and they blazed with a terrible anger.

She was really going to do it! This slender, woman-fragile girl was going to turn him out of her life. Deny him. Not see him ever again except perhaps a chance meeting on the street. Pride of manhood and other emotions he would not name rose up in overwhelming rebellion. The fingers of his hands clenched spasmodically.

Andrea wasn't looking at him now. The last burst of emotion completed her exhaustion. She had nothing left in reserve. She had made her appeal and if he chose to disregard it, she was defenseless. She stood before him in the eternal posture of the captive woman, head bowed for the yoke of submission. She was crying at last, slow, silent tears dripping in a steady stream. She didn't sob or make a sound, wasn't even really aware of the moisture on her cheeks.

He picked her up, holding her tightly in case she struggled, but she lay supine in his arms. He sat back down on the couch, arranged her comfortably in his lap, and began to kiss and caress her.

She was a pliable wax doll and her lips had all the exciting possibilities of a mannequin. No kiss of either tenderness or passion had the power to move her or make her respond. Even when his hand slid inside the neck of her dress to cup her breast, tracing the nipple bud with his thumb, she lay quiescent, spent.

It was passive resistance at its worst. He was defeated. She had locked all her responses behind a glass wall and nothing he could do now could move or reach her. If he stripped her naked and laid her on the rug to take her as a marauding Norseman might have taken a war prize in some convenient ditch, she would lie flaccid beneath him.

He lifted his mouth from hers, his hand from her full, warm breast and cursed. "All right, Andrea. You've won. No man enjoys making love to a rag doll."

He tilted her face back so he could see it clearly. Her eyes were closed, the steady tears leaking from beneath the tear-spiked lashes, but had her eyes opened at that moment, she would have been puzzled by the expression of intense and awful agony that carved lines in his face. Her eyes stayed closed. She did not see.

He looked at her for a long, silent moment and then put her aside. He stood up, looming over her. He could not leave her there on the couch. Her pallor bespoke total exhaustion and she might well lie there uncomfortably all night. He scooped her up, found the bedroom, grimaced at the single bed, and pulled back the spread, one-handed.

When she was tucked, dress and all, beneath the covers, he said quietly, "Andrea, look at me." Her heavy, reddened lids lifted slowly, so slowly, and she focused on him painfully.

"Good-bye, Andrea."

He turned and walked from the room, switching off the light as he went.

Andrea heard him go. Heard him cross the floor,

81

open the front door, and close it behind himself. The muted rumble of the elevator came next, dying away into empty, echoing silence. That was the way she felt inside. Empty. Echoing. The last quiet "good-bye" was a slowly fading echo and reecho somewhere in that vast loneliness.

She was hollow inside. It was a strange sensation, as though her outer skin stretched over nothing but a black vacuum. Cold and dark and empty. No pain, no joy, no tears, no laughter. Numb. The feeling extended itself into her head. She fainted.

Sometime during the faint she slipped insensibly into slumber. When she woke the next morning, it was hard to open her eyes. They were glued stickily shut, as though someone had tied her upper and lower eyelashes together in knots. She stumbled, half-blindly, to the bathroom and ran cool water over her hands, lifting cupped handfuls to splash over her face. The chill shock of the water drove the muzziness away and she lifted a dripping face to inspect it in the mirror. Ugh! If she hadn't already been depressed, the sight of her own face would have made her so.

She remembered it all. There was no comforting amnesia, so beloved of the novelists as a deus ex machina. She had sent Breck away and he had gone, without a backward glance.

What she had done had been right. It had been necessary, but it was like tearing herself in half. She had not known how *much* he meant to her until she sent him away . . . and he went. Futile *if only*'s chased madly through her tired brain. *If only* he'd refused to go. But he didn't. *If only* he'd said, "I can't lose you. I love you. Marry me!" But he hadn't.

He hadn't, she told herself drearily. She had accomplished what she had set out to do and now it was necessary to get on with the business of living. Just why escaped her right now, but presumably habit would carry her through. Habit turned on the shower and kept her under it until she emerged, drenched and shivering, but somewhat more wide awake. Habit made the coffee, which was all her churning stomach would accept.

It was one of her mother's very bad days, so Andrea need make no excuses for her pallor and grim-jawed silence. The nurses whispered sympathetically behind her back. They had all admired her devotion and unflagging solicitude, her inventive patience and her productive compassion for the other patients. They were sorry to see the strain and heart-wrenching business of watching a loved one slowly die lay its dimming pall over her normal vitality.

It took her mother three days to pull herself partway back up the dark slope she had slid so far down. Andrea had been by her bed long past regular visiting hours, holding the weightless, stick-boned hand. She wasn't trying to hold death back, far from it. She could ask no kinder release for her beloved mother. She merely gave what poor comfort she could, projecting warmth and love through that clasp, young hand to old.

She stayed each night until those fleshless fingers relaxed their frail hold on consciousness, no matter how late it was. She could have stayed past midnight, if necessary, with the nurses' blessing. A doctor's order was not needed to allow her the freedom of her mother's room. The nurses would have brought a bed in for her had she requested it, but she sat upright, hour after hour, in a hardbacked chair to help her stay awake.

By the end of the third day her mother had come back, as far as she was able, one more time. As Jeanne waxed, Andrea waned. She had not regained her accustomed color and she had lost weight. The hours by her mother's bed had left her with far too much time for reflection and she had gone over and over her few memories of Breck until they were threadbare.

She had heard nothing from him, nor did she expect to, and she tried to discipline herself into believing it was all for the best. She slept very badly and ate poorly and, if she was honest with herself, she had to admit it was due in part to concern over her mother's condition. But by far Breck and thoughts of him gave her the sleepless nights and stole her appetite. She was miserable and it showed.

Even when her mother rallied, Andrea continued to look haunted, and the nurses began eyeing her with concern. Andrea resorted to makeup, using more blusher than usual to put some color, artificial or not, in her cheeks.

On Wednesday night she took down the painting Breck had bought, although she had not yet been able to cash his check. She hadn't told her mother of the change in ownership, so Jeanne assumed the painting was going to Sylvia. Andrea didn't correct that impression. She found it impossible to speak of Breck to anyone, and to try to explain Breck's determination to have the picture was beyond her powers. She didn't really understand it herself.

On Thursday she left the painting at the framers, after extracting a promise from Kevin that he would notify Breck's office of the whereabouts of the painting. Kevin would charge her account once Breck had chosen the frame. She and Kevin together made several tentative choices and he laid the lengths aside to show Breck when he came. She could tell that Kevin was more than a little curious about this odd way of delivering a painting to a client, but he asked no questions. It was just as well. He would have gotten no answers.

She went back to her apartment for lunch, what she ate of it. While she ate, she scanned the day's delivery of mail. Bills, inquiries, junk mail, she sifted through it all and tossed it glumly on the table. She hadn't really expected anything else, but that little hope that does not die always burgeoned unbidden, determined though she was to quash it. She knew it was foolish. If he had anything to say to her, he wouldn't write. Breck was not a man to tamely write a letter. He'd phone or suddenly appear at the door.

"Andrea, stop mooning over the man like an adolescent! He wanted one thing from you and when he couldn't get it, he had no more use for you." The words echoed into silence in the apartment. Now she was reduced to talking aloud to herself. She'd given herself this lecture so many times the past few days, the tape should be wearing thin. Someday she'd even start believing it.

When she entered her mother's room that afternoon, she should have known. There was a pallid sparkle long absent in her mother's eye, and had she not been so glad to find that this was to be one of Jeanne's increasingly rare "good" days, Andrea would have reached the correct conclusion sooner. As it was, her mother's words were her first intimation of what was to happen.

"Andrea, dear." Her mother's unwontedly firm tone caught her attention at once. It had heavy overtones of "I know you're not going to like this but I want you to do it anyway." When she was a child, it usually presaged a visit to the dentist or to the doctor for routine inoculations. She watched her mother warily.

Jeanne, having caught her daughter's complete attention, waded in at the deep end. "Your father is coming by this afternoon, Andrea. I want you to stay during the visit."

"Mother!" She just couldn't let this pass without objection.

"Andrea, I want to see my husband and my daughter in the same room at the same time once more before I die. I know your feelings and you know mine. I also know what I'm asking of you, but I want you to do it." She reached weakly for Andrea's hand, and Andrea immediately responded, grasping the thin hand firmly. "Please, my dear. You gratify my every whim, and . . ." she continued with a ghost of a smile, "even those I don't know I have. Gratify this one for me too."

There was nothing Andrea could say.

When Devlin entered the room, bearing an ostentatious bouquet of long-stemmed red roses, Andrea thought she would choke on her own bile. The venomous look she shot at him, which her mother couldn't see, left him in no doubt whatsoever that she was here under duress. A red flush stained the back of his neck. Anger or mortification?

While he greeted his wife, Andrea watched the man who was her sire. He was tall and elegantly slim. She owed her own fine-boned elegance and coloring to his genes. He had a facile charm and ready wit, but to Andrea's critical eyes it was the shiny glitter of a mirror, giving him an illusive depth that had no reality. He was a taker and a user, selfish to the marrow, but it was not the innocent selfish egotism of a child. He was an adult egoist, interested in other people only as they related to himself. He took some twisted pleasure from the love Jeanne had steadfastly given him, and God knows he had given *her* cause to hate him. His betrayals littered their lives.

Andrea acknowledged her own share of guilt. In spite of her mother's words, had it not been for the presence of a child, might not Jeanne have left him finally and built herself a better life? Guilt and gratitude. Chains of love forged daily, and ones she'd gladly wear until death snapped the links.

So, she was present during the visit. She did not speak or look directly at her father. She had not looked directly at him since that first black glare when he entered, because now her mother watched the two of them constantly. She would not give her mother additional distress by showing her contempt with such blatant bluntness.

Andrea listened when he spoke to Jeanne, but never commented. Devlin was too canny to risk the snub direct. He knew even Jeanne's presence would not deter Andrea from rebuffing savagely any overtures he might foolishly make. His daughter despised him totally. She was the canker on his nearly nonexistent conscience, and when those clear gray eyes, like his own in color and shape but having a depth his own could never achieve, turned their incisive clarity on him, he always felt something within him blacken and shrivel.

"Devlin, you're looking tired." Jeanne's thin voice evinced concern. "Are you feeling well, dear?"

What grotesque reversal! Andrea writhed inside. She wasn't going to be able to take much more of this. If her father didn't leave soon, she would have to, against her mother's wishes or not. It would be better to go than be actively sick to her stomach. Even now the light lunch she had managed to choke down was assuming the proportions of a large lead ball somewhere near her solar plexus.

Andrea ground her teeth silently as Devlin reacted to his wife's concern for his well-being.

"It's that damned Breck Carson!" Andrea's head snapped up, but fortunately Devlin's attention was on his wife and he missed her involuntary reaction.

"Breck Carson? The new owner of the company? What's he done, Devlin?" Jeanne was curious.

Please don't let her mention that I've gone out with him, Andrea prayed silently. Her father was bound to hear, sooner or later, through the grapevine, but let it be later. She didn't think she could control herself if he gibed at her in front of her mother.

"He's got the whole company bustling like an anthill that's been stirred with a stick. He's in New York on business, but while he's gone, he has the auditors ripping the books to pieces. I think he plans to take the place apart completely and put it back together a different way . . . a top-to-bottom reorganization, in fact."

"How tiring for you, Devlin. I suppose you have to supervise it all while he's away. But a reorganization won't affect you, will it, dear?" Jeanne voiced the soothing concern that had always made her so valuable to his ego.

"Well, actually, I don't have anything to do with the upheaval directly," Devlin responded to Jeanne's question. "Carson has his own management team. He works with them to decide what exactly is to be done, but he usually doesn't turn them loose quite so soon or with such fervor. He's actually in New York to complete the final transfer. His people did a preliminary work-up on the company when negotiations began, and we knew there'd be some changes made, but it's most unusual to start this kind of operation before the final papers are even signed."

Andrea listened intently. Her father was worried about something, all right. She had caught faint traces the night of the company party, but the worry was now more distinct, more personal. Of course, her father always took everything personally. She fired a blind shot.

"It almost sounds as though Mr. Carson is looking for something, doesn't it?" she drawled. "Auditors at the books give rise to such unsavory and disquieting speculations. Perhaps someone's been cooking the accounts," she said to the room at large. She couldn't bring herself to address her father, even to set a sarcastic barb.

Narrow-eyed, she watched him pale and then flush dark red. Somehow she'd struck home! Things must really be happening at the company if the odor of malfeasance was wafting through the rarefied executive air. If there was a scandal, executive vice-presidential heads might roll, although she'd have presumed her father more than adept at survival techniques. He had the fine art of throwing a fellow passenger to any wolves gaining on the troika down pat. He'd even been known to brag about some particularly slick example of backstabbing in the privacy of his own home.

She considered the personal implications. Doing some lightning-fast calculations, she reassured herself that she'd be able to assume full responsibility for her mother's medical bills, should the need arise. It would mean working flat out, but the work would be good for her and it wouldn't give her time to think. She'd almost welcome the chance.

But, she shrugged mentally, it'd probably not come to that. Even if there was something rotten traced back to a man under her father's jurisdiction, she was sure he'd have a scapegoat ready to stuff down the wolves' throats, allowing Devlin Thomas to walk away without a tooth mark on him.

Her father left soon after, mouthing promises to come again in a few days. Andrea vowed *she* wouldn't be present the next time, whatever form of moral blackmail her mother brought to bear.

The rest of the week passed slowly. The forced meeting with her father was a darker spot in a uniformly black week. Even the weather was against her. When her car had a flat tire in the middle of a driving rainstorm, Andrea was contemplating shaking her fist at the heavens when a very gallant man stopped and changed the tire for her. He also asked her for a date, and she told him she was engaged to be married. He was very nice about it, if a trifle wistful. She felt rather guilty about deceiving him, but not guilty enough to accept a date with him. He'd probably turn out to be Jack the Nine-handed Wonder.

She still slept poorly, although her appetite had improved marginally. Johnny called several times, but she put him off, the first time because her mother was sinking so badly. The second time he called she told him she was swamped with catch-up work, now that her mother had improved.

She was behind, but it was mainly because she had developed a distressing tendency to sit and stare at blank pieces of paper instead of filling them with the required artwork. She told herself that if it wasn't so pathetic, it'd be funny. She was behaving like a Victorian miss pining away for love. Pep talks didn't do much good either!

CHAPTER FOUR

She was staring moodily out of the window, watching the rain sheet by. It was almost midmorning, but outside there was the crepuscular half-light of early evening. She had been up since six and had at last managed to get fairly deeply into the most urgent assignment. Yesterday, Saturday, she had received a query from the patient art director whose firm had sent her the commission. There had been several "I know you're busy, but . . ." phrases and, grimly determined, she had set her clock for the early hour the night before.

She had broken for coffee twenty minutes ago and the last of it was now cold and unappealing in the bottom of her cup. Her fingers were smudged and stained and her jeans and T-shirt were liberally spotted with acrylic paint. She had been trying out a spatter effect and it had worked.

In her preoccupation she hadn't consciously noted the elevator sounds, or maybe he just came up the stairs, but the sudden double knock startled her so much that she knocked her cup off the window ledge. She caught it before it shattered on the floor, and fortunately there wasn't more than a quarter cup of cold coffee left. Unfortunately, like blood, a little coffee goes a long way and she added coffee stains to the paint and ink adorning her clothes.

She looked over at the door, waiting for the knock to come again. Maybe she was having auditory hallucinations. The double knock resounded through the living room again, this time accompanied by a full-throated, "Andrea, open the door!"

"All right, all right, I'm coming," she yelled as she balanced the now empty cup back on the windowsill. Holding her wet T-shirt away from her midriff, she went hastily to the door and released the dead bolt.

When he heard the lock release, Breck didn't wait for Andrea to turn the doorknob. He thrust the door open, forcing her to leap agilely out of the way.

"What took you so long?" he growled. He looked at her closely. "You look terrible. You must have lost ten pounds, and you couldn't afford them."

"I spilled my coffee, and it was only five," she snapped back defensively, already badly off-balance. "I'm going to change my shirt. You can mop up the mess over by the window. It was your fault I spilled it."

"Was it hot? Did you burn yourself?" He grabbed her arm, and she wrenched it away. "Let me see, Andrea."

She backed away. "No, it wasn't hot, Breck. It was just the dregs of the cup I had while taking a break. I'm just wet," she finished as she turned and fled. When she shut the bedroom door behind her, she was breathing as though *she* had sprinted up the six flights of stairs.

He was really, really here. Big, blond, flesh and blood, and what did he want? She was excited and apprehensive at the same time. Her head told her to be wary, but her heart, which had cost her five pounds and a lot of lost sleep, could only race uncontrollably.

She changed into dry clothes as quickly as her shaky fingers would allow. He might just decide to follow her into the bedroom if he thought she was taking too long, and she had to avoid that at all costs. He had come back, but she didn't know why and until she did, she wasn't going to take any chances.

When she came out of the bedroom, she heard kitchen sounds and deduced that he had taken her literally and was cleaning up the spilled coffee. She hadn't really meant for him to do it. It had just been something to say on the spur of the moment. But, if he was occupied for the moment, perhaps she could scrub a bit of the paint and ink off her hands . . . and face, she added when she saw herself in the bathroom mirror.

She scrubbed away most of the spots and daubs, but she couldn't do much about the dark shadows beneath her eyes or the drawn hollows in her cheeks, which accentuated her cheekbones. She had to admit that she was just this side of being interestingly gaunt. Another three or four pounds and she'd have made it. From his comments at his first sight of her, Breck didn't approve, and would probably tell her so in greater detail as soon as she went back into the living room. It wouldn't do to let him think *he* had been the cause of a decline!

She dusted on a little blusher and rubbed on some lipstick, tucked in her shirt, and left the sanctuary of the bathroom.

Breck had cleaned up the spattered coffee and had the water boiling for more.

"Is all you have instant?" He indicated the jar of crystals disdainfully.

"Yes. I always put so much sugar and milk in it that it doesn't seem worth going the gourmet, grind-your-own-beans route. I drink it because it's hot and for the caffeine, not the taste. Instant coffee was invented for philistines like me." She nearly laughed out loud at the appalled expression that flitted across his face. "I gather you're a coffee snob. Just add an extra dollop of milk and another spoonful of sugar and you'll never know the difference," she advised him cheekily as she busied herself with clean cups and saucers.

He muttered something sotto voce and took the shrilly whistling kettle off the burner, setting it on a cool coil, while she spooned the dry coffee into the cups. He stirred his own with some violence, not taking her advice to add sugar and milk. She almost expected him to clutch his throat and cry, "Arrgh," after his first sip, but his control was equal to greater tests than her coffee.

He waited politely for her to precede him into the living room and when she sat down on the couch, close to one end, he sat down in the center and, considering his bulk, uncomfortably close. She sipped at her coffee nervously and tried to breathe normally. She could tell he was inspecting every shadow and hollow on her face and it wouldn't have surprised her if he had grabbed her wrist to take her pulse too.

As she had surmised, he pursued the subject of her appearance, which evidently displeased him greatly. "You look like hell. Been missing me?" This last was said with such pleased arrogance that Andrea was furious.

"No!" she snarled. "My mother was critically ill this past week and I've been by her side. Don't flatter yourself, Breck. I survived your absence very well, as I'm sure you did mine."

She hadn't meant to slash at him so viciously, and she regretted it the moment the words left her lips. Her hand went involuntarily to cover her mouth, as if to hold back more hurtful phrases, but it was too late to recall those already uttered. The grim set of his face told her she'd pay for those biting words, and her eyes were wide and apprehensive as she watched him.

"How is your mother now?" he asked stiffly.

"She's—she's better. She loses ground each time, but she's stable for the moment. The doctor had to increase her dosages again and that affects her heart adversely. It's a vicious cycle. The pain weakens her and the increased medication to ease the pain weakens her too."

Andrea sighed and pushed the hair back from her forehead tiredly. "It's really just a matter of time. Day after agonizing day she lies there, getting frailer and—" Her hands clenched spasmodically in her lap, but he didn't cover them or offer any comfort. "She was a lovely woman once. My father isn't attracted to any other kind."

She'd given him the opening he was waiting for. His face grew grimmer and sterner, and Andrea stiffened. He looked . . . savage, and then he smiled. The smile made her shudder. Suddenly she was terrified and she started up from the couch. She didn't get more than halfway up before he wrenched her back down beside him with a cruel grip on her forearm.

"Don't run away, Andrea," he said with silky menace.

"You're hurting my arm," she gasped. He eased his grip fractionally but didn't release her totally. His blue eyes were blazing at her, and she knew that she was about to pay for her injudicious taunt of moments earlier.

He smoothed the reddened skin of her forearm and his touch was oddly gentle, but his words were at variance with that light caress. "I am sorry, Andrea. I don't want to bruise this soft skin of yours. I now have a proprietary interest in keeping it unblemished."

"And just what is that supposed to mean?" She strove to keep her voice steady, but it quavered slightly. The triumph in his eyes was inexplicable. Surely he didn't mean to *rape* her? But his eyes were running over her as though he owned every inch of her, and her throat went dry. "Breck?"

His hand went out to cup itself around her throat, stroking gently up and down while she watched his face like a mesmerized rabbit. When it slid lower to press down in the vee of her shirt, exerting pressure until the button pulled out of the button hole, she drew in a shaky breath but stayed cautiously still. He was dangerous . . . she sensed it.

His fingers slid lower again, splaying out over the mounded swell of her breasts, his wrist resting against the second button, which was straining from the pressure. His little finger and his thumb spanned from nipple to nipple beneath her bra.

Andrea knew he felt the panicking thud of her heart. It throbbed beneath his warm, hard palm. "Breck?" she questioned him again, quietly, sensing that he was controlled by gossamer-thin threads and afraid to do anything to shatter those fragile strands.

He sighed heavily and slowly lifted his hand away, trailing his fingers across her skin to prolong his contact with her silken soft warmth. Now she noticed the etched lines of weariness that bracketed his mouth and saw that he too had shadows laid beneath his eyes. But where hers gave her an air of fragility, his merely made him look hard and dangerous.

The moment of incipient violence seemed to have passed, but she knew she must tread very warily indeed. Something was wrong, catastrophically wrong, and with a sinking heart she knew it was somehow connected with her father. Breck's face had changed when she mentioned Devlin in passing. He had become . . . triumphant.

"Breck," she said for a third time. "Please. Tell me what it is. What's happened?"

"Your father is a thief," he stated brutally. Her eyes rounded in shock and he smiled again, that mirthless, merciless smile that had so terrified her before.

"I don't understand," she whispered.

"It's very simple, Andrea, darling. We knew there was an embezzler in the company, in a position of trust, before we bought it. My team turned up traces during the preliminary investigation of the books before I closed the deal. The amounts are substantial and have been taken over a period of time, approximately three years, in fact."

He watched her face go bloodlessly white with almost clinical interest. Her eyes shut and her throat muscles rippled as she swallowed. When her eyes opened again, he continued.

"As I say, the amounts are substantial. Not enough to cripple the company, but it would have, should the drain have continued. We didn't know who it was, because it was necessary to do some rather concentrated digging to trace the thefts home to roost, and I wasn't prepared to do that until the company was mine."

Andrea remembered sickly her father's phrase about Breck's auditors "ripping the books apart" and his reaction to her gibe. He hadn't been tired. He had been in a flat panic! An embezzler escapes detection only as long as there is no suspicion. Once scented, all the paper twists and turns are futile. He leaves his track like dirty paw prints through the numbers, and all the auditor has to do is follow the trail back to his lair.

Lecher and thief. What a heritage! She felt fouled, ashamed to meet Breck's eyes. No wonder he had looked at her so oddly. The sins of the fathers . . . If he only knew the rest of it, he wouldn't stand to be in the same room with her.

She kept her head down, looking at her fingers, which were twisting and twining together with an independent life of their own. "Has he been arrested yet?" It was the conventional thing to ask, so she did, though she had no real interest in the answer. She should have, as Breck's next words made clear to her.

"Not yet, darling. That's why I'm here. His fate rests entirely in your hands." He was astounded when she began to laugh.

"Throw him in jail and drop the key in the ocean! Let him pay for his actions for once in his selfish, amoral life." There had been a touch of hysteria in her laugh, but the face she lifted to his was judicially calm. "I'll beg no mercy for him, Breck! He deserves none. Give him to the law." She might have been a Roman matron saying, "Give him to the lions." The tone was implacable, the gesture thumbs-down.

The woman was astounding. Tender and infinitely

loving with her mother, she was capable of an intensity of hatred he had not understood nor plumbed the depths of until now. For a moment he hesitated. Perhaps this was not the way. If she came to hate him as deeply as she did her father, what would it cost him? But it was too late. He realized that now. The mold was set, the die thrown, and he must go on as he began. None of these thoughts broke through his warrior's mask and he nodded slightly.

"As you will, but have you considered the effect on your mother when your father is arrested? She still loves him, I believe?" His tone was calm, merely pointing out an interesting fact.

Andrea went sheet-white. Her mother! How could she have forgotten? In her selfish, *blind* satisfaction, she had forgotten the effect her father's arrest and disgrace would have on her mother. Her thoughts scurried frantically. Maybe they could keep it from her. The nurses would help, as would the doctor. A convenient illness on her father's part, occasional deliveries of flowers in his name. Surely they could manage it for the short time still left to her.

Every one of these thoughts showed on her expressive face, and Breck was watching her intently. He relaxed slightly. It was going to be all right. Her reaction to her father's probable fate had shaken him, knocking his house of dream cards askew.

"It won't work, Andrea," he said gently.

"What?" she said abstractedly, still deep in plans. "What won't work?"

"You won't be able to keep it from your mother. If your father is arrested, she'll find out." His tone was still gentle. He could afford to be gentle now.

"No, she won't," Andrea said decisively. "It won't be easy, but the nurses and doctors will help. We'll censor the newspapers. I generally read them to her anyway. She'll be told he has a cold and can't visit, and I'll send her flowers and messages in his name. She . . . she hasn't long," her voice broke on the words, "and I can keep it from her. I have to. She's borne enough for his sake."

"You won't be able to keep it from her," he repeated with gentle persistence. "She'll find out."

"How?" snapped Andrea. "I've just told you—"

"Because I'll make sure she does, Andrea," he promised her.

She couldn't believe her ears, but one look at his face told her he meant what he had just said. And he could do it, she knew with a sinking heart. Anyone ruthless enough could get through the lax security of the nursing home. They could guard against accidental enlightenment, but not against someone determined to bring the news to her mother.

"Why, Breck? Why?" It was a cry from the heart. "Do you hate me so much?"

"Hate you, Andrea, darling?" His voice was silkily smooth again. "On the contrary. I don't hate you at all. I want you rather desperately, in fact."

She could only stare at him uncomprehendingly. He continued, his voice deepening savagely. "You've tormented my dreams and tortured my days. I hear your voice in other women's voices. The scent of your hair teases my senses . . . a memory I can't expunge. You haunt me, coming between me and my work and my pleasures, and so I'm going to exorcise you. I'm going to take you, to satiate myself with you until I no longer want you. Since you won't come to me freely, you'll come to me under duress, but come to me you will."

"You're insane," she whispered.

"Perhaps." He shrugged, and then his lips quirked, but there was no mirth in those blue eyes, which raked her face. "Just like the song says, 'Mad about the girl.'"

She scanned his face thoroughly. He had to be joking or bluffing or . . . He wasn't. She was defeated and she knew it.

"All right, Breck. You win. Spell out your terms." Her voice was passionless and level, reflecting her sudden numb acceptance of the unbelievable.

"You'll come to me?" he insisted.

"Yes."

"All right. I won't prosecute your father. He'll be forcibly retired, but no criminal charges will be filed. In spite of all precautions, slipups do occur, and if he was charged, your mother might hear of it. Besides, it wouldn't look right if I prosecuted my father-in-law."

Andrea's head jerked up. "Father-in-law?" she repeated.

"Of course. You weren't interested in any other arrangement. You've won, Andrea. You'll get a ring and all the legal benefits, and I'll get . . . you. I'm paying a high price for you, my freedom and over one hundred thousand dollars. That's approximately how much your father stole. See that you're worth it."

Her face seemed to hollow and tauten, the clean, firm bone structure showing with precision beneath the suddenly pale cheeks. "This marriage. It's nothing more to you than a legalized affair? A necessity because of my moral scruples against climbing into bed with anyone other than a legal husband?"

He shrugged. "You made the terms clear last week, Andrea. I'm prepared to abide by them."

"And if I will not marry you?"

"I will prosecute your father to the fullest extent of the law and make sure your mother knows about it." She could discern no emotion in his voice or face. He was simply stating facts.

"Even though you know what it will mean, would do, to her?"

He met her eyes firmly. "Yes. I want you."

Her eyes closed briefly and when they opened, they were a flat, dull gray, all light quenched. "You win, Breck. I hope your victory turns to ashes in your mouth, but you win this round."

He relaxed back on the couch. There was no triumph in his eyes. They were hooded and guarded. "We'll be married this Wednesday. I'll make all the arrangements."

A smile that bared her teeth stopped the rest of his sentence. "Oh, no, Breck. I won't *marry* you. When I marry, if I ever marry, it will be to a man I can love and respect. You see, I still believe in marriage, as an institution, in spite of the none too cheery examples I've seen. If I marry, I plan to marry for life. When I make my vows, I'll mean them and do my best to keep them."

He made an involuntary motion that she quelled with a lift of her hand. "I said you've won," she assured him. "I'll come to you. I'll be your mistress, but I won't be your wife. Until my mother dies, I'll be your mistress. When she can't be hurt anymore, you can prosecute my father and leave him to rot for all of me." Her words fell stony cold on his ears, beating against his skin like so many icy pellets of sleet.

Now her eyes blazed, burning bright and hating hot. "You'll have the use of my body, Breck, until my mother is dead, but that's all you'll have of me. Not one word of tenderness, not one ounce of compassion or concern. If you're tired, if you're hurt, if you're sick, plan to go elsewhere for succor, because you won't find it with me! Those are *my* terms, Breck, and they're the only terms you'll get from me."

"And what will your mother say? Won't such an arrangement upset her?"

"My mother won't know. You'll see to it. If she finds out, our *bargain*"—the sneer was perceptible—"is at an end. She's insulated from the world, sedated because of the steadily increasing pain, and my father and I are her only visitors. You'll make sure he realizes it's in his interest to keep quiet about our arrangement."

He capitulated. "As you will, Andrea. I'll arrange to have your things moved to my apartment. You can keep this place as a studio, until I can arrange to have one set up for you at my apartment. Once you have finished whatever commercial assignments you're still obligated to do, you can begin to paint seriously full-time."

He got up and began to pace. "Do you pay your mother's medical bills? I'll take over those, so you won't need your commercial commissions, and I'll take over the rent on this apartment as well. Give me the name of your bank and I'll arrange to have a monthly allowance paid into your checking account."

Andrea was off the couch in a flash and confronting him angrily. "You didn't listen to me, Breck. I'm to be your mistress, not your wife. My studio and apartment stay as they are. I won't live in your apartment with you. You can visit me, but I support myself and I'll take nothing from you . . . no presents, no furs or jewels or whatever are the perks of a mistress. Our bargain has only two factors: you promise not to prosecute my father while my mother lives, and for that promise I will pay you with my body."

He flinched and she laughed bitterly. "Too crude, Breck? How shall I dress it up? What words would you like for me to use to describe our forthcoming relationship?"

His fists clenched. "You've got a shrewish-sharp tongue, my girl," he said through gritted teeth.

"It must be the company I keep," she threw back at him.

"Give me a key to this apartment," he ordered her.

She turned away and walked over to the kitchen, where she rummaged in a small drawer. She pulled out a metal ring with several keys attached to it and took one off, returning the others to the drawer. She walked back to confront him, and the hand that held the key out to him trembled slightly.

He grasped the key, hand and all, and jerked her into his arms. His kiss was hungry, punitive, and bruising. She didn't struggle, but neither did she respond. When he let her go, she swayed slightly and raised her hand to feel her puffy lips.

"I have another engagement tonight," he informed her. Her eyes flew up to his face, their expression unreadable. "A working dinner with my bankers," he continued smoothly. "I won't see you until tomorrow, probably late in the afternoon. We'll go out to dinner, unless you prefer to cook a meal for me." His voice was mocking.

She glared at him.

"No? Ah, yes, that must come under the heading

of wifely duties, which you are not obligated to perform. Pity. Your father said you're an excellent cook."

"I go to visit my mother every afternoon, Breck," she warned him. "I'll continue to do so."

"Of course," he agreed. He dropped another kiss, lighter this time, on her lips. "Until tomorrow, my darling."

He shut the door behind him softly, then winced as it shook and the sound of shattering glass and splashing liquid came clearly through the panels. He shook his head and moved off down the hall, thinking, I hope she gets the coffee stains out of the rug.

Andrea stood looking at the dripping door, her whole body shaking. This couldn't be happening to her. It must be a nightmare that she'd wake from in a moment. She couldn't have just promised to become Breck Carson's *mistress!*

She bent mechanically to pick up the shattered pieces of the cup she had hurled at the door. A sharp-edged splinter pricked her finger and she sucked the little welling drop of red. It was true. Real blood.

More carefully she picked up the bits of cup and then got a dishtowel to mop up the brown splotches of coffee. She moved as though she were suddenly an old woman, stiff and jerky and incredibly ancient. Oh, Breck, her mind cried. How could you do this to me, to both of us? We should have come together in love and tenderness and trust, not lust and disillusion.

"I can't do it." She spoke the words aloud, flinging them into the air of the empty apartment. "I won't! I won't be like my mother!" It was the ultimate irony, and the tears began to stream down her face as she thought back to the days immediately after Jeanne's accident.

She knew her father had been seeing still another woman, but he had been more blatant than usual and he and her mother had quarreled. In a frenzy of humiliation and despair, Jeanne had driven off in the car, to be brought, broken and crushed, from the shredded ruins of her car several hours later. The police had said it was an unavoidable accident, not her mother's fault. A diesel hauler, with an inexperienced driver at the wheel, had jackknifed when he applied the brakes too swiftly, trying to avoid a car that cut in front of him. Jeanne had been caught in the resultant accident.

No, not her fault. Andrea knew why she had been out on the road that day. She knew whose fault it was and she told him, her young face twisted in rage and hurt. She had often heard her mother cry pillow-muffled tears in the night when her father had "worked late," and she had seen her mother's face when a jeweler's bill for a bracelet and earring set she had never received came to the house by mistake.

And then, stung by guilt and the ruthless mirror of truth his daughter held before his face, Devlin Thomas did the unforgivable. He told her the truth of her birth. Perhaps in some twisted way he meant to drive a wedge between the woman he called wife and the daughter he had sired, but instead it finished him completely and forever in his daughter's eyes. Where she had despised, now she hated. She had packed her belongings and left his house that night.

Jeanne was not her blood mother. Devlin had sired her on one of his mistresses, and when the girl, for she had been little more than that, had died in childbirth, he had brought the child to Jeanne. They had no children of their own.

Jeanne had named her and loved her and had never by word or deed ever been anything but a true and loving mother. Devlin had used them both. Jeanne to care for his chance-sired child—he had admitted that he had tried to get the girl to abort the unwanted baby but she refused—Andrea to tie Jeanne more tightly to him, had it been necessary. Jeanne loved the child and would do nothing to break the rapport between them. Devlin did not say it, but Andrea knew him well: knew he would have held the threat of revealing her parentage over Jeanne by implication if nothing else.

Daughter of a lecher, child of a whore. Soon to be concubine to a man she had been close to loving. Had she only herself to consider, she might well have slashed her wrists and been done with the pain of living. Instead she wept, bitter, hopeless tears and deep, racking sobs. She lay on the living room rug, curled in an embryonic ball, and cried until her tears were burned dry and she could breathe only in great gulping gasps of air that seared her lungs.

When the sobbing abated, she climbed shakily to her feet and wove her way into the bathroom to hang limply over the toilet while her abused nervous system took its revenge. She retched until nothing was left, splashed water on her face, and went to the phone. With shaking fingers she dialed the number of the nursing home, identified herself to the nurse who answered, and said, "Tell my mother that I'll come to see her this evening. I won't be able to come this afternoon, but I will stop by soon after supper." She listened for a moment and then said, "No, nothing's wrong. I've just had a bit of car trouble and it won't be fixed until late this afternoon. Please don't let her worry. I'll be there tonight without fail."

Andrea knew the nurse didn't believe her. She couldn't make her voice sound normal, but the nurse wouldn't alarm Jeanne. She'd make the excuse believable. It was the first time Andrea had ever missed an afternoon visit, but she had no choice at all. She couldn't see Jeanne while she was in this state. Another debt laid to her father's and Breck's accounts.

After she hung up, Andrea went into her bedroom and drew the drapes at the window. The darkness was a haven, a cave to hide in, a place of short oblivion. She undressed in the dark and climbed into bed, pulling the covers up over her head in a temporary retreat from a reality she found unbearably painful.

When she woke, she was resigned. It was all very well to cry, "I will not!" to the empty air, but it didn't change the situation. The mermaid was hooked and gaffed and the first searing rasps of air were excruciating.

Andrea knew what she had to face. Disillusionment. An unwilling attraction to a man who was arrogant and callous and ready to use her for the gratification of his desires, as her father had used her real mother.

"He would have married you," a little voice whispered mockingly.

"But only because he thought he couldn't have me any other way," she rejoined with bitter realization. "If coming to him in lust will be degradation and shame, what hell would a marriage founded on such a basis be? What sadistically refined torture!"

And with these spoken words, she made her plans. She knew the worst now. She was no longer torn apart between her head and her heart, divided by hope and wishes. Breck was inescapable while her mother lived, but when she died, the mermaid would rip herself from the hook. Though it ripped out her heart as well, she would swim away into the untraceable depths, and no bait would tempt her up toward the sun again.

The visit to her mother went better than Andrea had expected. Jeanne seemed to accept her tale of a fairly minor mechanical defect with equanimity, although Andrea wasn't sure how much was due to her histrionic ability and how much was due to the increased dosages of painkiller. Jeanne was slipping away from life steadily now, making no effort to delay her going. Andrea knew her time could be measured in weeks only, and very few at that.

The next morning Andrea rose very early. She had an incentive to work now and she intended to finish as many commissions as was humanly possible before her mother's death. She would need as much cash as she could gather together, readily available, at least enough to carry her for a while until she was earning again. When she knew the end was near, she would notify her clients to hold their assignments until she sent her new address. She would also caution them not to reveal her whereabouts to *anyone* without her specific permission.

Her initial lease on the apartment had run out and her month-to-month rental would prove no barrier when the time came for her to leave. Her furniture could go into storage. It was good, but there were no sentimental attachments. Someday, if she wished, she could send for it. Anything else, her pictures and clothes, would go with her in the car. Her rather spartan life-style the past few years hadn't left her many personal possessions, and what there was, was portable.

She worked swiftly and with intense concentration, something she hadn't been able to do for far too long, it seemed. The work she had started yesterday was done before her morning break. She'd mail it and a short cover letter to go with it on her way to the nursing home this afternoon.

She dived back into her work. While she was busy she didn't have to think about the evening . . . and Breck. Anytime her thoughts strayed to him, she got a queasy sensation in the pit of her stomach. She was inexperienced but not ignorant. Modern school theories being what they were, she had a complete, clinical grounding in the biological functions of the human body . . . all of them. But the translation of theory into practice was another thing altogether.

In spite of, or because of her background, she had hung on tenaciously to the dream of the one man, the antithesis of her father's type, who would cherish and value her as a woman and a person and to whom she would cleave for the rest of her life. Her unwilling attraction to Breck had shaken her preconceived dreams, and the reality of what she was about to do filled her with self-loathing.

To be carried away by the passion of the moment, overwhelmed by inflamed senses, seduced, in fact, would be easier to bear in the long run than this cold-blooded barter of her body. Breck would take her with premeditated passion and what was worse, he might even be able to make her respond, resist him though she would! Ruthlessly honest with herself, she had to admit that, for Breck alone, she felt the stirrings of a woman's curiosity toward a man. Something deep and primitive woke within her when she looked at him, something her fear of her sensual heritage could not quite quell. She didn't *want* to be like her biological parents, a slave to her desires!

She wanted more out of life, a deep relationship that touched on all levels, not just the physical. She hated Breck for being unable or unwilling to give her what she wanted and for perhaps destroying for all time her ability to ever find such a relationship with another man.

So, she would run. When her mother died, she would leave, totally cut loose from her past life and do her best to completely block it from her thoughts. Maybe in time, unhampered by ties of duty and love and hate, she could at last become the woman she wished to be. New places, new faces: they would be her curative. Somewhat comforted by her plans, she worked on.

She ate lunch on the way to the nursing home, succumbing to the indigestible efficiency of a drive-through hamburger chain because she was pressed for time. She still had to pick up her daily knick-knack for Jeanne, and the finding of just what she wanted might take some looking. Jeanne's increasing weakness and dimming vitality made the task of finding something to rouse her interest ever harder, and Andrea finally resorted to a new music cassette of some classical guitar selections by Roderigo and Albéniz. The crisp, intricate fingering was attention riveting and should distract Jeanne for a while at least.

Jeanne was pleased with the new tape and they played it several times during the afternoon. They decided that the young guitarist did not yet have the mature precision of Segovia but that his youthful fire and exuberance made for a stirring performance. Andrea promised to try to obtain more of his tapes, very pleased that her mother was so responsive.

She stayed longer than was her normal practice, both to make up for the shortened visit of the day before and from an unexpressed reluctance to go back to her apartment. She knew when she went home she would again be prey to the fears and anticipations of what the coming evening would bring. When she went back, she would have to prepare for Breck's arrival and all that that portended.

She parked the car in its accustomed slot and with dragging footsteps entered the elevator. She hadn't the energy to tackle the stairs as she usually did. She slumped against the wall as the elevator creaked and groaned its way upward. Maybe it'd get stuck between floors and she could spend the night, alone, on its hard, gritty floor. She laughed grimly. Breck would probably climb down the cables hand over hand to get to her.

No, there was to be no escape for her. As women had been from time immemorial, she was chained captive for a conquering warrior. Dressed up with flowers as that first invitation had been, if invitation was indeed the proper word, or phrased with all the naked power of the victor as that last ultimatum had been, she had known all along what he wanted, meant to have.

Suddenly a grim smile twisted her mouth. She was remembering the frustrated fury in his voice when he told her, "No man enjoys making love to a rag doll." Perhaps, even if she could not prevent what was to come, she could at least ensure that Breck took no pleasure in her. A limp and passive body beneath his, a body that might belong to "anywoman." With a sure instinct she knew that she could inflict a grievous wound by merely lying unresponsive before his drive to possess. He might say he desired her body, but the shell without the substance of her mind and spirit to fill it would avail him nothing. Could she do it? It was her only defense. She had to try.

She opened the door to her apartment, stepped inside, and froze in shock. A desk she'd never seen, a beautiful, massive walnut rolltop, was shoved against one wall, papers protruding from its cubby holes. A black, businesslike phone and a small dictating unit sat on its paper-littered surface along with a used coffee cup; one of her coffee cups. Beside the couch various components of a stereo system had been arranged and there were record and tape cassette holders next to that.

She heard movement in the kitchen and swung to confront the intruder. Breck came out of the kitchen, a coffee pot in hand. It was not her coffee pot. She didn't own one.

He really doesn't like instant coffee, flitted insanely through her mind.

He walked calmly over to the desk and poured himself another cup of coffee. Then he lifted the pot inquiringly in her direction, eyebrow quirked.

"How was your mother this afternoon, Andrea?" he asked politely. When she didn't answer immediately, he continued, "You look tired. It's just as well I've decided we'll eat in tonight."

She could only gape at him. Her eye was caught by several cartons of books and a partially assembled bookshelf. He noticed her glance and explained, "I didn't get around to putting the shelves together. There were several phone calls and some things that had to be taken care of right away. I'll do them tomorrow and then we can get rid of the cartons.

Your bookshelves didn't have enough room for my books too."

"You can't—" Her voice failed. She licked her lips and tried again. "You can't just move that stuff in here. This is my apartment. You have no right to—to —"

"To live here with you?" he finished for her. His grin was devilish. "Well, since you won't live with me, I will live with you. Luckily your bedroom is large and there is plenty of room for the king-size bed I had delivered and the extra chest of drawers. That chaste single bed has been sent to the Salvation Army. Since we won't be having guests, we don't need a guest bed. I put the extra linen in that cupboard in the bathroom, but we'll have to get a spread for the bed later. I doubt if we'll be able to match the fabric of the drapes, but it should be fairly easy to coordinate some solid color for the time being. I also got us some new towels. I like big thick ones, and yours all seem to be small and fairly threadbare."

"I must be going insane," she whispered. Then her voice strengthened and she hissed, "Get out, Breck. Get out of my apartment!"

He put the pot down carefully on a stack of papers and folded his arms negligently, leaning one hip against the side of the desk. "Just what did you envision, Andrea?" he drawled mockingly. "That I would visit you once or twice a week, stay an hour or so, and depart?"

"I tried not to think about you at all," she snapped.

He laughed, enjoying her helpless, seething, *impotent* fury. "Oh, no, my darling mistress-to-be." He seemed to savor the words. "I want more of you than that. I intend to have much more of you than that.

115

While you're mine, you'll be all mine. Whenever I want you, I'll take you."

His face hardened and his lips thinned into a cruel line. "You'll see no other men while you're my woman, and that includes John McKay. I'll be here to make sure of that, although I think McKay got the message," he informed her with unmistakable implication.

"What have you done? What did you tell Johnny?" Her voice was a croak. This was unbelievable.

"He called a little while ago, to ask you out, presumably. He seemed surprised when I answered the phone. Thought he had the wrong number, in fact." Breck chuckled slightly. "Of course, he didn't recognize my voice, but I assured him that he did indeed have the right number. He identified himself and I did the same. I also told him I lived here now too and I'd be glad to give you any messages when you got back from visiting your mother at the nursing home. There was no message," Breck finished with savage satisfaction.

Andrea could have scratched his eyes out. She'd never be able to face Johnny again. "You promised that no one would know. You lied to me!" Furious tears burned in her eyes and her hands arched into claws. She sprang at him, out of control, intending to do as much damage to him as she possibly could. At that moment she hated him with a hatred she had reserved only for her father.

He sidestepped her rush easily, pivoting to one side with catlike agility. He encircled her with steel-hard arms, imprisoning her outstretched arms by her sides with easy strength. She kicked and struggled until she was breathless with rage, but he held her without hurting her in any way, merely confining her to keep her from hurting either of them.

When she had calmed slightly, he said quietly, "I didn't break my promise, Andrea. I only agreed that your mother would not know. All of this could have been avoided, you know. I would have married you. I will still marry you. I have no desire to humiliate you, but I will not connive to keep our relationship a secret. I have no plans to sneak into and out of your warm bed, to leave your arms and drive back across town to a cold, empty apartment."

He turned her to face him. There was an odd, guarded look on his face, but she would not lift her eyes to read it. "Andrea, shall we be married after all? You have only to say the word and I'll arrange it still."

Andrea was hot and cold by turns. She didn't really even listen to Breck's words, so deeply affected was she by the knowledge that to the world she had now been proclaimed this man's plaything, his whore. She was her real mother all over again, she thought wildly. What was bred in the bone and blood always came out, struggle how she would to avoid her fate. Now all that was left to her was to hurt this man as badly as he had hurt her.

She leaned back as far as she could in his pinioning arms and looked him squarely in the eyes, her own a flat, bleak gray. "I hate you, Breck Carson. I'll never forgive you for this. I won't marry you! I won't tie myself in any way to a man I despise as much as I despise my father. You've forced me into this situation and now you've branded me before the world, before a man I liked and respected. I might even have wanted to marry him someday," she deliberately inserted to strike out at him.

She would never have married Johnny. He had been a friend, not a lover, but Breck was a possessive man and she knew instinctively that to link herself with Johnny was to drive a dirk through a weak chink in his armor. She wanted Breck to writhe as she was writhing and she would use any weapons she had on hand to make him bleed.

She succeeded all too well. His eyes blazed at her and his grip tightened until she could have groaned with the pain. "So you choose to be my mistress rather than my wife—" he began in furious tones.

"I don't *choose* to be your mistress," she interrupted him fiercely, determined to prick him again. "If I had free choice, I'd never set eyes on you again!"

"But you don't have free choice, Andrea," he ground out between clenched teeth. "You have no choice. You've agreed to become my mistress and your choice is made. You have a lot to learn about being a mistress, Andrea, darling." His voice had dropped to a menacing purr and she started to struggle fiercely again, terror in her wildly twisting body.

He swept her up into his arms. She might as well have been caressing him for all the effect she was having against his massive strength. He continued in the same purring tone as he looked down at her, his eyes flaring with triumphant possession, "It will be my pleasure to teach you all you need to know, and your first lesson will begin right now."

CHAPTER FIVE

He strode over to the bedroom door, carrying her easily, and shouldered it open. When it slammed shut behind them, Andrea went rigid in his arms.

The bedroom was dim, shadowed, but not dark. Andrea watched in horrified fascination as Breck strode toward a bed that seemed acres wide. It had been made up with darkly patterned sheets and matching blankets. He swept the top covers back with one hand and then dropped her, gasping, on the bed.

She immediately tried to scramble over to the other side of the bed to get away, but he caught her before she had covered even a quarter of the distance. He pulled her firmly back where he had dropped her and loomed menacingly over her, gigantic in the dim room.

"There's no escape now, Andrea. You'll only hurt yourself if you fight me." His voice was implacable and his hands went to the buttons of his shirt.

This was really happening to her. Her stunned immobility had the quality of some small wild creature petrified by the lights of an onrushing car, hypnotized by its swiftly approaching doom.

"Don't bother looking at me like a doe about to be shot by the hunter, my sweet, desirable mistress," he informed her grimly as he pulled the unbuttoned shirt out of his jeans. "You'll go to your fate willingly. The little death will be most enjoyable, I promise you."

Her eyes were riveted to the masculine perfection of the naked torso exposed beneath the shirt he was removing. His chest was smooth, with plates of strong muscle layered over the rib cage, and the bunched power of his shoulders and biceps as he removed the shirt told her how he had quelled her ineffectual struggles so easily. Small flat nipples broke the smoothness of his skin and a faint line of golden hair ran down from his navel, disappearing into his low-slung jeans.

The artist in her was forced to respond to the sculptured grace of broad, muscled shoulders tapering into narrow waist, but the inexperienced girl felt her throat go dry as his long-fingered hands moved toward the snap and zipper at his waistband. For the moment he merely hooked his thumbs in the belt loops and then his hands were moving again, toward her!

Like a rag doll, she lay passive as he unbuttoned her shirt, pulled it from her unresisting body, and stripped off her bra as well. He ran an exploratory, caressing hand over her breasts before loosening her skirt, removing it and her shoes and tossing them all in a heap on the floor. He finished stripping her, and when she lay naked to his gaze, he stood for a long moment admiring the graceful sweep of her long-legged body against the dark sheets.

"More beautiful than I imagined," he said huskily and began to strip off the rest of his own clothing. He didn't take his eyes off her the whole time. Even when he sat beside her hips to remove his shoes, he stayed half turned toward her, eyes roving restlessly over the length of her.

Even had he turned his back to her, Andrea would not have tried to bolt again. A fatalistic calm had come to her aid and she was blessedly numb, detached from what was happening to her. Later she would hate again, would rage and strike out with wounding words, but now she was not even embarrassed at their mutual nudity. No man had ever seen her thus, and while she had drawn from live models in her art classes, theirs had been a sexless angle and curve of line, not the heated touch of firm skin over sliding muscle and long, hard bone, mingled with the slightly musky scent of aroused male.

Her breathing was even and her pulse seemed to slam through her veins in an achingly slow, deep rhythm. Breck bent to her, lifting her further toward the center of the bed, and slid in next to her. She shivered once, convulsively, at the initial touch of his hands on her body as he moved her over, but made no other sign of awareness.

He grasped her chin in one hand, turning her face toward his, and forced her to meet his eyes. There was a curiously blank blindness in her silver-gray, dark-pupiled stare, as though she looked through and beyond him. He studied her face closely and then smiled mirthlessly.

"You won't escape me that way, my darling Andrea. I'll pull your spirit back from whatever far distance you seek to send it. Your mind is anchored in your beautiful body and here it will stay, stay to share and enjoy what I'm going to do to you now."

He began to caress her lightly, feather-touch strokes that goose-pimpled her skin, sweeping from her shoulders to her hips in delicate patterns, bringing to life every sensor in her skin. He watched the pupils of her eyes expand and darken involuntarily.

"I may hurt you a bit this first time, Andrea," he murmured softly, "but I'll pleasure you too, as you will pleasure me."

He did not speak again during that long, slow seduction of the senses, but watched her intently for the betraying signs of quickened breathing and hardening nipples, the little gasps she could not control and the whimper escaping through softly parted lips as he teased and touched them with lips and tongue.

His hands, his mouth tantalized and tormented her, learning every throbbing inch of her, gently, inexorably possessing her before he actually took her. When at last he moved over her, he could no longer see her eyes. They were closed. But her arms went around his neck to pull him to her and her mouth opened beneath his own in a wordless, hungry passion that told him what he wanted to know.

He caught the small pain cry in his mouth, swallowing it, and the subsequent little moans of pleasure as though they were delicious bites of some honeyed fruit. When she came at last to that pinnacle of delight and began her slow slide down to the aftermath of languorous lethargy, he let his own iron control slip free and he too slid down gloriously, after catching a glittering star from the heights of pleasure.

Andrea lay against Breck's chest and listened to his heartbeat beneath her cheek and ear. Her body felt heavy, yet paradoxically featherlight and alive. Later she would hate both Breck and herself, but just now it was too much effort and her weighted eyelids sank down. She slept, slept to wake refreshed as she had not for long months.

Breck pulled the covers over them as the room and

their heated bodies cooled perceptibly, and with Andrea held firmly against his hard length, he slept too. He would wake instantly if she tried to move out of his arms.

When next he woke, they were sleeping spoon fashion and the room was dark, not dim. The temptation to explore the delights his hand was cupping was almost overwhelming, but he regretfully desisted. Andrea was still deeply asleep and the tired pallor of her face when she had come back from her mother's bedside was still etched in his memory. He settled himself more comfortably and waited for her to wake up naturally.

Andrea woke to a cocoon of warmth and pitch black. She started to stretch, cat content, but ran up against an unyielding warm obstruction up and down the length of her back. There was a weight across the side of her rib cage and there was a hand cupped firmly around her breast, the fingers of which were lightly teasing the nipple! She sat up with a stifled scream, and a husky chuckle broke the silence.

"Surely you haven't forgotten me so soon, Andrea, darling?"

She groped blindly for the bedside lamp, but met only the wide expanse of mattress and more mattress. She felt Breck's weight shift on the mattress beside her and with a click, shaded light flooded the room, making their eyes squint as they adjusted after the darkness.

She was sitting up in a huge bed, naked to the waist—and below—in her own bedroom. Breck lay on his back beside her, hands behind his head, regarding her with appreciative eyes and a calm, guarded look on his face. The covers were rumpled around his waist too, but if his naked chest was

123

anything to go by, he was in a like state to herself. Suddenly memory came flooding back and she began to burn with a dark, hot blush.

"Oh, my God!" she moaned and covered her face with her hands, leaning forward into her drawn-up knees to rest her forehead. It had really happened. He had made good his promise. He had taken her and she . . . she had *responded!* All memory of the past pleasure was wiped out. All she could think of was that she was now no better than her natural mother. She began to cry, deep, wrenching sobs.

Breck listened for a moment in consternation. This was no maidenly lament for lost virginity. She wept as though her very soul had been reft from her body, heart-deep sobs torn from black anguish. He moved to grasp her shoulders, to pull her back into his arms to try to soothe her. She was tearing herself apart and he had to make her stop.

His touch, his hands on her shoulders made her stop. She rounded on him like a virago. "Damn you to hell, Breck! You've made me no better than my mother. You've made me no better than the promiscuous slut she was." She began to laugh hysterically. "Like father, like daughter. Like mother, like daughter. What's bred in the bone comes out in the blood." It was almost like a chant, and her eyes were silver fires.

There was nothing else he could do. He slapped her sharply across the cheek and she went abruptly silent, her head jerking back and away from the blow. She looked at him unblinkingly, the mark of his hand a red smear of stung skin across her chalk-white cheek.

"I'm sorry, Andrea," he apologized soothingly. "You were hysterical, and it was the only thing to do to snap you out of it. You didn't know what you were saying. I know you hate your father, but you don't hate your mother, Andrea. You didn't mean what you were saying about her." His voice was gentle, consciously calming. He didn't dare gather her to him, lest she go out of control once more and he didn't think he could bring himself to slap her again.

An indescribably bitter smile spread across her mouth. "I meant every word of it, Breck. And every word was the truth. You thought I was talking about Jeanne, didn't you? That good, brave woman who is mother of my heart but not of my blood." She watched comprehension creep across his face. "You're beginning to understand, aren't you, Breck? Why I refused to have an affair with you until you blackmailed me into it, for Jeanne's sake."

She slid off of the bed and walked over to the closet curtain, moving stiffly but with determination. There was a proud poise about the long line of her spine and she was unselfconscious of her naked glory. She slid back the curtain, idly noting that some of Breck's clothes now hung tidily next to her own. She pulled out a silvery blue velour caftan and slipped it over her head. The room was cool with the evening chill and the smooth warmth of the soft fabric was comfortable.

When she turned back to the bed, Breck was just snapping his jeans at the waist. He hooked his shirt off of the floor and thrust his arms into the sleeves, but didn't button it up. His feet, like her own, were still bare but she didn't wait for him to put his shoes on. She left the room, moving on silent feet to the kitchen, where she poured herself a tumbler full of white wine.

She was just lifting the glass to her lips when Breck

came after her, his feet in socks, but still shoeless. He watched her take several deep swallows and got a glass down from the cupboard for himself. He poured two fingers of neat scotch into the glass, knocked them back, and then poured two more, adding ice at last as an afterthought.

Still without a word between them, he followed her into the living room and watched her switch on several lamps. She gestured for him to sit on the couch, beneath the mermaid's picture, and she crossed to lean against the newly installed desk, where her face and upper body were shielded in the shadows. She drank several more swallows of wine and then began.

"Jeanne is my father's wife, but she's not my mother," Andrea confirmed bluntly. "I'm the child of one of my father's many mistresses. An accident, the unfortunate result of one too many nights of passion. He tried to get her to abort me, but she wouldn't, and so she died giving birth. I believe she was just barely twenty when she died. Rather young to pay such a high price for promiscuity, but then most women who have much to do with my father seem to eventually pay a pretty high price." Breck's face went taut at the soft savagery in that quiet voice.

"He brought me to Jeanne and she became my mother in every way but blood." Andrea's voice broke chokingly and then steadied. "Have you any idea what it must have cost her to take me into her home? Me, the visible proof that her husband, the man she loved, had given another woman his child? When, after more than five years of marriage, he'd never given her a child to swell her belly or rock in her arms? He'd deliberately refused her children and then brought her his bastard."

Breck watched Andrea's hands twist mindlessly, a visible lie to the calm monotone her voice had assumed. "Jeanne took me in," she continued. "She accepted me and loved me. I am her daughter, by her choice and mine. My father sowed me in another's body, but my mother, Jeanne, gave me life. Her choice was made soon after my birth, when my father placed me in her arms. My choice was made the night I left my father's house forever. It was the night after her accident, when we knew she would live . . . and how she would live."

She moved forward into the light, and he saw her face matched her tone, no flicker of emotion to break the calm mask. Only her hands betrayed her still. They twisted and clenched upon themselves.

"He told me the truth about my birth that night. I accused him of being the cause of Jeanne's accident, and he retaliated by telling me that it wasn't my concern, because she wasn't my real mother." Breck made an animal sound deep in his throat, but Andrea plowed relentlessly onward. "They'd quarreled about the blatancy of his relationship with his current secretary—no, not this one now, she's only reigned for three months so far, I believe. Jeanne was upset and she went for a drive to calm herself. The accident was an accident. The police were very specific, but she would never have been out on that freeway if it hadn't been for the quarrel. My father is morally if not physically responsible."

She drew in a shaky breath and finished, "And that is why I hate my father and love my mother Jeanne. And because she still loves him, God alone knows why, I won't let him go to jail while she's alive and could hear of it. If it weren't for her, I'd see him rot in the deepest dungeon ever dug."

Andrea gulped the remains of the wine in her glass and went back into the kitchen. Breck heard the clink of glass on glass and knew she was pouring herself another measure of wine.

There was a long silence and then he heard a drawer opening and the rattle of cutlery. He leaped convulsively off the couch and made the kitchen in five gigantic strides. Andrea regarded his precipitate arrival with astonishment. Breck looked at the sharp knife dangling from her right hand and stiffened.

Cautiously, watchfully he started toward her. "Let me have the knife, Andrea. That's no solution." Balanced on the balls of his feet, he estimated his chances of getting to her quickly enough.

She looked at him blankly. "What?" Then she seemed to realize where his eyes were so firmly fixed and she looked down at her hand. Her face took on astonished comprehension. She gestured with the knife and began to laugh. He didn't relax at all.

She tossed the knife on the counter and walked over to the refrigerator, opened it, and took out the two marinating steaks he had put in there earlier in the afternoon. "I presume these are intended for dinner tonight?" she questioned him over her shoulder. "Well, if they're cooked under the broiler with that much fat around the edges, the fat will splatter and make a terrible mess. Unless cleaning ovens is your hobby, I was going to trim the fat off and start them cooking. . . ."

She began to deftly trim the meat, wielding the wickedly sharp knife with a dazzling expertise. "I've only had cups of coffee and an appalling hamburger to eat all day and I'm hungry. You can wait to bake a potato if you want one. I'm going to broil a steak, have some green salad and some of the garlic bread I have in the freezer."

Suiting action to words, she pulled a broiler pan out of a cabinet and slapped the first steak down on its surface. She looked back at him and gestured to the second steak, which she had also trimmed. "Do you want yours cooked now too, or do you want to wait? A baked potato takes a little over an hour, and you'll have to wait awhile before you can eat."

"I'll take mine now," he responded automatically. She tossed the other steak beside the first.

"There's a boiling bag with cauliflower au gratin in the freezer." She looked his bulk up and down, evidently deciding that he needed a supplement to the menu as it had been outlined. "Do you want it?" He acquiesced readily and she began to assemble the meal, working with quick efficiency.

Without being told, Breck found plates and silverware, and following her pointing finger, pulled open a drawer to find a selection of tablecloths and napkins. Within an incredibly short time they were sitting down to a meal. Breck opened the bottle of excellent Cabernet Sauvignon he had brought to complement the steaks, but had to drink it alone. Andrea stayed with her white wine.

"I'm a wine philistine too," she commented when she refused. "I don't care for red wines particularly. In fact, I rarely drink at all, but when I do I just stick with Liebfraumilch. It was the first wine I ever tried. I've tasted others, but still prefer the Liebfraumilch. If it's not available, I have been known to switch to Green Hungarian or Chenin Blanc, but generally I just skip it. Alcohol's a fool's trap."

Andrea ate silently for a while and then continued, "So's suicide, Breck. I gather you thought I was going to slice my wrists dramatically and messily all over the kitchen awhile back. Did you think I had cause?" she said unexpectedly.

She watched the dark red run up under the bronze skin. Her attack had caught him off guard. He had been lulled by her matter-of-fact preparation of the dinner and her calm discussion of the wine. He looked at her closely and saw the opaque glitter was back, turning her gray eyes into silvery reflective mirrors, which shut him off from her thoughts. Gone was the clear, candid gaze. He could only read what she chose to let him know.

Andrea watched him from behind the shutters of her eyes. For once his face was open to her, as hers had once been to him. If it had been her innocence he had desired, then he should desire her no more, for it was well and truly dead. The past hours had killed it as surely as that sharp knife she had used on the steaks could have stilled her heart had she chosen. She was a woman now, by his making, and her girlhood had died forever in his arms.

He was wary, fearing, expecting another hysterical outburst. Her revelations had shaken him. No man could hear what she had revealed and remain untouched; uneasy at the very least and torn to the very depths if he loved the woman. Andrea didn't deceive herself. Breck didn't love her, but he desired her. Therefore he would be vulnerable to a certain extent, bound to her to at least a point because of the pleasure they had shared. She could wound him if she chose.

"I wouldn't kill myself because of you, Breck. As Lady Macbeth said, 'What's done cannot be undone.' I have gone so far for Jeanne's sake, I'll see it

130

through to the bitter end. I'll keep the bargain. See that you keep yours."

She finished her food, carried her plates to the kitchen, and loaded them in the dishwasher. She passed back through the dining area, where he still sat, toying with the remains of the wine in his glass, without sparing him even a glance. Not too much afterward he heard the water running in the shower.

When he came to bed, much later that night, she was sound asleep. She had not bothered to put on pajamas or a nightgown. Perhaps she didn't wear one normally. He didn't know, but somehow the unconcerned nakedness was an insult in itself. He yanked the sheet down from her waist, intending to shake her awake, but the outflung innocence of her hand as it rested by her head caught his attention. It looked so defenseless, the long, graceful fingers relaxed and slightly curved as a child's hand might curl during sleep.

He stood regarding the long, clean sweep of her spine and the taut arc of her buttocks. She slept on her stomach, one leg slightly drawn up and flexed, her head totally off the pillow, which was half off, half on the edge of the bed. He pulled the pillow wholly back onto the bed, but didn't tuck it back beneath her head. He went in and showered and when he came back into the bedroom, she hadn't moved an inch. He sighed, climbed into bed beside her, and pulled the covers up over them both. He switched off the bedside lamp, pulled her up against his chest, arcing around her almost protectively. It was a long time before he fell asleep, his hand cupping her breast possessively.

When he woke the next morning, the bed was cold and empty beside him. She was gone. He flung back the covers and, barely stopping to pull on his jeans, strode into the living room. It was nearly eight o'clock and there were no signs of her in the kitchen, unless he counted the still slightly warm kettle of water sitting on the back burner. He headed for the studio and thrust open the door.

She didn't look up at him as he stood framed in the doorway. He could tell his presence had an effect on her—he hadn't missed the almost imperceptible stiffening of her shoulders—but her hand was steady as she continued working. It looked like the illustration for the cover of a book. She continued working for several minutes more until she had finished a row of intricate scales on the body of the medieval dragon she had been outlining in green and gold.

He walked closer and regarded the nearly completed beast. It was a roguish dragon, with a whimsical and knowing eye. He could almost swear it was preparing to wink at the rather timid-looking knight who was confronting it.

"It's for the cover of a children's book," she spoke casually, as if he had voiced the question aloud. *"Peter and Percival.* Percival's the dragon, rather on the order of Ferdinand the Bull. Peter is Sir Peter, a knight who can't seem to get the hang of accomplishing the requisite knightly endeavors in good order. When he went after the Holy Grail, he came back with a beggar's tin cup, and the maiden he rescued turned out to be the baker's daughter, who had an unfortunate partiality for her father's wares, to the detriment of her waistline and complexion. He doesn't fare much better against Percival, who is an indolent and lazy beast at best and highly averse to being impaled on the end of Peter's jousting lance. A most uncooperative and unsporting dragon, in fact."

She handed him a sheaf of ink line drawings and said, "These are the illustrations for the book itself. Even Peter's horse, Parsley, doesn't have much time for him, and the weight of Peter's armor aggravates his sciatica problem." She began to work again.

Breck leafed through the drawings and chuckled over the long-suffering resignation of the rather plump war-horse, who had a definitely unmartial gleam in his eye, especially as he reached for a tempting apple on a nearby tree, oblivious to the desires of his rider to be away in search of adventures. He admired again the deft economy of line and clean precision of her touch. Each sketch was a small, perfect work of art.

"I hope the publishing company who commissioned these has the foresight to hang on to these originals after the book is published. Someday they'll be worth a lot of money," he said dryly.

She shrugged. "They don't take long to turn out. I did these this morning. I'll have this "—she gestured at the cover painting—"finished by lunchtime and in the mail this afternoon."

He noticed the empty coffee cup on the floor beside her, but there had been no signs of a meal, either here or in the kitchen. As if she had read his mind, she said, "I think there are still some eggs in the refrigerator and there's a package of sausages in the meat drawer. Help yourself. I don't have a toaster, but I find that running it under the broiler works pretty well." She kept on working steadily.

"How long have you been working this morning?" he questioned her.

"Since six. I always do when I'm working. I'm usually too tired by evening to do commercial quality, so I work in the morning when I'm fresh." She added a small touch of red to the dragon's right eye. He was definitely going to wink at Peter any minute.

"How do you like your eggs?"

She shuddered slightly. "I don't. When I must, I eat them scrambled, but when I'm working I never eat breakfast. A fried egg is an abomination, with that disgusting yellow eye staring balefully up at you. It's even worse when you break the yolk and it spreads all over the white. Ugh!"

He left before she put him off his food for good. She didn't come out until almost ten-thirty, and then only to make another cup of instant coffee. He had been working at the desk, making phone calls and dictating letters at a staccato pace for his secretary to unravel later. If it hadn't been for the occasional sound of his own voice, the apartment would have seemed deserted. No sound came from the studio, and it was the flicker of motion as she went toward the kitchen that caught his eye, rather than the silent pad of her bare feet.

Before she went back into the studio, he asked her, "Are you working against a deadline?"

All she said was, "Of sorts," and went back to work.

Andrea had been perfectly truthful. There was no hard-and-fast deadline for this particular assignment. The book was months away from publication and all that was required was reasonable speed, but the deadline was of her own making. She still intended to get through as much as was humanly possible, and now it would serve a double purpose.

More than ever she was determined to leave as soon as Jeanne died, and she would need money. It would be much harder to escape Breck's vigilance with him right here in the apartment. She hadn't planned on *that* at all! He had been correct and she foolishly naive to think he would indeed be satisfied to visit her once or twice a week and leave, but it had never entered her mind that he would *move in* with her! If it had, she might have agreed to transfer over to his apartment so that her own apartment could remain inviolate, a haven from him.

Now she would have to either resign herself to decamping with nothing but the clothes on her back when the time came, or devise some plan to circumvent his guardianship. It never entered her head to believe that he would move out after Jeanne died. His very actions negated that hope. He would leave her when *he* decided, not at the nominal end of her term of servitude.

Her studio was the only haven she had left. Breck had taken possession of the rest of her life and her surroundings. Only behind the door of her studio was she partially free of his pervasive influence.

As best she might, she intended to pretend he was not present in the apartment. She would keep to her regular schedule and habits, resolutely not allowing him to disrupt the daily routine she had evolved these several years. As for the evenings, she would meet them as they came.

She put the finishing touches on the cover illustration and left it to dry. The sheaf of drawings she interleaved with protective clean sheets and sealed in a cardboard-backed envelope. She'd pack the cover illustration the same way and then they'd all go into a larger, padded mailing bag for safe shipment.

When order was restored to the studio, she went into the bedroom to get clean clothes, intending to shower and get ready to leave for the nursing home. Breck was deep in conversation on the phone, so she

135

escaped without hindrance to her shower. She took the precaution of dressing fully before she came back out, determined as she was to give him no opening for implementing that unmistakable gleam of desire she saw in his eyes every time he looked at her. It had been like a hand reaching out to stroke down her spine when he had looked at her from the doorway this morning as she was working. It had taken all her self-control to continue filling in the scales with a steady hand.

When she came back out, Breck was waiting for her. Sometime during the morning he had shaved and showered and was now dressed in casual slacks and an open-necked knit shirt that clung to the virile lines of his torso. What a sculptor's model he'd make, she thought, striving for detachment.

"Finished for the day?" he questioned her casually.

"With work," she agreed cautiously. "I'll grab a bite of lunch and go on to see my mother." She started to walk past him to the kitchen, but he laid a detaining hand on her arm. She froze, quietly still.

He frowned slightly but his voice was expressionless. "I'll take you to lunch. I want to meet Jeanne, so I'm going with you to the nursing home."

"You can't!" she gasped, shocked. "She's not strong enough for visitors. I won't have you upsetting her."

"I won't upset her, Andrea. Would you rather I see her alone? I can go in the morning if you'd prefer." His voice was hatefully bland.

"You know I wouldn't," she snapped. It was useless to argue with him. He bent about as much as a granite monolith! "All right, you can come," she agreed ungraciously, "but if it's one of her bad days, you won't be able to see her. I mean that, Breck." She looked fully at him, adamant.

"Of course. I'm not an unreasonable monster, Andrea," he said, chiding her gently.

The look she threw over her shoulder as she moved past him left him in no doubt that she would be willing to debate that particular point anytime he cared to. She missed the sadly wry smile that tugged at the corners of his mouth.

They lunched at a seafood restaurant where the shrimp were large and succulent, and the cocktail sauce spicy enough to take the skin off the roof of your mouth, or so the warning on the menu promised. While they ate, Andrea explained her practice of taking some present to her mother each day. She confessed that it was becoming harder every day, as Jeanne failed, to find something diverting. Breck thought for a moment and said, "I have an idea. We'll see what you think of it after lunch." He would say no more and they finished their meal, talking of other things.

He took her to a shop that sold small, motorized kinetic sculptures. She chose one that combined the soothing, ever renewing wave action of breakers on the shore with a softly shaded spectrum of changing lights. He would not let her pay for it, saying briefly, "My idea, my treat," and she left it at that.

At the nursing home it turned out to be a "good" day for Jeanne, so Andrea went in to prepare Jeanne for the idea of an unexpected visitor. To Andrea's unexpressed surprise, Jeanne did not seem at all disconcerted or curious about why Breck Carson would desire to visit her. Andrea had the uncomfortable thought that her mother would shrewdly draw her own conclusions. She could only hope that they wouldn't necessarily be the right ones.

Breck didn't let his shock at Jeanne's appearance show by so much as a muscle flicker when he came into the room. He gravely and gently took her frail hand in his large, warm one and smiled charmingly down at her. His manner was the perfect blend of concern and interest, and Jeanne visibly expanded beneath his attentive manner. He kept his visit just the right length, too, leaving before Jeanne's slender store of strength was taxed.

He told Andrea he'd see her later, leaving the impression that they had come separately but would see each other for an evening date. Andrea had to admire the finesse with which he layered so many meanings into a few simple sentences. She knew he would be waiting for her whenever she left Jeanne's room, and she shuddered to think of the impact he'd be making on the nurses while he waited for her. She sighed. A steamroller was a featherweight in comparison to Breck when he set out to accomplish something.

She spent the rest of her time with Jeanne, fielding penetrating questions concerning her feelings about Breck and the state of their relationship. To divert Jeanne from the truth, Andrea was forced to imply that she might be seriously considering marriage with Breck, but that it was really too soon for that sort of decision for either of them. Jeanne had not missed Breck's possessive air with Andrea—it was as natural as breathing for him—and Andrea was sure that he had deliberately, for reasons of his own, encouraged Jeanne's belief in the romantic qualities of their relationship.

It wouldn't do any good to tackle him about it.

138

The damage was done, and since he had met Jeanne, she would at least evaluate any rumors that got through to her from the standpoint of their possible marriage rather than an illicit liaison. For such small mercies Andrea supposed she should be grateful, since the big ones were obviously not destined to come her way.

As she had surmised, Breck had an appreciative audience around him when she finally left Jeanne. She stood watching him for a moment, unnoticed, and was puzzled by something in his attitude. He was being polite, but there was absolutely nothing more than courteous interest in his manner to the several women who were obviously trying to attract more of his attention than he was willing to give. Two of the nurses were what are colloquially called "stunners," and Andrea would have expected him to show a masculine, appreciative awareness at the very least. They might have been sixty-year-old grandmothers for all the awareness Breck was displaying.

Though none of the group had yet noticed her, and she had made no sound, Breck suddenly looked up, directly at her, and his expression changed dramatically. Now there was awareness aplenty. She felt a hot blush spread from her cheeks down her throat. He excused himself with courteous brevity and came toward her, reaching for her hand and drawing her to his side in one smooth motion. The women he had left so precipitately exchanged knowing looks and shrugs. Ah, well, Andrea deserved a little luck in her life, was their obvious conclusion.

"Are you ready to go, sweetheart?"

She shot him a fulminating look, which bounced off his bland smile. There was a suspicious twinkle at the back of his eyes, which warned her that if she provoked him, he might do something really outrageous.

"Yes, Breck. I'm ready," she replied coolly. She said good-bye to the various nurses still standing around and allowed Breck to escort her solicitously out to his car.

"Did you have to make it so obvious?" she hissed.

"Yes," he said simply. Which left her with precisely nothing to say.

They ate dinner with little conversation on either side. Andrea was still angry, and Breck seemed deep in contemplation of some not particularly felicitous thoughts. Andrea didn't try to find out what was bothering him—she seemed to come off on the short end of the stick in any exchange they had—and as far as she was concerned, he could stew in his own juice, the hotter the better.

When they were back at the apartment, Breck turned to her and said, "Go get into something comfortable; that silver-blue thing will do. I'll pour you a glass of wine. No wonder you look so tired. A schedule like the one you keep would put an elephant under." He gave her a light push toward the bedroom.

Andrea went. If he was in the kitchen pouring drinks, he wouldn't be in the bedroom watching her dress, or undress, and she was longing to "get comfortable," as he put it. She wanted nothing more than to curl up on the couch and listen to music, to escape the complications of her life for even a short while. Somehow she didn't think Breck was setting up a big seduction scene on the couch. His voice had had an impersonal, almost kindly quality, as if he suspected that too much more pressure on his part would shatter her into a thousand sharp fragments impossible to jigsaw back together again.

She didn't take any chances, though. She dressed hurriedly in the caftan. It was her favorite lounging outfit and better still, was not particularly seductive. She didn't realize that the color deepened the gray of her eyes and lent a luminescent quality to her skin, and that Breck would probably think she looked seductive in a sack.

When she went back into the living room, Breck was lounging at ease on the couch, a glass of scotch balanced on his flat stomach, staring at the ceiling. He had put on Saint-Saëns's Third Symphony and was keeping time with one waving forefinger. As before, he seemed to sense when she entered the room, because he turned to look at her, though any sound of her entrance would have been covered by the music.

He rose to his feet, picked up her glass of wine, and walked over to hand it to her. She took it, carefully avoiding contact with his fingers. He didn't comment, but merely took her free wrist and led her back to the couch, standing before her until she sat down. She sat and contemplated her wine.

Breck sat down next to her, positioning himself comfortably in the angle of the couch back and arm, and then carefully pulled her back to lean against him, supporting her in turn in the angle of his chest and arm. She held herself rigidly for a while, but her spine began protesting at the unnatural strain, so she finally relaxed against him, wiggling a bit to get comfortable.

"Now drink your wine and listen to the music," his voice drawled in her ear as he laid the side of his cheek against her temple.

It was actually pleasant. He made no demands of her, just held her gently as though he enjoyed being next to her, and she felt her tension and apprehension gradually drain away. When he got up to change the music and replenish her wine, she waited patiently for him to return and then went back into his arms without protest.

The idyll lasted for several hours, until at last her eyelids grew lead-weighted and she began to yawn, half stifled little cat yawns. Breck chuckled and lifted her to her feet. He pointed her toward the bathroom and said quietly, "Go get ready for bed, Andrea. I'll lock up and turn off the music. Go on, scoot."

Whether he was being tactful or not, he didn't come into the bedroom until she had had plenty of time to drag out and don an old granny gown, high-necked and voluminous, that she only wore in the dead of winter. As he had surmised, normally she slept nude, but it was one thing to appear naked before him in anger and quite another to contemplate doing so tonight, she found.

When he came into the bedroom, he caught her just climbing into bed. At the sight of her cloth-enshrouded form a startled oath burst from him and he began to laugh. "What in hell's name have you got on?"

"It's my nightgown," she asserted with precarious dignity, her eyes beginning to spark.

"I thought it was a tent. Take it off."

"No!"

"All right," he said mildly. She gaped at him, and he began to take off his own clothes. It was the work of moments and she was still standing staring at him in shock when he finished and advanced toward her. She began to back away automatically and ran up against the edge of the bed, which she had forgotten was directly behind her. She started to topple backward, overbalanced, until he reached forward and gently pulled her back upright. When she was steady on her feet again, he grasped the gown in his two hands at the neck opening and calmly split it from neck to hem with one rending motion. He pulled the ruined gown the rest of the way off of her and dropped it on the floor.

The rest of the night was a duplicate of the previous one, except that this time there was no pain before ecstasy. She resisted him passively until she could do so no longer. He was patient and persevering, and he wooed her with an attention to her responses, building an edifice of passion slowly but thoroughly. At last he tipped her over the edge of delight and only then did he follow after her, to finish holding her tightly, gasping and spent, a close tangle of welded bodies. The last thing Andrea clearly remembered was Breck pulling the covers up over their intertwined bodies and tucking the sheet and blanket firmly around them both.

The pattern of their days and nights was set for the next several weeks, except that no more of her gowns suffered the fate of the first. She slid silently from bed each morning, thinking him still asleep, because his arms always slackened to release her. She didn't know he watched her exit from the room each morning through slitted eyes, enjoying the unconsciously sensuous sway of her hips as she left him to shower and begin her day's work in the studio. He would rise an hour later to shower, shave, and eat his solitary breakfast.

The rest of the morning followed much the same pattern as the first, she in the haven of the studio and he at the desk. He gradually managed to extend the time she allowed herself for a midmorning break, but it was subtly done, each extra minute added with stealthy caution.

Andrea was aware that Breck seemed to have taken over the ordering of her life, but she was powerless to stop him. She could not keep him from visiting Jeanne, and he went many times with her. Even on the afternoons that he went to the office instead of to visit Jeanne with her, they still shopped together for her daily present. He dropped her at the nursing home and picked her up, and no demur seemed to dissuade him. They ate lunch and dinner together, sometimes out, sometimes at the apartment. He was handy in the kitchen and, better yet, unselfconscious about it.

They went to the framers together to pick out a frame for Breck's picture and Andrea watched Kevin's eyebrows rise when she walked in beside Breck. She met his speculative glances with a stony stare of her own, and he wisely made no unfortunate remarks. Breck didn't miss the little byplay and it seemed to amuse him no end. Andrea was icily civil the rest of the afternoon. Fortunately it was one of the days Breck chose to go to the office, so she was not forced to dissimulate before Jeanne.

That night, Breck took her to another play, again a first night, but when he asked if she wanted to go to the cast party, she declined. He laughed and they went dancing afterward instead. The next morning she overslept, and Breck took care to confirm her erroneous belief that he had been asleep on previous mornings when she had "escaped" to the studio, by making thorough and prolonged love to her. This time she actively fought him, but the end result was the same.

The days passed. The silent struggle continued. She resisted; he ruthlessly overcame. In itself, her continued resistance was a victory of sorts, but Andrea knew only that she seemed to lose every encounter with Breck. He blocked every bid for freedom she made and eroded the areas she tried to keep separate from him. He began coming into the studio at odd times, standing quietly near her, watching her as she worked. It was nerve-racking, but when he asked her if having him watch made her nervous, pride forced her to deny it. He came in more often.

The dichotomy of her emotions was tearing her apart. Her mind was again at war with her body, and the conflict was like to destroy her. The fact that she was Breck's mistress was a raw acid wound across the fabric of her self-respect, but the touch of his hands on her body and the stroke of his lips and tongue at her breast made the time of passive resistance each night grow ever shorter. Someday soon, unless she could get away, she would come eagerly to his arms and something would die forever within her. The thought terrified her.

The time of stasis was coming to an end. Breck was having to spend more afternoons at the office, and Jeanne's final days began to run out with merciful rapidity. Breck had been unable to accompany her to see Jeanne for the past four days, and Andrea's talk with the doctor confirmed her private belief that the end was very near.

She obtained the doctor's promise that any inquiries about Jeanne's condition would continue to be met with the standard formula, "as well as can be expected," and she promised to inform her father of her mother's steadily worsening condition herself. Her plans were made. All she needed was the chance to implement them.

When Breck picked her up that afternoon from the nursing home, she knew something was about to happen. He was in a black mood, and she felt a burgeoning hope. Perhaps whatever was its cause could be turned to her advantage. If he was preoccupied with business problems, whatever they were, might his vigilance lessen just that necessary fraction?

Hope made her all the more cautious, and when Breck asked about her mother during their evening meal, she replied warily. "She's much the same. Failing more rapidly, of course, each day just that much weaker and more ready to go. Dr. Scofield increased her medication again and she's able to sleep somewhat. We don't talk much anymore . . . I just sit and hold her hand most of the time."

"I see," he said thoughtfully. "Can he give you an educated guess about how much longer?"

She was instantly alert, but careful not to let it show. "A week, two weeks, a month at the outside," she answered dully. "He thinks the increased sedation will slow the end somewhat, because she rests more, has more surcease from the constant pain, but as I told you before, it also weakens her heart. When she reaches the critical point, it'll be over very quickly." Now she uttered a deliberate lie. "His best estimate is about another two weeks, but . . ." she shrugged and spread her hands helplessly.

"I see," he repeated again and ran an agitated hand through his hair. He reached over and grasped her hands, commanding her attention. "Andrea, I'm going to have to fly to New York for three days. I've

146

put off the trip as long as I can, but it can't wait any longer. I'm booked on a flight tomorrow morning."

"Oh," was all she could say, but deep inside a surety was born. This was to be her chance. Call it fate, call it belated redress, but sometime within that three-day span she knew, with a deep, undeniable instinct, that the time would come for Jeanne and for herself. She looked down at the clasped hands to hide her expression, not looking up until she was sure she could control her eyes.

"Andrea, if I thought the end was near, I'd stay, no matter what. I know you think you're prepared for this, and I know it will be nothing but a release for Jeanne, but I don't want you to go through this alone."

Her eyes flew up to meet his and there was nothing but sincerity and concern in the blue fire of his gaze. It was nearly her undoing. Suddenly she wanted to throw herself against him and ask him to stay, to be her bulwark and her comfort in the dark days she knew were ahead.

"Do you want me to stay, Andrea? Do you agree with the doctor's estimate?"

His voice was so gentle, so softly concerned, that she nearly gave in. Tenderness was much harder to fight than passion. Then she caught sight of her ring-less left hand and her resolve stiffened. He was her lover, not her husband. She was his mistress, not his wife.

The eyes she lifted again from their clasped hands brimmed with tears and her voice was husky. "I agree with the doctor's estimate, Breck. Go on to New York. Jeanne and I will be all right while you're in New York."

Then she cried. He scooped her up and carried her

over to the couch, where he sat for a long time, holding her close, letting her cry out all the accumulated tensions and regrets. Though he didn't know it, she cried too for the times she would not be able to cry in his arms after Jeanne was gone. Finally, exhausted and hiccuping like a child, she was able to stop.

He carried her into the bedroom and undressed her, tucking her into the bed with tender care. He brought a cold washcloth to bathe her face and left her for a while in the dimly lighted room until he had taken care of the dishes and locked up for the night. When he came to her that night, she met him at last with an unreserved passion to match his own.

It was her farewell to him and an unspoken avowal of feelings she would not name, dared not put into words for the sake of her sanity. He whispered that he wanted her, needed her, called her darling and sweetheart in the darkness, but never beloved. In the silence of her heart she named him love, but the words never crossed her lips.

They made love again early the next morning with a passionate savagery Andrea would have thought herself incapable of. Last night had been farewell. This was for memory.

CHAPTER SIX

Breck packed, and she made his breakfast, even going so far as to eat a slice of bacon to keep him company while he consumed the two sunny-side-up eggs she had cooked for him. She had arranged them side by side and had placed a curved slice of bacon beneath the two eggs to simulate a crooked mouth. She burst into a peal of laughter at his expression when he first looked down at his plate, and laughed again when he immediately ate the bacon and shoved the eggs around on the plate.

He grinned at her and commented, "It might be safer to stick to cereal when you're making the breakfast. Good thing I don't have a hangover this morning!"

She drove him to the airport and waited until his plane was airborne, a rapidly diminishing dot in the sky.

When she got back to the apartment, she called the nursing home and received the report she had expected. Methodically she set about packing. There really wasn't much she wanted to take with her: clothes, her paintings and business papers, and the two sketches she had made of Breck. She would do an oil of him someday when the pain had faded a little.

When she had packed all she planned to take with her, she took several loads down to the car, filling the trunk and locking it. The rest could wait. She stopped by her bank on the way to the nursing home and came out with a sizeable bundle of traveler's checks. She also filled the car with gas and had the attendant check the oil, water, and tires. She was ready.

The night was very long. She sat by Jeanne's bed, leaving it only for the length of time it took her to call her father. She resolutely ignored the feminine voice she could hear questioning him in the background and said quietly, "Jeanne's dying. Do you want to come?"

They kept vigil, one on each side of the bed, each holding a wasted hand. Just before dawn, Jeanne woke once more from her stupor, but it was to Andrea she looked as her eyes dimmed and blanked. It was Andrea who closed her eyes and pulled the sheet over the peaceful, pain-free face, and then called the nurse.

Andrea and Devlin walked outside, into the corridor, together. Andrea turned to face him, her expression unrevealing. "Good-bye, Devlin." She turned to go.

He caught her arm. She looked down at his hand grasping her elbow and her lip curled. He removed his hand as though her arm had suddenly flared white hot. "I'll arrange the funeral," he said. "I'll let you know the time and details later."

"Don't bother. I won't be there."

Shock aged his face. "What do you mean you won't be there?" he croaked.

"I'm leaving town. I won't be back for the funeral. You'll have to play the grieving husband without my supporting role. Perhaps your secretary can wear the mourning black in my place."

"You aren't going to attend your mother's funeral?" He seemed to find the thought incomprehensible.

"No. I honored her in life. She has no need of my presence now. I leave the public mourning to you." Bitter scorn dripped from her voice.

"You can't leave town!" Naked panic hoarsened his throat. "What about Breck? You can't run out on him!"

"Amnesty's over, Devlin." She smiled with wolfish enjoyment. "You really are despicable, you know. Willing to barter my body to escape the consequences of your own actions. Well, understand me, and remember what I say. What I did, I did for Jeanne, to save her one more bit of pain in the hell she endured for those long, long years. She's gone now, and I'm free. No man will ever use me again for any reason whatsoever, and I hope Breck Carson puts you in jail for the rest of your life. And if he does, I hope you live to be a hundred years old."

She drew in a deep breath and said with stunning emphasis, in a dead-level, icy cold voice, "The worst curse I can think of to lay upon you is that you get everything you deserve."

She turned and walked away from him, head high, and never looked back or faltered.

Andrea drove back to the apartment, brought the rest of her things out to the car, locked the door behind her, and went down in the elevator for the last time. She left no note for Breck. There was nothing to say.

She drove for several hours, not really caring about her direction for the moment, and stopped at

151

the first motel she came to. After she had registered, she went into the impersonal room, carrying only an overnight case. She made sure the door was securely locked behind her, dropped the case on one of the beds, and took off all of her clothes. Then she crawled into the nearest bed and slept the clock around.

When she woke the next morning, she felt physically better, but there was a persistent ache deep in her throat, as though she were perpetually on the verge of tears but unable to cry. She wished she could cry, but she knew if she did, the tears wouldn't be for Jeanne. They would be for Breck. They would be for herself.

He would have heard of Jeanne's death by now. She knew he would have made arrangements to be notified of just such an event, not trusting her to get in touch with him, as she had not. He would not be surprised to find her gone. The fact that she had not called to tell him about Jeanne would prepare him for her flight, and she rather imagined that Devlin would be in for a very uncomfortable time when Breck came back.

Breck wouldn't prosecute Devlin, even though Andrea was now no longer his mistress, and technically their bargain was at an end. She had merely taunted Devlin with the possibility to see him squirm a bit. Breck would see that Devlin never again had any position of influence, and the odor of theft would waft about him for the rest of his life. That would be punishment in part, but never enough, never enough. Time and old age would do the rest, she supposed, and with that she dismissed Devlin Thomas from her mind.

Breck would look for her, and do a thorough job

of it, Andrea was sure. He would not easily let go of what was "his" for as long as he wanted it. He was not yet ready to let *her* go, but for the sake of her self-respect she had to go, to cut him out of her life and do it thoroughly.

Andrea showered and changed into comfortable clothes. She had a long way to go. While she ate her way through a large stack of waffles and the side order of bacon that came with it, she pored over the maps she had extracted from the glove compartment of her car. After she had determined exactly where she was, she could plot the most direct route to her destination. She was happy to discover that she hadn't come too far out of her route, and it would be comparatively simple to reach the interstate she needed.

As Andrea had expected, Breck had indeed made arrangements to insure that he be kept informed of Jeanne's condition. Andrea's intervention with the doctor had thrown his plans awry and he did not hear of Jeanne's death until his secretary called him out of a meeting in New York at midafternoon. She secured her job by that one act of initiative, because it was through her love of gossip that she was able to pluck the news off the grapevine.

Miss Jenkins was a romantic at heart. She knew that there was a *relationship* between Breck Carson and Andrea Thomas. She also knew that Breck had fired, without reference, two men he had overheard discussing that relationship crudely. Witnesses who saw the incident said that it had been only through some thin tendril of self-control on Breck's part that the two men escaped being broken into pieces by a ragingly furious Breck. No one dared protest the summary firings, least of all the two men involved. They considered themselves lucky to have escaped whole-skinned and were content to seek work elsewhere.

When Miss Jenkins heard that Mr. Thomas's wife had finally died, via the consequent speculation about the possible change in status of his erstwhile secretary—she had stayed to work for the company when Devlin was "retired"—she immediately began to try to reach Breck. She waded through layers of secretaries, endlessly repeating her refrain of family emergency until she penetrated even the board meeting.

Breck thanked her sincerely for her efforts. He'd find out later why his other sources hadn't notified him, but right now his primary efforts were directed toward getting hold of Andrea and getting back to her. He preempted the nearest secretary, who happened to belong to the company treasurer, and set her to arranging his flight connections. He spent fruitless minutes dialing the phone at the apartment and listening to it ring. He would not let himself think of possibilities when there was no answer.

When his flight connections were completed, he had the secretary contact the nursing home, but she could find out nothing there other than the bare fact of the confirmation of Jeanne's death and that both her husband and her daughter had been with her at the end. Breck's face was a savage mask.

There was time for nothing more if he were to make the flight the secretary had managed to book for him. There had been only one seat left on the plane and it would be his.

Breck went directly to the apartment when he arrived. When he went in the door, his eyes went immediately to the wall over the couch. His face twisted and his eyes closed in an intense spasm of pain. The wall was blank. The mermaid was gone.

With dragging steps he went into the bedroom and pulled back the closet curtain. Only his clothes hung on the rails. He sank down on the edge of the bed, his head dropped in his hands, palms against his forehead.

Andrea was faring a little better. She was fortunate enough to locate a small beach house at a reasonable rent. The mermaid had returned to the sea, or at least as close to it as was humanly possible.

The house was elderly, but had been well maintained and the silvery, weathered boards that sided it pleased Andrea's aesthetic eye. A grass-spotted sand dune ran right up under the front porch, which was raised on stilts. The house was compact, but it had two bedrooms upstairs, both of which had a marvelous view of the sea in all of its moods. She chose the larger one for her studio, and since the house was only sparsely and partially furnished, did not have too much rearranging to do to give herself the maximum amount of working space.

She didn't hang the pictures she had brought with her. She turned the mermaid and her watery world to the wall and left her there. For the first week that she was in the house she did no work at all. She walked the beach, ate when she had to, and slept when she could. After a week, she was sleeping better and her appetite had improved. Something is better than nothing.

Andrea was sitting in her favorite spot overlooking the ocean when she decided it was time to begin working again. She had come every day to this spot to watch the thrashing waves tear themselves to bits on the rock teeth that stuck, like jagged incisors, from a spine of rock lying offshore a hundred yards away. The thunder of the surf answered something stormy and dark that churned in the pit of her stomach.

Today, at last, she felt an easing and the tears began to run silently down her cheeks. She sat there for a long while, fat tears plopping with salty splashes to mingle with the ocean spray on her clothes. When she rose, she felt empty and drained. Not healed . . . only time and work could do that for her now, but *ready* to be healed. She had exorcised the festering hate and those tears had carried away the last remains of the malignant hatred that had stunted her emotional growth and had twisted her and her relationships with other people. For the first time she was truly free . . . and believed it.

She walked back to the house with a lighter step and thrown-back shoulders. Now she had a plan of action. She had letters to write and a pattern of living to begin. She had lived an abnormal life for so long that she was going to need time to throw off old habits and routines. She had skipped a normal part of her adolescence and had been catapulted by circumstances into a maturity, lopsided though it was, that had left her unbalanced, mature in some areas, dangerously adolescent in others. It was time to remedy that.

She wrote her letters, informing her various selected clients of her new address and adjuring them to release her location to *no* one. She reinforced that instruction with the implied threat that, were her privacy breached, she would do no further work for the offender. She was explicit enough and her work was valued so highly that she had no fears that they would do anything but guard her privacy with zealous attention.

She sent a letter to the owners of her apartment building to acquaint them with her decision about the apartment. When these letters were done, she felt such a sensation of relief that she nearly bubbled with it. The old life was gone and though it would be hard, she was determined to build herself another. The healing had begun.

For the first week after she began to work again, she concentrated on her commercial accounts. She wanted to have a firm financial base established before she began to paint seriously, and too, she was not ready to undergo the emotional trauma that such paintings, especially the ones she knew must be painted, were going to cause her.

She gave herself time. There was no urgency. The time for decisions would come, to be sure, but this was a time of renewal and rebuilding, and she must do it right. For the first time in her recent life, she was at peace within herself.

She also began, slowly, to enter into the life of the small community closest to her house. She stopped to chat at the small grocery store where she bought her supplies and at the post office/general store, where she bought everything else and picked up her mail. From there also she sent off her completed commissions, and thus satisfied general curiosity about her means of livelihood.

She knew she was an object of curiosity to the small community, an attractive single young woman who lived alone and had discouraged any but the most fleeting personal contacts when she first arrived. She revealed nothing of her personal history, except that her mother had recently died and she had felt in need of a change of scene from unhappy associations. She set no time limit on the duration of her stay.

This satisfied the inquisitive and cut off most of the probing questions out of tact because of her recent bereavement. The rest she took care of with a level, icy stare, which had a tendency to dry the words in the mouth of the importunate inquisitor. Andrea at her most quelling could be formidable indeed. She was gravely friendly but not ebullient, and her reticence had the not surprising effect of imbuing her with a tantalizing air of mystery.

The alert bachelors noted this exciting addition to the feminine portion of the population, and she began to receive invitations to beach parties and other local affairs. Most she declined, but she did, after much thought, accept a few, those where she did not feel the need for an escort. She mingled well but allowed none of the unattached males at the various parties to attach themselves to her permanently. She came alone and left alone, even if she was never alone while actually at the parties themselves.

When she had lived in the beach house for a month, Andrea set up her easel and began to paint. The first one she did was the view from her favorite spot overlooking the ocean. She put into it all the turmoil and torment that had racked her as she had sat looking out at the shredded waves. It was a wild and disturbing picture and tended to make those who viewed it in later years rather uneasy, although they couldn't define just why. Critics considered it an anomaly in the body of the majority of her work, but that only made it more desirable. She never sold it and rarely exhibited it, but when it was on public view, it invariably commanded attention and persistent offers.

She devoted less and less time to her commercial art, accepting only book and cover illustrations and a few selected, very lucrative commissions, which took little actual time to complete. She lived very simply and found her wardrobe, as it stood, to be very adequate to the small social demands she placed on it.

At last she began to accept an occasional date for dinner or a movie from among her more persistent admirers, but rarely with the same man twice in a row. None of her escorts tried to breach that intangible air of personal isolation. She could be an entertaining companion for an evening, but the slightest hint of any personal element or sexual overture on the part of the man brought an impenetrable, invisible barrier thudding down. She was prepared to be a companion, perhaps even a friend, but not a girl friend.

There was a woman's awareness in her eyes, but none tried to take advantage of it. Andrea was secretly amused many times, though not a flicker of it appeared on her face. She was a woman. Breck had made her one. She had known passion and had satisfied a man's desire, as he had hers, she wryly acknowledged to herself. She was no longer protected by that invisible air of innocence, and her escorts unconsciously reacted to the loss of that indefinable defensive barrier.

The loss of innocence had not left her undefended, however. Her experience with Breck had stripped her of innocence, but in its place he had left her with an awareness of the powers her woman's body wielded over men. Eve's knowledge, Lilith's knowledge:

blood-deep, bone-bred heritage of any woman who understands her own nature and has come to terms with it. Andrea was coming to terms with herself and if the maturation process was at times painful, it was also inexorable.

By the end of the fifth month, Andrea had a respectable number of canvases completed, almost enough for a small show. She was tanned and vitally alive, and although there was an unmistakable maturity about her, in some indefinable way she was also younger and more carefree than she had been since her early teen-age days, as though she had somehow managed to recapture a portion of her lost innocence.

It was time to begin the picture of Breck. It was the final test she set herself, the proof of complete healing. Like the exorcism of a haunting ghost, she would purge her subconscious of any lingering traces that could conceivably come between her and the life she hoped would someday be hers.

She had known this day would have to come and she had gathered her strength to meet the challenge she set herself. She had gone out with other men, though she had carefully allowed none of them to exact more from her than she was willing to give. This was her period of mourning, her metaphorical wearing of black, both for the loss of Jeanne and of her own girlhood. With the completion of the picture she now intended to paint, she would know whether it had come to an end.

She began to take long walks along the beach again. The summer had fled and the salt spray that whipped her skin had added a chill bite. Several storms, harbingers of winter's approaching inclemency, lashed at the little house. It creaked and groaned and the windows rattled like chattering teeth, but apart from an icy draft or two, which sent Andrea to the general store for a tube of caulk, it remained the snug haven it had been for her months of exile.

She withdrew from the social life of the town once more, retreating into the impersonality of her first few weeks residence. She pleaded pressure of work, not wishing to have to resort to incivility, and was adamant about refusing all invitations, no matter how pressing.

Once again she ate, slept, and took long walks, but with a difference. This time she worked on the picture as well. It was as painful as she had feared it was going to be, and it took her almost a month to finish it.

She finished it late in the afternoon and when she had laid on the last brush stroke, she paused for a moment and then turned away. She gathered together her materials and began to clean up, working mechanically and consciously avoiding looking at the picture. Tomorrow would be soon enough.

She fixed herself a scratch meal and then took a postprandial cup of coffee with her out to the porch, which faced the ocean. She pulled up a battered mission rocker, as weathered as the wood of the house, to within comfortable distance of the railing. She sat down, cradling the warmth of the cup between her hands and balancing the base of the cup on her stomach. She propped her feet up on the railing and tilted the chair back on its rockers.

The nearly full moon was rising from the watery depths of the ocean and she watched the silvery path spread across the gently heaving bosom of the ocean as it lay beyond the sand dunes. The ceaseless wash of the waves formed a hypnotic accompaniment in the night and she let her eyes flicker shut. She was so tired.

The next morning she rose early and went for a short morning swim. The water was breathtakingly cold, but it left her tingling and awake. Suddenly she was ravenously hungry. She fried bacon and scrambled eggs and ate them with relish. There was no pain from her memories and when she climbed the stairs, it was with a firm, unhurried tread. Her hand on the doorknob of her studio was steady and her face, as she stood before the painting, was calm and composed.

She looked at the canvas for a long time, assimilating the total message it had for her. When she turned away at last, it was with a sigh of relief. She was truly free. The long days and nights had been worth it. Disillusion and sorrow had scoured her deeply, as the potter's hands hollow the cup spinning on his wheel, but the capacity of the vessel is enlarged by the oft painful treatment. The long months of voluntary isolation had purged her of the bitterness and hatred. Old loves and old hates had drained away, leaving her empty, ready to be filled with a new, untainted emotion.

Love could never be the innocent unfolding it might have been. Too much had happened that could never be wiped away; her dreams had been too ruthlessly smashed to be put back together in their old forms. Her gills had metamorphosized into lungs and her old environment was forever barred to her. It was time to build herself a new life.

There was no reason to delay. She notified the real estate agent who managed the rental of the house that she would be vacating the cottage within the week. She had the car serviced and made her good-byes while she waited for it. She had deliberately kept the threads that bound her to this place tenuous. She had always known this was an interim, an interlude between her old life and the new one she would fashion for herself. She had shed her old responsibilities and the new ones she was ready to assume would be those of her own choosing, not those thrust upon her by events she could not control.

Once again she packed her clothes, but without the haste that had governed her earlier departure. Now there was no hurry. She was not running away ever again. She arranged for shipment of the majority of the canvases, taking only two new ones in the car with her, plus the ones she had brought with her.

Two days after she had stood before Breck's picture, she locked the door of the beach house for the last time, got in the car, and drove away. There were no backward glances.

Breck parked his car and got out wearily. Six long months had passed since Jeanne's death. If Andrea had mentally characterized him as an ancient Norse warrior, he was now a warrior for whom the battle had not gone well. Lines of strain were graven deep in his face. His mouth was tightly drawn, evidence of the exercise of now habitual control; a man who bears suffering because he has no way to alleviate it.

Andrea had been correct. He had looked for her most thoroughly. Every avenue had been explored, each ending in stone walls or a welter of false alarms. Andrea had chosen her clients well. None would jeopardize their relationship with her and release her new address. There were no secretaries to be suborned, because she had foresightedly provided that knowledge of her whereabouts be confined to one or two high-level executives of the departments concerned, and there were no return addresses for prying eyes to note. She had even contrived that the postmarks be blurred by smiling sweetly at the mail clerk each time she mailed off a package.

It was bitterly clear that she had planned every move well in advance, even to making sure that no news about the deterioration in Jeanne's condition was released. She had ably fulfilled her vow. When Jeanne died, she cut with ruthless precision all the ties he had sought to bind around her. He had no doubt that even had no fortuitous—from her point of view—business trip intervened, she would somehow have contrived to escape his enmeshing net.

The bait had not been sufficient to trap the mermaid after all. She had swum tracelessly back into the depths, leaving the man empty armed on the shore. Had she gone back mortally wounded by her experiences on land? Had the time she had spent breathing air forever destroyed her ability to live in the tranquil deeps? What price was *she* paying for *his* arrogant decision to snare the mermaid, regardless of the cost to her?

He had hoped to bind her with passion, to lock her with him in a mutual web of enchantment, but had he only succeeded in opening her perceptions to the sensual pleasures and potentials of the flesh? Would she sate the hungers he had aroused in her innocent body with another man? The thought of her in another man's arms clawed his gut with savage persistence. She had responded to him in spite of her hatred. Would she respond to another out of love or even a mere desire for comfort?

Was she pregnant? He had taken no precautions

against it and had found no evidence that she had thought of doing so either. In fact, he scathingly reminded himself, he had hoped to make her pregnant, to bind her to himself in that way. She would marry him for the sake of the child, he had reasoned.

Was she now growing large with his child? He knew her well enough to know that if she were, she would bear it and raise it. Would he ever know whether a child of his body walked the earth? What if she died of it? Women did. Her mother had. In spite of doctors and hospitals and modern medicine, women still died giving birth to the fruit of a man's lust for the warmth and wonder of their bodies. Andrea was slim-hipped. What if? What if?

He shook his head, seeking to chase away the phantasm, guilt born, which had haunted him for six months, long, aching, lonely months. He still turned in the night, reaching automatically to enfold her warm, lithe body, finding only cold, empty space. It was slowly killing him and he had only himself to blame. Like a greedy, spoiled child, he had reached for that which was not his, but which he desired above everything he had ever wanted. Mea culpa, he reminded himself wryly.

The elevator shuddered to a halt and his footsteps echoed hollowly in the hall. He inserted the key and walked in the front door of the apartment, his eyes going automatically to the empty space over the couch. It was sheer reflex now, compulsive and conditioned.

He took another step, tugging to loosen his tie, before his brain registered the message his eyes were telling him. He stopped dead still, afraid to move, afraid even to breathe. His lids dropped down over his eyes, sealing him within a black, still world, a world in which a small, wavering, ever so fragile pinpoint of light began to burn. After a moment that seemed eons long, he opened his eyes slowly. Perhaps he had finally gone mad. "Hope deferred maketh the heart sick". . . and perhaps the eyes hallucinate?

The picture was there, hanging in its accustomed place. He walked jerkily over to it, his hand outstretched to touch the surface, where the mermaid flirted with visibility. His fingers met the reality of canvas and paint, dragging slightly as he swept them over the painted texture.

He stepped back from the couch and swung to face the rest of the room. His head lifted alertly, straining to catch a whisper of sound. The stillness was complete, not even the stirring of an air current to carry a drift of the presence of another human being.

Had she come, and finding him still resident, gone? No! She must still be here. He strode into the kitchen. Empty. Their bedroom next.

There was a new painting hanging over the bed, but the room was empty. He saw three suitcases on the other side of the bed and he stalked over to investigate. From the weight of one he hefted experimentally, he decided they hadn't been unpacked. A quick check behind the curtain of the closet confirmed his guess. Only his own clothes hung there.

That left the studio. The door was closed, but that was not unusual. He kept it that way. It had been her sanctuary, the place she had done her best to keep free from his presence. He had known what it had meant to her even when he deliberately invaded it while she worked. He castigated himself as he had so many times before. He had been unwilling to allow her even a corner free from his imprint, forcing himself here as he had forced himself on her unwilling body.

His hand turned the doorknob, and the door swung open at his touch. At first he thought she was not here either. The room was quiet and there was no flicker of motion to draw the eye. Her easel stood again in the center of the room, a canvas propped on its support. He could not see its subject; the back of the canvas faced the door.

She was standing by one of the windows, looking down at the ground. You could see the parking area from that window. She had watched him park his car and enter the building. She knew he was here, but she didn't turn to face him immediately.

Breck drank in the sight of that slender figure clad in shirt and jeans with ravenous eyes. She stood in profile, backlighted by the window. She did not carry his child. That was immediately obvious from the slim perfection of that narrow waist and flat stomach.

There was no perceptible tension in that lithe figure as she turned gracefully to confront him. There was a new maturity and calm certainty on her face, and no surprise evident as she looked coolly and directly at him. He could not read her expression at all, save that it held no hate or fear.

"Hello, Breck."

Her voice was just the same, low-toned and slightly husky, with a soft slip of syllables, which nevertheless kept a precise pronunciation so that each word remained clean and distinct. He watched her lips move and then be still. Was there just the trace of a small smile on them in repose?

"Andrea." He could say nothing more. His voice

clogged in his throat. So many questions to ask, but for now he was content to look and look again.

Andrea read his face with wondering eyes. The time had not been easy for him and the marks six months had clawed in his face were plainly and deeply carved. I'll bet he's made life hell at the office. I wonder how Miss Jenkins is faring? she mused silently.

"You came back." The statement was a question. Breck's voice was dry in his throat.

"It's my apartment, Breck," she reminded him noncommitally. "I've paid the rent for it these past six months."

"I know."

Every month the travelers checks had come in to the apartment owners, impersonal and untraceable. Apart from that initial letter, which informed the landlord that she wished to maintain the tenantcy of the apartment on a month to month basis for an unspecified length of time, there had been no further communication with her. They had been instructed to contact a certain publisher if there were any messages concerning rent increases or other matters pertaining to the apartment, and a message would be transmitted to her.

Breck had contacted the publisher and requested that they transmit a message from him. They refused, explaining that she had told them specifically to transmit only those messages relating to the apartment, of the nature she had outlined in her letter to the landlord.

The import was brutally clear. She wanted no communication with her past life. She was cutting herself completely adrift from prior associations, and only the frail link of the month to month rental and those regular checks tied her in any way to old affiliations. That link she could sever at any time, and might. She had taken everything of personal significance with her when she went, leaving only haunting phantoms behind to torment him.

So he had stayed. He slept in the bed that they had shared and reached for her in the night. He ate at the table and sat on the couch and worked at the desk. Each day when he came in he looked at the spot where the picture had hung, never expecting it to be filled again.

Andrea moved toward him with the same elegant economy of motion that he remembered so well. His heart leapt in his throat, but she merely passed by him, out of the studio, carefully not touching him in any way. He followed hastily, unwilling to let her out of his sight for an instant.

She went into the kitchen, where she began to heat water in her teakettle for coffee. She got out one cup, and then glanced at him over her shoulder. "Do you want some instant coffee? If you want perked, you'll have to do it yourself."

"I'll take instant."

She got down another cup and spooned coffee crystals into both cups, adding sugar and milk to hers as she waited for the water to come to a boil. When the kettle began to whistle, she poured the water in, stirred both brews with the same spoon, and handed him the cup with the unsweetened black coffee. She picked up her own and wandered out into the living room.

She surveyed the room and commented, "You haven't made any changes. Do you still have your own apartment?"

"Yes," he replied warily. "I imagine that the dust

169

is inches thick there by now, but I've kept it. I own the building. You never saw it, but it's the penthouse apartment."

She nodded, unsurprised. She had never made any effort to inquire into his business dealings or holdings. She knew he was wealthy and had many interests, but all of their relationships had been on such an intensely personal level that what he did with the part of his life separate from her had never had a chance to enter into their relationship. It had been a side issue, unimportant at the time.

She sipped her coffee thoughtfully. "I'm not your mistress anymore, Breck."

She said it so casually, so quietly, that it took a moment for the impact of her words to strike him. When they did, he blenched, his body jerking slightly with the invisible blow her words dealt.

Then his eyes narrowed and he braced himself. He would fight for what he wanted. He would not give her up.

Andrea watched his reaction. She saw the effect her words had on him, saw him absorb the blow, accept it, and began to prepare to contest her pronouncement. Her eyes grew frostily chill. Had he learned nothing during the six months she had been gone? Did he still think to force her to his will?

"What have you been doing these past months, Andrea? You look very well." Breck kept his voice level and calm with immense effort. She didn't look well, she looked lovely. She was relaxed and tanned and so heart-stoppingly beautiful that she made his very bones ache with the effort he was making to control himself. He wanted to hold her and kiss her and bury himself so deeply in her that they became one, indissolubly.

170

"I've been painting," she informed him dryly. "I have almost enough canvases for a show. Another month or so and I'll be ready. I took your advice, you see. I decided to concentrate on my serious painting."

"But where were you?" he insisted. He felt a driving need to know in detail all about her life these last months. Had she left someone important behind her when she came back to the apartment? Would she return once a show was arranged?

"I went to a small town on the Carolina coast and rented a beach house. I've been there the whole time." She smiled slightly to herself and said deliberately, "It was a very friendly little town. Everyone was most kind and they made me feel welcome."

"I'll bet," he muttered to himself, black jealousy gnawing deeply into him.

Andrea turned away, lifting her coffee cup to her mouth to hide her twitching lips. Still the same possessive Breck. She began to wander aimlessly around the living room, straightening a cushion on the couch, running a forefinger across the surface of the desk and arching an eyebrow at the dust that adhered to her bare fingertip. The apartment was clean and tidy, but Breck was obviously not a white-glove inspector. She wondered if he "did" for himself or if he'd hired a part-time maid. He was perfectly capable of fending for himself. She'd discovered *that* about him when they'd lived together, and he had no hangups about pushing a vacuum cleaner around or wielding a sponge mop.

Breck had had enough. "Andrea, stop that!" he exploded.

Her head jerked up in shock. Breck's eyes were spitting blue fire and he looked dangerous. He faced her, legs spread and hands on his hips, head slightly jutted forward in an attitude of belligerent exasperation.

"You've been gone six months without a word, then you suddenly appear, and all you do is make faces over my housekeeping. Good God, woman, I've been going slowly insane over these past months and you come in as cool as . . . as a damned cucumber! I want to know exactly where you've been and who you've been with and . . . oh, God, Andrea . . . you've got to let me kiss you!"

He surged across the space that separated them before she could react to his words and plucked her empty cup out of her hands with one hand. With the other hand he grasped her waist and pulled her toward him, sending her off-balance so that she lurched against his chest. He tossed the cup to the carpet, where it cracked but did not shatter, and used the hand thus unencumbered to finish pulling her up against the length of his body.

Andrea's mouth opened to protest hotly and that was all Breck needed. He kissed her with a reckless thoroughness that knocked the breath from her body and the stiffening from her knees. The unexpectedness of his assault on her senses pulled an initial response from her and for a long moment she reacted mindlessly to the starving ferocity of his kisses.

Her involuntary, instinctive response affected him strongly. He groaned and pulled her tightly to his intensely aroused body, his arms steel bands at her waist and shoulders. The tightness of his hold broke the momentary sensual delirium that was bidding fair to swamp Andrea's reason.

She began to fight him with a determined vigor, pushing at his shoulders and wrenching her mouth from beneath his. "Let me go, Breck!" she gasped, shoving fruitlessly against the encompassing strength of his powerful arms and shoulders. "Let . . . go . . . of . . . me!"

His arms slackened their crushing hold slightly, and she jerked away from him, panting and dishevelled. She pushed the hair back out of her eyes and glared murderously at him.

"Ahhh, that was nice." He grinned, unabashed and unrepentant. "It was nice even after you stopped cooperating," he said, bending down to rub his shin where she had kicked him as she struggled. His next words were slightly muffled by his stooped position, but she heard them clearly enough. "And while you did cooperate, it was heaven."

She couldn't retort that there had been precious little cooperation on her part, because it was so patently untrue. When their lips had met, even with such bruising force and ferocity, a torrent of passion had passed between them. It was sensual magic at its most potent, and she could not deny its existence between them. But she was no impressionable young virgin now, to be swept into a maelstrom of mindless surrender, so she was able to smile coolly at him and acknowledge his thrust.

"But you'll notice I quickly stopped cooperating, Breck, and the next time you try to leap on me like that, I won't cooperate at all from the very beginning. We'd better get something clear right now, Breck. I said it before, but it obviously bears repeating. I'm not your mistress anymore. Jeanne is dead and nothing will ever force me into such a situation again. I'm dependent on no one, answerable to no one, and that's the way it's going to stay. I'll be no man's mistress, especially yours!"

"Oh, yes you will, Andrea," Breck assured her in a goaded voice. "But there's something else you're going to be first . . . my wife."

CHAPTER SEVEN

Andrea, her mouth opening to hotly refute his arrogant assurances that he would succeed in making her his mistress once more, snapped it shut suddenly. She looked at him uncertainly, unwilling or unable to believe she had heard him correctly.

Breck rumpled his shining helmet of hair and pulled at the tie knotted at his throat, seeming to realize for the first time he was still in his suit. He hadn't even shed his coat, so preoccupied by Andrea's return that everything else had been forgotten.

"Blast it, Andrea, I hadn't planned to yell it out at you that way!" He took off his coat and vest and tossed them on the dining table, followed by his tie, which promptly slithered to the floor. He ignored it. He undid the first three buttons of his shirt and rolled back his shirtsleeves to mid-forearm.

"You make me lose control. You always have." He grinned a trifle sheepishly. "I guess you always will. Whenever I'm around you I react with my emotions instead of my brains—you turn those to mush —and see where *that's* gotten me." This time his smile was bitterly rueful.

Andrea bent to pick up the cup he had tossed on the carpet, and when she straightened back up, her face was guarded and watchful. She hadn't said a word since he had flung that pronouncement out between them like a gauntlet thrown down in a challenge to mortal combat. When she did speak, her voice matched his own for rueful overtones. "Just where has it gotten you, Breck?"

"It's gotten me into the position I'm in now, where the only woman I've ever loved and wanted to marry probably hates my guts," was his simple reply. "I want to marry you, Andrea. I want you for my wife, not my mistress."

"Why? Because you have no other hold on me, no way to force me to your will, so you offer marriage as a last resort?" Her voice was cutting.

"No! I've always wanted to marry you, from that very first night at the dance. I was jealous of McKay, afraid he was someone special to you. I wanted to take you home myself that night and I was only very slightly reassured when you said he was just your date."

He rubbed the back of his neck, trying to order his words coherently. "I would have asked you out the following night, but I was committed to go to New York for two weeks. The best I could do was maneuver you into going to Devon's opening night and go on from there."

They were still standing, facing each other like two antagonists getting ready to square off. Breck looked around a little helplessly, then gestured toward the couch. "Look, honey. I can see this is going to take some time. Sit on the couch and I'll get you a glass of wine and me a drink. I promise not to pounce again." He smiled slightly, but his eyes were sad and a little anxious.

"All right, Breck," Andrea agreed with surprising mildness, and some of the hair-trigger tension eased out of Breck's big body. She handed him the cup she still held and he carried it and his own cupful of cooled coffee back into the kitchen.

Andrea kicked off her shoes and curled up in a corner of the couch, awaiting his reappearance. She heard the clink of glassware and the opening and closing of the refrigerator and freezer doors. Soon Breck came back out, carrying the two glasses carefully. He handed her the nearly brimming glass and she took a sip. Liebfraumilch. She had seen the unopened bottle in the refrigerator when she had investigated earlier, rummaging for a snack. Put there by Breck as a sort of hostage toward her hoped-for return?

Breck sat down at the far end of the couch from her, cradling his glass down between his big hands, dwarfing it. He looked moodily into its amber depths and was silent for a while. Andrea merely watched him, prepared to wait until he was ready to speak.

He began abruptly. "Well, you went out with me, all right. Twice. And after that you weren't going to have anything to do with me. You meant it. I could tell."

The words were jerky, each one a piece of him ripped out by a barbed hook. "I was panicked . . . frantic . . . and so I behaved just about as badly as I could. I tried to make you respond to me sexually, to make you admit that you felt this magic as strongly as I did." He leaned forward and put his forearms and elbows on his knees, staring at the floor between his feet.

"I didn't know about all of your family history, but that was no excuse. When you just lay in my arms, so white and exhausted, I hated myself. You couldn't have despised me more just then than I did.

So I left. It was all I could do. Then I committed the greatest folly of all."

He got up and began to pace up and down. He tossed off the rest of his drink and set the empty glass atop the desk. "I tried to force you into marriage, and it blew up in my face. Andrea, you *have* to believe me. I wanted to marry you, not make you my mistress, and I would never have gone through with my threat to have your father arrested and Jeanne informed of his crimes. It was all bluff, and you called it.

"I thought that if I could get you to marry me, it would give you a chance to get to know me, to let me prove to you that I wasn't the sort of man your father is." His grating laugh hurt her to hear it. "Instead I turned out to be worse than he is, because I love you more than my life and all I did was hurt you, hurt you so badly that you ran away rather than let me comfort you when you needed it most.

"I don't know how to describe how I felt when you agreed . . . not to marry me as I had schemed . . . but to be my *mistress,* and for an extra fillip added that you'd never consider marriage with a man like me."

He sat back down on the couch and looked directly at her, the first time he had done so since he had started his explanation. "I was trapped. By now you hated me so much that if I had let the thing drop, you'd never have spoken to me again. You would never have believed I loved you and really wanted to marry you, and even if you had credited it, you'd only have laughed in my face."

There was stark agony on his face, and Andrea automatically stretched out a hand to him. "No! Let me finish it all. It has to be said, and done with." He

178

continued, "So, I agreed, still hoping to get you to marry me. I was going to court you, if that's not too old-fashioned a term . . . take you out to dinner, dancing . . . and then you exploded another bombshell. I was to be allowed to visit you discreetly once or twice a week, like some cheap whore, and leave. I could have strangled you!" His expression was so ferocious, she believed him implicitly.

"I moved in with you. I was determined to make you get to know me, but I was also going to try my best not to force a sexual intimacy on you against your will. I hoped my forebearance would intrigue you, get you thinking about *why* I wasn't making love to you. It was sheer desperation, and when McKay called I let jealousy and my masculine territorial instincts goad me into making my claim on you very clear to him. It got rid of him, all right, but the price was too high. You found out, ripped into me, and—" His gesture said it all.

"All I could do then was hope your response to me was a sign that on some deep level you didn't hate me totally. If I could get you pregnant, or if, by living with me as my wife in daily intimacy, you could be brought to consider a marriage to me as something less than a fate worse than death . . . Oh, hell, Andrea . . ." he expostulated. "I had you. You slept so sweetly in my arms every night. . . . You were *mine,* and I was going to do everything in my power to keep you forever." He grinned at her, a tired twist of his mouth. "If I could have lived with you for seven years, at least you would have been my common-law wife."

His voice was draggingly husky, but he finished somberly. "When you left after Jeanne's death, I paid for every mistake. What if you *were* pregnant? You were so vulnerable . . . what if you married someone on the rebound? I never knew I had such a fertile imagination. I'd run the gamut of every conceivable horrible possibility, and still wake sweating in the night with some new, devastating nightmare. You'd disappeared without a trace and believe me, I followed up every faint trail, even the most unlikely. I was resigned to waiting until you became a famous artist and tracking you down that way." He smiled, but his eyes were deadly serious.

"The only hope I had was this apartment. You kept the rent up . . . but even if you hadn't, I would have. In fact," he said rather sheepishly, "I've bought this building. As long as you kept up the rental, it was a link. So . . . I lived here and I waited."

"I meant it to be a link." She spoke so softly that he wasn't sure he had heard correctly. "I meant it as a message to you, Breck. Perhaps I didn't expect you to still be living here, but if . . . if you really cared about me, I knew you'd see the apartment as a sign that I'd come back to it someday. I didn't know how long it would take me or when I'd finish what I had to do, but I always planned to come back here."

Now it was Andrea's turn to search for words. She sipped meditatively at her wine, wine she had not touched during Breck's whole long recital. She decided the best thing was just to tell him baldly and hope he was able to understand.

"You know my family history, Breck, but I don't know if you can comprehend just what that situation did to me. I suppose I always knew that I didn't have a normally happy home life. Even though Jeanne loved my father, his endless affairs and betrayals still left their mark. How could they fail not to? They often fought, though not in front of me . . . but a child

180

knows . . . and while Jeanne was all the mother a child could want or need, Devlin was a sometime father. He'd lavish attention in spurts and ignore me the rest of the time. I could never trust him as a child.

"As I grew older I began to understand the root of the tension between Jeanne and Devlin, and I also caught on that he was using me as a weapon against Jeanne. Those periods of attentive fatherhood always coincided with a crisis point between my mother and my father." Her lips twisted in a bitter grimace. "I was the ultimate blackmail weapon . . . knuckle under or he'd tell me the truth of my birth, was the message to Jeanne. Of course, I didn't understand until later just what threat he held over her, but I knew I was involved, was being used somehow to bring my mother to heel. From simply not trusting him I began to despise him. It made me very wary of all man-woman relationships and I never allowed myself to have a serious boyfriend."

Breck hadn't moved a muscle. He listened attentively to every word, concentrating as he had never concentrated before. What Andrea was telling him now would determine the course of their ultimate relationship. If Devlin Thomas had stood before him just at that moment, he might have killed him. Breck did not minimize his own culpability, but Devlin Thomas had a hell of a lot to answer for.

Andrea continued, sipping occasionally at her wine. "Then came Jeanne's accident and all the sordid revelations. I can't explain . . . there are no words . . . Oh, Breck, I felt so dirty and so guilty. Had Jeanne stayed with Devlin for my sake? What a heritage I had. . . . Would I someday come to be just like my father and my real mother? Added to the strain of Jeanne's condition and everything else, something

181

snapped inside me. I began to hate Devlin, and that kind of hate is self-destructive. It twisted me inside and twisted my reactions to people . . . men in particular. Those three years of watching Jeanne's agony just made it worse."

She smiled slightly at him. "Then you came along. I was attracted to you, and you knew it. I'd never felt that way before and I fought it. When I was afraid I was losing that fight, I decided for my own peace of mind, I would never see you again. You see, I was sure you weren't thinking in terms of anything but an affair. To me you were a Viking, Breck. You'd take a woman as a warrior's recreation but leave without a backward glance. You were self-contained, self-sufficient, and I never thought of you in terms of marriage. Twisted perceptions . . ."

"Not so twisted, Andrea," Breck interjected softly. "That was the type of man I was before I met you. I'd never wanted commitments before."

She looked sadly at him. "I really hated you, Breck, when you threatened to hurt Jeanne. I didn't see it as bluff and I hated you, so I set out to hurt you in any way I could. I taunted you, used Johnny as a weapon, and precipitated the very situation I—we—both really wanted to avoid. I bear my guilts too, Breck."

She was feeling drained. These revelations were exhausting her and Breck noted with concern the pallor of her face and the tired droop of her shoulders.

"Andrea," he interrupted her, "when did you eat last? Let me heat you some soup or fix you a sandwich."

She smiled softly at him, and for the first time since she began to talk, Breck felt some coiled spring of tension relax slowly within him. She couldn't still hate him so much and smile at him like that.

"I had a snack while I was waiting for you to come back. I want to finish this, Breck, to clear away all the debris."

"At least let me get you some more wine." He leaned toward her and took the empty glass. Their fingers touched, and Breck's laid on hers for a momentary caress. She didn't jerk away, and he was again heartened.

When he came back with a less brimming glass than the first one, she continued her narrative. "You were right in a way, you know." He looked at her in comical astonishment, and she laughed slightly. "While I was living with you I certainly had to see you as a man, and get to know you. I couldn't escape you. You were everywhere. You were gentle with Jeanne, considerate of me, and even when we made love"—she met his eyes without blushing—"I couldn't stop responding to you. I knew that I had to get away, so I laid my plans, and when Jeanne died, I ran. I needed to be alone, and I knew you wouldn't consider our 'bargain' at an end with Jeanne's death. Even then I think I knew you weren't just after a short-term affair, but too much had happened to me. I needed time and to be absolutely away from all past associations. In earlier times ladies went to convents. I went to the sea. I had solitude and work and time to think. I had to decide just what I wanted from life and I had to get rid of the bitterness that was warping me. I had to let go of my hate for Devlin before it destroyed me as a person."

Her face reflected a little of the agony of mind she had experienced, and small muscles clenched along his jawline. "It took six months and it wasn't an easy process, but I cut out the hate. What Devlin did to Jeanne can't hurt me anymore. She's dead and at rest and he'll go to hell in his own way. I've let go at last, and I know what I want now."

"What do you want, Andrea? Tell *me* now." He seemed to brace himself to receive a mortal wound.

"I won't tell you, Breck. I'll show you."

She rose from the couch and held out one hand. He took her hand in his and she led him toward the studio. They entered and as she led him around to face the canvas on the easel, she said, "This is the last picture I painted before I came back. When it was done, I knew I was ready to come home."

Breck stood in front of the picture, spellbound. It was a scene of an ethereal fantasy. Two figures dominated the center of a fairy beach. A man, garbed in clothes suggestive of a long-ago Viking rover, carried a woman in his arms and was looking down at her. The woman was clad in an iridescent gown, which was molded lovingly around her figure. Something about the drape of the fabric against her legs and feet gave the impression of a mermaid's tail. It was not blatant, but the suggestion was unmistakable. He was obviously carrying her out of the sea, and small waves still crisped about his feet.

The woman lay trustingly in his cradling arms and in her hands she held a jeweled cup, intricately chased. She was offering it to him, and he was bending his head to drink, his eyes locked with hers. The man was Breck, the woman Andrea. The look was love.

"It's called *The Mermaid's Cup,* Breck." She spoke softly. "I think Gibran said it beautifully when he spoke of joy and sorrow. 'The deeper that sorrow carves into your being, the more joy you can contain.' We've both been carved deeply by sorrow, my darling, but the cup has the capacity to hold full love at last. I am the mermaid, beloved. I offer you the cup of love, which never empties. Drink with me and of me and let us now share joy."

With an inarticulate sound of exultation Breck scooped her into his arms. As he carried his mermaid from the room his face was the face in Andrea's picture. The expression was love.

He carried her into the familiar bedroom, long uninhabited by both of them except in her saddest and sweetest dreams. He stopped by the side of the bed, swung her out of his arms, and slid her slowly down the waiting length of his body.

Andrea stood before him, head bent in an attitude of submission, as befits a captive, but she could hold the pose only for a moment. Breck tilted up her chin and searched her face with anxious eyes. What he saw, the love, the longing . . . all for him and for his touch . . . reassured him and he smiled.

With gentle, trembling hands he began to disrobe her, uncovering the only treasure that had reality and worth for him. His hands lingered over the globes of her breasts, cupping, caressing, delighting in the silky texture, which had no equal and no substitute. His thumbs traced and lightly flicked her nipples, which grew taut and aching beneath the expert stroke.

Andrea's eyes no longer watched him. Her eyelids had drifted shut, the better to savor the tactile pleasures of the flesh she had denied herself and him these long six months. She had not forgotten. She could never forget, but the pale fire of memory bore light resemblance to the consuming heat that now licked through the cells of her body.

Regretfully, but eagerly as well, his hands left the soft weight of her breasts and stroked downward to complete the task of undressing her. When she stood naked before him, his hungry eyes feasted on each curve and hollow and sweep of warm skin.

Her eyes opened languorously to watch him divest himself of his own hindering clothes, a task he completed much more efficiently than he had the removal of her own. A small, quiet smile tugged at her mouth. Breck saw it and leaned forward to kiss it onto his own mouth. It came to his lips but stayed with hers as well. A smile, like love, multiplies when shared.

They faced each other, delighting in the preliminary feast of eyes before they lay down to the banquet of taste and touch and scent. Andrea lifted her arms, offering. Breck stepped forward and lifted her once again, tilting her head back over the hard strength of his arm so that her throat and breasts arched up to his heated mouth. She moaned softly and her hand came up from her side to press his head more firmly against the rich curve he was so hungrily exploring.

He sank to the surface of the bed and, with unforgotten and desperate intensity, began to make her totally his once again.

Andrea gave herself, holding nothing, no shred of self back. Breck's mouth at her breasts, the drawing kisses and little, licking nibbles sent her nearly wild with sensation and desire. She ran her hands frenziedly over the corded muscles of his back, pulling him closer, urging him to take what she was so willing to admit was his.

They should be one. She had left him that she might come back to him at last, able to match him depth for depth. Now she was ready, eager, to both give and receive the full range of love. As Breck drew her beneath him, she arched up to meet him with an intensity that matched his own. They made love, they made life, they made a marriage.

SPEND YOUR LEISURE MOMENTS WITH US.

Hundreds of exciting titles to choose from—something for everyone's taste in fine books: breathtaking historical romance, chilling horror, spine-tingling suspense, taut medical thrillers, involving mysteries, action-packed men's adventure and wild Westerns.

SEND FOR A FREE CATALOGUE TODAY!

Leisure Books
Attn: Customer Service Department
276 5th Avenue, New York, NY 10001